Praise for *City of God:*

"Just as the conquerors invented a language to describe an undiscovered landscape and to make it their own, Lins conquers with words the underground world of the favelas—frightening, maddening, claustrophobic, in reality only imaginable in fantastic terms. *City of God* is an irreproachable and necessary work, an impressive immersion in the dominions of Mr. Hyde."

—*El País* (Spain)

"Where a river had laughed between vegetable plots and mango and eucalyptus trees, the buildings and shacks of a favela packed themselves in. Violent death, alcohol, drugs took over, with samba to muffle the despair and kites to make the heavens again seem possible. . . . To write this novel, the author investigated organized crime in the Brazilian shantytowns for years. These crisscrossing stories reveal dreams of happiness that drown in blood under the Rio sun. A dense, compelling book, out of another world."

—*Geo* (France)

"Rio. It is not only sugar bread, Caetano Veloso songs, guys checking out gorgeous girls on the Copacabana beaches, the glory of soccer and Carnival. . . . There are also the favelas, impoverished neighborhoods clustered around hills and intimately tangled around the wealthy districts. . . . Paulo Lins's novel, published in 1997, blew up in the face of those who did not want to be confronted with this reality. . . . The novel recounts several years in the life of the City of God . . . ending in a terrible gang war worthy of a Scorsese film. A novel that opens the eyes and shows the enormous humanity that emerges, despite everything, from these children and adults plunged into drugs, crime, and poverty."

—*Libre Belgique* (Belgium)

"A novelized record, the fruit of thirty years of observations and ten years of research, narrating in multiple accounts the rise of gangs and danger in poor neighborhoods."

—*Libération* (France)

"Groups of down-and-out, slum-dwelling drug dealers, without a rigid hierarchy or defined codes of behavior . . . fighting amongst themselves in a process of permanent self-destruction. Paulo Lins portrays this universe with cutting realism. . . . [*City of God*] explodes in the reader's face as gusts of words, disturbing and enlightening the conscience."   —*Correio Braziliense*

CITY OF GOD

City of God

PAULO LINS

Translated from the Portuguese
by Alison Entrekin

BLACK CAT
New York

Originally published in Brazil as *Cidade de Deus* by Editora Schwarcz
Ltda 1997.

Published simultaneously in Canada
Printed in the United States of America

Library of Congress Cataloging-in-Publication Data

Lins, Paulo, 1958–
   [Cidade de Deus. English]
   City of God / Paulo Lins ; translated from the Portuguese by Alison
Entrekin.
      p. cm.
   ISBN-10: 0-8021-7010-2
   ISBN-13: 978-0-8021-7010-1
   1. Cidade de Deus (rio de Janeiro, Brazil)—Fiction. I. Entrekin,
Alison. II. Title.
   PQ9698.22.I574C513 2006
   869.3'42—dc22   2006047663

Black Cat
a paperback original imprint of Grove/Atlantic, Inc.
841 Broadway
New York, NY 10003

Distributed by Publishers Group West

www.groveatlantic.com

08 09 10   10 9 8 7 6 5 4 3 2

For Mariana, Frederico, Sônia, Célia,
Toninho, Celestina, Amélia (in memory),
Antônio (in memory) and Paulina (in memory).

A special thank you to Maria de Lourdes da Silva (Lurdinha),
without whose valuable help this novel would not
have been written. I dedicate the poetry of this book to her.

I thank Alba Zaluar for her constant encouragement
over a period of nine years. The idea for this book
arose from our conversations, and her support
made it possible for me to write it.

Paulo Lins

GLOSSARY

Most of the characters in this book are followers of the Afro-Brazilian religion Umbanda, which contains elements of *macumba*, Roman Catholicism and South American Indian practices. The definitions below pertain specifically to Umbanda.

orixá (orisha) — generic designation for the divinities worshipped by the Yoruba from the southwest of Nigeria, Benin and the north of Togo, taken with the slaves to Brazil, where they found their way into a number of Afro-Brazilian religions, including Umbanda.

Exu — messenger of the spirits.

exu(s) — each of many entities of an inferior spiritual plane, who oscillate between good and evil.

pombagira — a female exu, who speaks through a medium and is often consulted by believers seeking advice about the future, protection and/or revenge.

terreiro — indoor or outdoor site where Afro-Brazilian religious rites are held.

The original Portuguese term for "bundle" (of marijuana) is *trouxa*, which, according to the author, contained a small amount of marijuana, enough for approximately two joints. The marijuana was packaged for sale in whatever was at hand (plastic, paper, old sports lottery tickets), hence the choice of "bundle" as a translation for *trouxa*, which doesn't actually describe the material used in the packaging.

CITY OF GOD

HELLRAISER'S STORY
THE 1960s

Seconds after leaving the haunted mansion, Stringy and Rocket were smoking a joint down by the river in the Eucalyptus Grove. Completely silent, they only looked at one another when passing the joint back and forth. Stringy imagined himself swimming beyond the surf. He could stop now, float a bit, feel the water playing over his body. Foam dissolved on his face and his gaze followed the flight of the birds, while he gathered his strength to return. He would steer clear of the troughs so he wouldn't be swept away by the current and wouldn't stay in the cold water so long he got a cramp. He felt like a lifeguard. He'd save as many lives as he had to on that busy beach day and then he'd run home after work. He wouldn't be one of those lifeguards that doesn't get any exercise and ends up letting the sea carry people away. You had to work out constantly, eat well and swim as much as possible.

Clouds cast raindrops on the houses, the Eucalyptus Grove and the open fields stretching out to the horizon. Rocket felt the hissing of the wind in the eucalyptus leaves. To his right, the buildings of Barra da Tijuca were gigantic, even from afar. The mountain peaks were wiped out by the low clouds. From that distance, the blocks of apartments he lived in, on the left, were silent, although he imagined he could hear the radios tuned to programs for housewives, dogs barking, children running up and down the stairs. His gaze came to rest on the river, the pattering raindrops opening out in circles all the way across, and his irises, in a hazel zoom, brought him flashbacks: the river when it was clean; the grove of guava trees, which had been razed and replaced by new blocks of apartment buildings; a few public squares, now choked with houses; the myrtles that had been murdered along with the haunted fig tree and the castor-oil plants; the abandoned mansion with its swimming pool and the Dread and Bastion fields—where he had played defense for the Oberom under-thirteens—had given way to factories. He also remembered the time he had gone to collect bamboo for his building's June festivities and had to run for it because the farm caretaker had set the dogs on the kids. He remembered spin-the-bottle, hide-and-seek, pick-up-sticks, the model racetrack he'd never had and the hours he'd spent in the branches of the almond trees watching the cattle go by. He recalled the day his brother got all cut up when he came off his bike over at Red Hill, and how great Sundays had been when he went to Mass and stayed behind at the church to take part in the youth group activities, then the movies, the amusement park . . . He remembered the Santa Cecilia choir rehearsals of his schooldays with joy, which suddenly fizzled, however, when the river's water revealed images of the days when he sold bread or popsicles, pushed carts at the street market and the Leão and Três Poderes supermarkets, collected bottles and stripped copper wire to sell to the scrapyard so he could help out his mom a bit at home. It hurt to think of the swarms of mosquitoes that had sucked his blood, leaving lumps to be picked at with fingernails, and the ground with open sewers he had dragged his ass across as a little kid. He'd been unhappy and hadn't known it. He resigned himself in silence to the fact that the rich go overseas to live it up, while the poor go to the grave, jail or fuck-knows-where. He realized that the sugary, watery orangeade he had drunk his entire childhood hadn't really been all that great. He tried to remember the childish joys that had died, one by one, every time reality had tripped him up, every day he had gone hungry. He remembered his elementary-school teachers saying that if you studied hard enough you might make something of yourself, but here he was, disillusioned about his chances of getting a job so he could continue his studies, buy his own clothes and have a little money to take his girlfriend out and pay for a photography course. It'd be nice if things were the way his teachers had said, because if all went well, if he landed a job, soon he'd be able to buy a camera and a shitload of lenses. He'd photograph everything he found interesting. One day he'd win a prize. His mother's voice whipped through his mind.

'This photography game is for folks with money! What you need to do is get into the Air Force, the Navy or even the Army to guarantee yourself a future. Soldiers are the ones with money! I don't know what goes on in that head of yours!'

Rocket refocused his eyes, stared at Our Lady of Sorrows Church at the top of the hill and felt like going to Father Júlio to ask for all his confessed sins back in a shopping bag, so he could recommit them with his soul strewn across every corner of the world around him. One day he'd accept one of the many invitations to hold up buses, bakeries, taxis, any fucking thing . . . He took the joint from his friend's hand. His girlfriend's ultimatum that she'd break up with him if he didn't stop smoking weed echoed in his ears. 'Screw it! The worst thing in the world has to be to marry a square. It's not just the hoods who smoke weed, otherwise rock singers wouldn't do it. Jimi Hendrix was the biggest head of all! And what about the hippies? The hippies were all crazies from so much smoking.' He was sure Tim Maia, Caetano, Gil, Jorge Ben, Big-Boy— the big names in music—all enjoyed a bit of weed. 'Not to mention that nutcase Raul Seixas, singing: "People who don't have eyedrops wear shades."' Smoking weed didn't mean he was going to go out looking for trouble. He didn't like squares, and the worst thing was that they were everywhere, noticing if your eyes were red, or if you were laughing at nothing. When he argued with squares about pot he always ended the argument by saying that it was the light of life: it made you thirsty, hungry and sleepy!

'Want another one?'

'Uh-huh!' answered Stringy.

Rocket insisted on rolling the joint. He liked this job; his friends always praised him. He made the joint as stiff as a cigarette without using much paper. He lit it himself, took two tokes and passed it to his buddy.

On rainy days, the hours pass unnoticed for those with nothing to do. Rocket mechanically checked the time and saw he was already late for his typing class, but what the fuck. He'd already missed tons of classes, so one more wasn't going to make any difference. He really couldn't be bothered to spend an hour banging away on the typewriter, and he wasn't going to school either. 'The square of the hypotenuse of a right-angled triangle is equal to the sum of the squares of the two adjacent sides, my ass.' He was really pissed off at life. He suppressed a sob, got up, stretched to relieve the pain of having spent so long in the same position and was about to ask his friend if he felt like scoring another bundle of weed, when he noticed the river water had gone red. The red preceded a dead body. The gray of the day intensified ominously. Red swirling into the current, another corpse. The clouds blotted out the mountains completely. Red, and another stiff appeared at the bend in the river. The light rain turned into a storm. Red, yet again followed by a carcass. Blood mixing with stinking water accompanied by yet another body wearing Lee jeans, Adidas sneakers and leeches sucking out the red liquid, still warm.

Rocket and Stringy stumbled home.

It was the first sign of the war to come. The war that imposed its absolute sovereignty and came to claim anyone who didn't keep their wits about them, to pump hot lead into children's skulls, to force stray bullets to lodge in innocent bodies and make Knockout Zé run along Front Street, his heart pounding like the Devil, holding a blazing torch to set fire to the house of his brother's killer.

Rocket arrived home afraid of the wind, the streets, the rain, his skateboard, the simplest things; everything seemed dangerous. He knelt by his bed, threw his head on the mattress, clasping his hands together, and in infinite supplication begged Exu to go and tell Oxalá that one of his sons felt doomed to eternal desperation.

In the past, life was different here in this place where the river, carrying sand, innocent water snake heading for the sea, divided the land on which the children of the Portuguese and the slaves trod.

Soles of feet grazing petals, mangos swelling, bamboo thickets shredding wind, a big lake, a lake, a pond, almond trees, myrtles and the Eucalyptus Grove. All this on the other side. On this side, the hills, the haunted mansions, the vegetable gardens of Little Portugal, and the cows on both sides living the peace of those who don't know death.

The branches of the river, which split over near Taquara, cut diagonally through the fields. The right branch cut through the middle, while the left—separating The Blocks from the houses and crossed by a bridge over which the traffic of the neighborhood's main street flowed—cut through the lower part of the fields. And, as the good branch returns to the river, the river, branching off, zigzagged along its watery path; a stranger who traveled without moving, carrying away loose rock crystals in its bed, allowing its heart to beat on rocks, donating water to the bodies that braved it, to the mouths that bit its back. The river laughed, but Rocket knew well that every river is born to die one day.

This land was once covered in green with oxcarts defying dirt roads, Negro throats singing samba, artesian wells being dug, legumes and vegetables filling trucks, a snake slipping through the grass, nets set in the water. On Sundays, soccer games on the Dread field and drinking wine under the light of the full moon.

'Mornin', Lettuce Joe!' Cabbage Manoel had said one day at dawn. But Lettuce Joe had not answered; he had just watched the first flight of the herons to the sound of roosters crowing and cows lowing.

The two Portuguese descendents tended the Little Portugal vegetable gardens on the inherited land. They knew that blocks of apartments were to be built in that area, but not that work was to begin so soon. They worked as they did every day, from five in the morning to three in the afternoon, talked about nothing, laughed at everything, whistled impossible *fados*, loved the different types of wind, ate dinner together, and together they heard the men in the car with the white license plate, in first gear, say:

'We intend to build a new place on your land.'

'Come, good wind! Put another smile on my face!' Lettuce Joe was to think later. 'Another wind, without homeland or compassion, has taken away the smile this soil gave me, this soil where men with boots and tools arrived, measuring everything, marking the land . . . Then came the machines, destroying the Little Portugal vegetable gardens, scaring the scarecrows, guillotining the trees, land filling the marsh, drying up the spring, and all this became a desert. All that is left is the Eucalyptus Grove, the trees on The Other Side of the River, the haunted mansions, the cows that know nothing of death and sadness in the wake of a new era.'

City of God lent its voice to ghosts in the abandoned mansions, thinned out the flora and fauna, remapped Little Portugal and renamed the marsh: Up Top, Out Front, Down Below, The Other Side of the River and The Blocks.

Even now, the sky turns blue and fills the world with stars, forests make the earth green, clouds whiten landscapes and mankind innovates, reddening the river. Here, now, a slum, a neo-slum of concrete, brimming with dealer-doorways, sinister-silences and cries of despair along its lanes and in the indecision of its crossroads.

The new residents brought garbage, bins, mongrel dogs, *exus* and *pombagiras* in untouchable bead necklaces, days to get up and struggle, old scores to be settled, residual rage from bullets, nights to hold wakes over corpses, vestiges of floods, corner bars,

Wednesday and Sunday street markets, old worms in babies' bellies, revolvers, *orixá* pendants, sacrificial hens, sambas, illegal lotteries, hunger, betrayal, death, crucifixes on frayed string, racy *forró* to be danced, oil lamps to shed light on saints, camping cookers, poverty to desire wealth, eyes to see nothing, speak nothing, never the eyes and guts to face life, to sidestep death, to rejuvenate anger, to bloodstain destinies, to make war and to get tattoos. There were slingshots, photo novels, ancient floor cloths, open wombs, decayed teeth, brains riddled with catacombs, clandestine graves, fishmongers, bread-sellers, seventh-day Mass, smoking guns to erase all doubt, the perception of facts before acts, half-cured cases of the clap, legs for waiting for buses, hands for hard work, pencils for state schools, courage to turn the corner and gambler's luck. They brought kites, asses for the police to kick, coins for playing heads or tails and the strength to try to live. They also brought love to ennoble death and silence the mute hours.

In one week there were thirty to fifty new arrivals a day; people bearing the marks of the floods on their faces and furniture. They were put up in the Mario Filho Soccer Stadium and came in government trucks, singing:

> *Marvelous city,*
> *full of enchantments . . .*

Then people from a number of *favelas* and other towns in the state of Rio de Janeiro came to inhabit the new neighborhood, which consisted of rows of white, pink and blue houses. On the other side of the left branch of the river, The Blocks were built: a complex of blocks of one- and two-bedroom apartments, some blocks with twenty and others with forty apartments each, all five stories high. The red shades of the beaten earth saw new feet in the hustle and bustle of life, in the stampede of a destiny to be fulfilled.

The river, the joy of the kids, provided pleasure, sand, frogs and eels, and was not completely polluted.

'Look at the bag of myrtle berries I got!'

'I've already picked mangos and jaboticabas. Now I'm gonna get some sugarcane from The Other Side of the River!'

The children discovered marbles, and themselves in the process:

'Bags I go last . . . if I getcha I'm king!'

'Everything goes!'

'On four fingers!'

'I'm throwin' it!'

'Get outta the way!'

'It moved! You're dead!'

'I'm next to the triangle!'

'Obstacle . . . go around!'

'Nothin' goes!'

Flying kites:

'Don't go, your line's too short.'

'I'm gonna try and tangle him.'

'No way! Go for his tail and line.'

'I can't. The glass on my line's not sharp enough.'

'You've gotta pull him up.'

'I'm gonna drag him.'

'He'll hitch you up.'

'Here goes!'

Playing games:

'One hit, 'cos there's a new It!'

'One hit!'

'I hit him and everyone else does too!'

'I hit him but no one else does!'

'Jump the graveyard wall!'

'The graveyard's on fire!'

'Every monkey on his branch!'

'Send a letter to your girlfriend.'

'Out of ink!'

'Freeze!'

'One hit, 'cos there's a new It!'

'One hit!'

They found one another in hide-and-seek and tag, had castor bean wars on The Other Side of the River, swam in the pond and played boats and Journey to the Bottom of the Sea. They headed into the fields, competing for ground with snakes, toads and cavies.

'Wanna go to Red Hill?' asked Rocket.

'Where's that?' asked Stringy, holding a bucket of water.

'Down where you were, near the spring. We can climb up and run down like in cowboy movies.'

'OK!'

They headed off from behind The Blocks, having invited a couple of friends. Rocket's brother, seeing the kids getting ready for a new adventure, thought about putting his bike away to go with them, but then decided to take it at his buddies' insistence. They crossed an area of dense bush, where new blocks of apartments were later to be built, and found themselves at the left branch of the river.

'I'm goin' for a swim!' said Stringy.

'Let's go straight to Red Hill. We can swim later!' said Rocket.

'We're better off swimmin' now, 'cos our clothes'll dry and our moms won't know we were in the river,' argued Stringy.

'Scared of mommy?' asked Rocket.

Without listening, Stringy threw himself into the water and his friends followed suit. They waded out to a certain point and swam back with the current. Stringy wouldn't come out of the river, and swam into and out of the current. They dunked one another and played American submarine and Captain Hurricane. The morning had reached its peak, invading the branches of the guava trees and bringing in its wake a land wind that swept away the rain clouds one by one. The finches sang.

It was as if they had moved to a large farm. In addition to buying fresh milk, picking vegetables in the garden and collecting fruit in the wild, they were also able to ride horses through the low hills along Gabinal Road. They hated nighttime, because there was still no electricity and mothers forbade their children to play outside after dark. Mornings were cool: they caught fish, hunted cavies, played soccer, killed sparrows to barbecue and broke into the haunted mansions.

'Let's get a move on and go to Red Hill!' insisted Rocket's brother, already on his bike.

They didn't take Moisés Street in case they bumped into one of their mothers fetching water from the spring; instead they went behind the houses and scrambled up the hill.

Red Hill had been mutilated by excavators and tractors when the houses and first blocks of apartments were being built. The clay taken from the hill was used to landfill part of the marsh and to roughcast the first houses. When it was still untouched, the hill had stopped very close to the riverbank. It now ended at one end of the Council Projects, where some of the Short-Term Houses were, on the road connecting the blocks of apartments to Main Square. From the top, one could see the big lake, the lake, the pond, the river and its two branches, the church, the Leão supermarket, the club, the Rec, the two schools and the nursery. You could even see the clinic from that distance.

'I'm goin' down on my bike!' announced Rocket's brother.

'You crazy? Can't you see you're gonna smash yourself up down there?!' warned Stringy.

'Don't worry, man, I'm a pro!'

He got on his bike, leaned over the handlebars and took off down the hill. After a while he stood on the rear brake, put one of his feet on the ground and spun the bike. His friends clapped and shouted: 'Cool, cool!'

He repeated the feat several times, to the spectators' delight. His eyes watered with the speed, but he didn't stop showing off. He got so carried away that he took off downhill again, pedaling ten times to pick up speed. It went wrong. He hit a hole, lost control and came tumbling off: bloody nose, body skidding across the ground, dust in his eyes . . . But the subject here is crime—that's why I'm here . . .

Poetry, my teacher: light the certainties of men and the tone of my words. You see, I risk speech even with bullets piercing phonemes. It is the word—that which is larger than its size—that speaks, does and happens. Here it reels, riddled with bullets. Uttered by toothless mouths in alleyway conspiracies, in deadly decisions. Sands stir on ocean floors. The absence of sunlight really does darken forests. The strawberry liquid of ice cream makes hands sticky. Words are born in thought; leaving lips, they acquire soul in the ears, yet sometimes this auditory magic does not make it as far as the mouth because it is swallowed dry. Massacred in the stomach along with rice and beans, these almost-words are excreted rather than spoken.

Words balk. Bullets talk.

Squirt, Hellraiser and Hammer ran through the Rec, went into Blonde Square and came out in front of Batman's Bar, where the gas delivery truck was parked.

'Everyone quiet or I shoot!' ordered Squirt, holding two revolvers.

Hellraiser positioned himself on the left of the truck, Squirt on the opposite side. Hammer went to the corner to keep an eye out for the police. Passersby sidled off; when they got farther away they quickened their step. Only the two old ladies who had gone to buy gas at that exact moment did not budge. They looked as though they were glued to the spot, trembling, saying the Creed.

The delivery men put their hands up and said the money was on the driver, who at that very moment was trying in vain to hide it. Hellraiser watched him. He ordered him to lie down with his arms out, frisked him, took the money and gave him a kick in the face so he'd never again try anything smart.

Hammer told everyone the gas was on him and they didn't need to bring empty gas bottles to exchange for full ones. The truck was empty in minutes.

'C'mon, let's head up this way,' suggested Squirt.

'No, let's go through the Rec—it's more open. Then we can see everyone . . . and let's get Cleide to take the guns,' said Hammer. 'No way, man!' answered Squirt. 'Real gangsters've gotta stay armed. I'm not gonna run around without nothin'. You never know if someone's gonna show up and try to grab our money. We don't know who's who round here, man! You think we're the only gangsters in this place? Everyone here's from the *favelas*! There's even guys from out of town holed up round here. And what if the pigs show up? How're you gonna deal with them? Fists ain't gonna do the job!' concluded Squirt without slowing his pace.

Cleide, who was at Batman's Bar at the time of the holdup, decided to follow them at a distance.

Hellraiser didn't say a thing. Something made him remember his family. His dad, that piece of shit, was always drunk on the slopes of São Carlos, his mom was a pro in the Red Light District, and his brother was a faggot. His slut of a mother was OK. She was known for her strong personality, didn't take any shit, kept her word and was respected in Estácio. Nor was his dad his biggest problem, because when he was sober the kids didn't draw on his face with chalk or take his shoes and, in spite of everything, he was good with his fists and a lead drummer in the samba school. But his brother . . . that was really fucked . . . Having a faggot for a brother was a huge tragedy in his life. He imagined Ari sucking off migrant laborers down in the Red Light District, taking it up the butt from the guys in São Carlos, jerking off sailors and gringos in Mauá Square and fucking rich assholes in the Lapa fleapits. He couldn't accept that his brother wore lipstick, women's clothes, wigs and high-heeled shoes. He also remembered the fire, when those bastards had arrived with burlap bags soaked in kerosene, setting fire to the shacks and taking potshots in all directions. That was the day his God-fearing grandmother, old Benedita, had burned to death. She was already bedridden because of an illness that kept her flat on her back all the time. 'If I hadn't been such a little squirt,' thought Hellraiser,

'I would've got her out of there on time and maybe she'd still be here with me. Maybe I'd have been a sucker with packed lunches and all that shit, but she's not here, right? I'm here to kill and die.'

A day after the fire, Hellraiser was taken to his aunt's employer's house. Aunt Carmen had worked as a maid at the same house for years. Hellraiser stayed with his mom's sister until his dad built a new shack in the *favela*. He hung around between the sink and the laundry tub the whole time and that was where he was when he saw, through the half-open door, the man on TV saying that the fire had been accidental. He felt like killing all those white bastards who had phones, cars, fridges, ate good food and didn't live in shacks without running water or toilets. Nor did any of the men in that house look like faggots, like Ari did. He thought about cleaning the whities out, even their lying TV and colorful blender.

When they passed in front of the Leão supermarket, Hellraiser noticed some boys playing soccer on a dirt field and turned to his friends:

'Hey, there might be some crazy bastards over there. And they might even be as crazy as me, but more than me, no way, know what I'm sayin'? I don't take shit from no one. If a guy gives me a hard time, I fill 'im with lead. C'mon, dare me to give those dickheads over there a hard time.'

'Dare ya!' said Squirt and Hammer.

They went over to the clinic. To their left were the boys playing soccer.

'Hey, stop that ball and send it over this way, 'cos now it's mine. If you don't the shit'll hit the fan,' threatened Hellraiser with his gun cocked.

A startled kid brought him the ball. Hellraiser juggled it, controlling the ball with both feet, tossing it up onto his chest, from his chest to his left thigh, then his head.

'The guy's good—he's got talent!' said Hammer.

After making the ball dance for several minutes, Hellraiser finally kicked it high into the air. It would have landed square in the middle of his chest—but like hell it would! He pulled the trigger and it fell, lifeless. Hammer and Squirt fell down laughing, but Hellraiser remained serious, looking around with an irate expression that gave continuity to the sound of the gunshot. He imposed silence, glaring quickly into each face as if they were all responsible for his miserable life. After a few seconds he turned his back on them. His friends followed him.

Niftyfeet, Shorty and Pelé were smoking a joint down by the river's edge.

'They let 'em sell almost everything and then caught up with 'em Out Front. They made some good dough, gave everyone gas cylinders, then gave those guys that play soccer down at Blood-n-Sand a hard time. Pass the joint, man!' said Pelé, enthused by the prospect of also holding up the gas truck.

'Where's Blood-n-Sand?' asked Niftyfeet.

'That little dirt field near the supermarket.'

'Who're these hoods workin' the area?' asked Shorty, handing the joint to Pelé.

'It's Squirt, Hellraiser and Hammer. I know Hellraiser from São Carlos, Squirt's from round Cachoeirinha way, and Hammer—if he's the one I think he is—is from Escondidinho,' replied Niftyfeet.

'All I can say is the next truck's mine, right? There's enough to go around, long as no one gets greedy!' warned Pelé.

'Careful, 'cos Hellraiser's a handful. If you cross him, you gotta have attitude or the shit'll hit the fan! But if you mention my name, he'll talk to you . . .'

'It don't work like that with me, man!' interrupted Pelé. 'I ain't scared of no barkin' dog. I ain't lookin' to pick a fight with no one, but if someone comes along throwin' their weight around, there won't be any talkin'. I'll give him what he's got comin'!'

'Everyone's gotta respect each other. We've all gotta feel that the enemy's the police, know what I mean? I don't wanna see my friends fightin',' warned Niftyfeet.

'Pigs!' said a voice from an alley between the Block Thirteen Short-Stay Houses.

Niftyfeet took off over the State Water Department bridge, doubling round the left side of the lake with Pelé and Shorty in his wake. They reached the part of the marsh that had survived the landfills. Their running startled a snake, but it went unnoticed by all three. They headed for the haunted fig tree, where they could smoke another joint in its branches and watch the police inspecting the Short-Stay Houses.

The milkmen had already passed. The children were watching *National Kid.* Those who didn't have television sets went to their neighbors' windows to follow the adventures of the Japanese superhero. The sun had already distanced itself from the Grajaú Range and an angry wind held up the kites zigzagging through the sky. Small clouds of red dust were born and died along the streets of beaten earth, children in uniform going home from school filled the landscape. It was already midday.

Up Top, at Hammer's house, the gang split the money while Cleide made vegetable soup, saying:

'The driver went from white to red. I'm surprised he didn't shit himself . . . I felt sorry for him, you know. But it was funny. I felt really sorry for those old ladies, the poor things were shakin' like leaves. I'm surprised they didn't have a stroke.'

'But I didn't even point the guns at 'em!' said Squirt.

'So what? Just seein' the guns, they could've kicked the bucket right then and there.'

'But they liked it when it was time to get the gas,' said Squirt.

'No they didn't. When everyone started crowdin' around, they hotfooted it out of there,' said Cleide.

Squirt moved away from his friends. He thought about going into the bathroom, but then decided to go outside. A sadness accompanied his steps; he wasn't listening to what his friends were saying. He shivered, went to the back of the yard, sat with his head against the wall of the house and allowed the tears to roll from his eyes. It wasn't the old ladies that had made him sad; they just made him remember another occasion, when he had gone to hold up the gas delivery truck alone and the police had appeared at the same time. There was no way he could run without shooting and that was what he had done. One of the bullets from his gun hit a baby in the head. He saw it reel in its mother's arms and they both fell to the ground with the impact of the shot. In an effort to relieve his guilt he told himself over and over that the crime had been an accident, but he was filled with desperation at having killed a baby every time he remembered it. He knew he could repent of his crime and go to heaven, but even so, that was a really big crime. He had always heard his parents talking about mortal sins. There was nothing he could do, he was going to rot in hell. He looked at the sky, then at the ground, and concluded that God was far away. Planes flew high and didn't get anywhere near heaven. The Apollo 11 had only gone to the moon. To get to heaven you had to pass through all of the stars, and the stars were really fucking far away. If hell was below ground, it was much closer. He feared God's wrath, but was keen to meet the Devil; he'd make a pact with him to have everything on Earth. When he felt death was near, he'd repent of all his sins and come up trumps on both sides. It'd suck if he died suddenly. He decided to stop thinking shit and headed back to his friends.

Squirt had been brought up in the hillside *favela* of Cachoeirinha. He had wanted to be a gangster so he'd be feared by all, like the gangsters where he lived. They were so feared that his chicken of a father didn't even dare look them in the eye. He liked the way they spoke, the way they dressed. Whenever he went out to buy something, he prayed for someone to be playing samba at the corner bar so he could hear the gangsters freestyling. Until he was fifteen, he had been forced to attend the Assembly of God Church. He always told his parents he didn't like that life of endless prayers, and having to attend service with them. He hated it when their house was the setting for religious gatherings and meetings of people from their church. He wanted to be like other kids in the *favela*. He wanted to take part in the June festivities, eat Saint Cosmas and Saint Damian sweets and get Christmas presents. He wanted to parade with the percussion section of a samba school, but none of this was allowed in his religion. They said Carnival was the Devil's party. The Devil was the one who understood things. One day Squirt decided to abandon the Church. He tore up his Bible, did the same with the pamphlets and confronted his parents, who insisted he remain in the faith. As time went on, Squirt began to smoke weed on the slopes of the *favela*. His first thefts were in his own home, then at the supermarket until he got involved in armed robberies. The neighbors commented among themselves that Squirt wasn't ugly, he was treated well at home, his father didn't drink, and went from home to work and back home again, and there was that son of his looking like a rabid dog. He was trigger-happy, mugged locals and raped the neighborhood girls. He was a real bastard.

'So, tomorrow I'm gonna do the gas truck again. I don't wanna stay broke, 'cos the pigs might show up and we ain't got nothin' to keep 'em quiet. Comin' again?' said Hellraiser.

'Comin',' replied Squirt.

Hammer said no. He thought doing jobs two days in a row was too risky.

'The police are gonna be on the prowl,' explained Hammer, 'just waitin' to bust hoods. I'm lyin' low.'

'If today was Gasbrás day, tomorrow's Minasgás day,' said Squirt, ignoring his friend's prediction.

The night belonged to choruses of crickets and the wind that brought enough cold to make people desert the streets. A few boozers were drinking in the corner bars. Between one pool shot and another, they listened to a comedy program on the radio. The gangsters fell asleep thinking about the holdup the next day. The morning was not long in coming. The job went smoothly, but this time it was carried out by Pelé and Shorty. Squirt and Hellraiser arrived at the same time as the police, who shot at them. Squirt ran behind the clinic, through the movie theater and up Middle Street. The police followed. Hellraiser headed down the right branch of the river. He even stopped along the way to take off his red T-shirt, leaving just the black one he had on underneath, to throw the police. He turned right past Augusto Magne School, trying to look as if he was running for another reason, and arrived Down Below, where Pelé and Shorty were squatting on the corner counting money:

'Hey, man. Where'd you get all this shit?'

'What's it to . . .'

'Hand it over, 'cos I saw you take off when the pigs showed up, and for your information, it was us that was gonna . . .'

'Fuck off! You outta your mind?' said Pelé, without missing a beat.

'Don't gimme any crap or blah-blah-blah. Hand it all over, or the shit'll hit the fan!'

'What's up Hellraiser? What's up Pelé? What's the problem?'

At the sound of Niftyfeet's voice, Hellraiser lowered his gun and Pelé followed suit.

'Just as well you haven't crossed paths before. I knew sparks'd fly. Let's head over there for a drink,' said Niftyfeet.

Up Top, Squirt was having a shoot-out with Boss of Us All. The policeman refused to give up trying to catch or kill Squirt. He had already loaded his two revolvers several times and swore when Squirt returned fire. No one was hit. Squirt took a man's car, drove down Main Street and headed for Freguesia, where he dumped it. He returned to the projects through the bush to meet up with Hellraiser and the others.

'Niftyfeet! Shit, man! I haven't seen you for fuckin' ages.'

'Yeah, man . . . It's been years. You been getting into trouble, man?'

'So was it you that did the truck?'

'No. It was them guys over there.'

'Fuck! You know I almost got shot 'cos of you guys.'

''Cos of us how come?'

'If you hadn't held up the suckers, the cops wouldn't've been there. You shoulda warned us . . .'

'Did you warn us yesterday?'

'Course not! We didn't even know you . . .'

'Right, man . . . You're full of shit, you know that?'

'Full of shit, my ass! One more word out of you . . .'

'Hey, cool it,' interrupted Niftyfeet. 'No one's guilty of nothin' and let's cut this squabblin', alright? If you wanna stand around squabblin' for nothin', it's the cops that's gonna get lucky. There's enough for everyone . . . I don't want my friends feudin', and I'm tellin' you—you gotta be friends. If you start this nonsense of feudin', soon the area'll be crawlin' with pigs. I've already told you: I don't want anyone feudin'!' said Niftyfeet, with the authority of one who knew his order would be accepted. Everyone respected him; no one would ever oppose the Salgueiro Samba School's best dancer. No one ever raised their voice to the best-known rogue in Rio's *favelas*. Even Big, the most dangerous gangster in the city of Rio de Janeiro, respected him. They'd bow to any request Niftyfeet made. They stayed there, drinking beer. By mid afternoon they were acting like close friends, playing pool and heads-or-tails, and improvising sambas:

Up on the hill,
Where the playin' is hard
Drinkin' beer,
Smokin' weed,
Playin' rounds of cards.

Families from several of Rio's *favelas* arrived at the new housing project. The chance to own their own home and finally establish themselves was an enticement, but the distance and poor living conditions that were available led many to reconsider. While on the one hand workers had to wake before dawn and walk two miles to catch the bus at Freguesia Square, on the other, every child who arrived was guaranteed to fall in love with the place: if it wasn't the guava trees, it was the avocado trees; if it wasn't the Eucalyptus Grove, it was the haunted mansions; if it wasn't the pond, it was the lake; if it wasn't the river, it was the big lake; if it wasn't the swamp, it was the sea at Barra da Tijuca.

Those who knew the projects well could walk from one end to the other without having to take the main streets. Squirt and Hellraiser liked to flash their guns at the police on patrol, then head into the alleys firing shots into the air. The police gave chase, but, unfamiliar with the twists and turns of the labyrinth, they got lost. When this happened they would often shoot at one another. The gangsters would double back and fire from another alley, making the police dizzy. They only did this when Boss of Us All wasn't around. It was best to stay home the days he was on duty, because he was as cunning as the Devil and knew the projects well.

Smaller houses were built in one area on The Other Side of the River. There were the Dread and Bastion pitches, where the soccer teams held games and tournaments. On the same side, to the right, was New World, an old area of plots where there was a bakery that gave the kids bread on a sale-or-return basis to sell door-to-door in the projects. It was the breadsellers who woke the neighborhood, shouting: 'Bread for sale, bread for sale!' Paulo Cachaça and Breadman Lolo, the only adult breadsellers, spent the mornings crying their wares:

'From Copacabana I trudge, to sell bread in the city of sludge.'

They both sold bread until eleven, then spent the rest of the day drunk.

The milkmen also rose before dawn, clanging away, shouting that they had fresh milk for sale. The popsicle sellers only appeared when the morning was at its peak. The housewives watered plants; water was abundant. There was none of that tin-of-water-over-the-head business. They planted vegetable patches and gardens, and washed the kids and dogs down with hoses.

Few gangsters circulated during the day; they preferred nights for playing cards, smoking joints, playing pool, singing sambas to the rattling of a box of matches, or even chatting with friends. Only Squirt, Hellraiser, Pelé and Shorty were seen during the day. Holding up gas trucks, smoking weed on street corners, flying kites with the kids, playing soccer with the cool guys. Other thieves preferred to operate in the South Zone, where the rich were. They robbed tourists, shops and wealthy-looking pedestrians.

Up Top, old Teresa had set up a den to cater to the few pot smokers in the projects. Madalena already sold weed Out Front, but it was hard, because she didn't have a good supplier. As a result she couldn't stock enough weed to keep up with demand, even though it was small. On Middle Street, Bahian Paulo opened a bar: the Bonfim, open every night of the week. The gangsters played cards, smoked weed, drank Cinzano-and-*cachaça* and snorted the odd line of coke. They ate fried fish, chicken gizzards, crackling, sausages, hard-boiled eggs and bean soup prepared by Bahian Paulo's wife. Couples swayed to the sound of the phonograph, and every so often trotted out some dance steps on the sidewalk.

Out Front, Batman's Bar was the hangout of the project's first pot smokers. This was where they met to chip in to buy weed to smoke in The Plots near the projects, in the bush, or even in the street when possible. Orange, Acerola, Jackfruit, Mango and Green Eyes' favorite place for smoking was The Plots. They enjoyed walking up and down the tree-covered slopes, hanging out in the bush telling each other funny stories, picking fruit from the trees. The Plots were not watched by the police, the houses were few and far between and there were dozens of hiding places where they could have a smoke.

A new community sprang up as a result of fights, soccer games, dances, daily bus rides, religious ceremonies and schools. The groups from the different *favelas* integrated within a new social network thrown together by circumstance. At first, a few groups tried to remain insular, but the tide of events soon led day-to-day life down new paths: the soccer teams, the project's samba school, the carnival groups were born . . . Everything worked to integrate the inhabitants of City of God, paving the way for friendships, disputes and romances between these people brought together by fate. Teenagers took advantage of the notoriety of the *favelas* they had lived in to intimidate one another in fights or when playing games, flying kites and competing for girls. The more dangerous their *favela*, the easier it was to command respect, but soon everyone knew who the suckers, con men, hoods, workers, gangsters, stoners and cool guys were. Those least adapted to the new society were the gangsters. The only ones who integrated were those who had been lodged at Mario Filho stadium as a result of the floods. This was the case with Squirt, Hellraiser and Hammer, and guys who had done time together.

No *favela* had its entire population transferred to the project. The random distribution of people between City of God, Vila Kennedy and Santa Aliança, the two other housing projects built in Rio's East Zone to take in the flood victims, tore apart families and old friendships. Many refused to move to City of God because they thought it too isolated. But the inhabitants of Ilha das Dragas and Parque Proletário da Gávea flocked to The Blocks, where they adjusted more easily.

On Saturdays there were dances at the club, where the gangsters, pot smokers, sluts and cool guys hung out. The bands played songs by Jorge Ben, Lincoln Olivetti, Wilson Simonal and others. The club directors managed the best soccer team in Jacarepaguá, made beef stew and *feijoada* on Sundays for members and organized excursions, competitions and indoor soccer tournaments. The directors prepared dozens of bottles of caipirinha, nylon-panties and jaguar-milk. They bought beer and snacks to sell during the dance, the most important social event around, although most residents did not attend because they knew people got up to no good there.

One Saturday, Hellraiser arrived at the dance in a rush, looking for Hammer. He wanted to tell him some good news. Squirt had got lucky in a robbery down Anil way. He'd landed two gold chains, a pair of wedding rings, a .38-caliber revolver, three pairs of Lee jeans and a leather jacket. Hellraiser went into the dance without paying, searched the entire dance floor, the bar and the washroom, but was unable to find his friend. He thought it was strange. Cleide had seen him there. He was leaving when he bumped into Niftyfeet:

'How's it goin', Niftyfeet? Seen Hammer around?'

'He went home 'cos the pigs're here. There's a Detective Beelzebub around askin' everyone if they know you, man. They've already been Out Front, Up Top, Down Below, they've been here . . . It's this nonsense of holdin' up trucks in the area.'

'Are they in a car or a van?'

'A van.'

'How many?'

'Three, I guess.'

Hellraiser scratched his head, visibly worried about the police. He thought about getting out of there, but doubted the cops would return to the club. He decided to relax and said:

'Let's go wet the whistle!'

'Real men don't wet the whistle, they have a drink!' joked Niftyfeet. They were heading toward the club bar when Detective Beelzebub came in with two other police officers, dragging a sobbing Cleide. Hellraiser ran to the middle of the dance floor, bumped into couples dancing to the sound of the group Copa Sete and knocked over chairs and tables. Beelzebub let go of Cleide and went after him. Niftyfeet strolled toward him, gave him a shove to slow him down, then apologized, saying it had been an accident, but

Beelzebub tried to cuff him. Niftyfeet dodged him without much effort. The other police officers got involved in the fight, but Niftyfeet delivered a stingray-tail kick to Detective Carlão, a sweep to Officer Baldie and a half-moon to Beelzebub, then left, not in a big hurry, crossed the bridge over the right branch of the river, turned into an alley and disappeared downhill.

'Got more than you reckoned for?' shouted Lúcia Maracanã, laughing, to rile the detective even more.

Hellraiser ran into the women's bathroom, climbed onto a toilet seat, scaled the low wall separating the cubicles, punched a hole in the asbestos ceiling and left the club. From the roof he saw Cleide making a beeline for the top of the hill. He followed Hammer's wife. They ran past the church, reached the priest's house, turned left, right, right again and threw themselves into the river near The Sludge. Old Teresa saw them go past and busied herself turning off lights and closing doors and windows, assuming the police were right behind them. Cleide and Hellraiser reached The Other Side of the River, crossed two dead-end streets, left the project, reached New World and stopped to rest in a vacant lot.

At the club, Detective Beelzebub was frothing at the mouth. He fired a shot into the air in an attempt to frighten Lúcia, who was still laughing on the dance floor.

'Who's this black slut that's laughin'?'

'It's me, okay? You gonna tell me I ain't allowed to laugh?'

'Where's your ID, you cheeky bitch?'

'Here!' answered Lúcia, holding out her ID.

'I want workin' papers, or I'll stick you in the slammer. I'll take you down to the station so the chief inspector can charge you with vagrancy.'

'Gonna charge a woman with vagrancy? Why don't you go after the guy that smashed your face in, you asshole?'

Beelzebub flew at Lúcia, grabbed her left arm and dragged her across the dance floor. She swore, bit the detective, threw herself on the ground, thrashed about and demanded to know why she was being arrested. Beelzebub said nothing and just punched her before shoving her into his van. The music had stopped, and most of the dancers were leaving. The club president approached the detective, who was frisking some kids at the entrance.

'Can I have a word with you, sir?'

Beelzebub said nothing.

'I'm the club president,' he continued. 'Perhaps I can help with something.'

'Fine. Here's the story: there's been a few holdups in this jurisdiction and the chief inspector asked for somethin' to be done about it, right? They're even doin' it out around Anil. A delivery truck can't even stop here without them showin' up. It's some guys by the name of Squirt, Hellraiser and Hammer. I've already been given the full rundown. I'm gonna arrest or kill the lot!'

'But you could lay off a little here at the dance. After all, this is just a club like any other . . .'

'Bullshit. There's only whores, gangsters and weed heads here. Decent people don't come here.'

'Yes they do. I'm a decent person and I'm here,' interrupted Vanderley, going up to the detective. 'I'm in the Army, I don't smoke weed, I work for a living. I'm here having a good time and then you turn up firing shots, arresting women, causing a huge commotion . . .'

'Where're you from?' asked Beelzebub.

'I'm in the Parachute Regiment of the Brazilian Army and I'm a club director.'

'Right, but don't get in the way of my work or I'll have a word with your captain and make life fuckin' difficult for you.'

'Watch your tongue with me, you don't have to swear! I'm talkin' to you nicely. I ain't lookin' to get in the way of anyone's work, but I don't have to let the police in if I don't want to. I'll stand at the door in uniform and I'd like to see someone come and lay a hand on me!'

'Look man. You think you're gonna be in the Army forever? You think I'm afraid of a soldier?' said Beelzebub, irritated.

'I'm a soldier and you're a dickhead! I can make it to president and choose your governor!' said Vanderley.

'I'll beat the shit out of you!'

'I'd only touch you with my foot, you fuckin' pig!'

'Enough, enough!' interrupted the club president. 'We're here to talk and find a solution for the problem. I want this to be a respectable place, a family place. I think we'd best head into the office to talk, without shouting,' he said.

They talked for an hour. The president explained to the detective that most people were decent, had jobs and their only leisure option was the dance. He was really keen to make it a family affair, and stressed that the club had good directors, people interested in the Jacarepaguá soccer team. Still tense, Beelzebub argued that he didn't know who was who in that place and that was why he had to come down hard on everyone:

'If I go soft on them, they go to town, know what I mean? Everyone here looks like a no-good, there ain't hardly any whites. There's just a bunch of mean-lookin' blacks. I gotta keep my wits about me.'

Nothing was resolved. Every so often, Beelzebub looked around, trying to keep his back to the wall and his revolver in his hand. Until another director came out with the final argument.

'You can come and collect a bit of hush money during the dance. Just don't ask for ID and don't arrest anyone. You can walk around the club, listen to music and have a soft drink, no problems, but let the dance flow. Alright?'

'Alright, deal!' answered Beelzebub, a little calmer. He let Lúcia Maracanã go when he left.

Over in New World, Hellraiser was listening to Cleide saying that Beelzebub had smashed in the door, fired shots in all directions and turned the entire house upside down. As he listened, he observed the way her dress, wet from the river, clung to her body. He imagined the taste of her thick red lips, and wanted to grab her and make her come right then and there, between the full moon and the bush. He'd screw her slowly, sucking her full breasts, then he'd move up to her mouth, running his tongue lightly across her neck; he'd lick her back, her thighs, her butt, her clit. He'd stick his tongue in her ear while increasing the movement of his steadily pumping hips so she'd call him sexy, hot, dirty. And he'd have her from behind, from the front, the side, her on top, underneath. He wouldn't even ask God's help. 'I bet she'd come loads of times,' thought Hellraiser. But no, he shouldn't be thinking those things; Cleide was his friend's wife and, besides, she'd never come on to him. She was a nice chick, who did everyone favors, and Hammer was a good guy, but if she gave him half a chance he wouldn't think twice and wham!

It was a sunny Sunday, and market day Up Top. It was the weather for kites to color the sky over the projects, the weather for children to grind glass into powder in milk tins, mix it with furniture glue, and coat their kite strings with it in order to cut the strings of other kites. It was already late morning when Hellraiser, Squirt, Cleide and Hammer met at the Bonfim. Between one mouthful of beer and another, Squirt told them how he'd pulled off the robbery.

'I told you I'd cased the house, didn't I?'

'Yeah,' said Hellraiser.

'So . . .' He took a long gulp of beer and ran his tongue across his lips. 'First I rode past and checked it was empty. There was no one on the street and it was too early for the sucker to get home from work. So I stopped . . .'

'Were you armed?' asked Hellraiser.

'No, I didn't have my revolver on me. I pretended to be the meter man and started shoutin', "Electricity!" No one came so I went round the back and broke the kitchen window and got in. Man! That house was amazing, there was shitloads of stuff . . . If I'd've had a partner, we'd've cleaned up. Then I split, got my bike and went really fast till I came off Jacarepaguá Road . . . So what's this I hear 'bout a commotion down at the dance?'

'Fuck! If it wasn't for Niftyfeet, we'd've been in the lockup getting the shit bashed out of us by the cops . . . And it was the Civil Police, man—they love a bashin'!' said Hellraiser before recounting what had happened at the dance.

When he said he'd spent the night in the bush with Cleide, his voice faltered because he'd thought all that shit, but Hammer didn't notice. Cleide complained about her ordeal, all wet, with those mosquitoes attacking her. She added that they'd only left the bush when they thought the police were no longer on their trail.

They decided to go to Batman's Bar for a beer. Squirt wanted to foot the bill as he had enough money to pay for everyone by himself. Hammer disagreed. He didn't want to drink Out Front because the police already knew who Cleide was and the robbery was very recent.

'If you're caught within twenty-four hours it's still considered "in the act",' warned Hammer.

They decided to stay at the Bonfim, in the street market, in the middle of the crowd. Squirt was in a festive mood that day. The whole thing had just shaken them up a little. The only thing bothering him was that the police knew where Cleide and Hammer lived. 'How'd the pigs find out? Who snitched? Hammer's gotta get the hell out of that place. He's gotta find a squat to hide out in Down Below, fast,' thought Squirt. He looked at his friend, noticed his concern and decided not to bring up the subject. The friends enjoyed themselves listening to Martinho da Vila, drinking beer and eating chicken gizzards.

Down at one end of the market, Lúcia Maracanã and Vanderléia stopped at the busiest stalls. Vanderléia held open her bag and Lúcia tossed the groceries in without the stall owners noticing. She did this on Sundays and Wednesdays. Lúcia didn't follow the example of her mother, who would go to each market at the end of the day to scrounge for greens and vegetables that had fallen on the ground, or beg stall owners for a little of this and a little of that. They filled the bag and went for a beer at the Bonfim.

'I know who snitched on you guys,' said Lúcia Maracanã when she ran into her friends.

'Who was it, who was it?' asked Hammer.

'It was that drunk that only talks to you when he's sloshed. He's your neighbor, man!'

'Who?' asked Hammer again.

'The guy that always wears red shirts, slicks back his hair with Vaseline and drinks peach cocktails. He's always here.'

'Ah, I know the one you mean . . . ! That motherfucker! I'm gonna bump 'im off, man!'

'Yeah, do it, man. Snitches deserve to die. If I see him, I'll do him myself,' said Squirt.

They spent the morning at the Bonfim drinking Cinzano-and-*cachaça* and beer. All Hammer could think about was moving. He couldn't keep his mind on anything else. Beelzebub and his side-kicks had turned his house upside down. They'd broken furniture, knocked over the fridge, ransacked his drawers, the wardrobe. Only his statuette of Saint George was still intact.

'Great Ogum!' said Hammer when he saw the state of his house an hour after Beelzebub had gone back to the club with Cleide, to try and get her to turn in her husband.

When he was still a child Hammer had promised himself that he wouldn't go without as he had when he was a kid living with his parents. The youngest of six brothers and sisters, only he had taken the risks to one day hit the jackpot. He had managed to hide his crimes from his family. Every now and then he got a job as an assistant bricklayer on construction sites down in Barra da Tijuca. He had calluses on his hands to show the police when they approached him. He played for the club soccer team, treated everyone with respect and tried to stop his pals from giving the other locals a hard time whenever he could. He had met Cleide when he was a parachutist in the Army.

'It was love at first sight,' said Cleide when she told her friends about her husband.

Hammer had never killed anyone and had never considered the possibility. He could even be arrested, but he'd only take someone's life if it was to save his own, even though he was a good shot. He was quick in getaways, good with his fists, discreet, well-spoken, and those who knew him said he didn't seem like a gangster.

The alleys were scorching that Monday. Stringy and Rocket had left school early because their teacher hadn't shown up. They hung around playing soccer with their friends down at the Nut Cracker. They staked out goalposts with two stones and called it mini-soccer. They took off their school shirts and played until 11:30, when *Speed Racer* came on TV.

Squirt, Cleide and Hammer went to Cachoeirinha to spend some time at Squirt's friend's place until things cooled down.

Hellraiser woke up late, thinking about holding up the gas truck. He went Down Below to put his plan to Shorty and Pelé. They decided to hold up the truck the following day at the Rec, because neither Boss of Us All nor Beelzebub would be on duty. They stuck together until late afternoon, scored some weed at Madalena's, played pool and drank beer.

Tuesday dawned with a blazing sun. Hellraiser, Pelé and Shorty met at around eight o'clock at the Rec. They waited for forty minutes for the gas truck to arrive.

'Looks like the bastards've figured it out!' complained Hellraiser, as he said good-bye to Shorty and Pelé. He headed toward Batman's Bar, where Mango and Acerola were chipping in to buy some weed. They were a bit short of cash and hoped Orange or Jackfruit would show to make up the difference. The milkman clanged past, the breadsellers shouted: 'Bread for sale, bread for sale . . .' Housewives were watering their plants. Acerola had left home early; he'd had breakfast with his younger brother and got ready as if he were going to school, but there he was, slacking off, wanting to smoke a joint so he could laugh the morning away.

'What's up, Hellraiser—everythin' alright?'

'Not so good, Acerola. The gas truck didn't show up . . . Things're lookin' a bit grim, man. If somethin' doesn't give soon, I'm gonna jump on the first sucker I see.'

Mango tried to convince Hellraiser to pitch in, but in vain. He already had some weed and didn't feel like getting stoned right then. He thought about giving the heads a joint, but since he didn't have much, he kept quiet. He was going to look for someone to mug or a shop to hold up. He said good-bye and headed up past the pharmacy. Acerola and Mango hung around waiting for a friend to show up.

As he crossed the right branch of the river, Hellraiser noticed a small crowd.

'Faggot, faggot, faggot . . .'

A white boy, toothless and shirtless, suggested:

'Shove a broom handle up his ass!'

At first Hellraiser thought it was funny, but when he saw who bore the brunt of the bullying was, he felt like hiding his face someplace where he wouldn't see anyone. But he couldn't turn a blind eye and keep on walking. He fired a shot in the air in a moment of lucidity, otherwise he would have shot at the crowd. It was Ari, in brown boots, a black leather miniskirt, yellow silk blouse, a flaming-red wig, large earrings and a blue shoulder bag, with an enormous beauty spot drawn on his left cheek. Yes, it was Ari, the Marilyn Monroe of São Carlos, his mother's son who wanted to be a woman. He looked like a samba school sprawled across the road. The two of them were left alone. A few people dared to go to the corner for a gawk. This time Hellraiser fired at them, but missed.

'Didn't I say I didn't want anyone here?'

'It's just that Dad won't stop drinking, he won't eat anything and he's always getting sick. Mom's pissed off and broke. That shack's awful and when it rains everything inside gets wet. We've heard it's much better here than there. Mom's tired of going up and down the hill carrying water. We want her to come and live here. I came to tell you and ask if you've got some cash so we can buy some medicine for Dad, 'cos I'm broke.' He straightened his wig and continued: 'I'm going up to your place to clean it up a bit, 'cos Mom's thinking about coming sometime this week.'

'You ain't comin', are ya?'

'No, for God's sake!'

'I'll get a woman in to clean up, man. I don't want no homos at my place. If you were a man it'd be alright, but you're such a faggot, pervert, queen, slut, homo, fairy . . .'

Ari didn't dare make a single objection to what his brother said. He remembered the time he'd disobeyed him and got lead in his foot. Hellraiser ordered Ari to come and talk only after midnight. And to enter without anyone seeing him. He turned his back on his brother, wanting to get away from him as quickly as possible. He walked aimlessly, reached the river's edge and crossed the State Water Department bridge. He walked through the bush until he arrived at the lake, where he sat for the rest of the afternoon. He rolled a joint staring into the water, thinking about Ari.

He remembered when Ari was born, everyone saying it was a boy. And the bastard had turned into a queer. He remembered how he used to carry him on his back along the paths of the *favela* when he picked him up from school or went to buy something at the shop. He'd tried to get his younger brother to play soccer, fly kites, climb trees and nothing—Ari was a big wimp, didn't chat up girls, got hurt for no reason and was afraid of everything. That was when Hellraiser began to suspect his brother might be a homo. As soon as he started going out at night, everything was confirmed. Several people saw him dressed as a woman in the Red Light District. He was once attacked by the residents of Maia Lacerda Street for carrying on with a sailor in a corner bar. Now there he was again with that faggot look of his. It'd be really fucked up if that fairy decided to live in the projects.

It was almost three o'clock in the afternoon on that cloudless Tuesday. Panela Rock, Gávea Rock and the Grajaú Range were fully visible, but they were not bigger than the pain of having a brother who was a faggot. He took one last toke on the joint and flicked the roach into the lake, that horizontal giant that drew in his gaze as if it were part of its watery body.

Hellraiser returned to the projects at nightfall. He had to send money to his mother. He couldn't say he'd send it later because he didn't want Ari to come back to City of God, and also because his father was sick. He went into the first shop he saw, since he didn't have time to choose a good joint to hold up. With his gun cocked, he ordered:

'Everyone quiet! Start handin' everything over or the shit'll hit the fan!'

The three men drinking beer didn't immediately obey him. They tried to talk to him. When they didn't readily comply, Hellraiser punched the one closest to him square in the face and ordered them to put their belongings on the counter. An old woman clung to a child, begging him, for the love of God, not to do anything rash. He collected the shop's takings for the day, the men's money and watches and the child's gold necklace, then left in his own good time. He strolled down Middle Street holding his gun in his right hand, sizing up people, shops and houses. Along the way he mugged those who looked well dressed and shot a kid that looked as if he was about to fight back.

He was an outlaw, he needed quick cash. In that situation he'd mug anyone, at any time, in any place, because he was prepared to confront anyone who didn't watch their step, have a shoot-out with the police or what-the-fuck-ever. Everything he wanted in life he would get one day with his own hands and macho attitude; he was a man through and through. He also had the strength of his *pombagira*, who gave him protection, because she would work some strong magic so he'd hit the jackpot when the time was right. With loads of money, the world is your oyster, you can do whatever you want whenever you want, all women are the same to a man with money, and the next day will dawn even better. The thing to do was to show up at the Salgueiro or São Carlos rehearsal hall wearing some really sharp threads and fancy footgear, order beer for the boys, buy heaps of coke and go round chopping out lines for his friends, send for a shitload of weed and roll joints for the cool guys, make eyes at the prettiest black girl and invite her for a glass of whisky, get an order of fries, toss a pack of smokes with white filters on the table, play with the key to his wheels so the chick would know she wouldn't be hanging around the bus stop later on, buy an apartment in Copacabana, screw doctors' daughters, have a phone and TV and hop over to the States from time to time like his aunt's employer. One day he'd hit the jackpot.

He turned on only the bathroom light, counted the money, checked the watches, chains and bracelets, wrapped some of the loot in a plastic bag and left it right there for that damn Ari to take, then stashed the rest under the bed. He was hungry, but wasn't about to make himself a sitting duck for the police—he imagined the pigs arresting him while he was having his grub. He lit a cigarette, remembered he had some weed down at the bottom of the yard, rolled a joint and puffed away with the happiness of one who has fulfilled his duties.

Hellraiser had lived among gangsters since he was a child over in São Carlos. He liked listening to their stories about holdups, robberies and murders. Even when he passed them at a distance, he made a point of greeting them. He never refused them favors, and gladly ditched school to help the movers and shakers: he cleaned their guns, wrapped up weed and, to get on their good sides, he sometimes used his own money to buy the kerosene they used to clean their weapons. When he got bigger he'd get himself a gun so he could get rich in robberies, but while he was still a kid he'd keep stealing his dad's loose change. He never noticed anyway because he was always shitfaced. His mom was no fool with money—she was really sharp. He liked his mom, even though she was a gossiping, foul-mouthed slut. The happiness and confidence he felt the time Spliff asked him to hide a revolver at his place grew a lot after Spliff was killed. That beautiful gun had been handed to him on a platter. He treated the .38 as if it held the answer to all his problems. A wild cure-all cared for with kerosene and a longing to hit the jackpot.

After his grandmother died, Hellraiser decided he'd never be broke again. Work like a slave? Never. He wasn't going to eat packed lunches and take orders from white guys, always doing the donkey work with no chance of moving up in life, waking up really early to start work and earn peanuts. In truth, his grandmother's death only encouraged him to continue down the path on which he had already taken his first few steps, because, even if his grandmother hadn't been killed, he would have followed the path that led him away from slavery. No, he wouldn't be a sucker on a construction site—he'd gladly leave that job to the guys who arrived from Paraíba dying of thirst. The third time he did a holdup he had a shoot-out with the police, but was lucky enough to come out unscathed. The idea of sweating it out on a construction site with the thirsty bastards from up north seemed more attractive, but like hell it was— the best gangsters have luck on their side. One day he'd hit the jackpot.

Not one of Hellraiser's victims reported him; only the boy he had shot had to file a police report because there had been a policeman on duty at the hospital where he was treated. Another guy who had been mugged played for Unidos, knew Hammer and was one of the cool guys. Aluísio had come from the neighborhood of Irajá, played tambourine with the local samba school and studied at the same high school as some of the heads who hung around with Orange. He felt humiliated, so he talked to some of the cool guys and told them his story, trying to get them to side with him, or at least establish a network of sympathizers. Regardless of whatever came of that, however, he was going to do something about it. He couldn't let a gangster give him a hard time, otherwise what would become of his life in the projects? People might think he was a wimp and he'd never hear the end of it. Things definitely couldn't be left like that.

It was already after two in the morning when Hellraiser saw Ari out front through a crack in the window. He opened the door without making any noise and gestured for his brother to be quiet as he entered.

'There's money, a watch and a chain for you to sell over in Estácio. Tell Mom if she wants to come, she can come tomorrow, because I'm already outta here, OK? Just tell her to say she doesn't know me, and everything'll be fine.'

Ari kept quiet; only his gaze wandered while his brother was talking. He thought everything was his fault. If he weren't a faggot, his brother would be living with them. As soon as he'd started cross-dressing, Hellraiser had taken off. He liked him. Deep down, he sometimes believed his brother was fond of him. Sometimes he didn't. He hated sex at that moment, blaming it for all of his misfortune. A silence that implied a hug or handshake descended upon them, until Hellraiser sent him on his way.

'Stay clear of the cops, OK? Look after yourself!'

Ari stepped into the City of God night, where various other silences were piled up in each alley. The night spilled across his restless gaze. He had to steer clear of the police. Anything even remotely out of place in the night was suspicious. He looked around. He decided to take off his heels so he could run when he noticed a man standing on the next corner. He made sure the money and jewelry were secure, crossed over to the other side of the road, slowed his pace and visualized his *pombagira*. The man didn't move, making Ari even more apprehensive. He'd wait until he was close to the corner, then take off running. Holding his purse in front of him and pretending to look for something, he got his pocketknife out of his pants, opened it and held it in his right hand, prancing along for all he was worth in the hope that the man on the corner would believe he really was a woman. He thought about turning back to ask his brother for help, but was afraid Hellraiser would say he'd been cruising. His potential attacker was less than ten yards away and he thought about making a run for it. His heart was the noisiest thing at that moment.

'Don't worry 'bout the swollen cunt and hairy asshole, you just gotta ram your pole!' said the man on the corner, revealing that he was completely drunk.

Ari turned the last corner, walked to the end of the street and went into the Doorway to Heaven, where Neide and Milk were having a beer while they waited for him. Ari paid the bill, hurrying along his friends from the Red Light District. They got into Milk's VW and headed for Estácio.

The clanking of the milkman woke Hellraiser. It took him a few minutes to remember everything that had happened, then he splashed his face with water from the spout in the kitchen and went outside holding his gun, without checking to see if it was loaded. He wasn't going to use it; he just wanted to intimidate the milkman.

'Hey, man! Get over here so we can shoot the shit.'

'What's up?' said the milkman.

'Think you can do me a favor?'

'Course I can!' he said nervously, trying not to look at the revolver or into Hellraiser's eyes.

'It's like this: you've gotta carry a mattress, stove, sofa, wardrobe and radio down to Block Thirteen. I'm gonna get myself a squat down there, then in you go, OK?'

'OK.'

'How many trips you gonna make?'

'From what you said, probably two.'

'So this is how it works then: get yourself organized over here and I'll get myself set up over there. I'll pick a squat quickly and wait for you there, OK man?'

'Uh-huh.'

Hellraiser picked two houses. One was for him and the other for Hammer.

The milkman was quick. Hellraiser left the wardrobe in the house reserved for Hammer and the rest in his new house. He gave the milkman a watch, paced around the living room with his hands behind his back, thought about his father's illness, his mother's legs climbing the slopes of the *favela* . . . He felt a brief sadness and opened the window; a ray of sunlight invaded the short-stay, motivating him to go out to get something to eat.

Before entering Dummy's Bar, he saw Black Carlos crossing Middle Street holding two bottles of beer. He called his friend over and quickly made up a lie. He said the police had blockaded his house during the night and that he was only alive because he hadn't done anything rash. He could never go back again because he couldn't afford to show up at a place the pigs were keeping an eye on.

'Hurry up and grab yourself one of those empty houses, man!'

'You think I haven't already? . . . I've already moved, man!'

They went to Black Carlos's house. On the way, Hellraiser asked a boy to run an errand for him:

'Go and get two bread rolls and a pound of mortadella . . . Take it to that house over there,' he said, pointing at his friend's house.

The boy was quick. They ate, drank, smoked weed and cigarettes and made small talk until Black Carlos told his friend to take a nap, after seeing him yawn several times.

'Good idea. I'm gonna head home . . .'

'You can get some sleep right where you are, man. I'm going out for a stroll, OK? You can stay as long as you like, no problem . . . This place is clean.'

Before leaving, Black Carlos told his friend that Lúcia Maracanã would come fix a nice dinner for them. Hellraiser thought about taking a shower and even headed for the bathroom, but changed his mind when he felt his head spinning; he was wasted on beer and good shit. He lay down, still dressed in his T-shirt, jocks and tapered pants.

He woke up at around two in the afternoon to the sound of Lúcia and Berenice talking. He showered. When he left the bathroom he checked out the unknown woman's legs. At first, the way he wouldn't take his eyes off her made Berenice uneasy. But as the minutes passed, she crossed and uncrossed her legs as much as possible. Lúcia talked about her carnival costume as she cooked.

'Did I tell you I'm gonna parade with the *sambistas*? I can't be bothered with choreography, having to rehearse every Wednesday, know what I mean? But not the *sambistas*. It's every man for himself and God for all. And all I'm wearin' is a little G-string, dance shoes, stockings and the top. This nonsense of wearin' lots of clothes just restricts your movements. I like to let my feet do the talkin'—spinnin' down the avenue like a turkey ain't my thing . . . This year I'm gonna parade with São Carlos, Salgueiro and the school from here. I'm goin' all in white so I can get into all three in the same costume,' she said.

Hellraiser was quiet, wondering if anyone had filed a report on his jobs. He regretted stirring things up within the projects themselves. Niftyfeet was always saying you shouldn't shit where you eat. But come to think of it, there was no two ways about it—it would have been impossible to case out a good joint, then hold it up, knowing his fag of a brother was in the area. Time was short. 'They'll probably do a composite sketch,' he thought. Although he was worried, he admired Berenice's body: her fleshy painted lips, a pair of tight little shorts showing off her round butt, her pointy, mouth-watering breasts, shapely legs, big eyes and soft voice . . . He got a hard-on.

Lúcia announced that dinner was ready, got out some plates and silverware, and helped herself to rice, beans, and ox-rib and potato stew. Berenice offered to serve Hellraiser. He gave her the thumbs-up with his right hand without taking his eyes off the house across the way. The clinking of plates and silverware also came through the neighboring window. Hellraiser watched an old woman cooking over a fire in her own living room for four grandchildren. Now they were eating beans and the smoke was making their eyes red. A sense of sadness sobered him, but Berenice's hand on his shoulder made him smile. She handed him the plate. He ate slowly, with his mouth closed so as not to do anything embarrassing in front of the woman he had the hots for.

Berenice was from the *favela* of Praia do Pinto, where she had been born and raised with nine brothers and sisters. When she was still a girl she had started stealing food from supermarket shelves in Leblon and Ipanema. Now she only stole from rich housewives at street markets in the South Zone. She was always inviting Lúcia to steal with her. She thought stealing food at the markets was child's play. The thing was to filch money, gold chains and bracelets. 'It's a piece of cake!' she repeated each time she and Lúcia talked about it.

When their mother died, each of the children headed off in different directions. Berenice went to live with Jerry Adriane in the *favela* of Esqueleto. She stayed with him until his body was found in São João de Meriti with fifty bullets in it and a sign hanging from his neck saying: 'I won't steal any more. Signed: White Hand.' Berenice moved with her father to City of God, where he drank himself to death. Now she was alone, wanting to start life over. She was tired of cooking for herself, sleeping alone. She wanted to have children as soon as possible because she already felt old. When she saw Hellraiser, she thought he was charming and allowed herself to be seduced by his words during that first meeting.

'Toss me a smoke!' said Hellraiser, and after Lúcia handed him one he added, 'You know, Lúcia's always had some hot friends.'

'So why haven't you set yourself up with one?' asked Berenice.

'So far none of them have made my heart beat faster!'

Lúcia sensed her friend's intentions, said she was going to Madalena's to score some weed and left the two of them alone. 'Looks like you're a picky one, then. Life's hard on people like that, don't you think?'

'To be honest, I think you're right, you know. And you know what? I'm gonna give it to you straight—I think my heart's chosen you. It's our stupid hearts that do the choosing, and when I saw you my heart took off like a racehorse,' declaimed Hellraiser.

'Yeah right, pull my other leg . . . A gangster's heart only beats in the soles of his feet and doesn't take off anywhere—it's always lyin' low.'

'C'mon, girl . . . Ain't you ever heard of love at first sight?'

'Gangsters don't love, they lust,' answered Berenice, laughing.

'It's a bit hard to talk like this . . .'

'Gangsters don't talk, they shoot the shit!'

'For chrissake, you pick the shit out of everything I say!'

'Gangsters don't say nothin', they give it to you straight!'

'I'm gonna stop wastin' my breath on you.'

'Gangsters don't stop, they take five.'

'Talkin' 'bout love with you ain't easy.'

'What's this about love, man? You're just bullshittin'!'

'Gangsters are fools when they're in love,' insisted Hellraiser.

'You're gonna end up convincin' me . . .'

They hung around talking until Berenice promised to think about it. Lúcia arrived with a couple of beers, a bit of weed and three papers of coke, to Hellraiser's delight. They talked for ages. Every time she gave him half a chance, Hellraiser tried to put the moves on Berenice. He knew you sometimes had to be persistent to win a woman over.

The hot sun had almost gone, the children brought in their kites, workers arrived on crowded buses, people who had night classes headed for school, the few afternoon breadsellers headed home and workers filled corner bars for their sacred drink. Aluísio got off the bus in Main Square. He didn't know what the story was with Hellraiser, but he didn't care if he was the meanest gangster in the world because he was going to kick his ass—Aluísio was hot shit with his fists too. He'd challenge Hellraiser to a fistfight if he had to. Real gangsters had to fight with their fists, otherwise they lost face, people looked down on them. He reckoned that if he wasn't at the Bonfim he'd be Down Below. On the way he ran into Orange and Acerola smoking a joint.

'What's up, man? Everything OK?'

'So-so.'

'Wanna puff, man?' asked Acerola, joint in hand.

'No, I don't smoke, thanks anyway.'

'That's right, I completely forgot.'

Aluísio took the chance to grumble to his friends. Acerola got angry when he heard what had happened. He said in an apprehensive voice that the gangsters had to respect the Boys. He said that if it were him, he'd beat the shit out of the guy to put some manners on him. He liked Aluísio, although he hadn't known him for long. He believed you could tell from a man's eyes if he was nice or not. He sensed sincerity in Aluísio's eyes and always saw him talking to everyone, and buying beer for the cool guys. He was a guy who never had problems with anyone, was always in the running for the best chicks in the area, and the guys he hung out with were the best. He decided to side with the one he considered a good guy. Orange backed his friend's decision.

They headed Down Below, as Orange had seen Hellraiser going into Black Carlos's house in the morning. Before crossing the square where the City of God Prospectors carnival group rehearsed, they ran into Niftyfeet having a good time at a pool table with two workers, knocking back a drink or two between shots to whet their appetites. Acerola took it upon himself to tell Niftyfeet what had happened and, seeing him all worked up, Niftyfeet decided to intervene.

'Let me have a word with him, but let's not all go at once, 'cos he might think we're gonna give him a hard time. You two wait for me here and I'll go with him.'

'Thanks!' they answered.

Niftyfeet advised Aluísio to tread lightly. He shouldn't be afraid, because Hellraiser didn't like that either, but if he came on too strong the shit'd hit the fan.

'I know how it is,' said Aluísio, like someone who understood how things worked. He visualized Father Joaquim of the Promised

Land of the Souls so everything would run smoothly. His protector never failed him in his hour of need.

The matter was easily resolved. Aluísio behaved as Niftyfeet had expected. When he said he was a friend of Hammer, Orange and Acerola, he received double what had been taken from him, along with the gangster's apologies.

Night made itself king of the hill. Moths clustered around every other streetlamp. Up Top, a gang of kids asked Bahian Paulo where the gangsters were. They wanted to celebrate their successes with the masters. That day, their eager little hands had made old people, pregnant women and drunks in the city center feel their vulnerability. They'd also begged and shined shoes in São Francisco Square. Pipsqueak, the one who always got the most money, was the leader of the gang. He lied to his friends to win their respect, saying he had already sent more than ten people off to meet their maker in the holdups he'd done alone. He looked up to Hellraiser, but adored Big, who was top dog in the *favela* of Macedo Sobrinho. If he managed to be like Hellraiser, soon he'd be like Big too: desired by women and feared by all. He considered Slick and Sparrow his best friends. When Slick was behind bars at Padre Severino, there were few occasions when his mother didn't take him money sent by Pipsqueak. When Slick got out of prison, Pipsqueak sung his friend's praises, saying he was the wisest and toughest, the biggest gangster of them all.

Bahian Paulo had only seen Hellraiser in the morning. As for Hammer and Squirt, he hadn't seen them for some time.

'Even the guy who snitched on them is showin' his face in the area again,' said the owner of the Bonfim, pointing at Francisco, who was drinking a peach cocktail at the other end of the bar.

The children went to old Teresa's to score four bundles of weed in the hope of finding a gangster to share it with. Then they headed down through the alleys. Night Owl went ahead, giving the rest of the gang the thumbs-up when all was clear around corners. If for some reason the police happened to appear, he'd continue on without signaling. Pipsqueak was the only one who carried a gun and he always kept it cocked.

Hellraiser was playing pool with Pelé and Shorty at Dummy's corner bar. When he saw Night Owl he shouted his name as if calling to a close friend. He was even happier when he saw the rest of the gang. He decided to greet each of them with a handshake and told them it was time for children to be in bed. He didn't stop at shaking Pipsqueak's hand and decided to hug him, slapping his shoulders not just in friendship, but also in admiration. After the reception, Pipsqueak said he'd come to let his friend in on a good one. He explained his plan. Hellraiser got excited and his excitement spread to Pelé and Shorty.

'We can even do it today. We just need to get a car . . .'

'No way, Pipsqueak! Saturday's better, 'cos there's more people there. More dough for us, right?'

They arranged to hit the jackpot late Saturday night. That Friday night, Pipsqueak would take Hellraiser and the others to case out the place they were going to hold up. They'd check the exits in case the pigs showed and choose the best place to park the car . . . The money would be divided equally between all four. Pipsqueak would be included just for having tipped them off. The job would be carried out by Hellraiser, Pelé and Shorty. They celebrated the success of the operation in advance. Hellraiser said the thing was to think positively so everything would work out alright. Carrots, another kid in the gang, asked for a soft drink and three pool tokens. Out of habit, he accidentally called the bar owner 'Bahian Paulo,' reminding Pipsqueak of the snitch.

'We just saw the guy who set the cops on you guys.'

'No way!' said Hellraiser.

'Yes way, man! He was at the Bonfim drinking beer.'

Hellraiser dropped his pool cue, went to the hole where he'd stashed his gun, gave it a once-over and headed into the streets in the dark of the moonless night. He went down an alleyway, passed the nursery, crossed the Nut Cracker, passed Augusto Magne School and continued down the road along the right branch of the river. He slowed his pace at each corner so as not to get caught off guard. The police were nowhere to be seen. He was going to bump off the snitch to set an example, because if he didn't everyone might start snitching. This was perhaps the most important lesson he'd learned from other gangsters when he was a boy in the *favela* of São Carlos. Hellraiser was brimming with hatred as he passed the club. All he had to do was cross the Rec, cut through the church alley, turn right, go down Middle Street and he'd be at the Bonfim.

Francisco was not completely drunk. He was sipping his peach cocktail and listening to Bahian Paulo's radio. He didn't notice Hellraiser.

Francisco had migrated from the northern state of Ceará to Rio de Janeiro with a job guaranteed. He worked on the construction of the Paulo de Frontin Bridge. He'd lived in the on-site accommodation during his first year in Rio, then managed to get a house in the projects with the help of one of the big-shot engineers working on the bridge. He'd sent a letter to his wife saying his brother was going to fetch her. His brother had gone by bus just the day before. The letter also talked about a good house with running water and a yard, and there was a school for the kids nearby, where, according to the neighbors, it was easy to enroll them. He had some money set aside for furniture. The only bad thing about Rio de Janeiro was that there were niggers everywhere, but he wanted her to come as quickly as possible because he was missing the kids so much. When he'd arrived in Rio, Francisco had been mugged before he'd left the bus station, and again two months later, in the Red Light District. Both times by blacks. When he'd heard Squirt saying he was going to do a house down Anil way, he waited for him to move away and said in a loud voice that if he saw a policeman he'd turn in that thieving cunt on the spot. He knew where the others lived and pointed at Hammer's house. Madalena, who had been drinking a beer at the other end of the bar, committed what he'd said to memory. The first chance she had, she told Lúcia Maracanã what had happened. Francisco hadn't been afraid to beckon to the police doing their rounds, to snitch that very same night on which he had sworn to avenge himself on that fucking race. He said he'd never liked niggers and after he came to Rio he'd begun to feel angry toward them. He argued with his friends, saying blondes were the sons of God, whites God had begat, mulattos were bastard sons, and blacks the Devil had shat. Telling the police where Hammer lived was his great act of revenge against that bunch of jigaboos.

Hellraiser asked Bahian Paulo for a shot of Cinzano-and-*cachaça* and told him he was going to teach Francisco a thing or two. He glanced up and down the street to see if the coast was clear, and ordered a peach cocktail for the snitch, like the heroes in cowboy movies. Francisco realized Hellraiser was there when he was being served. Wary of his gesture, he avoided looking at him and got ready to run. The next second he began to doubt whether he should run or not. Maybe Hellraiser only wanted to find out what had happened and everything would be alright after a talk. He'd heard many locals say that no one escapes a good chat. But, come to think of it, those guys were always serious when it came to business—he should be hotfooting it out of there. He worked out what path he'd take, breathed deeply and took off. Hellraiser, however, was faster. He headed Francisco off before he'd rounded the second corner.

'What's up, man? Are you too good for the drink I bought you?'

'No. It's just that I was on my way out already . . . um . . . um . . .'

'What you all worked up about? Relax, 'cos I just wanna talk . . .'

'I . . . I . . . I . . .'

'I my ass, man! You're a fuckin' snitch!'

'But . . . but . . . but . . .'

'But my ass! Let's head over there for a chat, I'm not gonna do nothin' to you, don't worry,' said Hellraiser, pointing at the square on Block Fifteen with his gun.

Francisco had no choice but to follow his orders. Hellraiser thought about White, his friends who'd had to spend time away from the *favela*, Hammer and Cleide's lost furniture. Francisco didn't hear the dogs barking or the sound of the record player coming from the Bonfim, which gradually became inaudible to Hellraiser too. In the square, a child holding a baby was waiting for his mother, who was on her way home from work.

The fearful sometimes puff up with courage when they become overly nervous. Francisco thought about his wife, his six children, the letter he'd sent and the death looming before him. Hellraiser's voice ordering him to recite a Hail Mary made him bold enough to jump on him in an attempt to grab the gun. His murderer dodged him and sent a bullet into his forehead.

He fired another three shots into the body already in the throes of death: eyes rolling, arms flailing. Blood ran down Francisco's forehead. Hellraiser took twenty cruzeiros from the corpse's pocket and the watch from his wrist and returned downhill along a different path to the one he'd taken on his way up. The child holding the baby took the opportunity to filch Francisco's shoes.

'Wanna see a stiff? Just take a spin Up Top.'

'You sent him off to meet his maker!' exclaimed Pipsqueak.

'I even landed myself some dough and a ticker—I got lucky! We'd better lie low now, 'cos soon the pigs'll being showin' up, man,' said Hellraiser, heading for the counter for a shot of Cinzano-and-*cachaça*. Maybe a drink would slow his racing heart, pulling him out of the terrain of remorse and leaving him only with the glory of having done in a snitch.

He downed the shot, lit a cigarette and insisted on paying the bill. The kids were looking for papers so they could roll a joint. Pelé and Shorty were playing a game on their last pool chip. Black Carlos arrived, saying there was a fresh stiff over by The Blocks. It had happened while some thieves were splitting the loot from a robbery. One had wanted a bigger cut for having cased the joint and ended up getting killed by his partner.

'Time for us to disappear, man. I just finished off the snitch Up Top!' said Hellraiser to Black Carlos.

They all headed off in different directions. Hellraiser thought about going to Berenice's house. He was sure she'd calm him down, but it'd take some nerve to knock on her door at a time like that. He decided to sleep at his new place.

All of the bars in the projects closed their doors. At the police post, Officer Jurandy and Marçal were asleep on the second floor. Downstairs, Corporal Coelho was reading *The Texas Kid Comes Back to Kill*. Over at The Blocks, the thief's mother lit seven candles around her son's body, removed the gold chain and Saint George medal from around his neck, recited the Lord's Prayer, a Hail Mary, the Creed and sang a song to Ogum:

> *Father, father Ogum,*
> *Hail Ogum of Humaitá.*
> *He won the great wars.*
> *On his earth we salute*
> *The horseman of Oxalá.*
> *Hail Ogum Tonam,*
> *Hail Ogum Meje,*
> *Ogum delocoh kitamoroh*
> *Ogum eh . . .*

Outside, snitches deserve a beating, but in the *favela* they deserve to die. No one lit a candle for Francisco; only a dog licked at the dried blood on his face.

When the rainy morning arrived, people on their way to work went over to the corpses to see if they were anyone they knew, then went on their way. At around nine o'clock, Boss of Us All, who had clocked on at 7:30, went to see the thief's corpse. When he pulled back the sheet covering the body, he concluded, 'It's a gangster.' He had two tattoos; on his left arm was a woman with her legs spread and her eyes closed, and on his right arm was Saint George, the warrior saint. He was still wearing Charlote flip-flops, tapered pants and a colorful T-shirt made by prisoners. At the other end of the square on Block Fifteen, however, when his steps brought him to the image of Francisco's body, a slight nervousness in his policeman's heart grew unchecked until it turned into all-out despair. The stiff belonged to a worker. Burning hatred seeped through his pores in a cold sweat. He suspected it was a fellow countryman. His suspicion did not betray him, for when he examined the dead man's ID he saw that he was from the state of Ceará. His anger was renewed and the flame of revenge kindled.

He asked around the area for information. Nothing. He headed down Middle Street, turned the corner behind the church and decided to cross the Rec. He stopped at corners, giving some people a frisking, others a punch in the face. Those who took off running got bullets—if they ran it was because they'd done something wrong. He appeared on street corners believing he was an exposed high-voltage wire. He was the thunder in the rain that was falling, he made the squares shudder, stretched the alleys—he was Boss of Us All in a fury, ready to avenge the death of a fellow countryman. Any gangster that crossed his path would die mercilessly. Before he reached Block Thirteen, he ran into two other policemen, who decided to accompany him.

Pipsqueak raced down Front Street on a bicycle trying to get to Block Thirteen before the police. As he turned down the street where the Short-Term Houses were, he ran into Niftyfeet strolling toward the bus stop.

'Hey, man! That fuckin' pig's lost it and he's headin' down this way. I've come to warn the boys. Where's Hellraiser?'

'He must be at his place. Know where it is?'

'Uh-huh.'

'So nip over there to let him know.'

A few minutes later, Pipsqueak and Hellraiser were hiding out in the Big Plot, a vacant lot near the exit on the road to Barra da

Tijuca, while Boss of Us All broke down doors on Block Thirteen and fired at windows. The old woman who lived with her grandchildren threw an aluminum plate at his head, and he responded with a shot, which hit her youngest grandchild in the leg. Boss of Us All swore at the top of his lungs and knocked over garbage cans. Killing a worker was really fucking unfair . . . The poor guy must have come to this hole of a big city for the same reason he had, and those niggers had finished him off like that. He broke down Lúcia Maracanã's door and saw her lying there, completely naked. Lúcia pulled the sheet up over her breasts and her eyes gave off a false sense of calm. For a second, Boss of Us All was relieved of his hatred as he admired her strong body, but he quickly got a grip on himself.

'Where's your man, you black bitch?'

'I ain't got no man, and you can't just go bustin' into people's places like this. And you know—that's why I don't like the fuckin' Military Police! Especially fuckin' northerners!'

Boss of Us All set into her with punches and kicks and Lúcia retaliated by biting him, but he managed to seize her.

'Let go of me, you filthy northerner!'

Outside, the other policemen were firing repeatedly at Pelé and Shorty, who jumped through the window of the house where they had been sleeping, turned down an alley, took a right and crossed the Prospectors' rehearsal square with bullets whistling past them. They cut across Main Street to try to get to Red Hill. Boss of Us All joined the chase, but he and the other policemen were losing ground with every step. Each shot that echoed in the fugitives' ears was in fact making their feet go faster. They were enjoying the situation. Later they'd tell their friends every detail of the getaway. They remembered *Bonanza*. Buffalo Bill and Zorro. From time to time they zigzagged like the heroes on TV. It was too bad the action wasn't on horseback like in films, and if they'd been armed they'd have ambushed their enemies from behind a tree to finish them off. They were good with marbles and slingshots, and with revolvers they left nothing to be desired. They climbed Red Hill and headed into the bush. The police tired of chasing them.

Down on Block Thirteen, the commotion spread from alley to alley. Some wanted to file reports, while others said they'd rather stone the policeman next time he appeared in those parts. Frightened, the children ran to The Other Side of the River to calm down under trees, in the lake, the pond . . . Housewives shouted, and news of the previous night's murders spread from mouth to mouth in the drizzle of that sinister morning.

The residents went to see the cadavers. A drunk amused himself by uncovering the snitch's face for each person who came to see. The afternoon teachers heard about what had happened from the children. The hearse arrived at around three o'clock. First, they removed the worker's body, then the gangster's. Boss of Us All passed through Block Thirteen from time to time.

'Here comes that bastard!' people warned.

The residents took to the streets. They said nothing, just watched the policeman's steps. Boss of Us All combed alley after alley. When he left, people hissed and cursed at him. He fired shots into the air and swore back.

In the Big Plot, Hellraiser ate the bread and mortadella Pipsqueak had brought him. He knew he had to stay there until the next day. Boss of Us All would only clock out at 7:30 the next day and Detective Beelzebub might show up at any moment.

'I'm going to Lúcia Maracanã's to get us some blankets so you can get some sleep right here, OK man?' said Pipsqueak.

'Good plan! While you're at it stop by Teresa's and get me a joint . . . And pick up a pack of Continentals without filters over at the Bonfim, and if there's time get my .38 from the top of the water tower, OK?'

'OK.'

'Got some money?'

'Yeah.'

'Go for it!'

Hellraiser shook the branches of the tree to get rid of the rainwater. Using a stick, he made a small ditch to divert the water from the place where he wanted to roll out his mat. He thought about Cleide, Hammer and Squirt; they'd undoubtedly hear about the snitch on the news. They wouldn't be turning up any time soon. A mixture of happiness and pain tore through his chest. Killing always brought back memories of the murders he'd witnessed throughout his life. It was always the snitches, the smart-asses, those who had their greedy eyes on other people's things and women, who bit the dust. There were those who were unlucky enough to die at the hands of the police or in holdups. He'd always heard gangsters talking about victims who retaliated—they deserved a faceful of lead, but those who handed everything over without trying anything smart . . . a gangster should at least leave the dickhead a little something to catch a bus with. 'The only ones that actually die are the motherfuckers who fuck things up for other people . . . No . . . I've seen tons of nice guys die, done in by their buddies while splitting the loot from robberies, or 'cos of schemin', tight-assed bitches or bar fights. There's even backstabbers who'll kill a man for nothin' just to get a reputation for being mean.' The fact that he'd lived his entire life witnessing murders for one reason or another relieved him of his pain that was not pain, because he imagined the news spreading that he was the one who had killed the northerner. He'd be feared more by other gangsters, the cool guys, the snitches. He liked seeing people afraid of him and laughed on the inside when someone crossed the street to avoid him, or when he asked someone a favor and other people offered to do it to get in his good graces. One day he'd be the most famous gangster in the place. He thought about meeting Boss of Us All head-on to settle the score with him. But no . . . He'd be buying himself a headache for the rest of his life. Killing a pig was like signing your own death warrant. The whole battalion would take to the streets until they killed the man responsible. The thing to do was lie low until the next day, especially since Beelzebub hadn't shown up yet. He might be preparing a surprise attack.

The rain left for good. A waning moon appeared in the sky behind the Grajaú Range. The silence of the night calmed him, as it had done since he was a boy. The crickets were chirping. If it hadn't rained, he could have sat by the river's edge, but the river was full and its banks were neck high in mud. He got the spot ready for the night. Pipsqueak arrived with everything he'd asked for and then left, saying he had a headache. Hellraiser ate the food Lúcia Maracanã had made him and smoked a joint. He hoped the night would pass quickly. The next day he'd see Berenice and surely find out whether she'd decided to be his girlfriend. He'd have that tasty black ass every possible way. She seemed like a nice girl. He needed a woman to cook for him, wash his clothes and fall into his arms whenever he wanted. He believed she'd accept his offer; she'd come on to him at Black Carlos's place, had insisted on serving him and had even flashed her legs at him. This had to work, as it was the only way he'd forget Cleide.

He thought about the snitch again. The scene of his last breath came back to him like a poke in the eye. He wished he were like Niftyfeet, who only stole far from the area, without attracting pigs, snitches and enemies, but this nonsense of catching buses every day like a sucker was fucked up—going around looking for a good joint to do over wasn't his thing. The best was to hold up a big shop and go for a long time without having to worry about money . . . Stealing from gringos was too hit-and-miss. He remembered Pipsqueak's plan. If all went well, he could furnish his house and there would still be a decent amount left over. People who go to motels don't go there broke, especially on a Saturday, the day to spend money.

The night brought a mild chill. Hellraiser covered himself, trying to get to sleep, but the mosquitoes stopped him from dropping off. His thoughts roved through the alleys of the projects, in a constant state of transformation. Families continued to come from Rio de Janeiro's different *favelas* and neighborhoods to the houses built around squares on vacant plots. Who were those people? Would any other gangsters be coming? Over at The Blocks there were already loads of them, as well as on The Other Side of the River. No one would be more respected than he was. He'd bump off anyone right then and there who tried to throw their weight around. This White Hand guy only worked in the Baixada region, so he didn't have to worry about him. The danger was that motherfucker Boss of Us All and Detective Beelzebub, but all he had to do was try and lie low on the days they were on duty, or always have some dough in his pocket; people had told him that they both accepted hush money when there was no one else around.

Pipsqueak arrived at nine o'clock with bread, coffee in a Coke bottle and news of everything that had happened in the last few hours. While he ate, Hellraiser discovered that everyone already knew it was him who had killed the snitch. Boss of Us All had prowled around all night long, busted Mango and Orange smoking weed, and told Orange's sister to rustle up two thousand cruzeiros, otherwise he was going to press charges. Pelé and Shorty had only shown up after the police had changed shifts. Detective Beelzebub hadn't shown his face yet and that wasn't a good sign; he might have changed his hours and could show up out of the blue.

Hellraiser hurried back to the projects. He wanted to go through how they were going to hold up the motel: who was going to stay out front; whether they were only going to hold up reception, or do the guests as well; whether they should call in one more partner; when they were going to case the area; where they would run to after the operation . . .

Acerola and Green Eyes collected money for one of the heads' mothers to take down to the station. Boss of Us All had said they could leave the money with the sergeant. He'd let them go. They had already raised half the money from friends; now all they had to do was go to Madalena's to ask her for help, because their friends had bought the weed at her den.

'Hey, you know those guys that bought some weed here yesterday? They got busted. Boss of Us All wants two thousand to let them go. We've already got a thousand. If you could help us out with the rest . . .'

'What guys? There were so many people here yesterday.'

'A white guy, he was wearing blue shorts, Bamba sneakers. The other . . .'

'Ah! I know—it's Mango, who lives over on Blonde Square,' said Madalena.

'That's the one!'

'Don't you think they might snitch on me?'

'If they were gonna snitch, they'd've already done it. The cops bashed the shit out of them all the way from Prospectors' square to the station and didn't stop until Mango's mom got there,' said Acerola.

Madalena gave them the difference after warning them that if they were lying their lives would be on the line, because she had the protection of the gangsters. Acerola and Green Eyes laughed sincerely. They'd never do such a thing. According to their rules, swindling people in their own neighborhood was a serious offense. A cause for disrespect and even death, depending on the case. They knew the gangsters would never forgive them, especially Ercílio, the dealer's own son, a gangster himself. It wasn't that they feared them, because if they were in the right they'd stand up to any gangster in the projects. They were only concerned about stirring up trouble for no reason, losing people's respect or snuffing it for real. They gave the money to Mango's mother.

Hellraiser stayed home all day on the lookout. Whenever he heard a car or unusual activity he'd check the street through a crack in the window with his gun cocked. Pelé and Shorty went to The Other Side of the River to fly kites with the kids. They hung around there until nightfall. Berenice left home early to get some money. She went to steal from the rich housewives in the South Zone street markets. She'd already decided to accept Hellraiser's offer. She wanted to have children, a family, her own place and a man by her side. She didn't think he was messing around; he really did want to move in with her. She'd look for him as soon as she got back. She arrived in Leblon at around eight o'clock, prayed that everything would work out alright, and walked through the streets without noticing the people who passed her. She was practically at a snail's pace when she felt a hand on her shoulder.

'What's up, man?' said Berenice when she turned around.

'Everything alright?' asked her friend.

Berenice didn't spend long with the taxi driver, an old neighbor from the *favela* of Esqueleto. She told him what she was going to do. He offered her a getaway ride to the neighborhood of Gávea.

She entered the market with a razor hidden in her hand and chose the busiest stands, where she could cut open handbags and remove purses. She was successful all three times. The first woman she robbed only realized what had happened when Berenice was already getting into her friend's taxi to go eat at a bar in Gávea.

'Everyone quiet or I'll shoot!' said Hellraiser to the occupants of a Chevrolet Opala parked in Taquara Square.

'Get out very slowly with your hands in the air!' said Black Carlos, pointing the .38 at the couple, who quickly obeyed.

On Friday, Pipsqueak, Hellraiser, Pelé and Shorty had gone to case the motel. It was a three-story building with two gates, a garage, colorful blinking lights everywhere, porcelain dwarves by the fountain in the garden and, on the right-hand side, the reception area, where an operator, manager, receptionist and two security guards worked. That was all they had observed the previous day. They knew there would also be cooks, waiters, chambermaids and cleaning and storeroom staff. They'd thought it best to take another man on the job.

They'd all go into the reception area together. They'd overpower the suckers easily, then lock them in a bathroom or something. They'd give the building a once-over to get the other staff members out of the way and would then go through the rooms and suites. If the pigs showed up, they'd make their getaway through the back, where there was a large area of bush, on the outer limits of the projects themselves. They'd only shoot to save their lives. If everything went well, they'd head for the neighborhood of Salgueiro, where they'd lie low for twenty-four hours.

They shook hands several times, made toasts with rounds of beer and kitchen-sink cocktails, shared a joint and snorted with the same straw, celebrating the opportunity to land a lot of money.

Pipsqueak was allowed to go only at the last minute; he was so insistent that his friends agreed to let a kid participate in a man's job. Although he knew he'd receive an equal part in the division of profits just for having cased the joint, what really made him happy was being able to go with his buddies. Black Carlos thanked them for inviting him to take part in the holdup.

'It's times like this that you know who your real friends are. Some guys try to pull a job off alone when they think they're onto the jackpot . . . I was thinking about having a quick one with my chick, but I'm gonna hang around to show you all my appreciation, know what I'm sayin', fellas?'

Hellraiser took the steering wheel of the Opala. He told the owners that if they went to the police they'd chase them all the way to hell if they had to. He also told them that they'd dump the car over in the Grajaú Range after three days. His intention was to get them to say, in the event that they went to the police, that the gangsters were heading for the Grajaú Range. They took the Rodovia Bandeirantes highway, with Hellraiser reminding everyone that they'd agreed not to kill anyone. If anyone tried to resist, all they had to do was club them on the nose with the butt of a gun and the dickhead would take a snooze on the spot.

It was after midnight on that full-moon night on the Bandeirantes highway, and the others were crouched low in the car. Hellraiser kept looking into the rearview mirror. The eloquence of the silence that spread beyond the roar of the car engine made him ask Black Carlos to check the guns; he didn't like silence at moments like this. He told Pipsqueak again that his job was to stay outside keeping an eye on the comings and goings. If the pigs showed up, all he had to do was go into the motel, shoot at the first window he saw and get out of there.

They entered through the back gate. At the front desk, there was only the operator, who was so drowsy her head nodded up and down as if bouncing in the air. She offered little resistance.

'How many people work in this shithole, bitch?' Hellraiser asked her, his left arm around her neck and his right hand pressing the barrel of his .38 into her head.

'Twelve,' she answered in a barely audible voice.

'How many've got guns?'

'The two guards and the manager.'

'Anyone upstairs?'

'Three chambermaids.'

'In the kitchen?'

'Four people work in the kitchen . . . Please don't kill anyone!' she begged.

'Where's the guards?'

'Everyone's in the kitchen. It's supper time.'

'If you're lyin' I'll blast your face off! What're those two doors there?'

'Office and bathroom.'

'So lock her in the bathroom,' said Hellraiser.

Then they all burst into the kitchen at once.

'OK, the shit's goin' down now!'

Hellraiser assured them that if they were all good boys and girls nobody would get hurt. Black Carlos took the guns from the security guards and manager. He, Pelé and Shorty tied up all the employees with nylon string. They knocked them out with punches and kicks, then locked them in the bathroom, where there were no windows. 'It's never been easier!' thought Hellraiser, who'd been worried about the time it would take to overpower them if they were all in different places. They'd got the lot in one fell swoop.

Hellraiser and Carlos headed for the second floor. In the office, Pelé and Shorty got the daily takings and valuables and took the phone off the hook like Hellraiser had told them to.

Outside, the night passed slowly for Pipsqueak. He wasn't nervous; in fact he never was. He really wanted to hear a shot inside the motel so he could emerge as a trump card in the plot of that game. He liked being a gangster. One of life's wounds in his soul had given him a thirst for revenge; he wanted to kill tons of people as soon as possible to get famous and be respected like Big over in Macedo Sobrinho. His hand glided across his revolver as the words of the most precise premise glide over lips: the one capable of silencing anyone who listens. He was wild, had a sixth sense and could shoot with both hands. He never lost a fistfight. He enjoyed provoking pain in others just for a laugh, since nothing weighed on his conscience. He was the despair of the storms condensed in the irises of each victim, the pain of bullets, death's prelude, a shiver down the spine, the cause of last breaths—and there he was, a mere lookout, feeling like a guard dog.

Hellraiser opened the door to 201 dressed as a waiter. He had demanded that the manager give him copies of the keys, as he'd planned the previous night before falling asleep. This son of Ogum, of Estácio and of the desire to get lots of money, was quick-thinking and calm. He had to hit the jackpot. The couple didn't notice the robbers come in. Hellraiser hit the man over the head with the butt of his gun and Black Carlos covered the woman's mouth.

'We don't wanna hurt no one, but if anyone tries to get smart we'll kill 'em, got it?' said Carlos, his voice wavering not only because holdups made him nervous, but also because he found it difficult to contain himself while holding a naked woman. They tied the couple up in the bathroom with sheets and cleaned them out. They got two hundred cruzeiros, two watches and a gold chain, and even went back to the bathroom to get the woman's earrings.

They entered 202. The couple was asleep. A brunette lying with her legs open filled Black Carlos's gaze; he'd never had such a sexy woman. Hellraiser was completely focused. He wanted to be as quick as possible. He noted a half-empty bottle of whisky on one side of the bed.

'They won't be wakin' up so soon!' he said.

He ordered Carlos to lock the door and chill out. He took two hundred dollars and a few cruzeiros from the man's wallet. From the woman's purse, just a checkbook and forty cruzeiros. He slipped the gold ring off her finger. There wasn't a single blemish on her body. She had a tattoo above her right breast, emphasizing its beauty. Black Carlos bit his lower lip and let one of his hands slide softly down her leg. She remained immobile. Hellraiser signaled his disapproval. They met Pelé and Shorty in the hall.

'Everything OK?'

'Everything OK,' answered Pelé and Shorty.

'OK, it's like this: gimme what you got downstairs, take the keys and go up to the third floor to make sure there isn't anyone else there . . . That bitch might be setting us up. Then you can do the rooms. Only shoot to save your life!' ordered Hellraiser, his eyes glued to the door of 203. The couple sensed the key turning in the door. They went in.

'Here's a drink on the house.'

'You should've buzzed first! You can't come in just like that!'

Hellraiser didn't utter a word, positioned himself in front of the man, removed the towel covering his revolver on the tray and said in a low voice:

'The shit's goin' down, man!'

The woman screamed. Black Carlos hit her in the nose with the butt of his gun. The man tried to fight back, but Hellraiser punched him, then stuck the barrel of his gun in the man's mouth.

'Wanna die, motherfucker?'

He removed the barrel from the man's mouth and gave him two blows with the butt of the gun to knock him out. They cleaned them out. On top of money and jewelry, they got a .32-caliber revolver. Everything was going as planned. He had to stay calm, work faster and continue getting lucky when surprising their victims, even the ones who were awake.

Pelé and Shorty didn't find a single staff member on the third floor. They glanced around nervously, afraid of being surprised. They stopped in front of one room and thought it better to do a different one. Their indecision cost them time. They decided to go by the numbers. They didn't know how to read, but counting was a piece of cake. They went into 301. Pelé and Shorty went for the occupants' noses, hitting them several times with the butts of their guns. They drenched the sperm-soaked sheet in blood. Two deaths splattered across the room.

They tied up the bodies and threw them in the bathroom. They took the man's taxi money from his wallet. There was nothing in the woman's purse. They thought it was a good amount. They forgot to take their rings, the woman's earrings and the gold chain around the man's neck. When they were about to enter the next room, they remembered they'd left the door open and went back to lock it. Nothing could go wrong. They went into 302. This time they found the couple sleeping. Just to be sure, they decided to bust their noses. They didn't take any lives this time. They tied up the couple and when they were about to clean them out, they heard a shot and the sound of breaking glass. They jumped through the window at the same moment as Hellraiser and Black Carlos and took off running together.

Over in City of God, a gangster looked at the creature moving with difficulty on the bed. He got up from the chair, reeling. He hadn't eaten in three days. He examined the knives he had in the house, chose the largest, sharpened it on the edge of the sink and lit a cigarette off the butt of the one he was smoking. He felt like having another shot and downed a glass of *cachaça* without tipping out a little for his saint. He smoked his cigarette compulsively, letting the ash fall on the hard cement floor. He ran his eyes across the rickety chairs, the spiderwebs on the ceiling; the sound of water dripping from the broken spout into the sink was as familiar as the broken lamp on the bedside table, a survivor of two floods. The fridge, propped up on a rock and two blocks of wood, shuddered, then went quiet forever. His emotions were a cauldron swinging back and forth between the two sides of his heart. For a second he considered not going ahead with it, but his determination to make his wife suffer had solid foundations, for since the day he had first set eyes on that disgusting creature, a desire for revenge had possessed his deepest thoughts; it had grown bitterly, multiplied itself unchecked and irreversibly installed itself in his heart. He knew the idea of letting things run their course would return, but he also knew it would leave, as his peace of mind had done. Women who fucked other men should rot in hell for all eternity. That bitch had to pay dearly. Although he'd never tell her, he loved her like a devoted dog—but now he hated her just as much. He'd become a mad dog.

'Why? Why?' he asked himself.

She hadn't had a penny to her name when he'd met her. He'd set up house for her, bought her clothes, sent her to a beauty parlor to do something about that unkempt frizz, and the bitch had gone and screwed another man. He thought about the affection he'd given that slut who couldn't find anyone to bring home the bacon, the nights he had gone out looking for sausages to cater to her pregnant woman's cravings, the times he'd placed his ear against her belly trying to hear the fetus. He imagined his wife running her tongue across the head of some white bastard's dick, spreading her cunt open for a white man's or a northerner's cock. She'd always liked whites. That's why she never took her eyes off the television during the soaps, where you never saw blacks. Whenever that Francisco Cuoco guy appeared on TV, she almost came.

The desperation of imagining his wife coming with someone else made him seek within himself the cruelest revenge. He ran his eyes around the room again, but this time he saw nothing. His fury had the same dimensions as his fever; he felt shivers and cold in that three-dimensional heat. He was thinking so fast he couldn't remember what he'd thought just a minute before.

Several times in dreams he'd seen himself meticulously carrying out his revenge. The fatalities were so specific, he didn't realize he was dreaming. When he awoke he had to look at that little shit again to be sure of what had really happened. When he came to grips with reality, that tumor, destroyed in his dream, recomposed itself more homogeneously.

He drank another glass of *cachaça* at leisure, a cruel smile on his face. His saint was forgotten again. He seized the knife with the speed of the Devil. Something had always told him that one had to begin certain deeds in a great hurry, otherwise they don't work, they have no effect. He placed the newborn on the table. At first the baby behaved as if it were going to be picked up. He held its right arm with his left hand and started sawing at the forearm. The baby thrashed about. He had to place his left knee on its torso. The baby's tears poured out as if trying to wash away its retinas, in an inhuman sobbing.

The murderer's spirit waged battle with itself, but he didn't allow himself to consider stopping his undertaking. He felt the pleasure of revenge and laughed just thinking about his wife's reaction. He didn't know who he hated more, the baby or his wife. His actions were automatic, as if he were grease, sucked in by the force of a set of gears.

Revenge determined the crime and the crime would bear, by its very nature, the mark of a red-blooded man's wounded pride.

He had a hard time getting through the bone, so he grabbed the hammer under the kitchen sink and, with two blows of the knife, finished the first scene of his act. The severed arm did not fall from the table; it stayed there within eyeshot of the avenger.

The baby kicked as much as it could, its cries a voiceless prayer without a God to hear them. Then it could cry out loud no longer, and its only reaction was a contorted face, the bright red that threatened to spring from its pores, and the kicking of its tiny legs. He cut the other arm slowly. That little white shit had to feel lots of pain. It occurred to him not to use the hammer anymore—the baby would suffer more if he cut the hardest parts slowly. The sound of the knife severing the bone was soft music to his ears. The baby floundered in its slow death. Its two legs were cut off with a little more work and the help of the hammer. The murderer raised the knife above his head to bring it down and split its defenseless heart in two. He knew that if he went to prison his cell mates would inevitably give it to him up the ass, because inmates loathe child murderers. But he wouldn't let anyone near his asshole. He could die, but become a faggot, never. That would be redemption for the traitor, and she only deserved eternal torment. No, he couldn't let that happen, he wouldn't be unlucky enough to get caught—he'd take off right away for some backwater town.

He put together the body parts as if solving a jigsaw puzzle, put everything in a shoe box and with unsteady steps headed for his mother-in-law's house. He pressed one of his palms to the left side of his chest to try to calm his furiously thumping heart. Contrary to what he had always done, he clapped his hands at the gate. His youngest sister-in-law came to the door and immediately called his wife. She had gone to her mother's place, two blocks from home, to get some fennel to make tea for the baby, who seemed to have colic. The murderer felt avenged; there were only a few minutes left before he'd see that woman suffering like a cow in a slaughterhouse, because that's what she was. He couldn't accept that his child was white, since he was black and so was his fucking wife. She came quickly, thinking about the baby; it was breast-feeding time. As she came over she asked where it was. Instead of answering, he waited for her to arrive, took the lid off the box and said:

'Give it to your child's father. You think you were gonna pull the wool over my eyes forever?'

In an impulsive gesture, the woman pulled one of the baby's arms out of the box. A mere trickle of blood connected it to the rest of the body. The woman fainted, the man fled. He was arrested a few days later.

Over in the Rec, a man lay in wait behind the club. At around 10 P.M., he'd told his wife he was going to a friend's to lend him a mallet and large knife, but he'd had a drink or two and there he was, alone, after midnight, preparing to defend his honor.

Two days earlier, he'd followed his wife when she left work. He'd been suspicious of her for a long time. He felt relieved when he saw that she went straight to the bus stop, but even so, he took a taxi to follow the bus, like a detective in a made-for-TV movie. Instead of getting off at her usual stop, his wife rang the bell at The Blocks. As she got off, she glanced around, without noticing her husband inside the taxi, and hugged a man who was always passing in front of their house on his way to The Other Side of the River. She gave him a kiss on the lips and, holding hands, they went into a block of apartments.

'I bet they're gonna screw at some friend's place,' he thought.

He went home to wait for his wife. She arrived, complaining that she was tired, and said she didn't want to do anything that night because her boss had worked her hard that day, making her stay back late. He agreed. The next night he went to the corner to see what time the guy passed. The bastard went past at two o'clock in the morning and even had the nerve to greet him.

Loverboy should have crossed the Rec bridge by now. The betrayed husband was crying by the time he saw a man appear on the corner by the Leão supermarket. He let the man draw closer to be sure it was really the guy that was fucking his wife. He adjusted his grip on the knife in his right hand, the mallet in his left, and crouched down, waiting for him to pass. He tiptoed after him and, with several blows, decapitated him. He took a plastic bag from his pocket, put the bloody head with bulging eyes in it, went home and threw it into the adulteress's lap.

Over at the motel, Pipsqueak walked down the second-floor corridor looking for victims. He wanted to rob, maim or kill someone—it didn't matter who. The guests, frightened by the shots, locked their doors. Pipsqueak broke down the first, the second, and stormed the third after shooting the lock, like the heroes in American films. A couple awoke to discover they were being shot at, although the bullets only grazed them. He cleaned them out. He broke into another room. The man tried to resist and got a bullet in the arm. He was trying to break into more rooms when he heard police sirens. He threw himself out of the window head-first, did a somersault in the air and landed on the ground ready to run.

He was happy as he ran into the bush, for he had actively taken part in the holdup. That's why he had faked the arrival of the police. He couldn't stand hanging around outside where time didn't pass, with everything going on inside. He'd hoped that a couple would turn up at the motel, because then he wouldn't have to simulate a situation in order to get involved, but nothing had happened for real; not the police, nor more guests.

Hellraiser, Black Carlos, Pelé and Shorty came to a halt in the bush. It was time to sort things out and split the loot, even though they hadn't yet counted the money or checked the value of the jewels, because if the police appeared and one of them was caught with all the goods, everything would be lost.

'Pipsqueak must've got caught. I didn't want to bring that kid,' said Hellraiser, mopping the sweat from his face. 'Now the shit's hit the fan, we'd better head back to City of God,' he continued.

'No way, man! Let's get on over to Salgueiro 'cos we might . . .'

'You wanna take a car now, with the pigs after us?' broke in Hellraiser in an authoritative voice. They walked on through the bush for a time in silence. After passing the Dread soccer field,

Hellraiser said they'd have to set aside Pipsqueak's share and, if he'd been caught, they'd send him the money in prison. They stopped at the foot of the haunted fig tree to divide the money five ways. Hellraiser bemoaned the arrival of the police.

'If the cops hadn't shown up, we would've got ourselves a nice little bundle! We would've hit the jackpot!'

'What if Pipsqueak snitches?' asked Carlos.

'The kid can be trusted, man. He won't snitch.'

The mosquitoes stopped them from hanging around for long. They headed for Block Thirteen to have a beer, smoke a joint and play pool. They went around the lake and crossed the State Water Department bridge in a hurry. As they turned into the first alley of Block Thirteen, they heard Detective Beelzebub's voice:

'If you guys touch your guns or run for it, I'll take you down right where you are!'

Ignoring the threat, they tore off down the alleys. A random pothead came along with a lit joint and, when he saw everyone running, took off too, but his steps didn't take him very far. A spray of bullets from Beelzebub's machine gun perforated his head. The man writhed in the burbling water of a blocked drain. Beelzebub ignored the others and went doggedly after Hellraiser, who reached the edge of the river, zigzagging back and forth. Before he'd got to the end of the first block, he turned into someone's yard and jumped the back fence into Middle Street. Boss of Us All was lying in ambush on the corner and joined the chase. As he ran he told the detective to leave it to him. Beelzebub begrudgingly went after Black Carlos, Pelé and Shorty again. Hellraiser, hearing only fire from a .38, figured that Beelzebub was no longer chasing him and decided to return fire. As he rounded corners, he waited for his pursuer to appear at the other end, then pulled his trigger. He wouldn't have done this had his enemy been carrying a machine gun, but in the case of a .38 against a .38, the smartest would win. Boss of Us All swore, saying there'd be no escaping this time. They passed Batman's Bar, rhythmically exchanging fire.

Mango and Green Eyes got rid of a roach and took off running when they heard the gunshots. Boss of Us All spotted another two police officers in Main Square and fired several shots to alert them. They joined the chase. In desperation Hellraiser invaded a house with the intention of taking a child hostage, but he was unsuccessful; there was no one at home. His breathless thinking reminded him that he had to jump walls, fences and climb onto rooftops to see where his enemies were and where they were heading. He thought it best to run for The Plots. His legs were slow to obey his head's commands. He decided to climb the first leafy tree he saw so he could recollect himself.

Down Below, Black Carlos, Pelé and Shorty were exchanging fire with Beelzebub and Officer Baldie. Furious over a defect in his machine gun, Beelzebub didn't want to catch the gangsters—he wanted to send them off to the pits of hell. Pelé and Shorty went wherever Carlos went, which irritated him. Carlos decided to lose them.

'Hey, I'm gonna double back and shoot him in the ass.'

He went around the block, took aim at the detective, fired and hotfooted it out of there. The shot grazed Officer Baldie. Beelzebub's ire took on a new proportion. He strode out into the gunfire and the gangsters retreated to The Blocks with Beelzebub on their heels.

Hellraiser had been up an almond tree for more than half an hour. Boss of Us All had seen him cross the street and head toward The Plots. The police officers figured that he couldn't have gotten very far. They decided to split up, and whoever found him first would fire a shot to warn the others. When he noticed Boss of Us All heading his way, Hellraiser moved in order to jump and take off running again. For a second he thought he should stay where he was. No, it would be better to jump and get out of there. His hesitation lost him time. There was no way he could keep running without getting hit. He knew Boss of Us All was a good shot. He settled back on his branch and bided his time. He visualized his *pombagira*. Now everything depended on her.

* * *

Boss of Us All searched the bush high and low. He remembered the flashlight he hadn't brought as he took one last drag on his unfiltered Continental and tossed it away. Then he crouched down to pick up the butt and lit a joint. He imagined Hellraiser would be far away by then. He might as well relax, since everything had gone wrong. He strolled along slowly, decided to sit under the tree where Hellraiser was and pulled on the joint.

He lit another cigarette, took off his cap, loosened his bootlaces and placed his revolver on an exposed root of the almond tree. Hellraiser tried to change position so he could shoot him in the backside and silently cursed the wasp flying around his head.

'Fucking hell! Why did the little bastard have to appear now?'

Pelé and Shorty arrived at The Blocks along with Beelzebub's bullets. To their surprise, Silva, Cosme and Biriba, gangsters from The Blocks, were also exchanging fire with other civil policemen. The police retreated when they arrived. But Beelzebub shouted:

'Let's kill the bastards!'

After stopping to catch his breath, he took aim at Pelé's neck and fired. One of the gangsters from The Blocks passed in front of him and fell to the ground writhing, a pool of blood forming around his head. A thin trickle filled the holes in the ground where Stringy and Rocket had played marbles that morning.

Cosme and Silva joined Shorty and Pelé, crossed Gabinal Road and hid in one of the haunted mansions. Detective Beelzebub checked the dead man's documents. He laughed when he noticed that the gun was one of many he'd given his friend Armando to sell. (Armando was a Military Police officer dismissed from the force for having killed his wife and her lover when he found them fucking in his bed.) He took the documents; they might be useful for forging something in the event that the guy didn't have a record.

Hellraiser let the wasp sting him. On his branch it was hard to find a position to shoot from. Boss of Us All leaned his head against the tree trunk. Tiredness made his eyes unsteady. The desire to sleep forced him up to go look for the other police officers. A little farther along he stopped to adjust his boot and heard the sound of someone getting a beating. They had caught three teenagers smoking a joint and drinking wine, while one of them played a guitar.

'You catch the bastard?' asked Boss of Us All.

'No, but we caught these potheads here.'

'Got any money on you?'

'Yeah, here, take it!'

'Now run and don't look back!' said Boss of Us All.

Up in the tree, Hellraiser had got rid of the wasp, changed position and was furious for not having managed to kill Boss of Us All. He stared at the distant police officers, who were dividing up the kids' money. He climbed down and made sure the money and jewels were secure. He walked swiftly through the night, crossed the river and took shelter at Nasty Jorge's place.

At the street market, talk of the previous night's shoot-out frightened housewives, who made sure their children didn't leave their yards.

Out Front, Mango and Jackfruit were listening to Acerola, who said there had been more than twenty Civil and Military Police officers patrolling the projects the night before. He said that in addition to the murders, a motel on Bandeirantes highway and two bakeries in Freguesia had been held up, an Army colonel's house on Pau Ferro Road had been broken into and two pharmacies in Taquara had been robbed. He finished by saying that it was a bad idea to get high anywhere in the projects because the pigs wouldn't leave anyone in peace until they caught someone.

'How do you know about all this commotion?' asked Green Eyes.

'I heard it on the radio this morning . . .'

Hellraiser left Nasty Jorge's place after one o'clock in the afternoon. He found Berenice at the market. He could tell by the way she looked at him that she was his. He planted a kiss on her lips, took her hand and they walked together down Middle Street. Back at home, he asked her to go look for his friends.

'Pipsqueak must've got caught, man! He still hasn't shown up,' said Carlos.

'I bet it was him that snitched,' said Berenice.

'No way, the kid can be trusted. He'd die before he snitched on someone!' said Hellraiser.

The gangsters had lunch, grumbled about not having hit the jackpot, and decided they'd better spend some time away from the projects; the police would continue to be trouble until they killed or caught someone.

'Truth is, no one knows if Pipsqueak snitched or not,' said Black Carlos.

They went to Salgueiro late in the evening.

On Monday, Saturday's crimes had made front-page news. A couple had been murdered at the motel. There had been no fatalities in the other holdups. After spelling his way through the news for his friends, Black Carlos got angry about the death of the couple. Pelé and Shorty stood up for themselves, saying they'd done everything Hellraiser had told them to. But the news of the motel robbery, the death of the baby, and the decapitated man emblazoned across the front page made them look courageous and fearless.

'Gangsters've gotta be famous to be really respected!' Hellraiser told Carlos.

In fact they were all proud to see the motel on the front page. They felt important, respected by other gangsters in the projects and in other *favelas*; it wasn't just anyone who saw his exploits stamped across the front page of a newspaper. And if they were unlucky enough to get caught, they'd be respected in prison for having pulled off a large-scale robbery. It was a shame their names hadn't been mentioned in the article, but at least it said that it could only have been the gangsters from City of God. Everyone who knew them would know they'd done it.

'It's better like that, you know, 'cos if our names were there, we'd have another investigation on our hands.'

Children took over the streets. They spent the mornings selling ice pops, and the afternoons playing. The school holidays, which arrived together with the heat, were always like that. Stringy and Rocket decided to sell ice pops that Tuesday. They got the goods on a sale-or-return basis at China's ice cream parlor on Edgar Werneck Avenue, near the projects. Their friends had declined the enterprise. They preferred to tie string to the ends of a broomstick, and throw it into the river to fish out the things washed along by the water. It was much more exciting than plodding around in the sun shouting, 'Ice pops for sale!' Fishing in the river for pieces of wood, oil cans, tree branches and all those other things required talent and luck.

Rocket sold his box of ice pops in a few hours and went to give his mother the money he'd earned. He went through the neighborhoods of Freguesia, Anil and Gardênia Azul, in addition to the streets of the projects. Stringy sold less than a third of his goods. He decided to give his fishing friends ice pops and consumed his merchandise while taking an occasional turn with the broomstick. Rocket didn't stay at home long; he'd earned the right to play until whatever time he pleased. He'd passed his end-of-year exams and now worked during the holidays to help out at home.

It was the time of year to go shopping, fix up the house, get your body in shape and make New Year's resolutions to stop smoking. End-of-year festivities always brought the hope that everything would work out from then on. The kids earned money by selling river sand to construction sites, and ice pops and bread in the streets. Some boys offered to weed yards and paint houses and apartments. Others collected bottles, wire and iron to sell at the scrap yard. Workers relied on their Christmas bonuses, gangsters on holdups and robberies, while Boss of Us All, Beelzebub and the other police officers concerned themselves with beating up potheads when they busted them, stealing stolen goods from thieves and demanding protection money from the den owners. The girls who worked the street markets in the South Zone sold their stolen goods personally.

Out Front, stalls were set up selling all manner of products. Pork Joe sold meat from his own pigs behind the Leão supermarket. The stalls gradually took over the main streets of the projects. December 24th, the men started drinking early and put their sound systems out on their windowsills when they'd done their last-minute shopping. The women divided their time between housework and visits to the beauty salons within the projects themselves. At midnight, families gathered together to cry for the loss of loved ones, then went outside to wish their neighbors a Merry Christmas.

The week passed in a festive atmosphere. Hellraiser, Black Carlos, Pelé and Shorty returned to the projects. They figured the pigs wouldn't bother them right after Christmas.

Niftyfeet, Jap and Black Carlos decided to rustle up some money in Copacabana on New Year's Eve.

'The best thing is to concentrate on the gringos. We can hang around the hotel then head over to Leme, right? But we can't stay near the Copacabana Palace the whole time—it'll be crawlin' with pigs,' said Niftyfeet.

Hellraiser gave Berenice money to buy the things they still needed so they could move in together properly. She spent the week asking him to take some time off from his life of crime. He still didn't have a police record and there was no reason why he couldn't get a job. She wanted peace and quiet so she could bring up their kids without any hassles. Hellraiser said he was going to keep at it until he hit the jackpot so he could set up a big business with lots of employees working under him, while he counted money and gave orders. Then he'd think about kids.

Pelé and Shorty didn't waste time making plans. All they could think about was the five papers of cocaine they were going to buy to see in the New Year. They told everyone they knew that the best coke was in Curral das Éguas, the neighborhood above Campo Grande in the West Zone of Rio, and whoever wanted some just had to give them the money because they were going there to buy it on the 31st, as long as they gave them a quick bump. Everyone got really fucked up on New Year's Eve and during Carnival. Some people only snorted coke on these two occasions.

Squirt, Hammer and Cleide arrived on the last day of the year to celebrate the New Year with their friends. Cleide didn't want to go Up Top to get what was left of the furniture from her old place.

'The thing to do is get loads of money and do what Berenice did—buy everything new. Right, gorgeous?'

'But only after January. Now everyone's spent everything and people ain't got two pennies to rub together,' said Hammer, adding that they were going to spend some time at Hellraiser's place until things were sorted out.

The first minute of the New Year arrived. The year of Xangô, winner of disputes, the most powerful *orixá*, god of lightning and fire, king of justice. It was the year to work hard for a stable relationship, health and lots of money. The just would be successful that year.

Before the sun had even set, people had raced for places on buses heading for the beach so they could create a midsummer spring in the night and the sea. They cast flowers into the sea to bring new currents into the lives of all the children of father Xangô. They sang a verse for each *orixá*, hailing them before the waters of Iemanjá. They set off fireworks for Xangô, the keeper of justice, millions of colors to imitate his brilliance and many prayers to give thanks for his protection.

In City of God, hands were clasped, and words of happiness bathed in wine were uttered. The police did not show up and there were no fights, gunshots or deaths. The smokers smoked. The cokeheads snorted. The drinkers drank. Everything in the blessed peace of the year that was beginning.

* * *

Being busy with the meetings of the different samba school groups, choosing costumes and rehearsing made January pass quickly. The gangsters got hopping. It was much more important to get money for Carnival than for the New Year's Eve celebrations. They held up bakeries, taxis, pharmacies, pedestrians and homes in nearby areas and within the projects themselves. Even Niftyfeet took any and every opportunity to get his hands on some dough. Pelé and Shorty were responsible for most of the holdups within the projects.

On a scorching Friday, the two of them were walking down Middle Street, outraged at the pittance they'd got holding up the gas truck and shops on The Other Side of the River. They decided to rustle up some more that night. Anyone who didn't have their wits about them was going to end up with empty pockets. They entered an alley and crossed the Prospectors' rehearsal square.

The boys from the carnival group were crouched on a corner playing cards. The idea of holding them up occurred to both Pelé and Shorty at the same time. They looked at one another and nodded to show they were thinking the same thing. The players, absorbed in the game, didn't notice their footsteps. The group had finished rehearsing a short time before. They had put away their instruments, smoked a joint and were trying their luck at cards. Pelé and Shorty ordered them to stop the game. They said they didn't want any games in the area so as not to attract the pigs. And now that they'd warned them, they were not only going to take the money from the game, but also whatever they had in their pockets. Luis the Tease, who was in the game, got up, looked them firmly in the eyes and said:

'What's the story? You think we're dickheads just 'cos we don't carry guns? No one here's givin' money to anyone, man! We're here mindin' our own business and you guys come along tryin' to push us around. Fuck off and leave us alone!'

Pelé and Shorty were surprised by Luis the Tease's words. They fell silent for a moment. They instinctively cocked their guns, but before they could point them at Tease, they heard Vidal's voice:

'It's like this: if you pull your trigger on one of us, you're gonna have to pull it on all of us, right? 'Cos we're gonna beat the shit out of you. We ain't buyin' this gangster crap! And if you kill us all there's still stacks of others to come and settle the score! Everyone here's respected in the area. Just mention the Prospectors and everyone knows who we are. This nonsense of pointing guns on us is a joke!'

The others went on in the same way at Pelé and Shorty, who shook to the core. They weren't game enough to kill them all, and felt that the Prospectors might well jump them. Shorty remained frozen, while Pelé argued:

'That's right—I seen you talkin' with Niftyfeet. You a friend of his?'

'What if I am?' exclaimed Tease.

'I'm gonna let this go 'cos of that, OK?' said Pelé.

'So no more jerking us around. You know it'll get ugly for you if there's any trouble, right?' warned Acerola, who until then had only glared at the gangsters.

They headed for Block Thirteen in silence. That episode had violently wounded their definition of themselves—real gangsters can't be pushed around. Especially since the guys had been unarmed. They saw that no one there had been afraid. The terrible certainty of truth, in what both Luis the Tease and Vidal had said, hurt, and not only damaged their status as gangsters, but also as men. Red-blooded men. They'd been afraid of Vidal and Tease's athletic builds. They knew that if they'd been challenged by either one of them to a fistfight, they'd have had the shit bashed out of them. That Acerola could've kept his mouth shut, since everything had already been settled. His threat had really rubbed their noses in it.

Pelé looked at Shorty again, who was walking along with his head down, his gaze marking his next steps. He thought about comforting his friend, without owning up to his own fear. But how could he without admitting that they'd had to pussyfoot around with guns in their hands? The only alternative was to lie to himself, and say the only reason they hadn't killed everyone was because of Niftyfeet. He tried to believe his own words as he said they'd have wasted them all if he hadn't known that Niftyfeet would be pissed off. Shorty agreed with his friend without looking him in the eye. He believed the lie as much as his friend did. They said good-bye half-heartedly.

Carnival Saturday arrived with a fine but constant drizzle, but it didn't dampen the Devil's party in the streets of Rio de Janeiro. Sunday was the day the festivities really got going with the samba school parades.

Lúcia Maracanã paraded with Portela, Vila Isabel and Unidos do São Carlos as well as the projects' samba school, Acadêmicos da Cidade de Deus, which was in the fifth division for the first time. Niftyfeet paraded with Salgueiro and Unidos do São Carlos. He could never parade with other schools because his own heart wouldn't let him. For him, Carnival was about more than merry-making—all year long, he spent his spare time at home practicing the samba steps that would dazzle the tourists he had robbed the day before the parade.

On Carnival Monday, Niftyfeet enchanted the crowds, parading effortlessly in the Dragon's Breath carnival group. He liked it when Dragon's Breath ran into the Bigwig of Ramos, its greatest rival, because there was always a brawl. The fight between the members of the groups smashed up bars and destroyed hawkers' stalls. Some took the opportunity to rob people in the audience and the samba played on. The Jará group had promised to help Dragon's Breath if they were around at the time of the fight. They called themselves blood brothers. The Bohemians of Irajá, however, didn't get involved in scuffles. They paraded in the city center, Madureira and Irajá.

City of God had no funding from the city council, which was why it didn't have a stage in the square. Stoopy, a local shop owner, took it upon himself to make the stage and hire musicians for the projects' Carnival. On the last day of the festivities, the samba school paraded down Main Street, along with the Prospectors and the City of God Angels.

Salgueiro came out on top. Even before the judges' points had been counted, everyone was already saying that Salgueiro would be champion.

Niftyfeet again won the prize for best *sambista*. He laughed and cried, drank, smoked heaps of really good shit and snorted the best coke to celebrate his victorious dance steps, the perfect-scoring percussion section and the most beautiful master of ceremonies and flag-bearer of the Carnival.

Stringy, Rocket and their friends said good-bye to the holidays in the Eucalyptus Grove. They'd woken up early that Friday morning. Rocket had promised to bring a frying pan. Stringy had brought the oil and the others had brought flour, sugar, matches, cold water and an instant fruit-drink mix. One busied himself lighting a campfire and preparing the raspberry drink, their favorite, while the others went into the Eucalyptus Grove armed with slingshots to hunt for birds.

They were sure that Pipsqueak (who had started showing his face around the projects again), Night Owl, Carrots, Slick and the other kids that hung around with them would not turn up there. They liked picking fights for nothing, ran off with the ball when other kids were kicking a ball around, stole their toys, smoked weed on street corners and conducted all transactions with their guns cocked. They saw the other gang—Hellraiser, Squirt and Hammer—as adults.

After their meal, they lay in the grass. The sun's rays sent shafts of light between the leaves. Over in the fields, the cows roamed back and forth. Cars went by unnoticed on Highway Eleven. The river flowed softly. The water snakes swam freely in the pond. The lake remained unruffled by the gusts of wind that the boys felt on their faces. Our Lady of Sorrows Church and the mansions looked more beautiful from there. The fishermen tried their luck in the big lake. The sky was reflected in the sea at Barra da Tijuca, embodying the metaphor 'bluer than infinity.'

Batman was an earthly superhero, you had to be on his side. Superman was the strongest of all the superheroes, but if National Kid wanted to, he could knock him out, no sweat, because his pistol beamed kryptonite and a shitload of other things. That Doctor Smith in *Lost in Space* was the biggest faggot. If a gorgeous naked girl appeared here in the Eucalyptus Grove, what would you do? You say 'but it's not' after everything I say. I thought my nose was bleeding . . . but it's *snot*. If you make a hole and dig and dig and dig and dig, you're gonna come out in China. I'm gonna be a doctor when I grow up. Well I'm gonna be a policeman, 'cos if anyone tries to jerk me around I'll arrest them. My friend's got a dog just like Rin Tin Tin. Miss Vera's the most beautiful teacher at school. Once I dreamed she was my girlfriend. Let's see who's got the biggest dick? This story about the stork is a load of bull, we come out of our moms' snatches. I went to Santa Catarina by air, the plane stopped when we were halfway there, my parachute wouldn't open and I was falling fast, so I told the manufacturer to stick it up his ass. Milk milk, lemonade, round the corner, chocolate's made. Think of a number, multiply it by two, add four, divide it by two, take away the number you thought of. The answer's two.

They stayed there until nightfall. Classes started the following week.

Right after Carnival, Hammer got lucky in a robbery over near Freguesia. He'd gone alone one sunny morning to hold up the employees of a mansion and had broken open the safe, grabbed jewels, a .38-caliber gun, dollars and a few cruzeiros that were on the dresser. He returned to the projects by taxi. When he arrived home, he told Cleide:

'Here, go buy us some furniture, and get yourself a nice dress. Go to the beauty parlor, get your hair done and fix up your nails.

But don't take too long, 'cos I wanna have my way with you!' he finished, narrowing his eyes and biting his lip.

'Where do I change the dollars?'

'Go see Bahian Paulo—he'll do it in a flash.'

The gas delivery men didn't worry about the holdups anymore, as only Pelé and Shorty carried them out. They even found it funny when the two of them made spectacular appearances from one alley or another in broad daylight, as if they were holding up a carriage or ambushing an enemy in the Old West. The delivery men already had something set aside for them. They'd leave with their guns pointed at their victims, and before turning the corner they'd fire shots into the air to intimidate them.

Hellraiser and Squirt made some good money from the five taxis they held up one Friday night. They'd agreed that the money would go toward guns and ammunition. They'd let Armando know that they would be at the Doorway to Heaven bar to make the transaction on Saturday morning. Beelzebub delivered the goods to Armando. As always, he warned the middleman that if he ever found out that his name had been mentioned to the gangsters, he'd kill him. The former policeman signaled his agreement. The transaction took place among Doorway to Heaven customers at ten o'clock in the morning.

Before saying good-bye, Hellraiser lowered his head and looked as if he were trying to decide on the best date for an important engagement. Armando and Squirt waited for him to speak. The time Hellraiser was taking to talk made them somewhat ill at ease. Then out of the blue he confronted the middleman:

'It's like this, man—you've been makin' a nice little bundle off everyone for ages, haven't you? A cop down in the Fifth Sector sent us a message sayin' he'd send us a box of bullets for half your price. That means you're makin' twice as much as you should. So this time I'm takin' the guns. Give us yours too and gimme back my money.'

Armando obeyed the villain in silence. Squirt was surprised by his friend's attitude, and he concluded that they'd just made a dangerous enemy. Ex-policemen were worse than gangsters, because their old buddies in uniform would always cover them when they got into trouble. It wasn't a good idea to go around making enemies. He decided to bump him off. Hellraiser frisked Armando and told him to get running. Without consulting Hellraiser, Squirt fired at the middleman, who zigzagged back and forth across the vacant lot next to the bar and entered the hush unscathed.

'Get 'im?' asked Hellraiser.

'Yeah, right. You go and make decisions without consulting me . . . That guy's all cozy with the cops. He's a dangerous enemy to have. We shouldn't have let him go alive . . .'

'Just as well you didn't waste him, 'cos I wanna know who his supplier is. How much you wanna bet that Beelzebub or Boss of Us All are gonna show up round here today? Let's get out of here and tomorrow we'll find out.'

Boss of Us All left home in a temper because he was broke and didn't like demanding food from shops, bars, bakeries and supermarkets like the other policemen did. He went to work without the slightest inclination to do anything. He dispensed with the company of his fellow officers on his beat. He wanted to get some money on his own. He went through the projects with his gun cocked. He was unlucky in his first attempts, as everyone whose papers he demanded to see was employed. He crossed over to The Other Side of the River. He wanted to bust someone smoking weed so he could extort some money. He noticed a boy quicken his pace when he saw him. Boss of Us All took two bundles of weed from his pocket and sized him up from a distance, to make sure he really was loafing around. He could have got some dough out of him by threatening to take him in for vagrancy in the event that the bastard had been arrested previously, but that'd be a lot of work. He'd have to call the Fifth Sector to get them to check, and his friend there would want a little something to do the job on the quiet. He decided to frame the boy as he was frisking him. Each time he said the weed wasn't his, Boss of Us

All thumped him with the butt of his gun. He'd only quickened his step because he didn't have signed working papers. Boss of Us All ranted and raved, saying he didn't like being called a liar. When he found out he lived with his parents, he didn't take him down to the station, but instead made the boy take him to his house so he could demand money from the family. And he did just that.

The boy's father had to ask for the neighbors' help to raise the money Boss of Us All demanded. Before heading back to the station, he went home to give his wife half the money. It was much more than he made as a Military Police officer. He arrived at the station in a better mood and told his friends that everything was calm in the area. He took off his boots, lay down and spent the rest of the day reading a trashy novel.

That same Saturday, Mango had waited for Acerola, Orange, Jackfruit or Green Eyes on the corner by Batman's Bar to smoke a joint, but no one had shown up; they were all with their girlfriends. He was dying to have a toke or two and then stay home under a blanket watching a flick in a spacey haze. Time passed and none of his friends appeared. He decided to go to Jackfruit's place, as he knew he had some weed at home. The day before he'd scored a shitload of weed in Curral das Éguas. The driving rain saturated his Lee jeans from the knees down, where his umbrella offered no protection. The electricity went off and on with every crash of thunder, frightening the dogs, the stray cats, the chickens in people's yards.

'Jackfruit!' he called anxiously.

'He's not here,' answered a child's voice.

Mango took the same route back, hung around Batman's Bar a while longer, strolled to Main Square, spent more than an hour watching the buses arrive and not one of his friends showed up to have a smoke with him. He rolled up the bottoms of his jeans, reopened his umbrella and hurried off to Teresa's place.

'She's gotta sell me some weed on credit!' he thought aloud.

Teresa was home alone; her daughters had gone to the dance at the club. She was packaging up the weed she'd bought in Curral das Éguas. She no longer had a supplier to bring the weed to her place, as Ercílio had done: he used to supply her in addition to his mother. Teresa had begun dealing six months after her arrival in the projects. Before that only her husband had dealt, but he was always drunk and spent all the money he made getting trashed day after day. Always losing money and marijuana; sometimes he didn't have anything to offer customers, so his wife and children had to go hungry. He was killed because he used to go around mugging random people to show how tough he was, making a lot of enemies in no time at all. One day he mugged a gangster, who then shot him in the head six times with a .38.

The only asset he left his family was thirteen pounds of marijuana, which Teresa thought about giving to their friends, but her girlfriends advised her to sell it. She'd be silly to just give it away to the heads. All that weed was worth good money.

That was how she was initiated into her life of crime. Her den, now well run, yielded better fruit. She managed to extend her house, change her daughters' rags for decent clothes and feed them better. She bought a sofa, wardrobe, fridge and had plans to buy a TV set. She had nothing to complain about; her life had improved considerably.

She was getting ready to go to bed when she heard Mango's careful voice through the crack in the window. She said she'd be there straightaway, after seeing him at the gate through the partly open door.

'How many you want, son?'

'I just want a bundle of weed, just one, but I'm kinda broke, you know? If you advance me one, I'll bring you the dough tomorrow before noon.'

'I don't sell on credit, but if you want to have a smoke with me, come on in,' said old Teresa.

In a flash her thoughts turned to seduction. For a long time her only sexual experiences had been solitary. Mango sat on the filthy sofa and looked around the room. He saw Saint Cosmas,

Do Um and Saint Damian lit by an oil lamp, an old crystal cabinet with a few colored glasses, a tea set, the coffee table covered in knickknacks, spiderwebs billowing in the slightest breeze. Old Teresa meticulously rolled a huge joint, aiming to get him stoned so he'd be easier to seduce. They lit the joint. Teresa said it was special weed. She offered him a shot of whisky and told him she had some coke for after their smoke. Mango loved the idea. He smoked quickly so he could get to the coke—so expensive and hard to find. Teresa suggested they go to her room, saying that one of her daughters might arrive home and she didn't want them to see her doing lines. She closed the curtains, sprinkled the coke on a warm plate, and got a razor down from the top of the wardrobe. As she chopped out a couple of lines, she told Mango that she didn't know why she was so fond of him, that she had never done coke with any other customer, and that he was the first and only one. Whenever he wanted a bump or a smoke, all he had to do was let her know.

'Why don't you take off those wet pants? Stick 'em behind the fridge. They'll be dry in no time.'

'Good idea!' he said.

He took off his shirt too, egging the old woman on in her game. His white skin was lit by the glow from the oil lamp coming through the flimsy curtain. Teresa went to fetch more weed.

'Let's have another joint so that when we do the coke we'll get really fucked up?'

She asked Mango to roll, while she cut out ten lines of coke on the plate. While he smoked, she let her hand slide down his leg. She did this several times. Mango's silence made her place her hand firmly on his right leg.

'Your leg's so hairy!' she said in a soft voice.

Mango remained quiet. Old Teresa squeezed her fingers, moved her hand closer to his hard-on and left it there. The joint was half-smoked. She slowly took hold of him through his underwear.

'Mmm . . . you've got a stiffy!'

She squeezed his dick and ran her hand up and down it. Mango acted as if everything was completely normal. She knew he had the energy to give it to her good. 'Isn't life great!' she thought as she made his cock spring from the clutches of his underwear. She took him straight into her mouth. Mango felt nauseous at first, but old Teresa's appetite made him come quickly. When he'd recovered, he asked her to do it again. They forgot about the cocaine on the plate, the joint in the ashtray, the rain on the roof. He rammed his dick into her. He didn't know why, but he remembered his mother, his girlfriend, his friends. . . . He tried to stop, but couldn't. He felt real pleasure acting out that scene. He slowly started to behave as if he were madly in love.

Teresa thrashed about the bed. Not even her daughters—who were young, didn't have varicose veins and saggy breasts, and had teeth—had got themselves such a handsome young man. Perhaps one day she'd be able to walk down the street arm in arm with him, introduce him to her friends as her husband, but no, that'd be hoping for too much. It'd be great if things stayed as they were. She had several orgasms. When she felt that Mango was about to come—although she knew that with his eighteen years he'd quickly recover and go for it again—she slowed her movements so he'd spend as long as possible on top of her. When he came, she eagerly took him into her mouth. She was happy.

Saturday mornings belonged to the soccer and pool players. The afternoons, like the mornings, brought no mysteries: the men either slept or stayed on in the bars, while the women—who had woken early, done the grocery shopping and cleaned the house— flocked to the beauty parlors after lunch. Saturday nights, which were always different, saw few things repeated, and unexpected twists and turns abounded because people wished things to be so. New experiences had to be sought at the right time and place. Saturday nights promised enchantments, new loves, the firming of relationships. Young people would hold potluck parties in their backyards, children would play until late and boyfriends and girlfriends would meet. The smokers knew which den had the best weed and which police officers were on duty, and kept a low profile when it was Boss of Us All and company.

The club was always the best option late at night, even for those who had serious girlfriends. They would go to the dance to find women to have sex with because, after all, men need an oil change every week. Only losers were content just having a smooch with their girlfriends.

Lúcia Maracanã went to the dance alone. She had ended a fling the week before.

'I'm not stayin' at home cryin' over no man,' she told herself when she decided to go to the club.

The dance was in full swing by the time Lúcia entered the hall, where The Daydreams were playing. She looked around for friends. The half-lit hall concealed vows of love made to the music of slow songs. When the ballads came on, not everyone would risk asking a girl to dance—only those whose footwork and swing were up to scratch would head for the dance floor to strut their stuff. Lúcia paired up with Niftyfeet and took the opportunity to tell him the reasons for her breakup. Her friend gave her a supportive hug, making some other women jealous.

'If them bitches keep lookin' at me like whores without a john, their faces'll feel the back of my hand!' she exclaimed in his ear.

The music stopped and that's exactly what happened: one of Niftyfeet's admirers, pretending not to see her, spilled a glass of beer over her. The fight started in the corridor and moved into the entrance hall, by which time the admirer had already lost her blouse, and had cuts on her face and a bloody nose. Lúcia fought like a man; she liked to beat her enemy down to the ground. No one separated them because they wanted to see the other girl without her clothes on. Niftyfeet put an end to the fight himself and took the jealous girl into the club office.

She was a tall brunette with green eyes and long hair. She worked at the Leão supermarket, lived in the New Short-Term

Houses, and was the oldest daughter in a family of five children. She had been at work the first time she saw Niftyfeet, and had been waiting for a chance to approach him ever since. After she had collected herself she said, without looking him in the face, that she had only done it out of jealousy. Niftyfeet smiled. Although he felt sorry for her, he was also proud. He invited her to go for a drink somewhere else, with the aim of having her that very night. They set out to find a bar that was open. They walked slowly, exchanging information about their lives until they reached a bar, where they had a beer.

It was already after two in the morning when Niftyfeet confessed he'd been attracted to her since the moment he'd set eyes on her. He said he'd even thought of asking her to dance but was afraid she'd say no. He was lying. She pretended to believe him. He was already imagining himself making her come and her calling him hot and sexy.

'Let's go to my place for a bite to eat. Know how to cook?'

'Yeah.'

Niftyfeet's house was tidy, as always. The girl cast her eyes over the nicely arranged new furniture in his living room. She examined his samba and soccer trophies. While he showered, she decided what to whip up with the ingredients in his well-stocked pantry.

The pea soup gave off a good smell late that rainy night. It was cold out.

Niftyfeet came out of the bathroom reeking of perfume, wrapped in a red and white robe.

'Go and have a quick shower . . . The water's nice and hot . . . It's a good shower . . .' said Niftyfeet.

After she'd showered, they ate, then Niftyfeet started by kissing her knees.

When the rain mixed with the morning light, he tried to go for it again. His lover complained:

'I've got a headache.'

'I'm not surprised, that crazy bitch really laid into you . . . Stay in bed here and I'll go over to the pharmacy . . . I'll be right back.'

The girl thought about the night she'd had: if it hadn't been for that Lúcia Maracanã woman, it would have been perfect. 'What a man!' she sighed. In addition to being good-looking, affectionate, polite and clean, he was good in bed. It looked as if he had a mother or wife to look after his clothes. She decided to make breakfast, but first she took a peek in his wardrobe to satisfy her curiosity. When breakfast was ready, she lay down. Niftyfeet was taking so long, but she didn't dare wait for him in the street. It'd be too forward for their first date. It was already eight o'clock when a single repeated phrase was borne through the air on a wail:

'Niftyfeet's dead, Niftyfeet's dead, Niftyfeet's dead!!!'

A gash appeared in the morning, made by a phrase with an intransitive verb and a dead subject. There were tears on every street corner. Theories that his death was a lie slowly fizzled out.

The girl fainted in an old woman's lap. Hellraiser, who had never been seen crying, let tears fall on his knees as he crouched in an alley. Lúcia Maracanã did not cry, nor did she utter a word. She suffered, frozen on her doorstep. Squirt, Black Carlos, Pelé and Shorty found out about their friend's death at the Bonfim. The news flew like a stray bullet through City of God.

Out Front, Niftyfeet's body was covered with a blue sheet and everyone who arrived lit a candle so that light, lots of light, would illuminate the mysteries of the path his soul had just embarked upon. It was the only way to help Niftyfeet, who had never let anyone down. He'd been the one to turn up at bars and pay for everything; he'd treated everyone with respect, given money to the kids, and had always been in a good mood. In front of him no one had dared pick on those weaker than themselves.

'Niftyfeet's dead—long live the red and white of Salgueiro Samba School, Unidos do São Carlos, and the carnival group Dragon's Breath,' rose a voice in the crowd.

At the police station, the driver who had run him over was answering the officer's questions:

'How can you drive in reverse without looking behind you!?'

'But I did look!'

'And how is it you didn't see the guy?' he asked again without getting an answer, while the mob outside shouted:

'Lynch 'im! Lynch 'im! Lynch 'im!'

People filled the street corners to discuss Niftyfeet's life and death. Incensed by the facts—and going on information from a reliable source—Lúcia Maracanã broke down the door of a woman on Block Fourteen. A week after being dumped by Niftyfeet, the witch had been seen at the graveyard burying a toad with its mouth stitched up and reciting the prayer of death. 'If I can't have him, no one will,' she'd told her friends. By the time Lúcia burst into her house, the woman had already fled through the backyard, never to return to the projects. That afternoon, the game between Unidos and Oberom for the Jacarepaguá Championship was suspended. Dodival, a friend of the *sambista*, went to break the news to the people at his favorite samba schools. The fine rain continued throughout his wake.

'More than two thousand people at the funeral! His girls were all there, all hot little pieces of ass,' Torquato told the drunks packed into the Bonfim that Monday. 'Even the Bigwig of Ramos carnival group sent flowers!' he finished.

'Really?! Why didn't you tell me earlier, man?' said Beelzebub when he heard Armando's story.

'I been ringing you for fuckin' ages and couldn't find you.'

Beelzebub left Armando in the living room, got a rope from the garage and a rock from the backyard and put them in the trunk of his car. He went back inside, got a gun, handed it to Armando and said:

'Let's go to City of God and get them guns back now.'

Armando stuck the gun in his waistband without asking any questions. They headed for City of God, exchanging few words along the way. Armando thought it strange when the detective didn't turn into the projects.

'Where you goin'?' he asked.

'Let's nip past Barra da Tijuca to pick up some more guys to help take out those cheap-ass thieves.' Before reaching the first bridge on Highway Eleven, Beelzebub's car started to splutter.

'Fucking hell! I'm gonna pull over to see what it is.'

He stopped the car at the river's edge. Beelzebub was the first to get out. On the other side of the river, Torquato was strolling toward the big lake with a fishing net. He recognized the detective. Protected by the darkness, he stopped to see what he was up to. Armando got out while Beelzebub examined the car.

'I'm gonna take a leak over there,' said Armando. He took a few steps and his heart started pounding wildly when he heard the sound of his partner's gun being cocked. He resisted the urge to turn, unzipped his fly, and a bullet pierced the back of his neck. The detective tied up his body, attached the other end of the rope to the rock, and sent it to the bottom of the river. He didn't know if Armando had been telling him the truth, but he would have been eternally suspicious if he'd accepted his excuse. Every man he didn't trust had to be killed. Now he had to kill Hellraiser and Squirt. He left the scene of the crime without noticing Torquato.

One hot afternoon Pelé and Shorty caught a bus at Barra da Tijuca. They sat at the back pretending not to know one another. They noticed the watches, rings, chains and bracelets worn by the other passengers. In the vicinity of Gardênia Azul, they cleaned out the passengers at the back, forcing them off the bus. Nearing The Blocks, they did the same with those at the front. Just before the Prospectors' rehearsal square they took the money from the conductor, then headed to the square to split the loot.

An Army sergeant, who had been on the bus, watched which way they went. Furious at having lost all his pay, he went home, got his gun and was lucky enough to run into the Civil Police van along the way. After hearing his story, Beelzebub got out of the van. They walked off quickly, the sergeant leading the way.

Over at the rehearsal square, Pelé felt that they shouldn't smoke a joint there, saying they'd better make themselves scarce. Shorty insisted that the police would head straight for the Bonfim, then Block Thirteen. It was safer where they were. His friend ended up agreeing.

Beelzebub caught sight of the duo as he turned the corner. He stepped back. He and the sergeant put together a plan to catch them, then he waited in ambush at the corner. The sergeant went around the block and turned into the alley leading to the square without being noticed by the gangsters. He walked slowly, his gun pointed.

The sunny afternoon was drawing to an end. Shorty was rolling a joint while Pelé recounted the money. A young boy, noticing the sergeant, jumped back, startling them. The sergeant fired and missed. The pair jumped the fence of a house and took two children hostage, making a chase impossible. The mother's voice and the sound of her crying forced Beelzebub to start negotiating. He promised that if they turned themselves in they wouldn't get a beating, much less be shot.

'Fuck! I told you it wasn't safe to stay here. Now we're gonna have to jump the back wall,' said Pelé.

'No way, man! It must be crawlin' with cops back there,' answered his friend.

'You're better off comin' out without a fuss, or the shit's gonna hit the fan!' said Beelzebub.

Shorty let the child go on an impulse, threw his gun over the fence, opened the gate and walked out.

'Stand against the wall with your hands up. I'm a man of my word!' said the detective.

At first Pelé thought his friend had done the wrong thing, but because he didn't hear anyone getting a beating and after hearing the detective say that if they returned everything they'd be let off, he thought it best to turn himself in. Pelé came out with his hands in the air. Beelzebub held out his hand and Pelé handed him the gun. The sergeant went into the yard to recover the stolen goods. The detective's smile hurt the gangsters.

'Now start walkin' side by side with your hands on your heads,' he ordered.

'But . . .'

'But, my ass!'

They followed Beelzebub's orders. The detective and sergeant looked at one another again and agreed everything without speaking a word. The first shot from the sergeant's .45-caliber pistol went through Pelé's left hand and lodged itself in his neck. The spray of bullets from Beelzebub's machine gun tore into Shorty's body. A small group of people tried to help them, but Beelzebub stopped them with another round of machine-gun fire, this time into the air. He walked over to the bodies and put them out of their misery.

Shorty had been born with jaundice in the scrublands of Pernambuco state. By the time he was five he had suffered from mumps, dehydration, chicken pox, tuberculosis and so many other illnesses that every time he rolled his eyes, fell into a cold sweat and shivered for hours and hours under the hot sun and blankets brought quickly by the neighbors, family members would begin lighting candles and placing them in his hands so he'd have light if he died, seeing as he was a pagan. Medicine had given up on him when he was still in his mother's belly, but he hadn't died as a fetus. He arrived in Rio de Janeiro at the age of twelve with only his mother, as his father had been murdered on the orders of a colonel he had been working for during the run-up to an election for mayor and city councilors. People said he had publicly announced his vote for the colonel's adversary. Shorty and his mother begged for years in the streets of downtown Rio until she was swept away in a flood in

Bandeira Square, where she and other beggars had been sleeping. The boy never forgot the scene—his mother was sucked through a manhole while he resisted the tug of the water by clinging to a post.

As life went on, Shorty worked as a shoe shiner, pushed carts in the street markets, sold peanuts, peddled porn magazines on trains, washed rich bastards' cars and fucked faggots up the ass in the Red Light District to hustle up some dough. This last employment enabled him to rent a shack in the *favela* Morro da Viúva. He and the kids from the *favela* got together to mug old ladies walking through Saens Peña Square. He got his first revolver with the help of a homosexual in the Red Light District whom he had fucked for two years. When he heard in a bar in the *favela* that whoever went to Mario Filho stadium would be given a bowl of soup at mealtimes in addition to a home of their own, he didn't waste time: he joined the 1966 flood victims and everything was as he had imagined. It was at the soccer stadium that he had made friends with Pelé, his trusty sidekick.

Pelé had been born in the *favela* of Borel. His father, who claimed to be the grandson of slaves, had been a strong, handsome man who worked as a garbageman and drank only on weekends. On weekdays he preferred to have a little puff on the slopes of the *favela*, where he was always respected by hoods and gangsters. A *sambista* with Unidos da Tijuca and a right back with Evereste, a second division team, Cibalena had always been chased by the women in his samba school and *favela*, and the female supporters of his soccer team. He used to brag among friends that he had children he didn't even know, but it was the women's fault, because they got pregnant on purpose to get him by the balls forever.

Pelé had been a victim of this underhandedness. He suffered when his mother sent him to look for his father, who refused to see him and claimed not to know him. He had been brought up by his mother alone—his maternal grandfather had thrown her out when she got pregnant. The woman whose house she cleaned had done the same. Desperate, she turned to prostitution, even before giving birth. She had friends who were prostitutes, and it was easy to get started in the profession. She then turned to crime, and began stealing from rich housewives in the Barra da Tijuca street markets. As time went on, she began to run drugs and arms for the gangsters in the *favela*, hiding cocaine and marijuana in her vagina to sell in Rio's prisons. She slept with the chiefs so she could traffic in the prisons. Pelé had never been to school. He was still a boy when he started stealing food at the markets and picking pockets in the city center. When he understood that his mother was a prostitute, he never spoke to her again. If he ever ran into those men with their sweets, sinister pats on the head and tomfoolery to keep him quiet, who locked themselves and his mother in the room in the house in the Red Light District where he'd spent his days, he'd kill them. He went to Mario Filho stadium so he'd be given a house because he'd already been condemned to death in the *favela*. By the age of fifteen he was a full-fledged gangster. He'd only give up the life when he hit the jackpot.

His mother didn't go to his funeral; she had caught a disease that the doctors were unable to diagnose and died a week after her son.

His maternal grandfather had the compassion to organize the funeral, but at the wake said that the brute had fallen into a life of crime out of sheer shamelessness. He knew several people who had been through worse things and were decent folk.

Their first blow came down on the left ear, then they laid into the entire body. The head was perforated by blows from a stick with a nail in the end. The left eye popped out. The four limbs were broken in several places. They didn't stop until they were certain their wild fugitive was dying. A woman begged them to have mercy. They ignored her. They placed the body in a plastic bag, crossed the bridge near The Blocks, went down Miracle Street and turned into the first alley.

'The bastard's movin',' said the boy carrying it.

They threw the bag on the ground and started beating it again mercilessly. The definitive blow, which smashed its head in, came with the help of a paving stone. They continued weaving their way through the alleys until they reached the gate of a house on Middle Street:

'Joe Meow! Joe Meow!' shouted Rocket.

Joe Meow came quickly with the money. He had been waiting anxiously for the delivery, as he still had to pull off its tail and head and chop the meat into cubes, season and skewer it. In addition to selling barbecued cat in the Red Light District, Joe Meow sold lemon cocktails, Vaseline, porno magazines and Japanese ointment. After they'd been paid, the boys went to the traveling fair next to the Leão supermarket.

Hammer expertly drove the Opala they had stolen just minutes before when holding up a timber yard on Geremário Dantas Street. Everything had gone just fine, but they had been unlucky enough to pass the Civil Police van on their way back to City of God. Beelzebub recognized Hellraiser in the backseat. The police fired at them, gaining ground on curves and losing ground on straight stretches. They went down Gabinal Road at seventy-five miles an hour until they reached Highway Eleven. Squirt told Hammer to take the road to the speedway. They managed to put a good distance between themselves and the police. Yelling at the top of their lungs they decided to head for Bandeirantes highway instead of following Hellraiser's suggestion to dump the car and take off into the bush. They arrived at the projects through New World and had time to cross the river.

The detectives had radioed for help. When they arrived at the place where the car had been dumped, they searched it and the nearby houses. Boss of Us All hadn't been on duty, but when he saw the police go past, he joined the chase, swapping his revolver for his partner's machine gun. He saw the three cross Middle Street. Squirt led the way with a bag of money tied to his right arm. Boss of Us All went around the block to surprise them and poked half his face around the corner. Squirt saw him, fired and jumped a wall. Hammer and Hellraiser followed. Boss of Us All went after them, enjoying the situation. The cackling of the machine gun riddled walls with holes, frightening the sparrows and every human being who saw or heard the chase.

Hellraiser and Hammer crossed Main Street and hid in The Plots. Squirt took a side street and almost got shot crossing Middle Street. He passed through the Rec, behind the Leão supermarket, crossed Jaquinha Square, turned into the street where the Augusto Magne Municipal School was and stopped on the corner, where he crouched down, expecting his pursuer to come that way. He'd send him off to meet his maker. He thought it odd that the policeman was taking so long and figured he was worn out.

Contrary to what the gangster imagined, Boss of Us All had taken the same path. Squirt didn't notice him coming up behind him with his machine gun aimed. Boss of Us All could have fired—he wouldn't miss a stationary target from that distance—but he wanted him alive so he could get him to talk. Squirt thought the policeman had stopped chasing him and decided to hide out at Lúcia Maracanã's place, but before he could get up, he felt the cold barrel of the machine gun against his neck:

'Drop the gun and hit the ground!'

Squirt dropped his gun on the ground and snapped back:

'No fuckin' way am I lyin' down! If you wanna kill me, it'll have to be standin'!'

In a quick move, Boss of Us All grabbed his gun, thumped him with the butt, handcuffed him and continued to beat him.

'Go ahead and kill me! Kill me!' yelled Squirt.

'I'm not gonna kill you, man. You're my buddy. You brought me a gun and all this money.'

Boss of Us All's irony stung Squirt like the dozens of eyes glued to him, watching Boss of Us All's trajectory of blows as he hauled him Up Top. In the vicinity of the Bonfim, Squirt decided to black out. When he threw himself to the ground, he realized the handcuffs weren't tight enough. If Boss of Us All gave him half a chance,

Squirt might be able to free himself. Boss of Us All didn't quite believe his fainting. He started kicking him. The other police officers arrived and joined in. An old man shouted:

'You're going to kill the boy. He might have done whatever he's done, but he's still human!'

'Hey, shut your mouth old boy. This thing ain't human—this here's an open sewer, a rabid dog!' answered Boss of Us All.

The Civil Police didn't stay in the projects. They received word via radio that a Fifth Sector patrol car was involved in a shoot-out in Vila Sapê and headed off in that direction.

Hellraiser and Hammer were still hiding out in The Plots. Night Owl, Pipsqueak, Sparrow, Carrots and Slick were strolling along the edge of the right branch of the river. They were on their way back from São Carlos with a load of cocaine for Madalena. From afar Slick noticed something abnormal was happening on Middle Street. He warned the others. They backtracked. Boss of Us All ordered the other policemen to go after the rest of the gangsters. Squirt was still pretending to be unconscious. Boss of Us All stopped thumping him. He was alarmed by the crowd around him: someone could suddenly take a pop at him in the middle of all that confusion.

'Hey, I don't want no audience!' he roared.

No one moved an inch. Some even hissed at him. He pointed his machine gun at the sky and pulled the trigger, but it didn't fire a single shot. Nervously he examined his weapon and realized he was out of ammunition. The crowd noticed and started chanting:

'He's out of bullets! He's out of bullets! He's out of bullets!'

Squirt half-opened his left eye, saw the policeman's distress and waited for him to move into a position where he could get him with a sweep kick. Boss of Us All was slow to fall to the ground and see Squirt turning into the first alley.

The crowd hissed at the policeman; he was always punching whoever he felt like in the mouth, framing people and feeling up women with the excuse that he was frisking them. Everyone knew that a few days earlier he had rummaged through a laborer's lunchbox with the barrel of his gun, looking for marijuana. Angry at the policeman's actions, the man had thrown away the food and been punched and kicked for disrespecting authority.

The pain Squirt felt did not stop him crossing the river. He hurt his hands freeing himself from the handcuffs, then went to the haunted fig tree and sat under it. His heart was racing. The sweat on his face and the river water stung the wounds on his body and his hatred was visible in his shaking and the expression on his face. His sight faltered. He was having difficulty breathing, the world was spinning fast, then he blacked out for real.

Boss of Us All headed back to the police station. The only reason he wasn't more upset was that he'd taken the money from the holdup. The agony of only remembering that Squirt's gun was in his waistband when he was already out of reach throbbed along with his heartbeat. He walked down Middle Street alone, firing the gun to frighten off people who stared at him. When he turned into the street that ran along the right branch of the river, an old woman threw herself at him, holding her grandson's dead body.

'Murderer, murderer!'

The word was a sharp pain in his ears. It had been a stray bullet from Officer Jurandy's gun right at the beginning of the chase. A few people started coming back into the street. Instead of hissing, they opted for silence. Every silence is a sentence to be served, a darkness to be crossed. Boss of Us All started shouting at the top of his voice that it wasn't him. He fired another shot to make the crowd back off. No one moved. The silence exploded again. For Boss of Us All their looks were the echoes of a horror he imagined to be the greatest of all. The grandmother, holding the body of the five-year-old boy, trailed after him as if to say, 'Here, take him, now he's yours.' Boss of Us All tried to shake her off by walking back and forth. Blood spurted from the boy's neck, formed arabesques on the ground and splattered onto the old woman's feet. It wasn't long before a van came to take the police officer out of that hell. As the van door banged shut the crowd hissed and threw stones.

The old woman saw everything spinning, felt her pores slowly opening. The ground slowly vanished from beneath her feet. She wanted to speak, cry, run into the past and snatch Bigolinha off the street. Her blood gathered speed in the straights of her veins, and built up at the curves. Sometimes it spurted from her mouth, or escaped from her anus. She could no longer see a thing: everything had become a light that burned in the flash of an instant. When the light subsided, the two bodies were covered with a white sheet and candles were lit.

The evening was just getting under way when Hellraiser and Hammer asked customers at the Bonfim what had become of Squirt. They fell down laughing when they heard how their friend had rid himself of Boss of Us All in such a spectacular manner. Now all they needed to find out was whether Squirt had managed to hide the money and where he was at that moment. They decided to comb the projects, but didn't find him.

Over on The Other Side of the River, Squirt was still sleeping on the exposed roots of the haunted fig tree. At midnight everything in the world stopped. The silence of things became overstated. Red steam came off the wounds made by Boss of Us All. Everything was very dark. Now the haunted fig tree swayed in its own private wind. The pain in his body disappeared, along with everything in the universe. Only the fig tree swayed, illuminated by a light that came up its trunk from the very ground. Above its leaves hovered a blond man with nervous blue eyes, staring straight into Squirt's eyes. In complete silence, he transmitted his thoughts to Squirt, telling him everything he wanted to know, and Squirt laughed, cried, was enchanted and agreed.

The den set up by Silva at The Blocks was already known by the addicts in the projects and neighboring areas, especially because the weed was sold on Gabinal Road, a busy place that was easy to get to. The police would hardly have suspected that someone would have the nerve to deal there. The den was only discovered by the police because Boss of Us All had busted two rich kids from Freguesia, who told the police every last detail about how it worked.

Cosme and Silva ran the shop in that part of City of God. They took turns selling, but they went to fetch their merchandise, packaged it and managed sales together. None of the other criminals in The Blocks dealt and they only rarely helped with sales or packaging. Silva had convinced Cosme to stop doing holdups and start dealing, arguing that the risks of the business were lower and the number of addicts had taken a fantastic upward turn.

'It's in the papers every day; only the blind can't see it! It's the brothel owners, rock singers and dealers that're making money, man!'

As the days passed, Cosme became convinced that his friend was right. He bought furniture, tiled the kitchen and bathroom, had his living room refloored, and he always had money on him. The den's turnover was astonishing; their clientele couldn't have grown any more. But they both knew that sooner or later the den would be discovered by the police. For this reason, every Saturday—when the turnover was the highest—they asked Flip-Flop, then ten years of age, to fly a kite and make it dip to the left if the police suddenly showed up.

One Saturday, Boss of Us All was heading toward The Blocks. As usual, he went ahead of the other police officers, leading the operation, checking out things he saw as he moved quickly along. This time he wasn't thinking about money—if he busted anyone he'd press charges. And if the bastard opened his mouth to say something, he'd pump his face full of lead. He appealed to his *pombagira* for help as he crossed the tiny bridge over the left branch of the river.

Flip-Flop dipped his kite and, as it was urgent, gave his friends a warning whistle. Silva and Cosme had time to put out the joint they were smoking and hide their weed under the planks of wood next to the wall of the building where they dealt. Boss of Us All saw what they were doing and hung back, together with the officers in uniform. The dealers could make a dash for Gardênia Azul or head down Gabinal Road, jump the wall of the country manor and hide out in the bush. They decided on the latter.

Acerola had bought two bundles of weed minutes before Boss of Us All showed up. He saw the police running and thought about making a dash for it, but there wasn't enough time. His only alternative was to throw the weed into the garden of a building. The police passed by without noticing his nervous face.

In the grounds of the manor, Cosme and Silva were attacked by two guard dogs. They had to kill the senseless beasts. The two minutes they spent doing this put them within firing range. They zigzagged between the trees, regaining the ground they had lost. They were still being followed when they reached the guava trees. They had to get through them and follow the trail to Quintanilha. Boss of Us All was panting heavily. His stamina was that of a middle-aged man and he was unable to keep up with the young men running from him. The other police officers also gave up.

When Silva and Cosme returned to The Blocks, they found a couple of gangsters waiting for them:

'What's up, guys? Is the coast clear?'

'Yeah, but the pigs took your whole stash.'

'What you talkin' about? They came after us!'

'That Iran guy didn't go after you, man! You split and he came along and swiped the lot,' said one of the gangsters.

Neither Silva nor Cosme believed them. Finding the whole story pretty fishy, they went to Silva's place to make up for lost time. There were eight pounds of weed and three ounces of coke to package up. They invited the two to help them with the packaging.

'Hey, let's send the kid for some whisky,' said Silva, already inside the apartment.

'Good idea!' said Cosme.

Silva stuck his head out of the window and motioned to Flip-Flop. The boy came running—he always worked for the gangsters like that. There were other errand boys, but Flip-Flop was the fastest and smartest, always ready for any task.

'Go and buy us a bottle of Royal Label and be quick about it!'

In the living room, they cut up the weed with scissors, bundled it up in sports lottery tickets and put it in a plastic bag. In the kitchen, Cosme and Silva were packaging the cocaine. They set some aside to snort while they worked.

At the entrance to the building, Flip-Flop was intercepted by another two gangsters:

'What's up, Blackie? Where you goin' with that whisky?'

'You know it's for the packaging, man!' answered Flip-Flop rudely.

'If the weed's already packed up, send ten bundles down here for us.'

Flip-Flop ran up to the fifth floor taking four steps at a time. As soon as Silva opened the door, he said:

'The guys want us to send ten bundles of shit down for them, OK?'

'Who?' asked Silva.

'Same ones as always,' the boy answered.

'Hey! Those guys are the biggest sponges, and they always get pushy whenever we're packaging. You think they can afford ten bundles just like that? . . . They're a bunch of clowns!' Silva concluded.

'Send 'em up so we can see what the story is,' said Cosme.

The gangsters were on edge when they arrived and shook everyone's hands as if they hadn't seen them in a long time. One sat on the floor in the living room, while the other took the only free place on the sofa.

'Who is it that wants ten bundles?' asked Silva.

The one on the sofa said it was him, but he'd still have to go home to get the money. He didn't budge. Cosme and Silva looked at one another, said nothing and continued packaging up the cocaine. The visitors said the police raid only happened because someone had snitched, and made a point of reaffirming that the policeman had taken the whole stash. They were the only two who spoke in that tense atmosphere. The weed packagers rolled joints from time to time. Everyone had a smoke, although the cocaine was reserved for the four working. The gangster sitting on the floor suddenly said good-bye to everyone and left.

'Cut me a line, man,' said the visitor as soon as his friend had gone and Cosme had locked the door.

Cosme told him to wait until he cut lines for everyone at the same time. The visitor asked for a shot of whisky instead. Silva told him to help himself. The bastard filled his cup to overflowing. He downed it in two gulps, while everyone else looked at him in disapproval for his arrogance. They acted as if nothing had happened. After smoking another joint, Silva cut five lines, snorted his and passed the plate to the visitor along with the straw made from a five-cruzeiro note. The visitor's drunken hands let the plate slip to the ground. A deadly mistake among gangsters. Cosme was about to fly at him, but Silva stopped him.

'C'mon, man, you gonna lay into the guy over a little coke? If it fell it fell, man . . . Forget about it. Let's have a beer downstairs to wash it all down.'

Flip-Flop was the first to go downstairs to see if the coast was clear. He checked the area, then waved to his friends. The five went down quickly, and headed toward the bar on Block Nine. It was a hundred yards away. They walked in silence past children playing hide-and-seek, cars on the road and first-floor windows. People were eating dinner and watching the evening soaps. Silva went ahead to see what lay in wait for them around corners. His eyes saw only the night stretching out along a poorly-lit alley. He turned to those following him. The visitor had time to see the full moon of Ogum hide behind a thin cloud a second before he received a bullet in the chest from Silva's gun. He spun and fell slowly, facedown. Cosme searched him but found only a bit of loose change. The body lay sprawled on the cold grass. Silva grew uneasy about the way the visitor's body had fallen after the shot. Those who fall facedown want revenge.

They returned to the murderer's apartment saying that someone who drops a plate of cocaine is asking to die. This argument relieved Silva of his distress at having killed a man, but deep down his real reason for eliminating the visitor was a different one: he believed he had pilfered their stash of weed. It had been obvious when the guy had wanted to buy ten bundles in one go, no doubt so he could show up with weed in the streets at any time without arousing suspicion.

Silva went to the kitchen, got the coke and told his friend he was going to cut up some more. He chopped out the lines himself, and again put forward his argument about the visitor's attitude. Real gangsters had to know how to come and go, and had to wait for the right time to make their moves. This thing of bumming other people's coke was for assholes. Maybe he'd dropped the coke on the ground for a laugh, so he could go around saying he'd paid them a visit, had a drink, a smoke, a bump and then thrown out the motherfuckers' coke too. He'd had his eye on that asshole for ages; he was always bumming coke and weed off people. Silva spoke in a didactic tone without taking his eyes off Flip-Flop. The boy nodded his head as though he understood what he was being taught. The murderer's conclusion was that the visitor had deserved to die.

After doing the coke, Silva got up and poured another shot of whisky for each of them, making it clear he wanted to be left alone. Cosme was the first to say good-bye, but his friend asked him to stay and help clean the apartment. Flip-Flop told the packagers it would be better for them to leave one at a time, because the police were probably already at the scene of the crime. They took his advice.

Silva was in a hurry because his wife had told him she'd be home early that Saturday. She knew her husband was mixed up in shady business, but she refused to receive gangsters in her house; she didn't like their talk and she was afraid the police might pay them a surprise visit. Silva, in turn, only accepted his wife's arguments after making her swear—with her feet together and without crossing her fingers behind her back—that no one would ever find out she was a prostitute and that she would never tell him how her night had been. But whenever she arrived home with lots of money he felt a pang in his heart, and when she brought him presents or looked tired he lost it—at times he wanted too much sex, while at others he wouldn't even look at her, picking fights over nothing. He tried to make her give up the night, but she said she'd only do it if he left his life of crime and got himself a decent job. She wouldn't mind struggling to make ends meet if she could live a peaceful life. Silva didn't give in. His wife, even less.

Cosme opened a paper of coke to buy time. He wanted to see his friend's wife arrive home. That black chick with her ample ass, strong thighs, almond eyes, shapely feet, hands with long, fine fingers, fleshy lips . . . One day he'd tell her how much he wanted her. He prayed the couple would have a fight so he could comfort his friend and put him off women for once and for all. After all, all women were worthless. He had been smart not to tie the knot with anyone; he was going to stay single his whole life. As long as his friend's wife wasn't his, he made do just looking at her, seeing her in a pair of tight little shorts and T-shirt with no bra underneath. He loved the way she talked, ate, laughed, used her eyes, lay on the sofa . . . Fernanda soon arrived, as expected. But she looked tired, which irritated her husband.

'Work hard?' he asked with a certain sarcasm.

Fernanda didn't answer. She just greeted Cosme then headed for the bathroom, where she counted her money, set some aside, hid it behind the cupboard and jumped into the shower.

They had already finished cleaning the apartment. Fernanda's secret admirer strategically opened another bag so he could see her come out of the bathroom in her tight little shorts, although her breasts were protected from his gaze by a T-shirt and bra.

She threw herself onto the sofa. Cosme chopped out six lines and passed the plate to his friend. When Silva lowered his head to snort, Cosme looked at Fernanda's foot, then ran his eyes up her body to her eyes, where he allowed his gaze to rest as if to say: 'I love you, I want you!'

Fernanda showed no sign of understanding the message in her husband's friend's eyes. After they had snorted coke, they had a shot of whisky, lit cigarettes and said good-bye. Silva didn't talk to his wife and went to bed without a shower.

Cosme shuddered when he saw the mother hugging her son's body. He turned, lengthened his steps toward the left branch of the river and hid the drugs and gun near the riverbank. He knew he'd toss and turn in bed if he tried to sleep and decided to walk until he felt sleepy. He couldn't get the image of the old woman clutching the stiff out of his mind, but fuck it—assholes deserved to kick the bucket. He crossed the bridge, wandering aimlessly. He prayed for daybreak to arrive so he could go ahead and open the den. He thought about Fernanda. If only she'd fall in love with him and suggest they get together. He'd run far away with her, someplace where he could give up this life of crime, have kids and get a sucker's job to make her happy. He walked around with his head down for several hours. The sun rose. Suddenly he remembered he shouldn't be roaming around at that hour because he'd already been busted by the pigs. That stiff in the dew would attract the police and he was reeking of weed. He headed towards the Eucalyptus Grove. He'd be safe there. A few breadsellers were crying their wares. The suckers were starting to head out for the daily grind.

A month earlier, two neighbors were chatting over on Block Fourteen:

'Don't your man lick you out? Girl . . . you're missing the good things in life. Before mine fucks me, he's gotta go down on me for about half an hour. And what about up the ass? You don't let him, do you. You don't know what you're missin'. It hurts the first few times, but afterwards it just slips right in. What you do is you get a banana, warm it up a little, stick it in your snatch and tell him to stick it in behind. It'll blow your mind. Ever tried a merry-go-round? Corkscrew? Choo-choo? Funnel? Finger? Sixty-nine? Bottle-stopper? Roly-poly? Traffic jam? Wet whistle . . . ?'

The northerner decided that when her husband got home, she'd suggest they try the pleasures of the flesh. But it didn't work. Not only did he not want to know about disgusting acts but he also gave her a beating so she'd stop thinking filth. Certain of the origin of these shameless ideas, he also forbade her to talk to the neighboring women. While he beat her, she thought about finding herself a man who'd indulge her. She'd get back at her husband by feeling real pleasure—but it'd have to be with a black man, because her neighbor had assured her that all blacks had big dicks. The more he beat her, the more she imagined a well-hung black giving it to her from behind with a warm banana in front.

The next day she didn't leave home. She made herbal compresses for her bruises, conditioned her hair with avocado and egg yolk to make it behave, and plastered her face with honey and lemon. A good remedy for blotches, blackheads and pimples. The day passed slowly as she plotted the betrayal. Yes! She'd have it off with the fishmonger and it'd be easy, because men were like mice: all you had to do was show them the cheese and they came running. She could wear a red baby-doll nightie and pull him inside when he came to deliver fish, or follow him to a safe place so she could jump his bones. Maybe a kid in the street could take him a note. It'd be easy if she knew his address; she'd turn up at his place before he went to work and catch him well rested, or if none of these things worked, she'd sidle up to him the next time she saw him and say: 'C'mon, big boy, let me have it!'

Two days later, although she was scared, the fishmonger was giving it to her from behind, with the warm banana firmly in place.

After work, her husband would go to Dummy's Bar to play pool and drink to each ball sunk in one of life's six holes. He took his time because a real man couldn't get home when he said he would; he had to arrive whenever he felt like it, smelling of a mixture of *cachaça* and the sweat of hard labor. He wished his wife were decent, as his mother had been. He didn't allow her to hang around in the street chatting with the nigger girls, forbade her to wear tops with low necklines and short skirts, and only let her wear long pants if they were really baggy and made of thick material, so no one could see the outline of her panties.

She didn't neglect her domestic duties, but she no longer cared about her husband and merely went through the motions when it was time for their unvarying sex. On two occasions she pretended to be sick at the fateful hour. After a few days, she decided to treat her husband normally, on her neighbor's advice. She acted as if she regretted the indecent things she had proposed. Her husband felt victorious; his wife had finally understood he was right. He started arriving home early. The following Saturday, after the grocery shopping, he took her to the amusement park. They ate toffee apples and sweet popcorn, shot at targets, tossed rings and rode on the big wheel. All to please his wife, who now really did remind him of his mother. On the Sunday, instead of buying that damn pork that he loved and she hated, he chose chicken, her favorite dish. She continued to receive visits from the fishmonger every weekday.

One Monday, he arrived at work early as always, and had already changed clothes when he was told there would be no work that day. He had a drink with his friends before heading home.

The fishmonger had already made his wife come three times and was resting up to start over again.

The husband got off the bus Out Front. He decided to buy a dozen limes so he could spend the day drinking caipirinhas and nibbling on fried sardines. His crazy wife had taken to eating fish like never before. If he felt like a bit of crackling or fried sausage he had to go to the bar. But that was fine, because after the belting he'd given her she'd become a respectable woman. He was happy.

Back at his house, his wife's lover was sliding and flicking his tongue across, into and out of her snatch. The first time she'd asked him to perform oral sex on her he'd protested. He imagined traces of her husband's spunk in there and leftover drops of piss. The second time, he went down on her more willingly, and even hurt her. The third time, he rubbed his nose in her, then got his whole face wet. From then on he did it hungrily.

The husband passed in front of the bakery, his legs casting shadows that expanded and shrank as he walked. He lit a cigarette when he got to the square on Block Twenty-Two. Before crossing the street to the Prospectors' rehearsal square, he stopped to shoot the shit with some friends. He walked another block and caught sight of the wall around his house. He thought about inviting his wife to take a walk around Paquetá Island, but no, it'd be better to stay home and take his after-lunch nap in his own bed—he usually took it on a plank of wood at the construction site. He turned onto his street and thought it odd that the radio wasn't on, because from that distance he could usually hear Cidinha Campos bellowing from the speakers, and his wife singing along. When he was two steps away from being enveloped by the shadow cast by the wall of his house he saw his damn neighbor peering at the unsuspecting street through a crack in her window. He fumbled about in his pocket for his keys, his fingers touched a box of matches, coins, a pocketknife and telephone tokens. He had trouble turning the key in the lock, then slowly pushed open the iron gate. The front window was closed, as were the bathroom door and window. The sand and stones he had bought were in the left-hand corner of the yard. In the pigpen, Margarida slept in the morning light, which stretched from the skillet with no handle to the basin with a hole in it. The chickens were quiet on their perches, a sign that they had been fed. In the small garden the sunflowers swayed in the breeze. The silence worried him; his wife wasn't one to sleep late. He went over to the left side of the yard looking at the ground. He lit another cigarette, walked to his front door, put the key in the keyhole and this time had no trouble turning it. There were no dirty dishes in the kitchen. In the living room, a shaft of sunlight defied the window and lit up a line of dust floating in space. The statue of Father Cicero, facing the door, was uncomplaining. The noise of water trickling in the water tank was the only sound in the tidy house. The smell of fish jarred with the cleanness before his eyes. The worn blood-red rug wasn't in its usual place. He adjusted it mechanically with his feet. He went into the bedroom and saw his wife lying on top of the polyester trousers he'd asked her to mend, pretending to be fast asleep.

'What's going on?' she asked when her husband shook her.

'The boss gave us the day off. The engineer kicked the bucket,' answered her husband, who, instead of making himself a caipirinha, put on a pair of shorts and went into the yard to dig a hole in the ground.

'For God's sake, you don't give yourself a rest, do you!' said his wife.

'I'm gonna make a cistern on the side here. This water tank's too small for my liking. If there's no water for a week we'll die of thirst.'

By about one o'clock in the afternoon, he had already dug a hole twelve feet deep. He decided to stop, have dinner and take a nap. His wife spent the day mending old clothes. Every now and then she thought: 'Since I started cheatin' on him this man's become a lamb.' Night came quickly.

The next morning, a plump sun in the sky, she went to the gate to chat with her neighbor after watering the plants:

'That was close, wasn't it?'

'Ah . . . But God looks after his own, my friend!'

'I think he smells something.'

'How many times has he come home like that without warning?'

'Just once, when he had a pain here,' she said, pointing at her arm, 'and a friend brought him home.'

'God gave you a helping hand. If I hadn't seen him at the super-market, he would've busted you . . . If I was you, I'd wanna make sure.'

'How?'

'Let's go to my sister-in-law's *terreiro* and have her call the *pombagira* for you.'

They left after dinner. They'd have to do everything quickly, because her husband sometimes got home before five.

'Ahh, pretty girl! I already know wot this earthly daughter wants to know . . . Just leave me a present at the crossroads, and the more ya go with the other guy, the more he'll believe ya,' the *pombagira* assured her, then cackled. 'So the banana thing worked then, girl?' continued the *pombagira*. 'Feels good, don't it? Here on earth the best thing is to fuck yerself silly. Since the one at home don't do it nice, ya had to find it somewhere else, right girl?' she cackled. 'Buy everythin' I tell ya to and leave it at the crossroads at midnight . . .'

'But I can't go out at ni . . .'

'Just give me apprentice the brass and he'll buy everythin' and make the offerin' fer ya,' finished the *pombagira*, cackling and sprinkling *cachaça* over her.

The next day, she waited less than half an hour after her husband had left for work and went after the fishmonger:

'Let's go to my place. Now I feel safe. We were unlucky yesterday.'

At first the fishmonger protested, but after listening to her, he put her on the back of his bicycle and they took off for her place. The street was full of children playing games and women having their morning gossip. The northerner was not the least bit shy about walking into her front yard leading the fishmonger by the hand. After she had opened her front door, the fishmonger grabbed her by the arm and gave her a hot kiss. Eagerly he stroked her private parts and she stroked his. Her lover was already un-buttoning her blouse when he received the blow that knocked him to the ground.

Before she could let out a cry of distress, she was gagged, then tied up and thrown into the hole her husband had dug the day before. He stabbed the fishmonger with his sharp fish knife and threw his body on top of his wife, who thrashed around in the bottom of the hole. He started covering them with earth. The gag came loose and she was about to cry out, but was stopped by a clod of earth that landed on her face. After covering them, the husband made a thick mixture of cement and black soil and threw it over the improvised grave. When the job was done, he grabbed his bag, checked his ticket and took off for his home state of Ceará, in the north.

Cosme didn't make it as far as the Eucalyptus Grove. When he saw the fire truck parked in Block Fourteen he stopped and joined the other onlookers. He almost took off running when a police car arrived, its sirens wailing. When the fright wore off he thought about going closer, but instead he asked a young boy coming from the direction of the northerner's house what had happened.

'There's two stiffs buried in that house there,' said the boy, without stopping.

Cosme thought it best to go home to bed and forget about selling coke and weed that eerie morning. He went back for his drugs and gun, then hurried home.

'Gotta talk to ya.'

'Make it quick 'cos I'm runnin' late.'

'Well, girl, it's like this: I'm nuts about you. Know what I mean? I just woke up and I been dreamin' about you. I been meanin' to tell you for ages, but I haven't had a chance . . .'

'What? What are you going on about? I don't get it . . .'

'I ain't been able to get you off my mind for ages. Know what I mean? If you leave Silva, I'll be your man.'

'You gangsters're all the same! My husband's own friend's got the nerve to come on to me!'

'I don't wanna stab him in the back. I really like the guy. But my heart's flipped for you. I'm gonna tell you something I've never told any girl, so you'll trust me.'

'What?'

'I love you!'

'I'm only gonna think about another man when Silva's dead. While he's alive, this body's his. See ya!' she finished, waving for the bus to stop.

Cosme crossed Gabinal Road without taking his eyes off that hot black piece of ass. He watched her go through the turnstile with that cleavage of hers, which enchanted the conductor. He continued slowly along the edge of the road, down the stairs and through the blocks of apartments with his eyes glued to the ground, his thoughts a jumble. He'd made a mistake. If she'd been interested everything would've been fine, but that heartless woman had been unmoved. What if she told Silva? He'd do him in for sure. This nonsense of hitting on a friend's wife and not screwing her was much worse because, whether he screwed her or not, the friendship was doomed. He felt like a dickhead, because there was no such thing as a difficult woman, but there were poor come-ons. He was so immersed in thought that his friend's voice made him start.

'What's up, buddy? Why ain't the den up and running?'

'Haven't you heard? This morning was really freaky. The area was crawling with pigs. There were two more stiffs over in Fourteen. A kid told me, so I split fast. Hey, let's go have a smoke over on The Hill, then we can open the den.'

Over on The Hill, Silva cut the rolling paper while Cosme broke up the buds. Silva scrutinized one of the haunted mansions. He was about to suggest to his friend that they change the location of the den, but he never got to say a thing, because a bullet from Cosme's gun pierced his left lung. The other ripped through his heart. The third entered the forearm of his already lifeless body. The murderer picked up the keys and took the gun from his friend's waistband. He was sorry for wasting his friend, but if he hadn't, he'd have been the one to die. He glanced around, went down the right side of The Hill, threw himself into the river, deliberately scratching his body, then ran to where he could find a friend.

'What's goin' on?' asked Flip-Flop when he saw the murderer in tattered clothes.

'I was up on The Hill smokin' a joint with Silva, when the cops showed up out of the blue . . . More than five pigs, I had to run for it . . .'

'What about Silva?'

'He went the other way. I don't even know if he made it, you know. All I heard was loads of gunshots.' He imitated the sound of the shots. 'Look, man. I'm getting off the street 'cos it's givin' me the creeps, know what I'm sayin'?'

While Cosme showered, he tried to think of a way for only Fernanda to know the truth. He'd already made plans to run away with her, have a load of kids and get a sucker's job. The crime he'd just committed didn't weigh on his conscience; it was bound to happen sooner or later. He was tired of seeing Fernanda asking Silva to give up that life and Silva not giving a damn. He'd often seen his friend leave his wife at home to hang around playing cards on street corners, smoke weed on the stairs of the blocks of apartments and every now and then screw some slut he'd picked up in the night. If it were him, he wouldn't swap Fernanda for any woman. He'd give up his life of crime right then and there. He knew how to lay a brick, build foundations and put up a wall. It wouldn't be difficult to find a job. He shaved carefully under the shower, slicked his hair back and headed for the apartment of the woman he loved. When she found out he'd killed Silva just to be with her, she'd fall into his arms.

He turned the entire apartment upside down looking for drugs and ammunition—he'd give it all to Flip-Flop, who could do whatever he wanted with it. He'd tell his friends he'd have to stay clear of the projects for a while because he'd heard the pig shouting his name when the shit hit the fan. He put what he found in a plastic bag. He half-tidied the mess he'd made, lit a joint and sat on the living-room floor to wait.

Fernanda arrived at three in the morning. She greeted him half-heartedly and went through the apartment looking for her husband.

'What's up? Ain't Silva here?'

'Nope. He went over to Red Hill to see if he can find someone to sell us some stuff. He'll be back soon . . . What about what I said to you? I'm not fuckin' around. If you stick with me, I promise I'll get a job. We can get the hell out of here and have a nice life—I'm not bullshittin' you. I wanna have heaps of kids with you. C'mon! Ogum'll protect us!' said Cosme with tears in his eyes.

Seeing his sincerity, Fernanda sat on the sofa, threw her bag to one side and took off her sandals. Her silence showed she was reflecting deeply on the proposal. After a few seconds, she said:

'I know you're serious. I've seen it all in your eyes for ages, but here's the story: Silva's my man. It's no use, this is where he lives.' She thumped her chest. 'I've felt like leavin' him a whole lot of times, but when push comes to shove I don't have the guts. I guess that's true love . . .'

'But he doesn't give a damn about you . . . He screws all them sluts downstairs. When he's pissed off, he smacks you around for no reason. I'll give you a life where no one'll be cleanin' guns before going to bed, heatin' up ammunition in the oven, killin' people, havin' shoot-outs with the cops . . . I'm ready to get a sucker's job. I don't want a life of cards, bundles of weed and papers of coke . . . I swear by this light that shines on us, by the strength of Ogum, that you won't go without a thing. I'll put rice and beans on the table with the sweat off my own back . . . I've prayed to Oxalá so many times for him to kill this thing I feel for you.' The tears started gushing. 'Give me a chance in this life!'

'But I don't feel anything for you. Silva's my man . . . I like the way he walks, his voice . . . The way he touches me, the way he asks for things . . .'

'Look, I'm gonna tell you somethin', but you can't tell anyone, 'cos I only did it for you.'

'What is it, man?'

'I pulled the trigger on Silva just to be with you. You said your-self you'd only have someone else if he was gone!' said Cosme.

Fernanda went quiet. She lowered her head, then leaned back on the sofa and looked Cosme straight in the eye.

'OK! Now I believe you! Let's get out of here.'

In less than an hour they had packed and left, never to return.

Only Silva's closest friends and family members went to his funeral, as everyone already knew about and disapproved of the crime he'd committed that Saturday.

The man he'd killed had been loved by all: he'd been friendly with the kids, made kites for them, respected everyone and had paraded with the Gávea Apprentices carnival group ever since he was a boy. Everyone who had come from the *favela* Parque Proletário considered him a friend. He was welcome for dinner at everyone's house and was always doing people favors. It was true that he had a few screws loose, took too many liberties, was some-times rude and did his small-time jobs, but he was incapable of killing anyone. He'd always said that if a victim tried to resist he'd take off running, but he wouldn't kill a sucker. At the wake, his mother was consoled by friends. They said the murderer would also die soon, because her son had fallen facedown.

Some of the cool guys had told Silva a few hours before Cosme killed him that he'd screwed up, because killing someone over coke was for old-time gangsters who weren't with it. Silva tried to ex-plain himself, claiming the guy had stolen his stash.

'Bullshit! You killed the guy for nothin'. I saw the cop find your stash with my own eyes, man!' said Jap, one of the cool guys, harshly.

Silva went quiet. He knew Jap was telling the truth. The cool guys stared at him for a while. Their silence told him he'd lost their re-spect. That was when it really hit home that he'd fucked up. His body's deep shudders betrayed his agitated soul. And worst of all, that damn intruder had fallen facedown. He decided to lie low. He got up from the curb awkwardly and was walking slowly home when he ran into his friend and was done in.

'Squirt knocked off three in that job he did over in Taquara and landed himself a wad of bills—all five hundred cruzeiros and up . . . We'd already rustled up a decent amount and headed off, but when we were goin' down this sketchy little street, he told us to stop the car and get out . . . He went alone, did the place and got lucky . . . Now he's started goin' out alone and comin' back loaded with dough sayin' he's killed two or three in one go. He's actin' really weird. Every Monday he disappears and no one can find him. People're sayin' he's gone nuts . . . He goes around sayin' he's hot shit. He's made Boss of Us All run for it heaps of times and he doesn't even split when he's in a shoot-out with the Civil Police. You should've seen it: Boss of Us All and Iran were comin' up Main Street and they hadn't even seen him, and he was over at Tom Joe's Bar havin' a cold one. When he saw the pigs, he crossed the street and told them to go get fucked, and he didn't even touch his gun. Then they started takin' pops at him but not one bullet got him! Then he opened fire on them. They ran for their lives and he just stood there laughin',' Hammer told Cleide a month after Silva's death, as they were going to bed.

'Stop hangin' around with him . . . You'll get yourself in trouble for nothin' and end up in the shit . . . I wish you'd give up this gang business. Every time you go out on a job I shit myself . . . Let's get out of here before it's too late . . . You could get killed just like that . . .'

'Watch your mouth! Knock on wood! You know I don't take risks. You're wastin' your breath!' said Hammer, and rolled over to show his wife that her predictions had irritated him.

They fell silent, but Hammer remembered the bullets that had already whistled past his ears, the times he had almost got killed

during getaways. He wasn't eager to cash in his chips or anything—
but get a sucker's job on a construction site? Never. Packed lunches
and catching crowded buses to be treated like a dog by the boss? No
way, not that. He remembered when he had worked on construction
sites in Barra da Tijuca. The engineer always arrived after lunch with
a hot chick in his car and didn't even say hi to the laborers. He'd go
around yelling his head off at everyone just to show off in front of
her, and the dickhead foreman, just because he earned a little more,
was always sucking up to the bastard. He'd stick with crime and would
never play into the hands of the pigs. He had to hit the jackpot so he
could buy a piece of land in the countryside and spend the rest of his
life raising chickens without a care in the world. Squirt was taking
being a gangster too seriously: for him, that was all there was to life.
All this shit of donning the Devil's cloak was a load of crap. Though
he did look like he had the Beast in his body . . . And what about his
eyes? They gave him the creeps. A crazy man's eyes . . . Hammer's
thoughts had almost faded into sleep when Cleide straddled him,
rubbed herself against him hard and whispered in his ear:

'Let's not fight! I only say these things 'cos I love ya.'

They lost themselves in one another until night ran into morning.

Squirt woke up early that Monday. He wanted to send a soul off
to the Beast fast, then take it easy at the beach. He hid behind a
garbage can near the Leão supermarket. He was waiting for someone well-dressed to go by so he could rustle up a watch or some
loose change. He looked around: he wanted to get to the beach
before the ten o'clock pickup game. Only badly dressed suckers
went past. He was impatient; he'd kill the first one he saw. He
didn't need money but, since he had to kill someone, there was
no harm in getting himself a bit of cash. He approached an el-
derly man who was walking along briskly. He didn't see Hellraiser
running toward him.

'Take everything in your pocket, stick it in my hand and lie on
the ground,' he said with his gun pointed at his victim.

Hellraiser ran to try and stop the crime. The policy of keeping the area clean had to be respected so the pigs would stop breathing down their necks. The police were always showing up. Even the Federal Police had been doing a few raids. Hellraiser asked him to let the man go. Squirt turned to look at his friend for a second, shook his head, then pumped the man's body full of lead. He took seven steps backwards, reciting a prayer which Hellraiser didn't understand. He stuck his gun in his waistband and took off down Main Street without saying a thing to his friend. He bought a pack of cigarettes at Batman's Bar and pitched in with Acerola and Green Eyes to buy some pot, but didn't wait for Green Eyes to come back with the weed. He took a taxi to the beach.

He didn't dare enter the cold water; after the game of soccer he climbed onto the rocks of the jetty, letting his thoughts roam. He saw a couple playing around in the water and thought about sex. He swore to himself that that night he was going to have a sexy chick from up north he'd had his eye on for ages. He left after two hours. He had a bite to eat at a bar by the canal in Barra da Tijuca. After another game of soccer, he went home, smoked a joint, showered and fell asleep.

At around 10 P.M. he woke up, got dressed, got his gun and left for the woman's place. He got into the house without any problems and her husband didn't fight when he saw his cocked gun. Squirt ordered him out. The man tried to argue and got a bullet in his foot. The woman didn't offer any resistance, nor did she cry out when he had anal sex with her. Squirt thought she was feeling real pleasure and imagined she was really coming. He left after an hour.

The husband stumbled to the house of a friend, who took him to the hospital. But he didn't spend the night resting as the doctor had recommended. He wanted to leave immediately, but he had nowhere to go. He'd have to save some money to return to his home state of Paraíba. He cried on his way home.

When he arrived there he found his wife lying on the sofa sobbing helplessly. If the bastard hadn't been armed he wouldn't have got past the front gate. He would have been man enough to floor the guy once he got his hands around his neck. He'd save up to buy a revolver and waste that evil bastard, that scum of the earth. His wife insisted they return to Paraíba as soon as they could. All they had to do was sell everything they had and take off. He didn't have the courage to ask what the bastard had done to her. Several times he wrenched his eyes away from the rumpled bed. He filled his glass with *cachaça* and downed it in a single gulp, repeating his promise of revenge with every minute that passed. He felt like shit for not having stood up to the thug, gun and all, but it was best not to make trouble; Squirt's hour would come. His wife wept uncontrollably. The pain she felt was greater than her husband's. She never imagined that she would one day have sex with a man that way, much less anal sex. She had pretended she was enjoying it to save her and her husband's lives. Those thugs killed mercilessly. It was almost morning when they made up their minds to return to Paraíba as quickly as possible. Her husband would work until the end of the month, and meanwhile they'd sell their things.

Squirt wanted to scrape together a pile of money so he could throw a party for his friends: a first-class spread on the day of the final of the Rio Soccer Championship. With any luck, Flamengo would thrash Botafogo with a shitload of goals. He'd buy ten papers of coke and ten or so bottles of imported whisky to celebrate Flamengo's victory. He wanted to get back in with his friends; he hadn't seen much of them since he'd made his pact with the Devil. He didn't need partners in holdups, but he knew they were true friends, although the next time one of them tried to stop him from sending a soul off to the Beast he'd have to get tough—he'd show them that things could get ugly. He had an obligation to send a soul to hell every Monday. He'd get rich, he wouldn't be killed by a bullet, the police wouldn't see him and false friends would become sitting ducks in his path.

Now he had to pull off a big job, hit the jackpot once and for all. He stayed home all morning. He cocked and uncocked his gun several times, practiced firing while lying down, ran through the backyard as if exchanging fire with someone chasing him, practiced target shooting with his left hand only—driving his neighbors crazy—and put the rest of his ammunition behind the fridge to warm it up. He repeated seven times that he was the son of the Devil, then hurried into the streets, straining to think of a place where there was lots of money. In front of Batman's Bar, he saw Orange hightailing it to Main Square.

'How's it goin', Orange? Know where I can line up a decent take?'

'Look, man, I'm in a hurry. I ain't got time to shoot the breeze!' he called back without slowing his pace.

Squirt didn't answer, but made a mental note to kill him one Monday. Orange had found out a few minutes earlier that his brothers and sisters had rushed their mother to the emergency room. Unconcerned about Squirt, he ran to the other side of the square, jumped into a taxi and took off.

Squirt wandered on. He didn't bother to look around, much less behind. He took the same route as Orange. He sat on a bench in the square, taking in the tiniest details of the afternoon. He remembered the woman from up north: he could have her whenever he wanted. The wind blew on his face; the sun warmed his body from the mild cold. He saw a bus go by carrying only the driver and conductor, and in a split second realized where there was plenty of money. He'd hold up Redentor Transport. He got up and headed for the taxi stand. If the driver didn't lend him the car without a fuss, he'd regret it. It was probably even best to kill someone to distract the police, and while they were busy he'd do the job.

He was crossing the street when he heard the sound of a car crash. Something made him head toward the scene of the accident. He fired two shots into the air. After frightening away the onlookers, he searched the car and took the gold chain from around the driver's neck. He was already beginning to come around, so

Squirt thumped him over the head with the butt of his gun so he'd keep sleeping. He found a revolver in the glove box, along with checkbooks and a pocket watch. He was already a few steps into the projects when he decided to go back and have a look under the seats, where drivers usually hid their most valuable objects. It didn't take him long to unearth two bundles of U.S. dollars. His smile traveled on the wind and scattered itself with the sunlight in the eyes of those watching from afar. He thought out loud:

'The Devil writes crooked with straight lines! Just as well that Orange hadn't stopped to talk. He might have suggested some worthless little dump.'

He strolled down Main Street, turned onto the street where Batman's Bar was and cut across Blonde Square. Over in Main Square, the Military Police had gone to the driver's aid. No one dared say a word about what had happened. The lamppost had been knocked but hadn't fallen, and there was a cut in the power supply.

'Hey, Squirt! What's up, naughty boy?' shouted Lúcia Maracanã.

'Shit! I was just thinkin' about you . . . Can you hide this for me?'

'Holy shit!' exclaimed Lúcia when she saw the dollars.

'Take some for yourself and if you see Hellraiser or Hamm . . .'

'Hammer's over there playin' soccer,' said his friend, pointing toward the Rec.

By the time he found his pal, the game had finished. They lit up a joint. Minutes later they were at Batman's Bar playing the best of three at pool. Squirt saw Orange going into the pharmacy. His desire to kill the pothead was rekindled, but he'd leave it for a Monday. He had never actually liked that little shit. He thought he was tough just because he smoked a little bit of weed. Who was he to say he didn't want to shoot the breeze? Not even the gangsters talked back to him. Orange's fate was tucked away in the barrel of his gun. Squirt lost the game because he wasn't concentrating.

The week flew by for the gangsters. A friend of Hellraiser's gave him a good tip-off. He told him that the wages for the construction site he was working on always arrived at lunchtime in a yellow Opala with only two guards. It was easy money. On Saturday, Hellraiser went alone to hold up the construction site and everything went according to plan—he even got the guards' guns. That afternoon, he sent a boy over to fetch ten papers of coke from the *favela* of Salgueiro. He spent the night doing lines with his friends. They were still at it at daybreak. Squirt sent another boy to rustle up another ten papers, and they carried on into Sunday night. At around four o'clock in the morning the *cachaça*-and-Cokes ran out. They went into the late-night alleys looking for a bar that was open.

'Only Noel'll be open at this hour,' said Hellraiser.

He was right. Only Noel's Bar was carrying on into that moonless night, along with a few drinkers.

'We'll have a *cachaça*-and-Coke,' said Hammer.

Noel poured the *cachaça* and Coke into the three glasses he'd just placed on the counter. Hammer asked for two one-liter bottles of Coke and a bottle of *cachaça*, and said he'd return the bottles the next day.

They went back along the river to Hellraiser's place. Real gangsters never take the same route twice. Gangsters only pass once. Gangsters are always on their way. Along the way they ran into a guy who was always sucking up to gangsters. The asshole was smoking a joint on a corner and insisted they have a puff. He wanted to be a gangster, but didn't have the courage. He talked like one, dressed like one, hung around them whenever he could, did them favors, ran errands. Those who didn't know him thought he was one. They smoked the ass-kisser's weed. The trio listened to him saying that the police had shot at Green Eyes Out Front, but the weedhead had been smarter than them and had slipped away through the alleys. When Squirt heard the name Green Eyes, he remembered Orange. He tried to bite his tongue, but couldn't help himself and said:

'Hey, when you see that Orange, tell him I'm gonna finish him off!'

His friends asked why. Squirt just answered that he had his reasons. They finished the joint and went home for more coke.

Monday dawned bug-eyed. The friends couldn't seem to go their separate ways. The only thing to do was to send for more, since everyone had enough money for shitloads of coke. Hammer hadn't done any jobs, but he'd worked all week on the construction of a garage in the neighborhood of Araújo. He wasn't flush, but he had enough to have a laugh.

Berenice woke up and went straight to the bathroom. She got washed and dressed and left the house saying she was going Out Front to wait for a friend who was coming to visit.

By early afternoon, Squirt was completely fucked up: when he tried to stand he almost ended up facedown on the ground. He'd been doing lines all morning, drunk *cachaça*-and-Coke and sent for a bottle of whisky, which was already half empty because he was showing off in front of Berenice's friend. Those who drink whisky have money. His headache outweighed his drunkenness, but he still trotted out a few old sambas accompanied by Hammer's badly played tambourine. From time to time he ogled Berenice's friend, who returned naughty smiles. She was the only reason Squirt was still there. And she, in turn, was waiting for him to jump her bones, as she had also taken an interest in him.

Somewhere around five o'clock in the afternoon, he put the moves on her. She was receptive. They left and went straight to a motel on Catonho Road. It was already eight o'clock by the time Squirt managed to have sex, then he had a quick bite to eat so he could return to the mulatta's body. There he stayed, completely forgetting the pact he'd made with Lucifer.

Squirt left the motel worried. By the time he'd remembered Satan it was already after midnight. It was the first time he'd let the Beast down, but he didn't think he'd have a problem with the Lord of Hell, he'd sent him extra souls on several occasions. The night was de-

serted. He got out of the taxi Out Front. He walked quickly down
Main Street checking his guns. Orange and Acerola were having a
beer at Batman's Bar. Squirt was only a hundred yards from seeing
them. As he passed Orange's house, he thought about breaking into
it and killing the little shit in his own bed, but like hell he would! It'd
be better to kill the northerner and grab his wife for good. He'd fuck
her little ass whenever he wanted. He'd force her to live with him,
because women were like dogs—they got used to their new masters
with time. He wouldn't let her want for anything at home and would
send her to the beauty parlor every weekend. Women liked money
and stiff dicks. The bitch had shimmied around eagerly on his cock
the first time. She'd enjoyed herself, otherwise she wouldn't have
come. He passed Orange and Acerola without noticing them. He was
walking so quickly that at times he practically ran. The Devil was a
cool guy—he'd see that he'd lost track of time, but had come through
the very minute he'd remembered their pact.

He turned into Middle Street with his heartbeat faster than his
steps. He was a man through and through, because he'd just had
the mulatta and now just the thought of the girl from up north was
giving him another hard-on. He'd have both of them. He crossed
over the right branch of the river, without seeing anyone or anything that caught his attention. He opened the wooden gate without a sound, then walked slowly over to the electricity meter and
turned it off. The cold that night made it difficult to manipulate
the wire he used to open the living-room window. First he stuck
his head in, then the rest of his thin body. Inside the house only
the silence bounced off the walls. Squirt thought he was doing
everything perfectly. When he opened the bedroom curtain, he saw
the woman asleep by herself. He went back into the living room
and went through the other rooms. No one. He went back into the
bedroom. First he stroked her legs, his dick exploding in his shorts,
then bent over to nibble at her neck. She writhed about in the bed,
murmuring softly. Squirt placed his gun on the bedside table and
began to undress. Without opening her eyes, the woman tossed and

turned in the bed, making him all the more excited, then her husband dropped from the rafters holding a knife. The first stab tore into Squirt's left lung, the second, into his right. The third, fourth and fifth tore his heart to shreds. The others had no effect; they represented nothing more than the fury of revenge fulfilling in destiny.

Only Lúcia Maracanã went to her friend's funeral; otherwise Squirt would have been buried without tears. His pals were afraid the police might raid the cemetery. There were no drums at his wake, no street-corner games, drinks, weed, coke, no promises of revenge. Squirt's parents only found out about their son's death eight days after he had been buried. The northerner returned to the state of Paraíba with his wife. He told people he'd finished off a local bastard with a knife.

The days passed, leaving traces, piles of memories, allowing unfulfilled hopes to die along the wayside. Mineiro, a friend of Hammer and Hellraiser, gave them a good tip-off: he told them his friend worked the till in a steak house on Taquara Square.

They made plans for the following Sunday. To get a car, Hellraiser had to kill its owner. The steak-house robbery went off without a hitch. They took off slowly so as not to arouse suspicion, but went faster and faster as they headed up Gabinal Road. It occurred to Hammer to dump the car and head down through Quintanilha, but his friend would say he was a big wimp, a worrier, jinxed even. They reached the end of the road without running into any trouble. Their feeling of success made them laugh. Hellraiser said he'd get a friend to strip the car, to rustle up some more dough. They followed the river to steer clear of the police station and turned down the road that ran along the right branch of the river. Happiness must be experienced intensely, so they headed for Teresa's to buy twenty bundles of weed to celebrate. Everything was going according to plan until a Robbery and Theft Squad car spotted them. At first Hellraiser didn't accelerate and they didn't even glance at the policemen to avoid looking obvious, but their ploy was in vain.

The police followed them. Hellraiser shifted into second and went as fast as he could, weaving in and out of the streets of the projects with machine-gun fire tearing into the rear of the Opala. It was impossible to return fire. They gained ground on Middle Street, dumped the car in the New Short-Term Houses, passed the Two-Story Houses and made it to the bush. The police split up. Two stayed to examine the abandoned car, while the other three went after them. Hellraiser and Hammer didn't open their mouths in the bush. They trained their minds on the *exus* that protected them. The minutes passed slowly while their hearts pounded, but the time it was taking the police to come after them put an end to their tormenting nervousness. Hellraiser's thoughts took off down several paths, but Hammer's followed a single line:

'I'm gettin' out of this life once and for all. If I don't I'm gonna kick the bucket or get screwed in the slammer. This crime business is for wackos.'

Hellraiser came out of hiding an hour after the chase. Hammer tried to convince him to wait a little longer, but his friend ignored him. He stayed there alone until daybreak; he didn't want to risk running into the police. At around nine o'clock, he slowly climbed down from the tree he was in, stretched, took a leak and started walking. He wanted to find Cleide so he could tell her he wanted to leave that place for good. He was a good bricklayer and could get a job whenever he wanted. He wanted to live in peace, have a kid and be happy with his wife. No, it wasn't fear he felt—he'd never been a coward, just cautious. It was just that this life of getaways and murders had become a pain in the ass. He spent the morning weaving his way through alleys until he reached Middle Street, where Boss of Us All was walking along with his machine gun cocked to take out hoods. The policeman had heard what had happened when he got to work. His determination to kill any gangster at all had nothing to do with the robbery. The murdered car owner had been his friend. Again, a desire for revenge gathered and smoldered in his heart. He correctly figured that the gangsters had already come out of the bush, so he walked down one side of the sidewalk alone, to attract as little attention as possible. Hammer never thought he would run into the police at that hour, imagining that both Military and Civil Police would be changing shifts. There were children playing in the alleys, others going to school, and people on their way to work that morning. He watched a boy walking along in front of him. His son would be as beautiful as that boy, but he wouldn't let him run around barefoot in tattered shorts and no shirt. He'd bring his son candy every day when he got home from work. The fresh morning breeze caressed his face, made his thoughts soar. His gaze followed the tips of his toes with each step. He didn't check the alleys and was unconcerned about danger, since he no longer considered himself a gangster. A dog barked. The reformed gangster clicked his fingers and the dog wagged its tail. He noticed some shame plants on the ground and went over to touch them with his foot, causing their leaves to close. Everything that happened to him was good and seemed to be converging toward a happy ending. The herons flew in the light, dry wind that whistled and sighed through the bare branches of the trees and blew across his face, giving him the impression that everything that had been bad in his life until then would leave with it. Boss of Us All strode along the opposite sidewalk with the jauntiness and eye of a killer, an attitude and expression that were typical of him. He had already crossed over the right branch of the river. He wanted to catch Hellraiser and Hammer together. They were the thugs who kept him on his toes most. There was a guy called Luis Sting who also had to be taken out so he could have a bit more peace and quiet. But wasting any gangster at all would be fine that day. He'd bet the other police officers that he'd kill one before noon. Passersby veered away when they saw him. He stopped to tie his boot, then continued, quickening his step, peering around corners before crossing intersections. Up around the Bonfim he slowed his pace, swept his eyes over the area and only saw a few drunks. Luis Gonzaga's voice on the radio calmed him a little. The sun burned his face.

Hammer whistled a song by Paulo Sérgio and thought about Cleide again—he was going to tell her that he'd get a sucker's job, come what may. Peace, peace and quiet for the rest of his life. He didn't allow dismal thoughts of packed lunches and crowded trains and buses to dampen his resolution. He felt sorry for Hellraiser, who would one day come to the same end as Squirt or rot in the slammer. Boss of Us All thought he was on a roll, because on his last shift he'd arrested two potheads and killed a bastard who had fired at him when he told him he was under arrest. He was feeling good about himself, and went around punching people in the face for whatever reason he saw fit. He was less than fifty yards from Hammer.

Cleide had already searched high and low for her husband. Now she was looking over the fence at the street, where she saw carts passing, kite strings being coated in crushed glass and glue, women gossiping, hoods on street corners and a honking gas truck.

Hellraiser had already woken up and counted the money. He was smoking a joint while he waited for his buddy to arrive so they could split the dough.

Staring at the ground, Hammer was imagining Cleide making him breakfast and a packed lunch when he passed Boss of Us All without noticing him, lost in thought. Boss of Us All didn't see Hammer go by on the other side of the street either. He trained his eyes on a boy he had noticed at the end of the street. Thinking it was Hellraiser, he sprinted after him. When he saw the policeman coming after him, the boy pulled his gun, fired and fled. The shot hit him in the arm. Boss of Us All kept running in spite of it, but he stopped when he noticed he was losing a lot of blood. He swore by the Devil that he'd kill Hellraiser the first chance he had.

Hammer walked calmly home.

'Deliver your soul to the Lord and you will live forever. Only Christ can deliver you from suffering and free you from the fires of hell. Repent your sins because Paradise awaits you! Hallelujah!'

Hammer listened in silence to the man in the navy-blue polyester suit clutching a Bible. It was only a few minutes after he'd arrived home and revealed his plans to Cleide. When the man finished talking, his followers all uttered words of similar logic, with the eloquence of those who repeat the same text day after day.

'What do I have to do to get all that?'

'Just accept Jesus into your heart!'

'What . . . ?'

'May we come in for a minute, sir?'

'Uh-huh.'

The man in the polyester suit sat on the sofa next to the other three Baptist missionaries. Hammer stood in the left corner of the room with Cleide by his side. Both listened while they preached the Gospel.

'Now let's hear the words of the Lord:

> *Psalm 91:*
>
> *He who dwells in the shelter of the Most High will rest in the shadow of the Almighty. I will say of the Lord, 'He is my refuge and my fortress, my God, in whom I trust.' Surely He will save you from the fowler's snare and from the deadly pestilence. He will cover you with His feathers, and under His wings you will find refuge; His faithfulness will be your shield and rampart.*
>
> *You will not fear the terror of night, nor the arrow that flies by day, nor the pestilence that stalks in the darkness, nor the plague that destroys at midday . . .'*

Everything in Hammer became bubbling, jubilant emotion when he heard these words. The speaker's sincerity was to Hammer as visible as his eyes. His very core had opened to the words of Christ. From his eyes—two bright celebrations—silent tears sprang and smiled in the wind rustling through every nook and cranny of the room. Each verse was a road tugging at his soul. A smile spread across his face. It was divine goodness beckoning him. The branches of the guava tree, the flowing river, the sea breeze, Cleide, the child he'd have with her, the stars in the firmament, the kites in the sky, the moon, the sad song of the crickets, everything, everything was created by God. Outside, the sun was blazing on street corners and all things were already different. Accepting Jesus was being able to be reborn in the same lifetime. His goal was to be happy so he could change the world with the teachings of the Lord. The miracle of conversion changed the metaphors of his face. Peace was present in all things. Cleide's feeling of happiness was also absolutely pure. The future had arrived to lodge itself in her heart.

'Love, God is love . . .' she stammered.

Hammer moved, without saying good-bye to his friends, one month after the visit from the missionaries. He gave up cards, his pocketknife, his gun, his vices. He stopped struggling against destiny once and for all. He told Cleide over and over that he had indeed hit the jackpot. He got a job at Sérgio Dourado, where he was exploited for a long time, but he didn't care. Faith shielded him from anger when he was discriminated against for being black, semiliterate and not having all his teeth. The prejudice he suffered came from people who didn't have Jesus in their hearts. He had two children with Cleide and returned to City of God to preach the Gospel whenever he could.

'How can a man just disappear like that without sayin' nothin' to his buddies? I always thought he was a bit of a joke, you know. He was always chickening out of things, a wet blanket, scared of everything . . . The biggest wimp!' Hellraiser told Lúcia Maracanã when he found out that Hammer had moved.

'They say he's turned into a born-again.'

'Yeah . . . I know. Night Owl told me. No way am I ever goin' in for that stuff . . . ! Accept everything the pastor says, be poor for the rest of your life and not care . . . That's for suckers, ain't it? But each to his own; if the guy's turned into a born-again it's 'cos he really wants to go to heaven, right? That's why he took off without sayin' nothin'.'

Hellraiser left Lúcia to her household chores and headed Up Top to find Luis Sting, his new friend. A twenty-year-old mulatto with reddish hair and thirty murders under his belt, he was strong, lanky, tight-lipped and mean-looking. He was known for his perversity throughout the *favelas* of Rio de Janeiro. He shot at residents for no reason, and mugged or threatened them just for the sake of it. The only reason he didn't know the Tender Trio was because he'd been in the slammer for five years. He told his friends he'd escaped one night during Carnival after overpowering two drunk prison guards. He was cleaning his gun when Hellraiser arrived:

'What's up man? Come in,' said Sting when he opened his door.

'I was talking with Lúcia Maracanã.'

'I was sitting here wondering if you're actually gonna get rid of that pig. There's people saying he's going around shouting on street corners that he's gonna do you in. Whenever he lays into someone, he asks if they know you, if they know where you live . . . You gotta get rid of this pig. If you don't . . .'

'I'm gonna take him down. If he was on duty, he'd die today! But leave him to me . . . Hey, wanna buy me a beer?' said Hellraiser.

They walked to the Bonfim, not watching their backs. Along the way, Hellraiser said Pipsqueak had shown up loaded, but had quickly disappeared. Pipsqueak was sharper, had more attitude. He'd make an ideal partner for them.

'I gotta meet this kid.'

'He said he's gonna show up again; you might already know him.'

'Uh-huh . . . So there's these guys, right? And they landed themselves a heap of dough in just one day . . .'

'You know that friend I was talkin' about?' interrupted Hellraiser.

'Yeah.'

'He's turned into a Bible-thumper, man . . . The biggest wimp!
Now he's gonna go round sayin' Jesus is the only savior. Makes you
wanna pull the trigger on him . . .'

'What was I sayin'?'

'Those guys that landed a heap of dough . . .'

'Oh yeah . . . But hey, these guys landed themselves a bundle of
cash real fast. They get a car and do three or four gas stations in
one shot. The best day's Friday. All we need is a driver, 'cos it's much
better than shops, bakeries and houses.'

The following Friday, they left before midnight to hold up two gas
stations on Bandeirantes highway and one on Taquara Square.
Carrots had to toss a coin with Night Owl to be the driver of the
operation. Sting wasn't easy on any of his victims. Even when they
offered no resistance, he shot them in the ass, hit them with the
butt of his gun and punched them in the face. The only one who
tried to retaliate got a bullet in his head. Sting didn't like well-
dressed whites. He thought they took the place of blacks in everything. First in the Baixada region and now in the projects themselves,
whenever he saw well-dressed whites, he mugged and abused them
to avenge the Negro, whose place in society they had stolen. He
didn't run from the police. He thought that was for wimps. 'I've
already bumped off loads of pigs that crossed me,' he'd say whenever he had the chance.

They repeated the holdups at a number of gas stations in
Jacarepaguá and Barra da Tijuca for a good while. Hellraiser only
came out of hiding on days when Boss of Us All wasn't on duty. He
hoped that as time went on the policeman would forget about him.
One night, he left Dummy's Bar half-drunk. He thought about picking up a slut to screw. He took a stroll around Block Thirteen, headed
up Middle Street, drank a Cinzano-and-*cachaça* and lit a cigarette.
His feet were all over the place and he decided to go home. He took
the same route back. When he lay down, everything was spinning
and he felt like vomiting. With the help of a finger down his throat,

he threw up the Cinzano-and-*cachaça*, beer and chicken gizzards. He put his mouth under the tap, slowly turned it on, rinsed out his mouth, splashed water on his face and lay down again. Within a few minutes he had fallen asleep. He slept well, even in the intense heat with the mosquitoes rattling in his ears, but suddenly Squirt was walking on fire, dressed in red and black and holding a pitchfork. Hellraiser tossed and turned in his bed. The place he was in looked like Block Thirteen, Block Fifteen, São Carlos. It was at once familiar and strange. The fire beneath Squirt's feet died down and leaped up toward him, then became blood, from which Niftyfeet, Pelé and Shorty emerged, wearing the same clothes as Squirt.

'What do you all want?' he asked.

'We've come to give you a warnin' so you won't get kicked outta life like us,' answered Squirt.

'Where are you?'

'It don't matter now, but if you don't wanna come hang out with us you'd better take out Boss of Us All,' said Squirt, while he and his buddies slowly turned to smoke. The smoke hung there for a few moments, then became a new pool of blood, in which Hellraiser saw his own body writhing.

He woke up shouting. The neighbors were frightened, but no one dared go and see what was happening at Hellraiser's place. It might be the police or an enemy. They stayed quiet under their covers. Hellraiser realized it had been a dream and went looking for Berenice. He remembered that she was at a friend's place helping with an abortion. The fragile early-morning light came through the curtain at the living-room window. His thoughts were completely focused on his nightmare. He got the coke from the bottom of the wardrobe and snorted it straight. He was so determined to get high that he didn't warm the plate in order to cut the coke out into lines. He did it all in one go, then rolled a joint to calm his spirit.

'What a fucked dream—I wonder if it's a warning?' he thought aloud. He'd never had a dream like that. It could only be true that it was going to happen. He had to kill before he got killed. He got his two revolvers, which he'd left warming behind the fridge so he could clean them down with kerosene. He noticed that he was low on ammunition and that the revolvers weren't in a good state. 'A gangster without a gun is like a whore without a bed.' He remembered the dismal but simple lesson he'd learned at a tender age from his mother when she didn't have a room in the Red Light District and his father didn't have a gun to rob with. He tried to control his body, which kept on shaking. But that bastard of a cop would have to light lots of candles to the Devil to get rid of him, because he was a tough nut to crack—he'd give him what he had coming.

Outside, morning brought life to the alleys, breadsellers, milk carts and school children. The noise of the day made him calmer. The threat of death makes any silence suspicious and every sound sinister. He heard the kitchen door handle turn, threw himself behind the wall between the living room and the kitchen, and cocked his guns. It was Berenice.

He told her about his dream before she'd even had time to sit down and relax. Seeing how strung out he was, Berenice tried to calm him:

'Let's go to the *terreiro* to talk to the *pombagira*, 'cos you're a bag of nerves and you haven't been there for ages.'

'That's true!'

On Monday night, Hellraiser went to Osvaldo's *terreiro* for a cleansing.

''Fraid of dyin', boy?! 'Fraid of turnin' into an *exu*?!?' cackled the *pombagira*. 'How long's it bin since ya last come to see me? I don' ask fer more than wot's agreed. I protect the boys and the boys don' give a damn 'bout me. When things get better the boys forget wot I asked fer. But it wos me that showed up in yer dream,' she chortled. 'Ole Black Boots wants to get rid of ya, but don' worry, 'cos I've got him on a string!'

Then she asked her apprentice to write Boss of Us All's name on a piece of paper, ran a dagger through the paper and placed it in a glass of *cachaça*. She puffed cigar smoke into the glass, cackled and continued:

'Go and bury this at Calunga Grande Cemetery on Monday and leave the rest to me. After twenty suns Ole Black Boots'll meet his end at the seventh crossroad he come to. Then ya come back to see me. Now drink a bit of this and in yer mind ask fer wot ya want.'

Hellraiser asked for protection from bullets, luck with money, lots of women in his life and health for himself and his wife, who, on the way to the *terreiro*, had told him she was pregnant.

He dreamed the same dream several times. Even with the protection of the *pombagira*, he was constantly on guard—he wasn't going to play into Kojak's hands. In one week, he had the dream seven times in a row and, to add to his desperation, that Saturday he heard from Sting that Wilson the Devil had been killed on the field next to the Doorway to Heaven. He had been surprised while playing soccer by Boss of Us All in civilian clothes.

'He could've thrown him in the slammer, man. He had him by the balls. But then he ordered him to the ground and pulled the trigger.'

'Was he alone?'

'Yeah. He swore with his foot on the stiff that you're next. And from the way he said it, it looks like the shit's really gonna hit the fan. Your days are numbered!' joked Sting.

'Give me a lend of that rifle there!' begged Hellraiser in a worried voice.

'I don't lend that to no one. But I can help you out with a forty-five. Know how it works? It's dead easy and whatever it hits, it kills. It takes hollow points. C'mon, let's go down to the lake for a practice. We can swing by my place for a smoke first.'

Only Sting talked while they smoked two joints. Hellraiser remembered his dream. He paced around his friend's living room. He didn't know why Boss of Us All was so eager to kill him. He did everything at speed, and even drank a glass of water with the swiftness of a thief. They set off for the big lake. Before the lesson began, Hellraiser ordered the children playing there to scram.

'This gun doesn't have a cylinder. It takes a magazine. Just press this lever here, see, and it comes out; to load it just stick it in here. To cock it, hold it here, underneath, and slide it back like this. If you just pull the hammer back, it doesn't cock, right? I'm loaning you this magazine here 'cos I trust you, otherwise I wouldn't. But keep your shit together and don't let the pigs get it, OK man? Let's see if you got the idea.'

Hellraiser turned the gun over slowly in silence. He visualized his *pombagira*, looked at the almost cloudless sky, two butterflies coming and going between the almond trees, the kids heading away to the Eucalyptus Grove. There'd always be things to get perfect in no time at all. He thought about asking his friend to help him ambush Boss of Us All, but he didn't feel comfortable about extending the invitation. Sting was a good pal, but they hadn't been friends long enough for him to help kill someone unless it meant he could rustle up some dough. If it were Squirt, he wouldn't even have to invite him—but if he could just stop dreaming about him for Christ's sake! He could always slip away from the projects, but the pain of chickening out would be endless. Berenice would like it, but deep down she'd think he was a wimp. Only the wind could be heard at that moment; it rustled the branches of the almond trees, the Eucalyptus, stirred the riverside grasses, made it hard for the herons to fly and blew across his skin. The *pombagira* returned to his thoughts. She'd have to work some strong magic for him. He'd already buried Boss of Us All's name on a piece of paper in the cemetery. Faith moves mountains—it would move Gávea Rock and place it over Boss of Us All's head. Now everything depended solely on his strength, his presence of mind. All he had to do was practice shooting with this thing he was holding. He took out the magazine, put it back, cocked the gun as Sting had taught him, took aim at the trunk of the most distant almond tree and fired. Bull's-eye, and satisfaction on Sting's face. He only missed two out of ten shots. He said that he'd already got the hang of it and that he wouldn't waste more bullets on the tree. He'd save the rest to pump into Boss of Us All's ass.

'Go ahead and practice some more—there's stacks of ammo back at my place,' Sting assured him.

Hellraiser spent the rest of that Saturday at home, but in the evening he felt like taking a stroll. He didn't think Boss of Us All would still be prowling around that day, because whenever he killed someone he didn't show his face. He left home with the .45 cocked. Everything in his path was suspicious. He ran into the cool guys smoking a joint on the corner in front of the nursery. He heard Green Eyes saying Dirty Dick's death was a shame:

'Dirty Dick was a good man. He wasn't cocky, always minded his own business . . .'

'I don't know who this Dirty Dick guy is . . . How come he snuck off?' asked Jackfruit.

'He'd lit a joint and didn't have anywhere to throw it.'

'He could've just put up his hand and tried to talk,' said Acerola.

'No way! Boss of Us All ain't interested in talkin'. He's been shootin' people left right and center!' said Mango.

They hung around bullshitting. Hellraiser warned them not to smoke in the streets when Boss of Us All was on duty. If they wanted to have a smoke without any hassles it was fine for them to just turn up at his place. The potheads mentally turned down his invitation. If the police suddenly showed up they wouldn't know any of them from a hole in the wall. By the time they'd explained who was who, the vultures would already be circling overhead. Hellraiser promised he'd kill Boss of Us All the next day. He swore so adamantly that only silence followed. The joint was already dying. Acerola glanced around, hoping to avoid unpleasant surprises. Hellraiser suddenly stared at Green Eyes and broke the silence.

'How come you're black and you've got green eyes?'

They laughed. Hellraiser finished off the roach, dropped it and stood on it. He left saying he was going to Teresa's to score a couple of papers of coke so he could stay up all night and surprise Boss of Us All when he was leaving work. The heads hung around a little longer.

'This shit makes you really sleepy, you know,' said Acerola.

'You really think Boss of Us All's gonna die tomorrow?' asked Jackfruit.

'I'm not stickin' around to see,' said Acerola, laughing too much.

'You're really shitfaced, man! You're gonna get home and raid the kitchen!' joked Orange.

Hellraiser drew close to the police station, his footsteps still shrouded in pre-dawn darkness. He'd spent the night getting wasted while Berenice slept. He bit his lips, checked to make sure everything was OK with his gun and visualized his *pombagira*. Outside, Saturday night was still in full swing, with improvised sambas in bars, street-corner romances and potluck parties in people's backyards. Oblivious to the night, Hellraiser had done too much coke. Berenice had lain there, unmoving, unaware of everything that was about to happen. Her husband was going to take out Boss of Us All. A cat on the roof had frightened him and he'd decided to turn out the living-room light so as not to attract attention. He'd knocked back a mouthful of brandy to perk himself up before heading out to finish off that shithead of a cop.

He positioned himself strategically so he could pull the trigger as soon as Boss of Us All went by. He couldn't miss from where he was. All he had to do was fire, then head up Red Hill, come back down through the neighborhood of Araújo, circle back through The Plots, pass the Doorway to Heaven, go down Main Street and hide out at Sting's place. If there was a chase he'd head into the bush, because no policeman in his right mind would risk a shoot-out in the bush. He waited there for his enemy for more than three hours.

Boss of Us All had breakfast at the police station and said goodbye to his fellow officers with the smile of one who has done a good job. It was cold outside. He took his first few steps rummaging about in his trouser pockets to make sure he hadn't forgotten anything. Then he opened his bag, had a last look inside, spat on the ground, picked his nose, rolled the snot between his fingers and ate it.

Hellraiser had already taken aim. He was waiting for him to walk another thirty feet, then bang—he'd send the bastard off to rot in hell. His finger was already beginning to pull the trigger when a car went past, blocking his view. He started again with shaking hands, then held his breath and fired. Boss of Us All threw himself to the ground and crawled to a post. As he got up, he heard another shot and saw the sniper make a run for it.

'Hellraiser, you motherfucker! Think it's easy to knock me off? Now we'll see who's who! C'mon, shoot then, go ahead and shoot me, ya faggot!'

The other policemen came to their friend's aid, and wanted to take off after the gangster immediately. Boss of Us All objected, saying it was his business alone and he'd take care of it that very day. He went back to the station, got his machine gun, slung his bag into a corner and left, weaving his way recklessly through the alleys. He correctly guessed the route Hellraiser had taken, and waited in ambush in an alley near the Doorway to Heaven.

When he saw he wasn't being followed, Hellraiser crossed the street feeling a little calmer, but even so, the misfortune of not having hit his enemy caused him to shudder in the face of a failure that could cost him his life. He'd baited the bear. He had to get out of there as fast as he could. He stuck his gun in his waistband. Hammer had been a gangster but he'd got out before the shit hit the fan. He'd go home for Berenice and take her with him to anywhere far from there—he'd even go to São Carlos. He looked up and saw a heron flapping across the gray sky. The real fear of death comes only when you're about to die.

Boss of Us All had already seen him. He scratched his dick and waited for Hellraiser to get as close as possible. Hellraiser walked with his head down. If he'd killed the bastard the world would be different now. He'd buy ten wraps of coke, a crate of beer and a shitload of weed to celebrate. He raised his head and saw a woman pass an alley and start running, pulling a child along by the arm. He snapped back to the present. He cocked his gun, doubled around the block and fired. Again the policeman got away unscathed and this time returned fire straightaway. Hellraiser ran to the corner and stopped. He knew his enemy was alone. Now he'd exchange fire, even though Boss of Us All had a machine gun. With the speed of a bullet, he visualized his *pombagira*. Boss of Us All's face peered around the corner. Hellraiser pulled the trigger. Boss of Us All ran out into the open firing his machine gun, riddling the wall Hellraiser was hiding behind with holes.

Boss of Us All's attitude made Hellraiser hesitate for a fraction of a second, then he quickly sprinted to another corner. The policeman came after him, his machine gun spitting out bullets. Hellraiser broke into someone's backyard, jumped two fences and took shelter behind a post. A man shook a child's head, trying unsuccessfully to bring him back to life. A hail of bullets had torn through his chest, perforating a lung. The man cried out to people running past, begging them for the love of God to help his son.

Boss of Us All looked at the child in the throes of death, but fuck it—better the child than him. He wanted to tear the gangster's body to shreds. Instead of taking the same route as Hellraiser, he took off around the block at a speed his old body had not managed for a long time. He saw his enemy as he finished replacing the magazine. He took aim, held his breath, fired and missed. Hellraiser sent lead flying and bought himself enough time to flee the battle scene. He decided it was impossible to face Boss of Us All when he had a machine gun. He wove his way through the alleys, down Middle Street and arrived home. Boss of Us All tried to follow him, but gave up before he even got to the Bonfim. The shoot-out now over, residents began to appear in the streets again. A friend of the family carried the child's body to the clinic. Boss of Us All went into the Bonfim. He asked if anyone there knew where Hellraiser lived. His question echoed between mixed drinks, *cachaça*, beer. The drinkers' silence was swallowed dry. He downed a shot of brandy, walked back to the station, got more ammunition and went home.

Hellraiser woke up at around two in the afternoon and raided the kitchen. Berenice thought her husband had spent the night holed up with some slut. Her jealousy made her sulk, but even so she served him some food and went outside to talk with her friends.

Boss of Us All didn't spend long at home. He took his wife to the bus station. She was going to spend a month in their home state of Ceará. Before his wife had even got on the bus, he hurried back to the projects and roamed the steepest alleys carrying a long-barrelled .38 and his machine gun. He prayed to his *exu* to make Hellraiser a sitting duck in his path. City of God was creepy—empty streets, no kites or sun in the sky. The street market finished early and the day passed slowly. The street corners lay in ambush. Boss of Us All gave up his search and on his way home saw a boy leaving the clinic with his leg in a plaster cast. He had broken it in a manhole without a lid while fleeing from the gunfire that morning. Hellraiser spent the rest of the day at home.

Monday dawned wounded. Rainy days seemed premature, if not aborted. The cold brought with it the pleasures of laziness. It was nice to stay in.

As soon as Berenice woke up, Hellraiser asked her to buy provisions, weed and coke, with the intention of spending a week holed up at home. No way was he going to let Kojak get him. He'd eat, drink, do lines and fuck his wife all week long. He figured Boss of Us All would cool down. He might even think he'd fled the *favela*. He was worried that some northerner might snitch on him. Northerners, who all sucked up to their bosses, were also snitches. A worthless bunch. They'd have you believe they shat flowers.

The idea of leaving the projects to save his life lasted all week long, although he knew he couldn't move house as it would attract the police's attention. He'd become aware that the only physical space that belonged to him was his body. He had to preserve it, but if he left the projects he'd lose face. He'd be a coward if he chickened out, if he wasn't man enough to waste Boss of Us All or die in a shoot-out with him.

'My husband died in a shoot-out!' Berenice would boast, or at least that's what Hellraiser misguidedly thought.

Boss of Us All roamed the entire projects day and night. He exchanged fire with Sting on Wednesday and managed to arrest two gangsters at The Blocks. He killed another over in Block Fifteen. By Friday, he already believed Hellraiser had left the projects, as his friends in uniform had figured. He relaxed.

'Where you from?'

'I'm from here, girl. Nobody knows me because I hardly ever go out, but then I haven't been livin' here for very long either.'

'Where'd you come from?'

'I used to live over in São Carlos and I also spent some time over in the Red Light District.'

'Who d'you know there?'

'Um . . . I know Milk, Cleide, Neide . . .'

'You know Milk? That's right! Is he still selling weed there?'

'No, the cops've got an arrest warrant out for him . . . He had to clear out for a while. Hadn't you heard?'

'And how's Neide doin'?'

'She's fine. Gone and got herself pregnant with a guy over in Turano and she's holing up with him over there.'

'So that's why she didn't parade last year . . .'

'No, it wasn't 'cos of that. The president of the section got on her case and she started ripping off her costume, then went for her tooth and claw . . . It was the biggest knock-down, drag-out fight.'

'Who's the president?'

'Dona Carmem.'

'Of course—that woman's such a bitch! She's pissed me off before too . . . What's your name?'

'Ari, but you can call me Ana Flamengo. What's yours?'

'Lúcia, but everyone knows me as Lúcia Maracanã. If anyone gives you a hard time, just tell 'em you're a friend of mine and everything'll be fine, OK? I'm goin' for a walk around. I'll come and talk some more before the end of the dance.'

Although on edge, Hellraiser went for a walk with his wife. He couldn't stand sitting around inside watching the clock tick any longer. He threw back a beer at Dona Idê's Bar, but didn't stay in any one place for very long. Against Berenice's wishes, he decided to look in on the dance. He went into the hall only after making sure Boss of Us All wasn't there, then roamed the entire club, accepting greetings in silence, always in silence. He wasn't in the habit of speaking when he was strung out. He stopped near the bar. One of the directors offered him a beer. He drank quickly, his eyes searching the darkest corners. His gaze came to rest on the transvestite. He'd never seen that woman. She might be a snitch. He was about to head over to check her out, but Berenice, who had followed his gaze, said somewhat jealously:

'Don't go, he's a faggot!'

Hellraiser again fixed his eyes on Ari. His skin broke out in a cold sweat. Yes, it was Ari—his mother's son who wanted to be a woman, right there in the middle of everyone. For sure they'd beat the shit out of him; they'd feel him up then bash his face in. He wasn't hanging around to see that. He pulled Berenice along saying something was telling him Boss of Us All was in the area.

They left the dance quickly and turned down the right branch of the river. Hellraiser approached crossroads and turned corners carelessly. He stared at the ground; if it opened he'd let it swallow him so he'd never again have to see Ari. Berenice walked beside him, taking all the precautions. As they turned down the last street, she glanced at her husband, who had allowed a few tears to escape from his red eyes.

Down at the end of the road, Boss of Us All's lips drew back into a murderous smile and he pointed his machine gun at that easy target. He'd kill the wife too. Those who keep company with gangsters go down with them. Berenice looked back down the street. She had time to jump on her husband and fall to the ground with him. The machine-gun fire snarled in their ears. Hellraiser returned fire awkwardly, managing to protect Berenice while she got out of the firing line. His first shot was way off mark. The second almost tore off the policeman's ear. Boss of Us All fired another round, then took cover. Even from the ground, Hellraiser fired five near-hits. Then he got up, slipped away, jumped two fences, crossed two streets, went around the block, reloaded his gun and crept up behind his enemy. He crouched on the corner and saw Boss of Us All heading away toward the club. He walked slowly home and went inside, his nerves in shreds.

Berenice looked at her husband. She could barely speak. Her most spontaneous gesture was to cry, allowing her entire body to shudder. Hellraiser wandered back and forth in the pitiful space that was his home. If that asshole of a cop discovered where he lived, he might surprise him in his sleep. And that fairy was around again pretending to be a woman. Ari was a cancer that ate at his stomach. What was that bastard doing at the dance? His place was in the Red Light District! Why hadn't Boss of Us All's bullets blasted his head off? It was the only way he wouldn't run into his brother again.

Berenice went into the bathroom, washed away the blood running down her arm, splashed water on her face and returned to the sofa. Her husband was sitting in the kitchen doorway. She thought about begging him to get out right then and there, but it'd be no use; Hellraiser was pig-headed. If she wanted to leave she'd have to go alone. Although she knew her husband hated women crying, she was unable to stop fresh tears from rolling.

Hellraiser stared at a dead ant. He couldn't say a thing about his wife's crying. She was the one who had saved his life and almost lost her own. Perhaps if he cried too, something at the core of him would change, but men didn't cry, especially in front of women. Men who cried were queers, like Ari. The oil lamp in front of the saint flickered in the wind. He heard a car and cocked his gun. If it was Boss of Us All he'd have it out with him until one of them fell. The car didn't stop. His thoughts returned to his brother. A vague feeling of tenderness ran through his soul, but his hatred for that faggot was reignited. Why had he shown up again? He would never confess, not even to the *pombagira*, that that bastard was of the same blood as he was. Berenice stopped crying. The silence was only broken when people went past and talked in the street. He moved closer to his wife and tried to resist the urge to hug her, but she held out her arms. He sat there suffering in silence with her.

Sunday brought rain, but looking out toward Barra da Tijuca one could see rays of sunlight poking through just above the horizon. Sting went to Hellraiser's place to take him a box of shells and his rifle. He didn't think it fair to leave Hellraiser with only a .45 when the enemy had a machine gun. He made a number of recommendations and implicit threats in their conversation about the rifle. They spent half an hour examining the weapon. It was easy to shoot and could fire one shot at a time or in bunts. Hellraiser decided to buy his friend a beer and roll him a joint in recognition of his gesture. As they smoked they strolled through the alleys and drizzle of an almost dead rain. They were both wearing Lee jeans and jackets. Hellraiser was carrying the .45 and a long-barreled .38, while Sting only had a .32. They headed up Middle Street. The joint was petering out, so they decided to salvage what was left of it. Hellraiser removed some tobacco from the end of a cigarette, replaced it with the roach, lit it, took two tokes and passed it to Sting.

The day was up and running with the Bonfim still open for the few remnants of the night. Whoever saw them moved away, afraid there might be a shoot-out at any moment. Beth Carvalho sang out from Bahian Paulo's phonograph. Torquato opened a beer. They toasted. Sting asked Hellraiser to use the rifle only once. Boss of Us All couldn't be allowed to see the gun and get away, and if he was with other policemen they'd all have to die. The thing was not to let anyone know about the rifle. The police couldn't be allowed to find out that the weapon was in City of God. Staring fixedly into his friend's face, he said that if he managed to kill Boss of Us All he'd have to cut open his body and retrieve the bullet, so no one would be the wiser.

Lucia Maracanã came over. She looked at Hellraiser, went over to the counter, asked for a glass and slowly poured herself a beer. Hellraiser asked what was up. Lúcia told him she was very worried, because Boss of Us All had shown up at the club saying that soon the Devil would have a fresh corpse and that he wouldn't sleep until he'd killed him. Hellraiser emptied his glass of beer in a single gulp. He turned to Sting with a knowing laugh. Lúcia continued. She talked about the transvestite who had left the club in a frenzy when he heard the shots. A shiver ran down Hellraiser's spine. Everyone had seen Ari. That dirty homo had had the gall to show up on his turf. The next time he saw him he was going to shoot him in the foot. He changed the subject, then said good-bye. He spent the rest of the day at home.

Monday dawned with a hot sun in the sky. Boss of Us All arrived at the police station earlier than usual. He greeted everyone half-heartedly, changed into uniform, got the 'cunt' (as he called his machine gun), examined it, loaded it, got more ammunition from the cupboard and hurried into the streets. He'd had nightmares all night long. In his dreams he'd seen Hellraiser ordering him to the ground while holding a gun to his chest. He'd woken up before two in the morning and had been unable to get back to sleep. His determination to eliminate the gangster that day was much stronger, but he didn't look around. He allowed his gaze to stretch out along the alleys, streets and lanes. He was sad; the nightmare had been a warning. Whenever he dreamed bad things, something shitty happened. His depression was not only due to his bad night. His wife had written to him saying she wasn't coming back to Rio de Janeiro. She was tired of that life of deaths. She refused to sleep any longer beside a man whose weapon was an extension of his body. A man without peace of mind; a murderer. She didn't want to wake up every night startled by the sounds of the world. That incurable ulcer had been caused by the fact that she could never be sure whether her husband would arrive home at the end of each day. Not being able to walk down the street without a worry had left her isolated, without any peace of mind. Being a policeman's wife made it hard to make friends. She spent her life locked away at home. And if she complained too much she got a beating.

Boss of Us All was wrought with anger at her betrayal. His thoughts dwelt more on his wife than on Hellraiser. He walked along with his head down. Acerola, Mango and Green Eyes put out a joint and passed by him unnoticed. He turned into Middle Street and went behind the supermarket. Life in his home state of Ceará had always been hard. He'd gone hungry throughout his childhood. When he was still a child, he would wake up before dawn to work, and only had afternoons free to study at the one school in the region, more than twenty-four miles from home. His father's death put the seal on his miserable life. He saw his mother have to start doing any work she could find to feed her children. He cut across a square and turned down the street that followed the right branch of the river. He might have been a carpenter like his youngest brother. He reached the river's edge. Those born in the drought country don't choose their profession, by virtue of their place of birth. He turned left and walked along with slow, steady steps. Deep down, he didn't like being a policeman. Everyone feared him, and when they didn't fear him they hated him. He lit a cigarette. But being a policeman was much better than dealing with drunks in a bar. He knew this from personal experience, as he'd worked in a bar in the city center before joining the police force. He walked down the middle of the street, something he never did. He remembered the times he'd had to rummage for leftover food when he'd just arrived in Rio. He turned into an alley where a few kids were smoking a joint on the corner. He told them they were under arrest, which was a waste of time. It only sent them running. He

couldn't be bothered chasing anyone. He'd only get moving if
Hellraiser appeared in front of him. His son had died of tuberculosis. He stopped at a bar and ordered a Cinzano-and-*cachaça*, then
left without paying. The lieutenant who had got him into the Military Police force was always asking for favors, for him to kill someone or other. One day he'd blast his head off. He crossed another
square. His wife had betrayed him. Another bar. He knocked back
another Cinzano-and-*cachaça*. The biggest scar on his body had
been made by his stepfather, who stole his mother from him and
made him leave school so he could work the whole day. Another
bar, where he drank another Cinzano-and-*cachaça*. The drought
in the Ceará backlands had bleached the color out of his deepest
dreams in the full bloom of his youth. He passed the Bonfim. He
had been married in the registry office in addition to the church.
He thought about going home. His mother had died of a snake bite.
He sneezed. He'd killed more than thirty people, but most of them
had been niggers. He coughed up phlegm. He wanted his wife to
come back. He spat. He ate sausages. His father used to beat his
mother. He continued down Middle Street. His stepfather had
beaten her too. One day he'd catch a gangster with more than ten
million in stolen money, take the jackpot and ask for a discharge.
He arrived at the Two-Story Houses. If he'd moved, his wife
wouldn't have left him. He walked through the New Short-Term
Houses. He'd never pay rent. A few gangsters took off running. He
fired to kill. He'd had whores in the Red Light District. He took
the road along the river's edge and lit a cigarette. His uncle had been
a policeman in Ceará. All the men in his family were tough as hell.
He'd kill Hellraiser with more than fifty bullets. The sun was getting hot. He took the first left. He'd never been afraid of any man.
His godfather was an important man in the Ceará backlands, a
farmer with many heads of cattle. If he went home he'd be guaranteed a job, but come to think of it he could find himself another
wife, and he still had it in him to have kids. He turned right. The
sun hid itself behind a cloud. His wife had left him. He thought

about going home where no one would see him to cry about the loss of his wife. The tears welling up in his eyes were his only defense. He wanted peace and quiet and then he died.

His murderer walked over slowly and fired a shot to put him out of his misery. He then ordered a cart driver to hand over his cart. Boss of Us All's body was thrown roughly into the back. The killer fired a shot to frighten the horse, which galloped off through the streets of the projects then slowed to a trot, trailing blood through the stretches of the afternoon that had just caught fire. The residents followed the cart, thronging to see the corpse. Boss of Us All's body was an endlessly gushing fountain. The horse kept stopping, but there was always someone to thump its hindquarters, making the spectacle continue. The procession turned onto Main Street. A few gangsters shot at his body and blood spurted out, hastening the October dusk and turning it ruby red. The mother of a pot smoker murdered by Boss of Us All took her chance to spit on his body. She was cheered. The cart turned into the street that ran along the right branch of the river. The crowd grew. A few thought they had lost a good policeman. Sting held up the procession looking for guns. He only got ten cruzeiros. The cart carried on. It turned the corner and arrived at Block Thirteen. The party took on a new dimension. People threw stones, emptied garbage cans over the body, clubbed it. The afternoon was still.

The procession continued as far as Dummy's Bar, where a police car arrived with two policemen, putting an end to the show.

Boss of Us All's murderer had been on his way to hold up a hardware store when he had seen him shuffling along with his head down. The chance to kill his brother's murderer had made him forget the holdup. He crouched behind a car, took aim and blew the policeman's brains out. He took the 'cunt' and returned to Vila Sapê, where he lived, celebrating his revenge.

Hellraiser heard about what had happened from his wife, but didn't go out to see the body; he just smoked a joint and had a few beers at home to celebrate.

*   *   *

A week after Boss of Us All's death, Rocket watched with a slightly sad expression as tractors and excavators worked in an uninhabited area behind the blocks of apartments. It was the place he'd played in most. It was next to the haunted mansion with the pool, where the guava, jaboticaba and avocado trees were. The rain had returned and was crying for Rocket, who, although he was watching the traces of his childhood being destroyed, was enchanted by the maneuvers of the machines that bulldozed boldo trees, shame plants, rose moss, fennel and sunflowers. He was too young to realize how much of his childhood was being carried away by excavators. He offered the workers cold water and asked to ride on the tractors. His days were filled with these adventures.

On Monday, Stringy and Rocket were talking, leaning against the wall of a building, which protected them from the biting wind blowing in from Barra da Tijuca.

'Jap said the Baron of Taquara and his wife appear every night at midnight in a coach over in the mansion on Gabinal Road,' said a wide-eyed Stringy.

'Bullshit! This stuff about souls from other worlds is a load of crap. Jap was just bullshittin'.'

'He's not the first one to say it. Everyone says so. He appears in a coach all jazzed up, with a huge blue beard, takes a spin around the manor and when it starts gettin' light he takes off. I believe it!' said Stringy.

'I couldn't care less about all that shit.'

'Then let's go there tonight at midnight!' Stringy challenged him.

'Yeah right. You think my mom'll let me go out at midnight?'

'My mom doesn't let me either, but I sneak out. You're just scared, you big wimp!'

'OK, I'll go. I'll be down here at quarter to twelve.'

'I'll have to see it to believe it!'

By 11:45 they had already crossed Gabinal Road and entered the grounds of the manor. They walked up the short cobbled path to the haunted mansion, peering into the nooks and crannies of the night. They sat down under a full moon that made its presence felt in the starry midnight sky. The silence was only interrupted by crickets, mosquitoes and the occasional car driving down the deserted Gabinal Road. They walked all over the manor. In a small, shaky voice, Rocket said that this story about haunting was bullshit.

They were about to leave when the moon became the midday sun, the houses and apartments gave way to enormous fields, the other mansions looked new, the river became wider, with clean water and alligators along the edges. In both of their throats were strangled screams that wouldn't come out. They saw the Negroes working on the sugar and coffee plantations. Whips stung their backsides. The Eucalyptus Grove grew thicker; it now had an imperial air. Up around Main Square a fountain appeared, where dozens of Negro women washed clothes. In the mansion on Watermill Farm, they watched the hustle and bustle of Dolores's kitchen during preparations for the Baron of Taquara's wife's birthday party.

Along came the Baron astride his chestnut steed, personally commanding the Negroes who were carrying a grand piano he had had sent from Paris as a present for his wife. There were forty Negroes carrying that beauty. While twenty carried the weight of the instrument, the others broke the lowest tree branches so it wouldn't get scratched. People came running from all over the countryside to see the grand piano.

No one noticed the boys. In perplexed wonderment they discovered they could pass through walls, fly and see through things. It was a journey into the past of the haunted mansion by the light of a full moon.

They took off and flew over all of the Jacarepaguá lowlands. They flew over the Pretos Forros range, the big lake, the lake, the pond and the sea. Rocket, who had always dreamed of flying, was now a cloud breaker. National Kid. Superman, Super Goof. Every now and then he would swoop down close to the ground, then soar back into the sky.

They landed again at the mansion. They unwittingly arrived in the torture room, where preparations were being made to amputate the leg of a runaway slave. Eyes bulging at the sight of the operation now under way, both Stringy and Rocket let out the scream long suppressed in their throats, attracting the attention of one of the foremen, who was clairvoyant and able to touch them. The man let go of the slave and rushed at them, wielding a whip. They ran through the labyrinths of the mansion, passing through many rooms, running normally, forgetting that they could pass through walls and fly. They were losing ground when they got to the main entrance of the manor and ran out onto Gabinal Road, older now, in their first years of secondary school, smoking grass while cadavers floated downriver.

After a prayer had soothed his soul, Rocket got out of bed and opened his bedroom window. The world was still gray, but the rain had passed. He looked to his left and saw a crowd at the river's edge. His depression continued—he had to do something to take his thoughts elsewhere. He went back into his room, still scared of everything. What kind of a miserable life was that? The ticking of the clock on the wall reminded him of a shoot-out. He headed for the living room. Perhaps his despondency would pass if he listened to music. He rummaged through his small record collection: Pepeu Gomes in the phenomenal 'Malacaxeta.' Of all the Boys, he was the only one who liked Brazilian music. He put the record on the phonograph, lit a roach he had stashed in his shoe and relaxed.

He thought about his friends at Brazil Central High School. He couldn't wait to go camping with the kids from school. They were going to catch the train to Santa Cruz, then the Macaquinho, a train with wooden carriages which would take them to Ibicuí, a beach to the south of Rio de Janeiro. The train followed the shoreline, crossing that paradisiacal region known as the Green Coast. Among the passengers there were always guitarists playing Brazilian music. The crowd that was into Brazilian music, theater and cinema was different than the crowd that enjoyed rock 'n' roll at the dances. As always, he'd take a tent just for him and his girlfriend Silvana to camp in, so he could snuggle up close to her during those days of fun. He'd also remember to take a roll of black-and-white film to record everything, canned food and three bundles of weed. It was such a blast getting a campfire going at the water's edge and getting wasted, shooting the breeze, singing songs and cuddling up with his girlfriend under the Ibicuí sky, which is full of stars because the absence of light brings the firmament down close to your eyes. Whenever he went camping, Rocket would lie on his back in the sand and make three thousand wishes on the thousand shooting stars that came to play within his field of vision . . .

He really did enjoy the company of his school friends, but when he was with the Boys from the *favela* he also felt at home. He laughed his head off at the crap they came out with and loved hiding out in the bush to smoke weed with them. And what about the dance? The dance was fun, everyone wearing hip-huggers, Reng Teng shirts, dancing and chewing gum. The kids from school didn't understand why Rocket got tattoos and bleached his hair.

Silvana was always asking him to change the way he dressed and stop using that *favela* slang, since he was nice-looking, studied and hung around people from Méier, the neighborhood where his school was. Rocket would come back at her with something and then change the subject, but deep down he agreed with his girlfriend, because the Boys were a little rough around the edges and hated Brazilian music. Most of them had never been to a rock concert, much less a play. They said the singers Caetano Veloso and Gilberto Gil were faggots, Chico Buarque was a communist and Gal Costa and Maria Bethânia were dykes. It was just bullshit; they didn't have the sensibility to understand the metaphors in their songs—they didn't even know what a metaphor was. Once they had told him that Caetano kissed men on the mouth and Rocket had immediately responded that he was breaking taboos. One of the Boys had answered back (just to be an asshole): 'Taboo—fuck you!'

* * *

Stringy didn't actually go inside; he started telling passersby, then went back to the river's edge with the crowd. They stood there staring at the corpses. Some people said they were all den owners, but most were silent, which was the best thing at times like that. The victims' relatives arrived in desperation and tried to pull the bodies out of the river, which had swollen due to the rainy weather that had lasted more than a week. Stringy stood there for a while watching that miserable scene. Suddenly, he looked at the sky, guessed the rain wouldn't come back, and took his wallet from his pocket. Counting his money, he saw he had enough to catch a bus to the beach, which is what he did. Nothing better than a swim to wash away the blues.

Within ten minutes his feet were leaving footprints in the wet sand by the sea at Barra da Tijuca. He went to the water's edge, made a hole in the sand, rolled his wallet in his shirt, put it in the hole and covered it again. He did thirty push-ups, sixty sit-ups and stretched. Then he dived into the high tide, swam through the breaking waves, rested, checked the direction of the undertow and thought about swimming a hundred yards against the current. He took a deep breath before swimming into the purest blue of his dreams.

The best way not to get tired was to let your thoughts dwell on something that had nothing to do with the sea, breathing or distance. He did his best, but was unsuccessful, because he remembered the public test for lifesavers that was coming up soon. Practice, practice—that's what he had to do every day. His father had been a lifeguard, so had his brother, now his turn was approaching. He swam well in the waters of Iemanjá. He went farther than he had planned without feeling tired, then returned to the sand. He went straight to the place he had buried his wallet and sat down. His thoughts returned to the river waters. He'd never die like that. Being murdered must be the worst death. He'd die in the sea . . . No, not in the sea! He'd die in his sleep when he was really old. He knew all the dead guys; they had sold marijuana and cocaine. There were even some who didn't sell anything, but they hung around the dealers. He imagined the police had done a clean-up. Lucky he hadn't been scoring anything when it happened. He fixed his eyes on a strip of blue close to the ocean. The rest was just clouds, although they were blown by a wind coming off the land, indicating that the rain was about to stop once and for all, and the Boys would no doubt hold a bodysurfing championship. He'd have fun practicing, although he knew he'd always win—he was the best swimmer of the lot. He had to pass the test for lifeguards. If he passed, he'd have a good reason to stop studying. He couldn't stand this nonsense of memorizing letters and numbers, but his mother insisted he remain in school. He felt like sitting there on the beach the whole day, despite being alone, despite the cold he felt. The ocean had become an extension of his existence. He'd had this love since he was a boy, not just for the sea, but also for rivers, lakes and waterfalls. It wasn't for nothing that he was nicknamed Indian; in addition to loving water, he was a straight-haired mulatto. He spent most of his time fishing and hunting, and to make some money he hung around near the seashore when the water was rough, collecting chains, watches and bracelets that bathers had lost in the water and the sea threw back up.

He thought about the Boys again: he felt like one of the gang, but only when they were bodysurfing. In fact, he didn't dress like them, wasn't the least bit attracted to the dances, and he'd never liked music. He only liked their love of the sea.

He stayed there alone trying to drown out what had happened. He needed to be alone and liked it. It was in his nature to seek solitude. The waves turned to foam on the sand. The wind blew the clouds. The next day would be sunny.

It was early morning. Rodrigo, Thiago, Daniel, Leonardo, Paype, Marisol, Gabriel, Rocket, Álvaro Katanazaka, Sir Paulo Carneiro, Lourival, Vicente and a bunch of other Boys met at the start of

Highway Eleven to hitch rides to the beach. They chatted about the bodies floating in the river. Marisol said it was the work of Tiny, Night Owl, Russian Mouse, Bicky, Sharky and Marcelo Baião.

The *favela* now had a boss: Tiny. He was the only one who could deal in the *favela*. He gave one of the dens to Carrots out of friendship, but the rest were his and Sparrow's. Teresa continued selling, but she only earned ten percent of each sale, like any other seller.

Marisol looked happy as he opened the bundle of grass he'd bought from Tiny himself. He said he'd never scored such a generous deal. He took the paper lining from his packet of cigarettes and rolled an enormous joint right there on the edge of the highway. When cars driven by young people went past, he held up the joint with one hand and asked for a ride with the other.

His strategy worked: the Boys climbed onto the back of a truck, expressing their gratitude in rowdy euphoria. The driver sped along and they smoked the joint, singing rock 'n' roll. White, long-haired and smiling, some were students, none of them worked and most were waiting to serve in the Army. Off went the Boys to spend the day at the beach, bodysurfing, smoking weed in the sand. That's why they stuffed their faces before leaving home. They'd spent their lunch money on weed.

Before hitting the water, they smoked another joint, laughed at the soul crowd and talked about designer shops and labels and how much they wanted to wear them. The coolest thing was buying the sports brands, but they were really expensive, and, perhaps for this reason, the sharpest. They dreamed of wealth, and wealth meant living across the road from the beach, having ferns in your living room, wearing designer labels and having a car with tinted windows and wide tires (not to mention a loud Kadron exhaust), having a purebred dog to walk on the beach every morning and afternoon, and buying eight pounds of weed in one go so you didn't have to keep making trips to the den all the time. If they were rich, they'd only buy imported skateboards, Caloi 10 bicycles and waterproof watches; they'd dance on the best dance floors and screw the hottest chicks.

As soon as Stringy arrived, the bodysurfing championship began. Flippers were not allowed. From time to time Stringy missed a wave on purpose. It wouldn't be any fun if he won everything.

Dusk fell slowly, the beach was already deserted. The Boys sat in the sand. It was time to smoke one for the road. Marisol remained standing, saying they'd have to arrive earlier at the dance the next Sunday to surprise their enemies. The trick was to spread out around the club until the Gardênia Azul boys got there. They'd wait a bit, then when their enemies thought everything was OK, they'd move in. They had to give those bastards from Gardênia Azul a thrashing so they'd learn not to try to feel up the girls from City of God, and especially not the girls that hung around with them.

As Marisol spoke, everyone was thinking about Adriana: brunette, perfect body, long hair, chiselled face and those thighs capable of giving any guy a hard-on. She was currently Thiago's girlfriend, and Thiago listened suspiciously to Marisol's plans. He guessed Marisol was taking up the cause just to win points with Adriana. You can't trust the next man when your girlfriend is beautiful and sexy. 'What I've really got to do is keep him as far away as possible,' he thought. As soon as Marisol paused for long enough, Thiago gruffly cut his friend off, said it was his business because the girl was with him, and he'd teach the bastard a lesson himself.

He got up after a silence and went for a dip. Marisol looked uncomfortable. He then said Thiago was right, but made it clear that it would be better if they were all together when he went to demolish the jackass. If the enemy tried to get heavy with him, they'd be around to step in. Marisol did, in fact, have his eye on his friend's girlfriend. If Thiago broke up with her, he wouldn't even wait an hour before putting the moves on that doll.

They sat around talking about past fights. They were respected over at the Cascadura Tennis Club because they'd smashed the shit out of the Pombal boys, winning the fight on enemy territory. The fight had started when one of them had stepped on Vicente's foot. Even though he apologized, the Pombal guy copped a left hook, alerting his pals, who came to his rescue. Reason enough for the City of God kids to go around laying into whoever they wanted at the dance. Even the security guards got a beating.

Pipsqueak had been born in the *favela* of Macedo Sobrinho. He was the second of three children. When he was four years old, his father drowned while fishing on Botafogo Beach, leaving the family in dire straits, as he had never had a secure job with benefits. Pipsqueak's mother was forced to go out and work and left the children in the care of relatives. He was brought up by his godmother in the house in Jardim Botânico where she worked as a maid. She wasn't firm enough, however, to insist that he remain in school. He hardly went to school in his first year; he would go back to Macedo Sobrinho, where he spent his days playing in the streets, still wearing his school uniform. The neighbors would tell his mother, who would in turn speak to his godmother about the boy's lifestyle, but none of it had any effect. She claimed that she had already asked her employer for permission to fetch him and take him to school, but she had refused, throwing it in her face that she'd already been extremely generous in allowing him to live in her house, and she couldn't do any more than that. His godmother didn't have time to keep watch over him during the day, when he immersed himself in children's games and ran errands for gangsters. His mother complained: 'The rich never help you see things through!'

Pipsqueak liked carrying guns to a point near a place that was going to be held up and delivering them to the gangsters. But his six-year-old mind didn't understand what he was doing. He knew it was wrong, but always having change in his pocket to buy sweets, football cards, kites, string, marbles and spinning tops made it worth it.

'Yes, it's wrong for a child to be involved in crime, but even worse is not having anyone to give him a little money to satisfy his childhood desires,' said the Chief Inspector of Gávea when he wouldn't let the detectives beat him up the first time he was caught with a derringer in a paper bag.

The boy was still living at his godmother's employer's house and wandering the streets of Rio's more affluent South Zone when he started mugging people. He already stuck his neck out carrying weapons for gangsters to use in their jobs, so he might as well risk the lot. He started mugging old ladies with blue hair in Leblon, Gávea and Jardim Botânico, pretending to be armed. With the money from his first muggings he bought a .22–caliber revolver from a friend in the *favela*. And so young women also became his victims, in addition to men, shops and whatever the fuck was around at the time.

He made a point of killing his victim the third time he mugged someone with the revolver, not because they'd shown any signs of resisting, but to feel the rush—and he laughed his quick, shrill little laugh for much longer than usual.

As he grew older, his life of crime intensified. He did holdups morning, afternoon and night, but the older gangsters from the *favela* often stole his takings. Even though he was armed, Pipsqueak didn't dare stand up to them: they were seasoned murderers, infamous enough to intimidate any beginner. Instead he swore revenge; a promise that he kept to himself, in the deepest possible corner of his spirit. While he worked hard to establish himself among the gangsters, his mother got herself a house in City of God almost as soon as it was founded, after passing herself off as a flood victim at Mario Filho stadium.

She was going to City of God no matter what. Having a house with electricity and running water for cooking and showering would make her life easier, even though she'd have to rise before daybreak to go to work: she'd leave food ready for her children and prayed that Our Lady of the Sacred Heart of Jesus would take care of them. Yes, she'd leave Macedo Sobrinho, the place that had made her life a misery, a place of heartless thugs who gave children guns so they could go around getting into trouble. She trusted in God, and believed Pipsqueak would settle down if she could get him out of that hellhole.

She moved to a house Up Top, taking with her dreams of peace, the will to face life alone with her three children, and the determination to make them good people, even if she had to stop sleeping and eating and just work. Life was hard but, being merciful and just, God was compassionate with the poor, which is why He gave her health and the ability to wash clothes, iron and cook very well. With this kind of faith, people were absolved of blame, and everything depended on God, the Holy Virgin and her own determination. She managed to get Pipsqueak's gun from him after talking, talking, talking, with teary eyes and a wavering voice, and so much listening, listening, listening, finally coaxed the voice of redemption out of his mouth: 'OK, OK . . . I'll work as a shoeshiner 'cos there's money in it, but I don't know about this learnin' to read bullshit!'

His mother set aside part of her wages and hunted high and low for a shoeshiner's stool, all of which cost much more than she had set aside. OK, then she would keep saving until she could make up the difference. After all, if everyone got their own way all the time the world would not be one. If she couldn't buy it that month, then she'd just have to wait until the following month, because that was God's will and she wouldn't complain, because God was too kind. For this very reason, before she had received the following month's wages, she heard the good news that over on Block Twenty-Two there was an affordable carpenter. She went after her good fortune as soon as she found out he was there, so close to home.

'Cheap!' answered the carpenter Luis Cãndido when she asked him the price.

He promised to deliver the stool that very week for half the amount she had set aside. He liked to talk, said he had made shoeshiner's stools for boys who were now well-placed men and told a number of other stories about shoeshiner's stools. Pipsqueak's mother smiled and felt comfortable enough to pour her heart out. She told him most of what was going on with her son, her eyes welling up with tears. She kept a grip on herself. The carpenter Luis Cãndido remained serious, because he was serious and always had been, because the lives of the poor were serious, social inequality was serious, corruption was serious, as was racism, the American invasion, cold capitalist propaganda . . . Serious man, serious woman, serious son, serious gunfire, serious poverty, certain death. Everything was very serious for the carpenter Luis Cãndido, who spoke seriously:

'My good lady, you can come get the chair tomorrow and you needn't pay.'

'But, sir . . . it's already so cheap, I . . . I . . . I . . .'

'You can come and get it, and if you're not afraid to walk the streets late at night you can even come tonight around midnight because your son's livelihood will be ready.'

'You're so kind, sir! May God reward your kind . . .'

'My good lady, I'll have you know I am not kind, much less do I believe in God. I'm a Marxist-Leninist. I believe in the power of the people, in grassroots movements, in uniting the proletariat, and—what's more—I believe in armed struggle! I believe in ideology and not in the God of the Catholic Church, who's used to keep the people quiet and to make lambs of workers. I bet your son's godmother's employer is Catholic, but why didn't she let your son's godmother take the boy to school? Why not help properly, as you said yourself? You must learn about Marxism-Leninism and help raise awareness so we can seize power . . . Don't you see what they've done to us? They put us here at the end of the world, in these little doghouses . . . This shoddy sewer system that's already clogged, no buses, no hospital, no nothing . . . nothing. What we've got are snakes coming up through the drains, and centipedes and mice wandering over our roofs. We must unite!'

The carpenter Luis Cãndido gesticulated, put on his black hat and took it off again, his eyes sparkling, glued to Pipsqueak's mother, who had never heard of Machoism-Leninism, or the proletariat. She only knew that the carpenter knew how things worked, had a good heart and was going to make Pipsqueak's shoeshiner's stool. She stayed a little longer watching that thin old man in a black suit, who from time to time taught his carpentry students a new secret of the profession through hand movements, without missing a beat in the conversation.

In his first few hours as a shoeshiner on São Francisco Square, Pipsqueak really did try to make his way in the profession. On a sunny Monday, he went with Sparrow and Slick—friends he had made the day he arrived at the projects—to make a living shining the shoes of the white bastards in ties in the city center. They took turns at the job. The boy stared down the first customer the whole time he sat on the chair. The hatred of poverty, the marks of poverty, the silence of poverty and its excesses were hurled through his eyes into his customer's face. He did try—he gave a special shine to the three pairs of shoes he polished. The fourth customer was suddenly pulled from the stool, whacked across the back of the neck and had his shoes, money, chain, bracelet and watch stolen. Before running away, Pipsqueak turned to a drunk lying on the ground vomiting.

'Keep the chair!' he said, laughing his quick, shrill little laugh, and took off through the streets of the city center.

Later, Sparrow went back to retrieve the chair, along with the cloths and shoe polish, and took it all to another point in the city so they could repeat the operation. They spent almost two months mugging customers.

The best place in the world was Estácio, where the Red Light District and São Carlos were. When they left the city center, the three would disappear into the depths of the Red Light District, where they sold the things they'd stolen, smoked weed and drank beer. It was there that they had their first sexual experiences. Then they'd head for São Carlos, where Slick had spent his early childhood and was well known. There was always a place to sleep whenever they arrived. City of God was too quiet, too far out in the sticks, too dark, everything finished early. São Carlos was cool; there was always drumming at the Unidos do São Carlos Samba School rehearsal square, someone improvising a samba on the slopes of the *favela*. When there was nothing going on in the *favela*, they'd head for the Red Light District. None of this jerking off in the bathroom business for them; they had sex with three different women in a single night. That was the place to live and spend money.

Pipsqueak managed to deceive his mother for quite some time, saying it was quicker to get to the city center from his friend's place, and lugging that stool home every day would make him very tired. At first his mother believed him, then she started noticing Pipsqueak's nervous face whenever he came home. His manners, his way of speaking, that quick, shrill little laugh, the wads of money in his pockets. And the friends who came looking for him she swore looked like thugs. Her mother's intuition—together with the evidence—was dead-on. When she eventually found a .32-caliber revolver hidden in the backyard, she decided to leave things in God's hands. First, however, she woke Pipsqueak up with a boxing about the ears. Holding the revolver and crying, she asked:

'What's this for? What's this for?'

'It's for mugging, killing and being respected!'

From that day on he never returned to his mother's house, staying either in São Carlos or with his godmother, who had also managed to get a house in the projects. On one of his visits to City of God, he made friends with Night Owl, Carrots, Hellraiser, Squirt, Hammer and the other gangsters, who liked hearing about his adventures in the city center, São Carlos and the Red Light District.

The day they held up the motel, Pipsqueak ran to Taquara, stuck his revolver in a taxi driver's face and made him take him to São Carlos, where he tried to set himself up for good.

After serving for two months as a snare for muggings, the shoeshiner's stool became known to the police, so they started doing pedestrians instead. From Estácio it was easy to go and mug people in the city center and the neighborhoods of Tijuca, Lapa, Flamengo and Botafogo. Pipsqueak went out to make a living every day. He didn't like being broke—that was for workers and shoeshiners. He squandered money on his friends in São Carlos: almost every day he bought several papers of cocaine, beer for the prostitutes and ate at what he considered to be the most expensive restaurants.

Sparrow, Slick and Night Owl, who had started hanging around with them, led the same life. Ari Rafael, a dealer in São Carlos, was jealous and began to hassle the new gangsters. Whenever the boys went to the den, he took their things, asked for money, and didn't pay them back. He started beating them up for no reason at all and charged a toll to enter the *favela*. Until one day Pipsqueak refused to sell him a gold chain for the ridiculous price he'd offered. Because of this he earned a beating and had all his belongings taken before being thrown out of the *favela* along with Slick, Sparrow and Night Owl. The four of them returned to City of God penniless and unarmed. It occurred to them to do a holdup on the bus ride back but Pipsqueak, who was depressed, thought better of it because it was an unlucky day.

'You broke? Why didn't you say so, motherfucker?! I was gonna give you some money, but you been racin' through so fast lately and haven't stopped to talk. All you been talkin' about is São Carlos, São Carlos . . . Remember that motel you tipped us off about?' said Hellraiser after listening to Pipsqueak.

'Yeah.'

'Well, man! I've got some dough for you, but I haven't got it all on me now.'

'I already forgot about it.'

'Don't look so down in the mouth, man. One of these days you can kill that Ari Rafael. You know Sting? He's a really good guy. He only goes in for good jobs and he's always ready to go for it. If you go up to him now and say: "Hey, wanna try for the jackpot?" and he'll be in right away.'

Pipsqueak looked seriously at Hellraiser, paced around in a circle in the tiny alley on Block Thirteen, looked around to make sure no one was coming, went over to the wall, unzipped his fly and took a leak. Hellraiser followed suit and explained with a smile:

'When one Brazilian pisses, we all piss!'

Ignoring his friend's joke, Pipsqueak said:

'You know this money you wanna give me? Tell you what— gimme a gun . . . gimme a gun, a long-barrelled .38, and forget the money. And take me to see this Sting guy now. I wanna talk to him right away.'

They headed down Middle Street in a hurry, as Pipsqueak only walked, talked, ate, mugged and killed people in a hurry; he only slackened his pace when he had money. During their walk Up Top their silence went uninterrupted. Hellraiser, who thought Pipsqueak was stronger, more serious and more violent in his behavior, whistled in front of his friend's house as the clock struck noon that sunny Wednesday. Sting didn't take long to ask them in. Before his visitors even had time to say why they were there, he said he needed to do a job.

'Can two go?'

'Yeah, but it's like this: if you gotta kill, you gotta kill—there's no getting arrested! The joint's got security. If we had one more partner . . . Where you from?'

'This is Pipsqueak, the kid I was telling you about. He's a good kid. He hasn't been around here for a while, but some guys over in São Carlos've been givin' him a hard time, and he's back here with us again.'

'So you're Pipsqueak? Everyone talks about you. It's a pleasure! Really nice to meet you! I'm just gonna take a leak, then I'll give you the lowdown.'

Pipsqueak's expression was less gloomy now.

'The place is over in Barra da Tijuca,' continued Sting from inside the bathroom. 'A really busy gas station. I've already scoped it out. There's a safe that the suckers stuff full of dough all day long. Then around six, two cars show up. One of them's got two suckers in it and the other one's got four. The first two don't have nothin' and the rest've all got guns. They pick up the dough and leave. We gotta round up the four, get the guns off 'em, grab the dough, get in the car and drive back . . .'

'Were you goin' by yourself?' asked Hellraiser.

'I was if I didn't get myself a partner! I don't like bein' broke.'

'You're outta your mind! Risking a joint like that by yourself!' exclaimed Hellraiser.

'I don't like bein' broke either, you know! But everything's fine. We're gonna get lucky . . .' said Pipsqueak.

'Sure you don't wanna come, Hellraiser?' asked Sting.

'No, man. I'm takin' things easy. I don't feel like it today. Go for it, man.'

Pipsqueak and Sting arrived well before six o'clock and hung around near the gas station pretending to be beggars. The cars appeared at 6:15 on the dot. They overpowered the four without much effort. To their surprise, the owner of the gas station reached for his gun and got a bullet in the chest from Sting's revolver.

'Open this shit quickly, man!' Sting bellowed at the manager, after collecting the security guards' guns.

Pipsqueak noticed one of the men sidling away, so he put a bullet through his head. He had to kill someone. He was really pissed at Ari Rafael, he was penniless, he couldn't go to the Red Light District to screw the pros, and there was that dickhead of a guard risking his life for money that wasn't even his. The manager opened the safe. Sting filled a bag, put it in the backseat of the car and broke the back window before taking off.

'If the pigs show up, let 'em have it!' he said as he sped along.

They hid the car in an alley and crossed Edgar Werneck Avenue taking just the money in the bag. They got themselves a plastic bag in the Prospectors' rehearsal square so it would be easier to carry the guns. Pipsqueak went ahead checking street corners. They stopped to let the thieves know there was a hidden car to be stripped. They arrived at Sting's house without any problems.

They laughed as they remembered the two they had killed. Sting said a good partner was like that: fearless and ready to kill. They would do it every day so they could scrape together enough to buy a house in the country. If they got the equivalent of two prizes in the sports lottery in one shot they'd be rich for the rest of their lives.

The sun was blazing in the cloudless Thursday sky. Well before midday Pipsqueak woke up at his partner's house, where he had settled down on the sofa after drinking a bottle of whisky, snorting twenty papers of coke and smoking five joints with Sting and Hellraiser the night before.

Looking into the bedroom, he saw Sting asleep holding a gun in his right hand and another in his left. He smiled. The guy was a good friend—he didn't give bad luck a chance and he was upfront. He got up, noticed he was sweaty and jumped into the shower. His head was pounding—perhaps he'd be better off sleeping a little more. He tried, then decided to rouse Sting. He awoke pointing both guns at Pipsqueak, who exclaimed:

'Shit man, you never chill out!'

'Yeah, man. Can't take any risks.'

Soon Hellraiser arrived with bread, milk and coffee, and a newspaper with a photo of the men killed in the holdup.

'Is it in the paper already?' asked Sting, surprised.

'Sometimes it takes a couple of days to appear . . . This time it was quick . . .' said Hellraiser.

'Know how to read? Know how to read?' Pipsqueak asked Sting, knowing Hellraiser wasn't a very good reader.

'No,' he answered, shaking his head emphatically.

'Then I'm goin' over to Sparrow's so he can read this stuff for us.'

Pipsqueak ate his bread without margarine and didn't wait for Sting to make the coffee. He ran to the corner and looked around, thinking it strange that there were no hoods hanging around at that hour. He felt something weird in the air and considered turning back, but he wanted to know what the paper said. He hurried to his friend's house and was lucky enough to catch him opening the gate on his way out.

Back at Sting's place, Sparrow read the paper, stumbling over the intonation of longer sentences. Even so, Pipsqueak sat on the ground with his head propped against the sofa, like a child listening to a fairy tale. What most worried him was the news that the police believed that the criminals responsible for the holdup and two fatalities were from City of God. His concern didn't last very long, however, because as soon as Sparrow had finished reading, Sting—without commenting at all on the content of the article— said that on Gabinal Road there was a printer's that paid its employees every Friday afternoon. They had to do another joint soon so they wouldn't run out of steam.

'We're the men for the job!'

'But we'll need a set of wheels, man. The guy that tipped me off said they've got this thing there that if you turn it on the police come runnin'. We've gotta go in, grab the guy, maybe even put a .22 slug in his leg so no one'll cotton on, and say we know about the thing, OK, man? Then we tell him to turn it off and move his ass.'

'What we can't do is leave the wheels here, OK? The kids didn't even have time to strip the other one 'cos the cops showed up too fast. Leaving the car here's too much of a giveaway,' said Sparrow.

'So we go on foot. We can leave through Saci Alley, head into the bush over at Gardênia Azul and spend a day and a night there . . . Remember the time you finished off that grass?' said Pipsqueak, looking at Hellraiser.

Over in the Sixteenth District Police Station, Beelzebub was compiling information on Sting. In addition to a composite sketch, he'd had anonymous phone calls telling him about one of his lodgings. Certain residents were not fond of Sting; he was trigger-happy, he harassed people for no reason, he had killed a guy after unfairly accusing him of cheating in a game of cards, he mugged people and refused to pay in bars, he'd raped women . . . There was going to be a raid the following Friday at noon on the house in which the four were now organizing their next job.

The gang spent the day inside. Sparrow arranged for an errand boy to go and buy them five meals, then they had an after-lunch smoke and examined the five guns taken in the holdup. As they had already noticed, one from the military stood out from the others.

'You just have to show this one here and the suckers'll hand everything over real fast!' said Sting.

Night always comes as a surprise to those who wake up late. They hung around planning and replanning the following day's operation. No one felt like doing coke. Their best bet was to have a smoke so they'd feel hungry, then stuff their faces and hit the sack, get up early, take a stroll to get a feel for how the day was shaping up and find out if Officers Portuguese, Lincoln and Monster were on duty. All they'd have to do was ask the heads, because they always knew everything—they even knew if the Civil Police had done the rounds. They went to bed after watching the Montilla Rum wrestling and two films on Sting's new TV. That queer Ted Boy Marino beat Red-Beard Rasputin again, just as the Black Horseman always beat his adversaries. Rin Tin Tin was always sniffing out the bandits, but it wasn't a problem—with a .45 in your muzzle, vultures become canaries, snakes become worms and roosters lay eggs. All hell would break loose when they got to the printer's.

They woke up early and had a quick slurp of coffee and a cigarette. No getting wasted before they did the job. They combed the entire project with restless footsteps. Orange said he hadn't seen any police in the street the night before or that morning. They found Night Owl, Carrots and Slick playing pool at Dummy's Bar with a carefree attitude that got on Pipsqueak's nerves, because real gangsters couldn't afford to be carefree.

'You're all screwing around, aren't you? Fucking around . . . If you wanna fuck around you gotta stick a lookout on each corner and keep a cocked gun at your hip!' said Pipsqueak jokingly. He was hoping, however, for Sting or Hellraiser's approval. He then ate three slices of mortadella that were sitting on a plate on the bar counter and asked Sting to show his friends his .45. The three were enthralled with the .45 and enjoyed meeting Sting, about whom Hellraiser had told them so much. Pipsqueak even tried to beat Slick in a game of pool, but when he saw he was going to lose, he stuffed the balls into a pocket, making his friends laugh.

It was already after eleven when they headed separately to the printer's as arranged. Everything went better than they'd planned. They didn't even need to shoot Sting's informer in the foot: in fact, they didn't even see him. They ran down Gabinal Road, turned into Saci Alley and went through the bush to the Big Plot without being chased. From the Big Plot they heard police sirens wailing desperately through the streets of the projects.

Beelzebub realized how unlucky it had been to raid Sting's house while the printer's was being held up. He was now sure Sting wouldn't return home and some lookout would tell him he had been there. He felt like breaking the police car radio.

'Now we're fucked. Coming here and not catching him'll just make him go to ground somewhere else, won't it?' complained Detective Beelzebub. He then asked for more detailed information on the holdup.

The only thing he found out was that the thieves had taken a lot of money. His mouth watered. His desire to find the hoods went beyond professional interest. If he found them he'd keep all the money and send them off to their graves. He waited around a little longer in the hope that Sting would return home. His intuition told him he was involved in the two holdups. After an hour he decided to scour every alley and every corner of the projects, but saw nothing unusual. The other detectives kept repeating that it was no good looking for him that day so he ended up telling the driver to head for the station, where the composite sketch of Sting was ready.

'It's him, didn't I tell you . . . ? It's him—the same guy that's been doin' all these places in Jacarepaguá, and from what they say on the phone, it's Sting alright! He's hangin' around with Hellraiser . . .'

'Let's wait—let him think everything's settled down before we do a raid. Keep your cool. Don't screw things up,' advised the chief inspector at the Sixteenth District Police Station.

Beelzebub didn't say a thing, tossed the handful of papers he was holding on the desk and left the chief inspector's office. He went into the kitchen, poured himself half a cup of coffee, went overboard on the sugar and drank the hot coffee slowly, making an unpleasant noise. He removed his gun from its holster and sat on an old chair. Every thought that entered his mind was violent, because he was violent, his name was violent, the way he talked, his thoughts. The idea of being able to order everyone around had always appealed to him. He lit a cigarette and glanced at a detective who had also gone over to the thermos. He continued to think about how to move up in the force without having to do a law degree. Maybe if he bought a diploma . . . He had to show them what he was made of, and that to be a cop you had to catch hoods, not go to college. Catch Sting—that's what he'd have to do, because he was the most wanted criminal in the Rio metropolitan area. His name was in the news almost every day: 'City Patrol,' 'The City Against Crime' . . . The police were asked to do something about him on every radio program that went to air.

The wind at Barra da Tijuca always blows colder than it does elsewhere in the city of Rio de Janeiro. Beelzebub zipped up his leather jacket and headed for the chief inspector's office. He told him he was going home to spend the rest of the afternoon nursing a headache. He took the composite sketches of Sting without consulting the chief inspector and drove home at a leisurely pace.

At home, he examined the pots on the stove. He wanted to eat something, but nothing looked appetizing. The job of superintendent was appetizing. He thought again about buying a diploma so he could make chief inspector and then become superintendent. He'd heard of a lawyer, Violeta, and a professor, Lauro, who sold diplomas; as soon as he had some time he'd look those guys up. He decided to rest up so he could go out that night in his own car to catch Sting and show up at the station proven to possess the mettle of a superintendent.

Over in the Big Plot, the gangsters were eating the bread and mortadella that Sparrow had bought. They'd split the money equally and planned new jobs. Hellraiser didn't think they needed to sleep out there in the bush. He was sure the police would have already arrested someone to pin the crimes on. He wanted to go home so he could screw his wife. Pipsqueak was against the idea and wanted to stay for two more days. He didn't want to play into Kojak's hands, because two big jobs in a row was enough to keep the police on the prowl day and night. All four of them felt like smoking a joint. Sparrow chided himself for not having swung past the den in The Blocks to buy some weed when he'd gone to the bakery.

'Who's going Up Top to get some?'

'No one,' Pipsqueak told Sting.

Pipsqueak argued that they needed to sleep to make time go faster. The craving for weed would pass. Sparrow gathered up some dry twigs that were lying around to make a campfire; it would keep the mosquitoes away and keep them warm, but Pipsqueak said the fire would attract attention.

'A little fire!' said Sparrow, with a mild chuckle.

He made the campfire, fed it with the dry twigs he'd piled up between his legs and sang several sambas. After a time, Sting and Sparrow fell asleep. Pipsqueak couldn't get to sleep and tried to start a conversation with Hellraiser, who couldn't get comfortable, wouldn't answer him, wanted to leave. He looked at Sparrow's watch. 4:30. Judging by the hour, he figured that if he tried hard enough he'd fall asleep. He found a place to lie down and fell into a light sleep until seven in the morning.

With his gun cocked, Beelzebub combed City of God on foot, passing in front of Luis Sting's house several times. It was always closed up.

At around six o'clock in the morning, he returned home and had the custard his wife had made him. He was going to head back to the station, but decided not to when she told him that the chief inspector had called and left orders for him to get back to the station as quickly as possible. He wouldn't take orders. He considered sleeping, but the thought of being able to say whatever he wanted to the chief inspector if he caught or killed Sting perked him up. He armed himself and went back to City of God. He parked outside the projects and went into the alleys full of children spinning tops and women gossiping or sweeping their doorsteps.

'The poor are like mice. Look how many children there are in this shithole!' he thought aloud.

He headed in the direction of Sting's house again, as if drawn there by fate. His tired eyes were out of kilter with the rest of his body, and his mind shook when he remembered the chief inspector and a terse conversation they'd had a few days before about his habit of beating up prisoners. The strong light of day made him put on his sunglasses, which covered more than half his face. He approached street corners stealthily.

Slick spotted him from afar, snuck off in the opposite direction and stopped at a corner to see where he was headed. He remembered the friends he hadn't managed to track down. The day before he had been to Hellraiser's place twice. He thought it best to go hide out.

From the first alleys up to Middle Street, Beelzebub's presence didn't cause the slightest alarm or perceptible fear in passersby. Their calm irritated him. He was used to the frightened stares and tension his appearances caused. He decided to walk more quickly, shake the peace of that morning, reinstate fear. He'd be superintendent if he bought a law degree.

'I'm outta here, OK? I'm gonna stop by Teresa's, score a few bundles of weed and get myself some decent shut-eye . . .'

'C'mon, Hellraiser! Give it a bit more time, man. Things haven't cooled off yet! The cops'll be around!' insisted Pipsqueak.

'If the guy wants to go, let him go!' Sting intervened.

'Fuck! You're really pigheaded, aren't you? You've forgotten that we done two big jobs, man! Have you forgotten that the job on Gabinal Road'll be hittin' the papers today? You're actin' like you don't know nothin'. The papers make the pigs all nervous, man! And they wanna bust someone no matter what. It's not worth the risk!'

'You're just scared I'll snitch if they bust me. Don't worry, man— I won't snitch!' said Hellraiser with a half-hearted laugh.

He got up, brushed the dirt off the back of his shorts, stuffed the money into his jocks, waved at his friends and left, his gun in his waistband.

'Stay here, man!' said Pipsqueak.

Hellraiser crossed the street and considered going straight down Highway Eleven, but decided it was better to take Gabinal Road, enter the projects through The Blocks and head for Red Hill. A cold breeze covered his body in goosebumps. The quiet of the streets terrified him. He liked activity, because things that are too calm suddenly get whipped up. Man is like that, like the sea, the sky, the earth itself and everything on it. He was afraid that something might whip up against him. Pipsqueak's words echoed in his ears. The morning was very calm and produced little noise. Hellraiser couldn't hear a thing. He was a character in a silent film. The rows of sunflowers in gardens, spinning tops in children's hands, cars going past on Edgar Werneck Avenue, the milk carts, the late May sun and the right branch of the river were all so familiar, so why was he so nervous? Why did he want to go back to his friends? A feeling of emptiness made him uneasy, sent shivers down his spine. He checked his gun and patted the money with shaky hands. He'd had that feeling many times, but only during shoot-outs, getaways and jobs. There was also absolute calm on Middle Street, causing his dread to grow, dread of nothing. And what was nothing? Nothing was sparrows darting from electric wires to rooftops, from rooftops to branches, from branches to walls, from walls to the ground and from the ground to out of the way of the footsteps of the people going past without noticing him in the alley he turned down on his way to Teresa's place. He could have given up on the idea of having a smoke, but a force was tugging him in that direction. From time to time, he felt as if his whole body was being punched and kicked. It occurred to him to draw his gun and kill the innocence the sun was spilling into the square on Block Fifteen, all the calm it offered him. He didn't know why, but tiny fragments of his life were suddenly flashing before him. The most vivid colors of the day became laden with much deeper meanings, scrambling his vision. The wind was more nervous, the sun hotter, his footsteps heavier, the sparrows so far from the people, the silence useless, tops spinning, sunflowers swaying, cars going faster and Beelzebub's voice whipping everything up:

'Hit the ground, asshole!'

Hellraiser didn't react. Contrary to what Beelzebub had expected, an inexplicable calm filled his consciousness, an almost abstract smile revealed the peace he had never known, a peace he had always sought in the things money could provide, because he hadn't, in fact, noticed the most normal things in life. And what is normal in life? The peace that means one thing to some and something completely different to others? The peace that everyone seeks even though they don't know how to decipher it in all its plenitude? What is peace? What really is good in life? He'd always been unsure about these things. But no one can say there is no peace in a beer at the Bonfim, in playing the tambourine in samba school rehearsals, in Berenice's laughter, in joints smoked with friends and Saturday afternoon pickup games. Perhaps he had gone too far looking for something that had always been right beside him. But can there really be true peace for one whose life had always meant floundering in the depths of poverty? He had been looking for something that was always so close, so close and so good, but the fear that a few drops of rain might suddenly become a storm had made him what he was—blind to peace, which had now come to stay.

Perhaps peace was in the flight of the birds, in the subtlety of the sunflowers swaying in people's gardens, in the spinning tops on the ground, in the branch of the river always leaving and always returning, in the mild autumn cold and the breeze blowing in. But there was always the chance that things might get whipped up in some undefined way, lash out at him and end up in the path of his revolver. But can one actually see beauty with eyes blurred by the lack of almost everything a human being needs? Perhaps he had never looked for anything, or even thought about it; all he could do was live the life he lived without any reason to be poetic in a world written in such cursed lines.

He lay down very slowly, without even feeling his movements. He felt an overwhelming certainty that he wouldn't feel the pain of the bullets. He was an already yellowing photograph with an unfaltering smile and the hope that death really did mean rest for one who had been obliged to make peace a systematic declaration of war. Beelzebub's questions were met with silence and an expression of melancholic joy remained in his coffin.

SPARROW'S STORY

THE EARLY 1970S

After Silva died and Cosme fled the Old Blocks, Miguel dealt for more than six years without too many problems. Since few gangsters were into dealing, and because The Blocks were quiet compared to the houses, there were only a small number of gangsters and few operated in the area. Miguel watched the new blocks of apartments going up, the arrival of the population of the *favela* Macedo Sobrinho, and the brutal institution of community living. Because the new residents all came from the same place, there was an existing network of friendships, and this gave them attitudes that segregated them from and irked the old residents.

Fighting broke out between groups of youths from the apartments and the houses. They fought over kites, marbles, soccer, girlfriends . . . The residents of the New and Old Blocks weren't on hostile terms, however, perhaps by virtue of their proximity. People often said the New and Old Blocks were all the same thing. The gangsters who had just arrived didn't steal there. But they did set up a den in Building Seven of the New Blocks the very day they arrived.

The den belonged to Sergio Nineteen, also known as Big, a gangster famed throughout Rio de Janeiro for being dangerous and fierce, and for the pleasure he took in killing cops. Big had also been a resident of the now extinct Macedo Sobrinho, but he hadn't moved to City of God, as he'd figured it would be too easy for the police to find him there. He liked living on the slopes, where he could watch everything from up high. He'd been in hiding almost everywhere in Rio de Janeiro, from the South Zone *favelas* all the way up to the North Zone, but the police had tracked him down in all of them. That was why he'd arrived in the *favelas* of Juramento in the neighborhood of Leopoldina, shooting at every gangster in sight, kicking down shacks and shouting that the one in charge now was Big: the Big who had taken over most of the dens in the *favelas* of the South Zone; the almost-six-foot-five Big, willing to take on five or six men at once with his bare hands; the Big who had a machine gun he'd got in a fight with a marine on duty in Maua Square; the Big who'd been cold-blooded enough to cut off his own little toe and hang it from a chain around his neck; the Big who killed policemen because he thought they were the biggest bastards of all—that bunch that served the whites, a bunch of poor guys defending the rights of the rich. He enjoyed killing whites, because whites had stolen his ancestors from Africa to work for nothing, whites had made *favelas* and stuck blacks there to live in them, whites had created the police in order to beat up, arrest and kill blacks. Absolutely everything that was good belonged to the whites. The president of Brazil was white, the doctor was white, bosses were white, the grandpa-who-glimpsed-the-grape in learn-to-read books was white, the rich were white, dolls were white and the fucking niggers that became policemen or went into the Army deserved to die just like every other white in the world.

Big left the den in Building Seven in the hands of his good friend Napoleon, who was on friendly terms with Miguel. They both sold their weed without worrying about whether the next man was selling more. The true test of friendship came when Miguel went to prison. Napoleon could have taken over his den, but he left Flip-Flop at the helm, precisely because he was the one who'd been Silva, Cosme and Miguel's errand boy. He'd grown up in the den, had earned the right to be the boss and Napoleon wasn't going to be the one to take it away from him. Flip-Flop was schooled enough in the running of a den and, although he'd grown up in the company of gangsters, was discreet and polite. He didn't feel the need to stir up trouble like most gangsters, he rarely went about armed and treated customers from all over the estate well. The Saint Cosmas and Damian candy he handed out was top quality. Besides the candy, he gave away clothes, children's books, toys and school supplies, and was always buying soccer cleats, socks and shirts for the Oberom Soccer Club, a team from right there in the Old Blocks. That was how he won over the residents. His den was discreet. To keep things low-profile, he didn't have a bunch of gangsters doing the packaging, and he had no partners so there'd be no backstabbing. He had no enemies. He was always sending a few bundles of weed over to the local gangsters and the cool guys. He was well liked.

The day the population of the *favela* of Macedo Sobrinho started being relocated to City of God, Pipsqueak left his godmother's house and went to live in The Blocks. No sooner had the government representatives inaugurated the New Blocks than he started squatting in one. He hung around the square greeting his childhood friends as they arrived. He made a point of shaking hands with the workers, slapping the veteran gangsters on the back, and feeling up the sluts. It had been ages since he'd seen those people, who'd known him back when he was still learning how to spin tops, play marbles and fly kites. He asked after a few people, rolled joints for the cool guys and introduced Sparrow, Night Owl and Carrots to the new residents. This made him feel good.

A few days after the inauguration of the New Blocks, Pipsqueak decided to celebrate his eighteenth birthday in Building Seven with a barbecue and beer for his friends.

His older brother, Israel, who was squatting in another apartment, arranged for a member of his samba group to play at his eighteenth. Pipsqueak got drunk and told the den to supply his friends and anyone else who went to buy drugs that day, because it was all on him. He'd come of age, having chalked up ten murders and fifty armed robberies. He owned thirty revolvers of every caliber and was respected by all the gangsters in the area. His ability to lead came not only from the fact that he was dangerous; it came from his guts, his desire to be the biggest, as Ari Rafael was in São Carlos and Big had been in Macedo Sobrinho. On his birthday, he gave revolvers to his childhood friends Bicky, Russian Mouse and Sharky, saying he knew where the jackpot was and that they were going to get it with him.

The night exceeded all limits, and the party was still going at daybreak. More meat, more pot, more coke and beer in the morning that dawned to the rhythm of samba. Since real badasses have to have money to spend down to the last penny, and then, when the money runs out, pay for whatever they want in gold, Pipsqueak traded gold chains for meat and gold watches and bracelets for cocaine.

Before the party was over, Pipsqueak slipped away in the company of Sparrow. They went into an apartment where everything had been prepared for their arrival. Candles were lit to Oxalá and Xangô, because Oxalá was the great father and Xangô was the *orixá* of Father Joaquim of the Cross of the Promised Land of the Souls, who came down from the spiritual plane to start the ceremony. But he wasn't the one with whom Pipsqueak was to speak. Father Joaquim soon went back up; he'd only come down to start the ceremony, greet the children of the earth, send a message to the medium and give the apprentice orders. He didn't work with hoods. The one who worked with hoods was the *exu* Street Keeper of the Land of the Souls, who came down after squabbling with other *exus* for the right to do so. He arrived cackling loudly, driving away bad energy, and drew a cross on the ground before greeting the children of the earth. He sprinkled *cachaça* on the ground, ate a candle flame, ordered the apprentice to roll up the cuffs of his trousers, and touched shoulders with the apprentice, first on one side, then the other, because the *exu* had to greet the apprentice first. It was the apprentice who looked after him, left presents at crossroads, bought *cachaça* and candles for the sessions, left offerings at Calunga Grande Cemetery and made sacrifices. He then touched shoulders with all the children of the earth present.

'Don't mess with *exus, exus* are not to be messed with,' sang Street Keeper of the Land of the Souls, hopping up and down.

Pipsqueak listened in silence to the chant the *exu* had started, which the devotees sang along with. First the *exu* granted the apprentice a consultation, asked for a sacrifice and a present at the crossroads, told him his path was clear, and passed on messages for the medium. He then called Pipsqueak over for a consultation.

'I'm the Devil, kid! I'm the Devil! If ya want I can get ya outta this hole, I can set ya up really nice, but if yer lookin' for trouble, you've come to the right place. I'll protect ya from snipers' bullets, I will, I'll save ya from Black Boots' claws, I will, I'll put brass in yer pocket and show ya the enemy, I will. Ain't that what ya came to ask for? Well then . . . But don't get smart on me, or I'll fuck things up for ya, I'll stick a fig tree up your ass, I will . . . I'll stick ya in a wooden overcoat, I will! All I want is a bottle of booze and a candle stub . . .'

Pipsqueak opened his mouth to speak, but Street Keeper of the Land of the Souls continued:

'Ya don't have to speak, ya don't—think about what ya want.'

Pipsqueak closed his eyes and lowered his head. He felt the power of the *exu*—who didn't mess around because he wasn't to be messed with—trying to take over his every thought. Pipsqueak was unusually calm and Sparrow cast him a worried look. Standing there, Pipsqueak strolled through light and darkness, through the center and around the edges, above and below, inside and out, straight and sinuous, through the lies and the truth of things. He could choose the world he wanted to be in; all he had to do was choose the lane he wanted to run along, the game he wanted to play; he could get out of that hole or dig it even deeper; he'd win any game under the protection of the *exu*—who didn't mess around because he wasn't to be messed with. It was there that a chosen fate truly took shape, a fate in which doubt would not exist. It was, in fact, a fate that life had drawn for him and that he now glimpsed through a harness, with his eyes closed and faith burning like the flame of the candle flickering in the wind that blew into the living room of the apartment; burning like the tip of the *exu's* cigar, casting its gyrating light on Pipsqueak.

When the *exu* started speaking again, telling him facts about his life that only he knew, he opened his eyes, then drank the *cachaça* the *exu* offered him and memorized the prayer the *exu* taught him. The others present couldn't understand a single word. He touched shoulders with the *exu* and left in silence. Sparrow accompanied him.

The holdups in Barra da Tijuca and Jacarepaguá made Pipsqueak enough money to live life without limits, to which he had become accustomed. But Napoleon and Flip-Flop squandered much more money than he did: it pained him to see the parties, the sweets they handed out during the festivities for the saints Cosmas and Damian, and the money they gave the Crown carnival group so it could parade for the first time in the fifth division. He saw that Up Top the dealers sold drugs as if they were selling candy to children. They threw parties that lasted for two or three days at a time and were open to everyone, and yet they did next to nothing themselves—they didn't leave the estate, nor did they hang around the dens—because they had suppliers to deliver and assistants to sell the drugs. Nevertheless—although he was the one who planned large-scale holdups, who cased joints to find out the best time to do jobs and subsequently got a larger cut when dividing up the loot, who went out alone and came back with valuable objects from the houses he robbed—he didn't have enough to make him, besides the most feared, the richest. He noticed that the number of pot smokers was growing by the day. So what was he waiting for, then, to take over Napoleon and Flip-Flop's dens? What was stopping him from taking over The Blocks, since it was his area? Because if he presented a good plan to his partners in holdups, he'd have their immediate support.

He thought about taking over Napoleon's den when he heard that Big had died in a shoot-out with the police in the *favelas* of

Juramento, but luckily he was prudent enough to spare him while he waited for the right moment to convince his friends. Napoleon had been well liked by people since back in Macedo Sobrinho and, shortly after Big's death, the Fifth Sector police kidnapped him, killed him and got rid of the body.

They actually did the job for him. Beto assumed control of the den in Building Seven because he was Big's brother, but from the moment he took over things went downhill. Beto squandered money without a thought for replenishing stock. He had to do hold-ups to buy drugs. Pipsqueak said the den in Building Seven was a mess. He said that if the den were under his command the local stoners wouldn't have anything to complain about. He talked to the cool guys about his intention to pull the trigger on Beto.

He started buying large amounts of drugs on credit at Beto's den and never paid. He also borrowed money from him and didn't pay him back so he could pick fights and kill him without falling out with the cool guys. But Beto never complained. On the contrary, he treated him with respect, leading Pipsqueak to conclude he was afraid of him.

'Hey, Beto borrowed my gun, then said he wasn't givin' it back,' Russian Mouse told Pipsqueak.

Pipsqueak waited until his friends were all together to say that Russian Mouse was a good guy and Beto was fucking around with him just because he was a kid. He was too close a friend of Russian Mouse's to let the matter go and he was going to take it up with Beto if he didn't return the gun.

One Wednesday morning, he waited for the dealer to wake up and invited him to go to The Hill, saying he'd hidden three pounds of coke there that he was going to let him have to give the den a boost. Israel, who was good friends with Beto, saw death in his brother's eyes. He knew him well and suspected that Pipsqueak was going to take out Beto on The Hill. Israel drew his gun and pointed it at his brother as one would at an enemy. Pipsqueak laughed his quick, shrill little laugh, then backed away and stepped behind a post. Israel told Beto to leave, keeping his gun pointed at his brother; Pipsqueak did the same. They'd duel to the death. But blood was thicker than water; Israel moved his hand away as he pulled the trigger. Pipsqueak laughed and swore at his brother, who ran as soon as he saw Beto turn the corner.

Israel couldn't let his brother kill his friend and knew that if he asked Pipsqueak to spare him, he wouldn't listen. He ran to the shops, but uncocked his gun when he heard Pipsqueak's voice ordering him to cut the funny business. They had a terse talk about it. Israel accused him of wanting to resolve everything with death— for him it was all about bullets. How on earth did he think he was going to kill Beto just like that if Beto was his friend and, besides, if everyone liked him? Pipsqueak ignored his brother and warned him to never again raise a hand against him, because the next time he'd ignore the fact that they were brothers and send him off to rot in hell.

Before Pipsqueak turned away from Israel, he saw his younger brother Good Life, who'd also moved to City of God, running toward him; he'd heard that the two were having a shoot-out. Good Life anxiously asked what was going on. After everything had been explained, he warned Israel of the risk he was taking. Pipsqueak was capable of killing him.

Pipsqueak knew Beto wouldn't be back: he'd only gone around acting like hot shit because of Big. He'd taken advantage of his brother's reputation, he wasn't as fierce as he made himself out to be, and he only got into battles with guys he knew were nothing to worry about. Pipsqueak arrived at Building Seven still holding his gun. He asked Otávio, a seven-year-old boy, to fetch Sparrow and, before the kid had even handed his spinning top to his friends, handed him a ten-cruzeiro note. The boy took the note, smiled and sped off.

'The den's already ours!' he told his friend cheerfully.

Sparrow shook his head and said:

'You're a nasty piece of work, aren't ya?'

He asked Sparrow to take Beto's assistant's merchandise, then spent the whole day working the den, flush with victory. With a lit joint in his mouth and a gun in his waistband, Pipsqueak served his customers. Whenever someone he knew arrived, he made a point of giving them an extra bundle of dope for free. He said this was Macedo Sobrinho, which had belonged to a big guy and now belonged to a little guy who, even though he was small, had as much balls as Big, or even more.

'This den, in the new Macedo Sobrinho, belongs to a little guy!' said Pipsqueak.

Yes, now he'd call himself Tiny; Tiny, since the police knew about a guy by the name of Pipsqueak, who didn't spare his victims in holdups, and who'd been considered dangerous since Hellraiser's day. 'Change of name—good idea.' He started saying Pipsqueak was dead and that the den in the New Blocks now belonged to a guy called Tiny. The other gangsters watched him with fear and admiration, some sitting on the curb, others leaning against the wall of Building Seven. None of them dared do what he was doing, and for this reason came to respect him as everyone in Macedo Sobrinho had respected Big. Money, he was going to make lots of money—there were users everywhere you looked and no shortage of suppliers to sell him drugs.

'OK, here's the story. We're pissed off at this Flip-Flop guy, know what I mean? Lots of people've complained about him, 'cause he gets shitfaced and talks shit about customers, his weed's always dirt, and he takes women by force, know what I mean?' He looked at everyone, but glanced at Sparrow at the end of every sentence, looking for support. 'The boys want to dust their noses and he don't stock coke in his den. When there's no coke in my den, they go to his, but they never find any. And what's even worse is that he's goin' around rapin' and muggin' folks here in the New Blocks. We gotta get rid of him, 'cause if we don't, some worker's gonna file a complaint and then the shit'll hit the fan for us too . . . Let's get rid of him, let's do it . . .'

Sparrow took the cue and agreed with his friend, although he knew the whole story was a lie. He knew Tiny had wanted to take over the den in the Old Blocks for ages so he could have complete control of that part of the *favela*. Tiny didn't mention money as a reason for wanting to take over Flip-Flop's den so he wouldn't have to share the profits with anyone except Sparrow, his best friend, the sort of friend who was already the godfather of his unborn children (he was sure whoever had a kid first would give it to the other to christen), the sort of friend who'd never bail out on you when you were in danger, the sort of friend who'd kill anyone that gave you a hard time. They hadn't arranged anything ahead of time, because good friends had to know everything about each other. Of all the gangsters, they were the only ones who'd been that way ever since they were kids, since the time they'd worked as shoeshiners in the city center, since their first holdup, since the days when they used to hang out together in São Carlos. A wink or a laugh or a scratch of the head said more than a whole sentence spelling things out. That's why Sparrow noticed Tiny's glances asking him to confirm that Flip-Flop was fucking things up. At any rate, even on his own, Tiny would get his pals to do whatever he wanted: he was always in charge of everything: he led the holdups, the robberies, the dividing up of loot, and even in their leisure time it was he who called the shots. Sparrow's words weren't as emphatic as Tiny's, but they were enough to decide that Flip-Flop should be killed that very night. Sparrow tried pulling him to one side after the decision had been made, hoping to convince him to let Flip-Flop live— they could just kick him out. Tiny's reply was short and direct:

'He's gotta go. He's a snake in the grass!'

'Fuckin' hell! All you wanna do is kill, kill, kill. You never try to find another solution!'

'Got a better idea?'

* * *

It was no later than 8 P.M. when Tiny and his friends hurried over to the Old Blocks looking for Flip-Flop, who'd opened his den early and given his assistant fifty bundles of grass he'd packaged himself before going to the beach where, as always, he'd stayed until around three o'clock in the afternoon. He'd kicked a ball around in the Big Plot before going home and had taken a nap after lunch.

He woke up in time for the evening shift at the den and, although he hadn't washed, went down the stairs two at a time. He went to the den, took seventy percent of the takings, and asked his assistant if it was worth replenishing stock. The assistant shook his head and said the police had already showed up twice and it had been hard to sell the fifty bundles. Flip-Flop looked around to make sure the police weren't nearby. He put the money in a plastic bag, hurried home, counted it and took a small amount to have a beer and play cards with.

The bartender opened the tenth bottle of beer while Flip-Flop shuffled the cards. The bartender told him the beer was getting warm and Flip-Flop dealt to the three people in the bar.

On the corner, Tiny's friends cocked their guns. Bicky whistled. Flip-Flop looked up. At first he thought it was the police, but realized it was Tiny when he waved him over. He felt a twinge inside and remembered the gun he'd left at home. He dropped the cards, downed the rest of his glass in a single gulp, and walked on wobbly legs into the middle of the street. He'd never imagined Tiny would kill him: he'd always treated him well and every now and then would send some weed over to his gang. He'd respected him, had never had any misunderstandings with the guys from the New Blocks, and was always buying the things they brought back from their holdups, which is why he'd never worried that they might betray or attack him.

Sparrow was the only one who wasn't holding a gun. The gangsters' silence and seriousness revealed their intention. Suddenly,

Flip-Flop pointed to the left, let out a cry and took off running to the right. He had wanted to give his enemies a fright. But his strategy didn't work on Tiny who, even from far away, shot him in the region of his right lung with a .36–caliber pistol. Flip-Flop kept dodging between the buildings before running into Building Four, where he sat on a flight of stairs. Tiny's friends were already heading off when they heard him shouting that Flip-Flop had tricked them. They obeyed his order to go after the fugitive, which Tiny repeated with a mixture of laughter and desperation. Over on Gabinal Road, a police van was heading toward Freguesia. The officer noticed all the scurrying around and told the driver to do a U-turn. The gangsters then ran toward The Hill, where they took cover.

'Fuck! The guy duped ya. That shoutin' and runnin' off was just a trick—he realized the shit was gonna hit the fan and set us up! I was the only one who didn't fall for it . . .'

'But the pigs really did show up . . .'

'The pigs only showed up afterwards, man! If everyone had pulled the trigger right then and there, he'd already be dead, but I got him. I did . . .'

They stayed put for a while. From where they were they could see the police van turning back into Gabinal Road. Tiny's intuition told him Flip-Flop was still alive and he thought about combing the Old Blocks to put him out of his misery. He walked a few paces toward the Old Blocks, then stopped suddenly, turned to Marcelo and said:

'Hey, Marcelo, you've never killed anyone. Go kill the guy! Take this .36, find him and even if you think he's dead, pull the trigger on him anyway. You've never killed anyone. Go and do it so you can see what it's like, OK?'

Marcelo hesitated and was about to protest when Tiny insisted at the top of his lungs:

'Go kill the guy! You're one of us ain't ya? Go kill the guy!'

Marcelo clutched the gun, his hands shaking, his heart racing. He had to follow Tiny's orders, because Tiny was the one who always gave him money to buy a pound of something or other, and it was Tiny who'd backed him up in his first holdup. His life had improved a lot since he'd started hanging around with Tiny. He cocked the gun and headed off, weaving his way through the buildings, carrying his fear, nervousness and all the cunning of his ten years together with the gun that barely fitted in his hands, with Tiny's voice accompanying his footsteps:

'Go kill the guy!'

The streets were deserted. Some people watched what was going on from behind their curtains. Marcelo crossed the square of the projects, staring all the way down every alley he passed. Flip-Flop had gone into hiding, there was no doubt about it. With any luck the dealer wasn't going to die at his hands. He was already turning around to go back when he noticed a commotion at the entrance to a building. He sprinted over. Inside, he saw people with desperation painted across their faces. He had to check it out. If he didn't kill Flip-Flop, Tiny would be pissed off at him, but if he killed him he'd be on Tiny's good side; he'd be respected. He had to kill someone, because Tiny had already killed someone, Russian Mouse had already killed someone, Beep-Beep had already killed someone, everyone had already killed someone and he was the odd one out. He'd be seen as a tough guy. Kill, kill, kill . . . A verb requiring a bloody object. Victims who fought back had to die, snitches had to die, idiots had to die. Kill. Tiny said:

'Go kill the guy!'

He galloped up the stairs and, on the fourth flight, found a woman giving Flip-Flop water. The woman noticed someone approaching; perhaps it was a relative who'd come to the dealer's aid. Without turning, she said he was losing a great deal of blood. Marcelo didn't hear what she said; he didn't hear or think a thing. Just Tiny's shrill little voice:

'Go kill the guy!'

Marcelo took a deep breath and, in a flash, ducked his skinny body under the woman's legs and fired six bullets into Flip-Flop's chest.

Two days after Flip-Flop's death, Tiny bought fifty pounds of weed on consignment from a supplier who showed up saying he could always bring him as much as he wanted, so he could sell the fattest bundles of weed in all of Rio de Janeiro. He told Sparrow that the sooner they sold the dope the sooner they'd make money. It was easy: the thing to do was build up a good clientele, then slowly reduce the amount of weed in the bundles.

In no time Tiny's assistant was receiving a supply of fifty bundles every half hour. Tiny gave him orders to trade weed for stolen goods, revolvers and any other items of value. Before long he already had generous wraps of good coke to offer his customers, who bought them with stolen gold chains, and guns of all calibers.

Business grew. The Blocks were easily accessible to customers from other areas, who lined up to buy good weed. Everything was on the up. The thieves always brought guns to trade for coke and pot, and Tiny's assistant worked with a gun at hand—assistants who weren't armed were amateurs. Sparrow was his only partner, as he was the only person he trusted. The others got their money in hold-ups. Money poured into Tiny and Sparrow's pockets. They needed to find someone who could read and write to manage the cash flow. He couldn't be a gangster, because gangsters were a waste of time—they'd stick it to you the first chance they got. It had to be a worker who was a friend of theirs, someone they'd known and liked since childhood, who'd never stolen, but who had attitude and balls, who could use a gun if he had to. Tiny mulled over the idea as he wandered aimlessly through The Blocks, looking everyone he saw in the face.

His face broke into a grin when he spotted Carlos Roberto from afar. Every now and then Carlos Roberto would stop to give him a few words of wisdom, and was always telling him to keep an eye on the hoods around him, because hoods were like snakes. In all the time he'd known Carlos Roberto, he'd never seen him shooting his mouth off among friends. He was the serious type, respected by the veterans and the cool guys. He hurried over to Carlos Roberto and made him a job offer, which he turned down. But Tiny insisted, saying he wouldn't have to lay a finger on a gun. All he had to do was manage the money so there'd always be enough to pay for the weed and coke. He also wanted him to supervise the assistants; nothing that was too much work or dangerous. He'd only have to deal with money and negotiate with the suppliers. He wouldn't have to package or buy anything. Carlos Roberto took some convincing, but since having a little extra cash in your pocket never hurt anyone . . .

'It's like this: Carlos Roberto's gonna be headin' things up here with me, OK? What he says goes. You're all gonna answer to him now, got it? You don't need to talk money with me anymore,' Tiny told the assistants in a meeting held the day after he arranged for Carlos Roberto to manage the dens.

Days in The Blocks went by as Tiny wanted them to: the dens doing business, gold piling up in a pillowcase he kept in a secret place, and he always ended up with the guns the thieves got burgling houses in Barra da Tijuca and Jacarepaguá. He banned stealing in The Blocks; anyone who mugged residents in the vicinity of his dens would die. To serve as an example, he killed a thief for no reason at all, then told everyone he'd killed the bastard because he'd mugged a resident, who didn't want to reveal his identity. The dead man was, in fact, the brother of a gangster who was already dead, who'd beaten him up and taken his loot from a holdup in Botafogo back when he spent his days in Macedo Sobrinho. Before killing his assailant's brother, he remembered having sworn revenge while he was being beaten up. Now he'd avenged himself and given the local thieves a fright—two birds with one stone . . .

'Muggin' residents is risky, 'cause they tell the cops on the quiet, then the cops come along and raid us.'

Tiny also wanted the residents to like him so that if he needed a hideout or helping hand, they'd be quick to come to his aid.

From time to time the boss of The Blocks took a walk Up Top, always accompanied by other gangsters, to find out who was dealing, if a particular den was doing good business, if the same supplier was stocking the dens there. He'd go to Teresa's den for his information, as they were very fond of one another. He liked it Up Top: it was the first place he'd lived in City of God, and it was where he'd met Sparrow, Slick, Luis Sting, Squirt, Hellraiser and Hammer. Whenever he walked through those streets, he remembered Black Charlie and Slick, who were doing time in Lemos de Brito Prison. One day soon he'd send them some money. He often showed up at bars and footed the bill for the cool guys, slapped his friends on the back, and invited them down to The Blocks for a beer. He moved around the entire area, but avoided passing in front of his mother's house, as he hadn't spoken a word to her in a long time.

One Friday morning, Tiny and his partners were biking through the estate looking for Carrots. They'd already been Up Top and to Block Thirteen. Tiny looked for his friend, who'd stopped hanging around with him ever since he'd taken to giving orders and yelling at everyone. He didn't know the real reason why Carrots had become distant, and imagined he was envious because he'd always done better for himself in holdups and robberies. Actually, Tiny had always thought Carrots a little weird; aloof. He often saw him shooting the breeze with friends, but whenever he saw Tiny he'd clam up.

Long before Tiny became the boss of the dens in The Blocks, Carrots had set up a den on Block Thirteen with Sting and had been running the den on his own ever since his partner had wound up behind bars. On Block Thirteen there was a bunch of youngsters who committed crimes both within City of God and elsewhere. Some of these kids worked as sellers for Carrots, whose den didn't do much business because customers from other areas were afraid to walk through the estate.

'Hey, seen Carrots around?' he shouted down the alleys Up Top, as if the question was directed at everyone in the bars, on street corners, in doorways.

'He's takin' a nap over at Rattler's place,' answered a teenage boy.

'Go wake 'im up, quickly.'

'I can't, I gotta stay.'

'You can't my ass, kid!' shouted Tiny, going over to the boy to clout him across the face. Then he asked:

'You goin' or what?'

'I'm goin', I'm goin'!'

The boy sped off through the alleys while Tiny had a beer with his men at Noé's Bar, always with his gun in his hand, glancing around. Carrots emerged on the street corner, strolling along in a pair of Bermuda shorts and no shirt. Tiny waved cordially, drinking his beer in small sips. Sparrow said that Carrots was getting fatter by the day. Carrots shook hands with each member of the gang and made a point of hugging Sparrow.

'You know it's us that's runnin' the show down in The Blocks?'

Carrots nodded his head.

'Well then don't let them kids over on Thirteen rob down there, got it? Tell 'em to do it somewhere else. It'll attract the pigs to both our dens if they keep workin' the area, you know. I bet . . .'

'Hey man, I mind my own business and no one else's. It's not my thing to go around givin' orders and I'm not the police either, you know. Go tell 'em yourself.'

'I came to talk to you 'cause I heard them kids was hangin' around your den,' said Tiny coldly. 'Seein' as it's not your problem, when they all start droppin' dead, don't come to me for help.'

Before Carrots could answer, Sparrow intervened:

'I knew you wouldn't want to get involved. You always did like to keep to yourself, but here's the story: tell the kids you like to lay off if they don't want any trouble from us, understand? We've come peacefully, know what I'm sayin'? We just want to see eye to eye . . . You don't need to give anyone a hard time or kill anyone, but have a chat with them kids, OK man?'

Then Sparrow quickly got on his bike and said:

'Let's go, let's go, let's go.'

Along the way, Tiny discussed the possibility of eliminating Carrots. He thought he'd been rude to them when they'd only gone to have a word with the guy, precisely to avoid a clash with him; he was an old friend after all.

'That's just the way the guy talks, man! He just don't wanna get involved, period. You warned him, didn't ya? All right! I'll have a word with them kids over on Thirteen . . . They listen to me . . .' said Sparrow.

They were passing in front of Batman's Bar when Sparrow said:

'Hey, I'm gonna swing by my place, OK? I'm gonna grab some clothes and I'll head over to The Blocks in a bit. Can you take my gun?'

He doubled back along the same path he'd taken on the way there, then took the road along the right branch of the river, went down an alley, turned left and came out on Edgar Werneck Avenue, where he lived, but braked his bike when he passed a kiosk where some guys were playing samba.

He ordered a beer, sat next to a man playing the *cavaquinho* and positioned himself so he could see the guy's fingers strumming the strings. He got friendly with him. After a while, it was he who led the sambas. He sang out loud, drank beer quickly, and insisted on paying for the beers ordered by the musicians. His expression of joy at being there grew with every passing second. Everything was going fine until two men arrived, looking as if they already knew Sparrow was there. They called him over. Their curt conversation lasted a little over ten minutes, until one of them gave him a shove. Sparrow stumbled back, but quickly found his balance again and flew at his attacker. The samba stopped when the fight started. Although slightly drunk, Sparrow leaped about, dodging the kicks and punches the men were now throwing at him. He was short and chubby, but he wasn't afraid to take on a big guy with his fists. He could even sprint off to his place to get one of his ten brothers to come and help him, but he decided to see the fight through to the end. Some people shouted:

'Two against one is chickenshit!'

People gathered around to see Sparrow beating up two men who were bigger than him. The fight was ending when one of them jumped behind the counter, grabbed a butcher's knife and flew at Sparrow, stabbing him twice in the stomach.

Sparrow tried to run home, while his enemies backed away amidst hissing and swearing. Sparrow fell before he'd gone a hundred yards, and asked someone to call a taxi, finding it difficult to talk. Acerola and Orange stopped a car on Edgar Werneck Avenue and made the driver take him to the hospital.

There was commotion over in The Blocks when Sparrow's own brother brought the news. He told Tiny what had happened and asked him for a gun.

'You don't need a gun, 'cause you're not a gangster. You need money.'

He turned and shouted:

'Russian Mouse, ask Carlos Roberto for money to pay for the hospital and Sparrow's medicine.'

When Sparrow's brother had gone, Tiny, somewhat confused, talked about several other things, then off he went, flitting from thought to thought without giving anyone a chance to cut in and without mentioning Sparrow's name in his agitated monologue. Sometimes he'd stare off into space, then come back gushing out his feelings, still reeling from the events. He fired shots into the air while chewing his lips, cocked and uncocked his gun, laughed his quick, shrill little laugh for no reason at all, wandered back and forth between all the blocks of apartments, ordered people to roll him joints, punched in the face anyone he thought looked like a jackass, and several times recited a prayer which no one could understand a single word of. Late in the afternoon, he ordered Bicky to buy thirty pounds of the best quality meat and threw a barbecue near Building Seven. No one dared ask him a single question, and he was the only one who talked in that tense atmosphere. He'd talk to himself and laugh after a long silence, and would order the gang to eat—because at this barbecue only the gangsters were allowed to enjoy the rare steak, its blood oozing from the corners of their mouths. Even the cool guys were excluded from the barbecue, which continued on into the night.

At exactly midnight, without explanation, Tiny got on his bike and quickly pedaled Up Top. He wandered through the darkness of that moonless night and found out from a reliable source everything that had happened. He went to Teresa's place and ordered her to stop dealing without telling her why, went to Block Thirteen, where he rudely gave Carrots the same orders with his gun cocked, then returned to The Blocks.

'Time for a bump, time for a bump . . . Gangsters need blow to stay wired . . . So they don't sleep on the job! Gangsters need zip, gangsters need blow . . .' he said over and over, laughing his quick, shrill little laugh.

The next morning dawned gray. Everything seemed slow in the sinister atmosphere that enveloped the people in the streets, who walked around with grave expressions in the omission of alleys and lanes, whose desertion made up the sadness of the day.

Down at The Blocks, Tiny was still snorting coke with his men. He was even more agitated than when he'd first heard what had happened to his friend.

It was noon on the dot when he told everyone to follow him. Some went by bike, others on foot, running along with their eyes wide open, teeth clenched, glaring into places both real and imagined, with the intention of instilling terror in the eyes of whoever Tiny wanted. Because he was the one who gave orders, he was the one who took the lead, with three guns, and decided which path to take. He was going to give his enemies the full tour of death.

They turned into the alley where Poison César's den was. Tiny asked a group of people on the street corner where to find him. A woman pointed at the bar. Tiny followed her finger with his eyes and saw Poison eating fried sausages, drinking beer and telling jokes.

'What's up, Poison César? Let's talk!'

When he saw fifteen armed men, Poison made a run for it, but one shot from Tiny caught him at a distance. Although he'd been hit, Poison disappeared down an alley, jumped two walls and hid under a car. Tiny's gang scoured the area but didn't find him. As they were leaving, they passed the car Poison was hiding under. The dealer, thinking he'd been found, begged them at the top of his lungs not to kill him, then handed his gun over to one of Tiny's men. Tiny laughed his quick, shrill little laugh and pumped three bullets into the bastard's head.

Valter's family celebrated Poison's death. Poison had killed Valter, a thief from Up Top, two days earlier, then lit candles around his body out of sheer malice.

Tiny and his men took off running again toward the New Short-Term Houses. They arrived shooting locks off doors and scouring all the houses and, just like the police, captured two dealers. They headed for Block Fifteen with their prisoners at gunpoint. Bicky and Tiny invaded Sparrow's attacker's house. The hauled him out of bed, hitting him with the butts of their guns, and took him with the other two to the river's edge.

'Hit the ground, hit the ground . . .'

'What's up, Tiny? . . . Don't do this, don't . . . What've we done? For God's sake!' said one dealer, already defecating, feeling his entire body tighten with the despair of one who finds himself in death's path.

The other two dissolved in silent tears amidst the members of Tiny's gang, who were also finding the situation hard to understand. They knew Sparrow had been stabbed, but they'd thought they were only going to take revenge on the guy who had stabbed him. Some of them wanted to leave. But who had the courage to go against Tiny? Bicky and Russian Mouse looked happy and thumped them with the butts of their guns when they raised their voices begging for mercy. The rain was light, the river ran a little faster, and Tiny's laugh was quicker, shriller and littler. He was unblinking, his head swinging back and forth toward every extreme of that moment.

The first of the three was brought down with blows and bullets. Several shots blasted his head open. Tiny rolled the still writhing body into the river with his feet. The first murder made the other two prisoners fall silent. The man who'd stabbed Sparrow fainted before his body was pumped full of bullets. He too was pushed into the river writhing. The last one suddenly jumped into the river and stayed underwater trying to hold on to something. When he came to the surface for air he took a bullet from Tiny's gun in the left side of his head. Before Tiny had even uncocked his gun, two friends of the executed dealers emerged from an alley; they'd come to ask Tiny to spare their friends. When they saw the bodies floating in the water, they asked what was going on.

'Come to make a request, have ya? Well I don't take requests! You carrying? Are ya?' asked Tiny.

'Yeah, but we're here in peace.'

'Peace my ass! Gimme your guns! Gimme your guns!'

The two looked at one another, put their right hands on the backs of their waistbands and stared firmly at Tiny, who, on hearing one of their guns cock, shot them both and yelled to Russian Mouse:

'Throw 'em in the river! Throw 'em in the river!'

They walked around Up Top firing shots into the air and ordering bars to close. As always, Tiny went around thumping people in the face if he didn't like the look of them, and warned everyone that he was the boss of those parts and anyone who set up a den in the area would snuff it. He told Teresa she could sell all the weed and coke she had, but afterwards she'd only be allowed to sell for him. He hung around a little longer then headed to Block Thirteen looking for Carrots.

'Come here, Carrots, come here, Carrots . . . Here's the story: I killed everyone Up Top, right? And it's like this: you're only gonna be the front man, got it? But only if you send some dough over to the slammer, got it? You gotta send money to Slick and Sting, OK? If you don't, you've had it!'

The rain gained new strength, its drops ricocheting on the rooftops like machine-gun fire. The water washed away the pools of blood by the river's edge and put out the candles around Poison César's body.

'But if everything that comes from the heavens is sacred, it doesn't matter!' said his mother after saying a decade of the rosary and giving up trying to keep the candles lit.

Above all, the waters came down to cry for Rocket and Stringy the day they left the haunted mansion and smoked a joint at the river's edge over by the Eucalyptus Grove.

A few hours after arriving back from the beach, where they'd replanned the beating they were going to give the gang from Gardênia Azul, the Boys from City of God showered and put on their designer clothes. Grouped together and dressed alike, they looked as if they were about to parade with the same samba school. Before reaching Main Square, they bought chewing gum and Halls cough drops. They chewed and sucked them, but kept some to offer the girls at the dance. As boys do.

Sunday night. Main Square belonged to the Boys and their childish games. Marisol was one of the first to get there. As the rest of his friends arrived, he ran through the plan of letting Thiago go alone to talk to the boys from Gardênia Azul. If there was a scuffle, they'd let their enemies have it.

They got on the bus singing rock 'n' roll. The white kids from City of God were going to get the dance at the Freguesia Olympic Club grooving. Thiago remained serious and sat in the front seat with his arm around Adriana. Marisol sat behind them. Although concerned with memorizing every little detail of their plan of attack, he sang in a loud voice, doing everything he could to get Adriana's attention. Every time he saw the couple being affectionate, he turned his face away so he wouldn't feel jealous.

When they got to Freguesia, they spread out in small groups. Adriana did what she'd been asked to, but nobody came on to her when she walked into the club. The Boys from City of God went into the dance discreetly and stayed apart even in the dance hall, confusing the guys from Gardênia Azul, who did the opposite, huddling together in a corner, oblivious to everything but themselves in that atmosphere of Led Zeppelin at full volume, lit joints and strobe lights.

Dancing along, Marisol went through the entire hall looking for the boy who'd had the cheek to feel up Adriana, that sexy piece of ass who'd one day be his, when she'd be treated with all the affection that a gorgeous girl like her deserved. He noticed the guy with his friends, who were now all in the middle of the hall, and crept over. 'I'll punch him in the face, then take off running to stir things up,' he thought, closing the short distance between them.

The punch floored the boy, and his friends didn't know whether to help him or go after Marisol, who shouted to the others for help. Within a few seconds, those who weren't from City of God were taking a beating. Sometimes there were four against one on that battlefield, where sounds of laughter mixed with those of desperation.

Daniel and Rodrigo held their enemies so Marisol could kick them. The best tactic was to throw them in the pool outside, and then, when they got out, beat up everyone who was wet. Some people raided the bar, some stole the belongings of those who'd been knocked out, or grabbed a hot chick for a quick smooch while the fight raged on, but others, like Rocket, made a run for it before somebody jumped them.

The security guards concerned themselves with safeguarding the ticket money and sound system, as they knew there was no way they could break up a fight involving more than a hundred people. The fight, which seemed to have ended in the hall, started up again in the street. At this stage in the brawl, people in nearby bars, at the bus stop, and taxi drivers were attacked and mugged, even though the Boys weren't using guns. Passing buses were pillaged. They broke noses, arms, legs and heads and left eyes swollen in such a short space of time for so many acts of violence.

After the fight they got on the first bus that appeared and forced the driver to take them to City of God, even though he had to change his route to do so.

On the bus, Marisol said he'd been attacked in the most gutless way. He'd caught it in the back of the neck from God knows where. The next time they had to give it to them the minute they arrived, so they'd never again dare attack one of the Boys from City of God. Out of the corner of his eye, Thiago watched Marisol, with his slanting eyes and tousled black hair. He sensed hostility when Marisol's gaze came to rest on him and desire when it came to rest on Adriana. He decided never to let his girlfriend out of his sight, because he knew guys lusted after her, not only Marisol but everyone who saw her wavy hair, fleshy lips, small breasts and shapely thighs. Marisol talked too much, repeated himself, gesticulated, laughed, and he was already planning another fight.

They got off the bus as soon as it had passed the bridge, and were careful not to go past the police station. Daniel suggested they score a bundle of grass in Building Seven, but quickly gave up the idea when Marisol reminded him it would be risky. The police were no doubt on the hunt for Tiny in The Blocks, because his gang had just murdered six people. Marisol looked around and saw that everything was deserted. They were the only people out and about after midnight. They were all immediately gripped by a feeling of fear.

Daniel and Marisol hung back chatting, after saying good-bye to the other Boys.

'Tiny killed them guys the day before yesterday and this morning he was dealin' over in Seven with his tail up . . . Every time he kills someone, he likes to do the dealing himself. He gives out free dope to everyone he knows . . . I showed up mindin' my own business, know what I mean? He saw me, stared at me for ages, then went: "So what'll it be? Buy one, get one free; buy two, get two free; buy four, get four free." Can you believe it? He said the dens Up Top are his as well.'

'Fuck! All of a sudden the guy's top dog in the area. I don't get it—how can a guy that's short, fat and ugly as hell be the boss of everything? He's worse than Sparrow.'

'Who's Sparrow?'

'The guy that got stabbed. He runs the show with Tiny and he's short and fat just like Tiny. But he's a bit nicer lookin'.'

On the Monday, Thiago woke up early and got ready to go for a jog. As always, he'd go to the beach, where he'd swim for a while, stretch and do some sit-ups. He set out at the time he'd promised himself before falling asleep—sleep that had also been preceded by feelings of jealousy, anger, insecurity and a determination not to lose Adriana. Before he reached the first bridge over Highway Eleven, he decided to turn back and follow his girlfriend to the bus stop.

She went through the streets swinging her hips so much in her hurry to get to the bus that the men she passed made sleazy comments and turned to look at her ass, irritating Thiago, who wanted to believe that the body everyone admired was his. Close to Main Square, he snuck up behind her and put his arms around her, giving her a fright. Hiding his jealousy, he said he'd spotted her a few minutes earlier. He walked her to the bus stop and, after making small talk, said he'd meet her after school, something he'd never done before. She didn't notice his jealousy and readily agreed, happy that her boyfriend was so dedicated. She gave him a big kiss before getting on the bus.

Thiago thought about doing a few more laps around The Plots to finish his run, since his jealousy had stopped him from going to the beach. But everything was fine now, because she'd agreed without hesitation. If she had a boyfriend at school she'd have been nervous or perhaps even against his suggestion. He ran fast through the streets of The Plots, now paved and occupied by lower-middle-class houses, although there were still many trees and secluded places where you could smoke a joint in peace. He sat on the highest branch of an almond tree and rolled a joint, taking his time about it, his thoughts on the men that turned to look when his girlfriend went past, the lustful looks Marisol had shot her on the bus, the looks her teachers might give her legs. She was without a doubt the prettiest girl at her school. He even thought about going back to study; he'd enroll at the same school so he could keep an eye on her all the time. He smoked the whole joint. His thoughts were now slower and his gaze contemplative. He noticed a nest on the next branch and was curious to see what was in it, but when he lifted himself up he realized how high he was and returned to the position he'd been in. He held on to the tree trunk more firmly and was afraid to climb down. This business of climbing trees to smoke dope was always the same—when they were fucked up, smokers were afraid to come down. He'd heard stories of friends who'd had to stay up the tree until their high had worn off. After a while he felt he wasn't as out of it. He relaxed and watched the sun's rays coming through the leaves, the birds playing on the branches. Everything was calmer and more beautiful. Things were always more evident after a smoke—how long had it been since he'd noticed the happiness of the sparrows, the beauty of life. The image of the sunlight in the branches would remain forever in his mind. He sang a Raul Seixas song, looked down again and clung to the trunk as firmly as he had before. He'd be better off climbing down to put an end to that paranoia once and for all. When he started to climb down he felt scared again, then he saw it was easy—it had all just been a head trip. He walked home willing time to pass quickly so he could go meet Adriana at her school.

He put on his best clothes, after shaving off his sparse facial hair, dousing himself in cologne and rubbing in too much of his mother's moisturizer so he could go out looking smart. He arrived at his girlfriend's school far too early and went into a nearby bar, where he bought two chocolates and a soft drink to kill time, without taking his eyes off the entrance to her school. He left the bar, went for a walk around the block and timed it. After three more laps she'd be coming out. He kicked stones, whistled several songs, thought again about going back to school, realized his sneakers were a bit worn, and strolled along with his hands in his pockets: the next time he'd arrive at the right time.

When Adriana saw him she hurried over, gave him a big kiss and asked when he'd arrived. Thiago stuttered a lie:

'I just got here.'

'Liar! I could see you pacing back and forth from the classroom. You're worried about something, aren't you?'

'I've only been here a little while . . . I'm not worried about nothin'. I was missin' you!'

'It's not "nothin'" Thiago, it's "anything"!'

He put his arm around her before crossing the street, then stopped at a bar to buy a cigarette, and decided not to keep his arm around her to see if some dickhead would come up and greet her with kisses, hug her, chat her up. He left the bar with the cigarette already lit. This time he walked along without touching his girlfriend, who the men in the street had started ogling again. Adriana made a point of putting her arms around him; she felt bad being checked out beside her boyfriend, who was now scowling. Unable to contain himself he said somewhat maliciously:

'You like it when guys look at you, don't ya?'

'Don't be silly . . .'

'Whenever a guy looks at you, you swing your hips even more!'

'Stop talking nonsense. That's why you came to pick me up, isn't it? You know all men are like that . . . Are you telling me you don't look at girls in the street?'

'Nope, I've only got eyes for you. I don't look at other girls, I don't think about other girls, all I want is you, just you . . .' he said affectionately.

They stopped at an ice-cream parlor before taking the bus back to City of God. Adriana said she was in a hurry because she had to go to a friend's house to work on a group project. Thiago listened without saying a word, but his mind was full of mistrust; he scratched his nose and swung his legs with a nervousness his girl-friend didn't notice. Was she making it up so she could go meet up with some boyfriend, or even Marisol himself? Women were the biggest liars!

'Where's your friend's place?' he asked, without looking her in the face.

'Over in Freguesia,' she answered in the same manner.

They said good-bye after Thiago said he'd meet her after school again, since he couldn't spend the afternoon with her as he'd planned. He thought about saying he'd take her to her friend's house, or arranging to go to the movies afterwards so he could check that it really was a group project she was working on. Standing on the corner of her street he tried to dream up a way to bump into her as she left her house. His eyes followed a ball some kids were kicking around the Rec sports area: he felt betrayed and tricked, although he had no reason to. As well as love, he now felt hatred for Adriana; hatred not only toward her, but toward the comments made by men in the street, Marisol's lustful looks, a rich boyfriend in Freguesia, her teachers, the bus driver, some bastard that caught the bus with her every morning. He wanted to stop feeling jealous, to feel so normal that he didn't even care if she had someone else. Rocket had once said on the beach that it was better to share filet mignon than eat a dog alone. What a joke! No man could accept that. If he went and got her pregnant, his chances of losing her would decrease. If he could find a way to be with her all the time, he'd feel calmer.

The sun made the atmosphere—still tense after the deaths of the six gangsters—even more heated. Thiago noticed Gabriel and Tonho at the other end of the Rec. He thought about leaving, as he wanted to be alone to think up a strategy so he could go with Adriana that afternoon. Then he realized his friends had already seen him. Perhaps he was better off going to shoot the breeze with his buddies to get that fretting out of his head. He sat down, leaned against a post, made an effort to change the expression on his face and held out his hand to his friends, squinting in the sunlight.

'We're here to tell you somethin'. D'you know there's gonna be a rock festival on a farm over in Magé?' asked Gabriel.

'No,' replied Thiago.

'Fuck! How can you not know, man? More than thirty rock 'n' roll bands . . . There's ads on Mundial Radio all the time . . . You're so out of touch! Everyone's thinkin' about goin' on Friday and not comin' back 'til Sunday. We came to see if we could take that tent of yours if you're not goin', know what I'm sayin'? Fuck, man—a whole bunch of girls goin' to a farm! You sure you're not comin'? I'm takin' ten bundles of dope and I'm gonna get shitfaced three days in a row . . .' said Gabriel excitedly.

'You know what there's shitloads of at these festivals? Mushroom tea. You drink a cup, smoke a spliff, pop a handful of pills and get shitfaced, man! I'm in, OK? But my tent's only big enough for two. We need . . .'

'No way, man—your tent's got room for ten, easy! All we gotta do is find two more, get a couple of gas lamps, buy some canned food, loaves of bread . . . And we need to see who's goin' so we can get things movin'. So let's have a look at this tent, then. Is it in good shape? C'mon, let's check out the tent, OK?' Gabriel rubbed the palms of his hands together as he talked, a cheerful smile stamped across his face. His black curly hair covered his shoulders and goosebumps covered his thin, springy body as he talked about the things he was going to do. He offered Thiago a hand.

They walked to Thiago's house with Gabriel making travel plans and calculating how much they'd spend over the three days. They had to tell Katanazaka, Rocket, Marisol, Daniel, Bruno, Leonardo, Breno, Sir Paulo Carneiro, Rodrigo, Chevy and all the girls.

They set up the tent in Thiago's backyard. Thiago completely forgot about his girlfriend. All they had to do was stitch up a tear on the left side and that was it. They rolled a joint, then went to Álvaro Katanazaka's place to tell him about the trip, their spirits even higher because they were fucked up. They made plans while eating the gnocchi that Mrs. Katanazaka had prepared. In the evening, they told their friends about the trip and what they still needed to do, so it would happen. They didn't want to lug too much weight around. The girls would carry the dope, Rocket had a tent and would borrow two more from his school friends, Daniel had a gas camp stove and everyone would take lots of blankets, because the place was cold. It was all set—if everything in the world could be resolved like that no one would have any problems. They went out to smoke a joint on a street a reasonable distance from Katanazaka's house, used eyedrops so they wouldn't give themselves away and went back to eat more gnocchi.

Marisol arrived at Katanazaka's house shortly after Thiago, Gabriel and Tonho had returned. Thiago thought about Adriana, but Marisol's presence reassured him somewhat; now he knew Adriana was not with Marisol. He barely spoke to him, however, and from time to time looked him up and down offhandedly, but without letting his eyes rest for long on his rival, who didn't notice his feigned indifference. They played pinball until well after midnight.

Thiago woke early, although he had gone to bed late. As always, he got ready to go for his jog. He took the same route as he had the previous day, but didn't follow his girlfriend. He waited for her to arrive in Main Square. They walked to the bus stop, where they arranged to meet again in front of her school. This time Thiago arrived a few minutes before school got out, wearing his second-best clothes, duly perfumed and armed with chocolates and chewing gum. He didn't put his arms around his girlfriend while he talked about the rock festival, trying to convince her to go. Although he was talking a lot, he watched the other men going past and stuttered whenever someone's eyes lingered on her, then pretended nothing had happened and kept talking. He stopped off at the same bar to buy a cigarette, and also bought two bottles of soft drinks, put four straws in each bottle and went to the door of the bar, where his girlfriend was waiting for him. He drank his soft drink keeping a certain space between them. To put even more distance between them he walked over to the farthest person he could to ask for a light, then got him talking by asking him something or other, and out of the corner of his eye watched his girlfriend, who smiled when a guy from school went past, said something, ran his hand across her neck and stroked her hair. Thiago galloped from the bar with the bottle poised so he could bring it down with all his strength on the bastard's head. The boy spun and fell to the ground, completely stunned. Before he could even get up, Thiago kicked him in the face and paced around his bloody, unconscious body. It all happened so quickly that Adriana froze, her eyes bulging and her mind straining to understand what had happened. A circle of people quickly formed around the student. Two men tried to grab Thiago, who tugged at Adriana in an attempt to leave with her, but a crowd had surrounded him, making it impossible for him to escape with her. He planted a left hook on the ear of the guy closest to him, ducked and dodged to slip the others and used the bottle to threaten those who tried to follow him. He got on the first bus that went past, while Adriana went to her friend's aid.

At the third stop, Thiago left the bus through the back door, threw away the bottle and wondered where to go. He thought about going back to get Adriana, but no—perhaps it was better to wait for her at home. The right thing would be to wait in the square, or he could take a bus past the scene of the incident to see what had happened. Could the guy have died? He began to realize he'd fucked up, his hot sweat slowly went cold, and an emptiness pulsed through his spine. Stupid, he'd done something stupid. How many times had he stroked a female friend's hair? How many times had he greeted girls with kisses? Girls who were, incidentally, also Adriana's friends. He regretted what he'd done. He waited there until a bus went past going to City of God.

'Have you lost it? Do you see what you did? You almost killed the guy! Never, ever look me in the eye again!'

'I thought it was that guy from the dance comin' onto you—I couldn't tell he was wearing a uniform! If I'd known he was your friend, I wouldn't've done nothin' . . .'

'Didn't you see he was from my school when he was on the ground?'

'I saw red, I didn't see a thing, I . . . I . . .'

'Stop lying, Thiago! You've been acting all jealous since yesterday—I've only just realized . . .'

'Jealous? What you talkin' about? I was just tryin' to help you and you go and turn your back on me. Fine! Forget it, then. I'm outta here . . .'

Thiago went down an alley, feeling even more defeated because his lie hadn't worked. Short steps, head down, hands in pockets, eyes full of tears. He'd gone and acted like a guard dog and ended up losing Adriana. What idiocy, what stupid jealousy, but if he talked to Patrícia Katanazaka, Adriana's best friend, sticking with his lie, showing how much he regretted what he'd done, maybe she'd talk to Adriana on his behalf. He had to make up with her before the trip. It was too risky to go off and leave that gorgeous thing alone in the middle of a bunch of men, especially now she'd started smoking weed. Some asshole would promptly offer to roll her a joint, then stick his dick in. He'd lie low for a while, then he'd go have a chat with Patrícia Katanazaka, and would even go as far as to cry in front of her if he had to. He went to Teresa's den, bought a bundle of weed and strode home.

He locked the entire house up from the inside, rolled an enormous joint and bitterly remembered the details of the incident.

If he could turn back the clock, he wouldn't even go meet her after school.

'Oh God, Adriana has to be mine again . . . What man isn't a fool for a woman? Just them northerners and niggers, who only pick up dogs. Anyone who had her would be jealous, of course they would! Let's see if she can find a boyfriend that loves her more than me . . . No way is she gonna find one and you know what, God? It's not just because she's gorgeous and sexy. She's sensual, it's the way she comes, her soft hands, the way she talks, dances, asks me for things. Please, God! Bring her back to me!'

Eight months, just eight months together had made him sick with love, insanely jealous. He sobbed, leaning his head against the wall.

'He cried so much at times he could hardly speak. I've never seen Thiago like that! I was scared he might even keel over. He talked so much! He said you didn't believe him and that he was only try-ing to protect you. He swore on his mother's grave that he was tellin' the truth . . .'

'But he could see the guy was from my school, he was so close, for God's sake! He hit the guy over the head with a bottle, then kicked him in the face. I haven't got the nerve to go back to school. I told everyone I didn't even know him. Just as well no one saw me with my arms around him . . . But tell me! Did he really cry in front of you?'

'He bawled his eyes out! You should've seen him: if I was you I'd go talk to him.'

Making up was easy: Thiago cried on his girlfriend's shoulder, but she forbade him to pick her up from school, which he agreed to immediately. She told him she didn't like this business of resolv-ing things by fighting, that even the fight at the dance had been unnecessary. She was afraid someone might get hurt and had even thought her friend from school was dead. Thiago nodded his head at the end of each sentence, with a feigned acquiescence that even fooled himself.

By Wednesday at Katanazaka's house, everything was practically ready for the trip. They were to leave Friday night. All they had to do was pool the money to buy supplies, change the gas cylinder, rustle up thirty bundles of weed, three packs of pills and talk about the cocaine that Marisol was insisting on taking. He said that in the United States all young people smoked and did coke, and the United States ruled:

'You can see it's the greatest nation in the world, and it's the country that's got the most heads. I mean, fuck, all their stuff is better than ours—jeans, rollerskates, skateboards, watches and heaps of other shit. And people here think they're hot shit, pah! . . . There's where it's happening, you know. You see Woodstock? Hot chicks everywhere, shooting up, snorting their heads off, smoking huge spliffs. Days and days of pure rock 'n' roll, man! In the United States they don't arrest heads. People even smoke in bank queues. So if listenin' to rock 'n' roll when you're high on weed is a huge trip, imagine what it's like when you're shitfaced on coke. I'd rather tell the guys to forget this crap of buyin' canned food and spend everything on coke, know what I'm sayin'?' As he finished he had a smile on his face, and so did everyone who was listening.

'I wanna have a toot too, but we've gotta have a decent amount, know what I mean? It's gotta be a good high. Like in that Gilberto Gil song: "The more glitter, the better".'

'Gil's the biggest head, ain't he? He was arrested down south with a shitload of weed on him . . .'

'It wasn't just him! Caetano, Bethânia and Gal too . . . Those women're huge heads too . . .'

'Seen the film?'

'*Sweet Barbarians*?'

'Yeah.'

'No.'

'Rocket's seen it and he said Gil ranks on the chief inspector, big time.'

'Does the film show him getting thrown in the slammer?'

'Yeah.'

'Ah . . . Then it's just for publicity.'

'What d'you mean publicity, man? You tellin' me that Gil, Gal, all them guys from Bahia don't smoke? Gil's the biggest head. But I dunno . . . I don't like his music that much. I just think it's a bit . . .'

'Rocket loves it.'

'Did he get the tent?'

'Hey! Rocket said there's a shitload of rich kids at his school that smoke dope at the theater, at concerts—whenever those guys do a concert, everyone smokes their heads off.'

'Janis Joplin died of an overdose, didn't she?'

'So did Jimi Hendrix . . . Remember when the teachers handed out that flyer with their pictures saying they'd died of an other-dose.'

'Not other-dose! It's o-ver-dose, dumbass!'

'That's when everyone got curious and started doin' it.'

'It was even on *Fantástico*, man!'

'It's fantastic, cunt of plastic, cock of elastic, the show of li-i-ife, it's fantastic.'

They'd always heard that rock 'n' roll was a way of life, not just a type of music, so for that very reason they got high on pot, coke, needles and tea during the seventy-two hours of round-the-clock rock 'n' roll that rollicked along in Magé. They saw huge colorful beasts, lost all notion of time, didn't eat, went around wearing only Bermuda shorts during the three nights of intense cold, planted handstands, did somersaults at the waterfall, and danced for five or six hours on end. Some people had sex until their genitals bled, they clapped at the beginning of songs and forgot to applaud at the ends of shows, went for hours on end without uttering a single word, danced naked, emptied their bowels in the river they drank from, had the constant impression that they were the happiest people in the world, lost tents, clothes, gas lamps, pots and pans, basically everything they had taken with them.

Rodrigo woke up three days later in the main square of a town he'd never seen before, next to two girls he didn't know, nor did they know him. Marisol only showed up two days after the festival was over, covered in scratches, with a broken tooth. Gabriel and Tonho found themselves locked up at the Leblon police station without the slightest idea of how they'd gotten there. Over the following days, memories of the festival flashed through the Boys' minds. The next rock festival was going to be in Miguel Pereira and none of them could wait. It was going to be wild.

After getting rid of the six people as planned and giving Carrots his orders, Tiny celebrated the success of the operation by firing a hail of bullets into the air in front of Building Seven, where he did the dealing himself until midday. He then sent his men on their way and went to lie low in the apartment of his younger brother, who was away with his wife. He spent the whole afternoon locked away trying to sleep, but his thoughts were racing, making any kind of rest impossible, because no matter what he thought about, his mind kept skipping back to Sparrow. How was he? Would he come back with that permanent smile of his, singing, always singing those funny little songs, those old sambas, walking quickly by his side and making him feel confident in the way that only he knew how? Yes, Sparrow was the only person he considered a friend, the only one who deserved his trust, even though he couldn't even explain to himself why he liked him so much, why he was so fond of him. But if Sparrow didn't make it, his death had already been avenged, and if he lived, he'd get two more dens Up Top, maybe even three. The truth was, he hadn't killed the six purely for revenge; he'd used the incident involving Sparrow so he could do something he'd been planning for some time. He'd taken advantage of the situation so he wouldn't have to convince his associates of the need for the operation. He thought it was better like that, because he wouldn't have to share anything with anyone in any of the dens that were now his and Sparrow's. That was why he'd decided not to tell anyone that he was going to kill the dealers from Up Top all at once, nor to let anyone else kill them. He was certain his friends would believe that revenge was the reason behind the bloodbath, because real friends have to avenge one another.

His dream of being the boss of City of God was there, alive, completely alive, achieved, extremely healthy, beside him on the sofa. He knew his own men were afraid of him and that was the way they should stay, so they'd never try to get smart on him and would always obey him. The thing to do now was to put good, cheap pot in his dens and always have coke on hand for whoever wanted it, because even though he didn't sell much, cocaine was expensive and it was a nice little earner. He thought about Ari Rafael, who'd managed to make himself a decent amount of dough in a short time with just two dens in São Carlos.

Dealing, that's where it was at, that's where the money was. He now remembered Jelly, manager of the numbers game in São Carlos, saying it was dealing that was keeping the numbers men from going under, because things had been looking down for them ever since the Military Police had started patrolling the streets (previously the responsibility of the Civil Police), because most of the Military Police wanted protection money from the numbers men, who, although they sent a lot of money to the police colonels, had no more peace. In addition to the Military Police, the Civil Police detectives and inspectors also continued to demand hush money. Jelly nostalgically remembered the times when things were organized; all the numbers men had to do was send a decent amount to one police station and everything ran without a hitch. They didn't have to buy coffee for the boys on the beat and beer for the foot police of each district, who, in turn, said that only the colonels made good money. The detectives said the same thing about the inspectors. Things were already bad for the numbers men and got a lot worse when the sports lottery appeared, taking more than eighty percent of the bets and forcing the numbers men into the drug business, which was starting to look promising, so as not to lose their income. It occurred to Tiny to send a wad of cash to the local numbers man, but he figured it wouldn't be necessary. He knew there was no den in the area that belonged to a numbers man; in fact, he didn't even know if the numbers men were still involved in drugs. What he did have to do was have a little talk with the suppliers so they'd bring him good weed and coke whenever he wanted, and ban thieving in the area so as not to attract the police.

His thoughts came back to run through the project streets: they went through the alleys imperiously and stopped to pose on street corners. Because they were his, that's right, he was boss of the streets, king of the streets, there, alive in the cards of that game, the game of guns, of danger, of anger. At the limits of violence, it was all so natural for him, so easy, and he tried to get to sleep, as if killing six people at once was normal. Truthfully, he was nervous, but this state of mind was due to the fact that Sparrow might die. Sparrow, his friend, together with whom he would be the boss of the streets of the projects . . . 'Projects my ass! This is a *favela*! That's right, a *favela*, and one hell of a *favela* at that! The only thing that's changed is the shacks, which didn't have electricity or running water, and here it's all houses and apartments, but the people, the people are like the people in Macedo Sobrinho, like the people in São Carlos. If *favelas*'ve got dens and a shitload of hoods, blacks and poor bastards, then this is also a *favela*—Tiny's *favela*.'

He got up from the sofa, walked slowly over to the mirror on the other side of the room, and noticed his gun wasn't in his waistband. He hurried back to the shelves, where there were mugs from beer festivals, a statue of Saint George, a few crystal glasses and some comic books. He put his gun in its rightful place, went back to the mirror and started muttering. At times he grew serious, as if he were firing at some asshole or other; at others he let out a slow, obscure laugh.

He went back to the sofa, lay his gun on the floor and tried to get comfortable, but he tossed and turned in that tiny space until he pulled up a stool, plumped up a cushion and leaned back on the sofa with his feet on the stool. He got up again, this time to light a cigarette, tasted cocaine in his mouth and ground his teeth. He thought about Sparrow again. He was the only reason Tiny hadn't put Carrots six feet under. He knew his friend wouldn't have been happy about it, but if Carrots' den started making lots of money he'd use his first step out of line as an excuse to do the bastard in. He remembered the den on The Other Side of the River and was ashamed to realize he was afraid of its boss, because he knew that Leaky Tap was a gangster respected all over town and wild as a dog; he had the contacts to put together a gang whenever he wanted and take The Blocks. And another thing; if he killed Leaky Tap and was unlucky enough to get caught, he'd definitely be killed in any prison he went to.

Leaky Tap's den wasn't actually all that great; it only sold weed to the heads in the *favela*. The den at The Blocks was the best of the bunch, so much so that even rich kids from the South Zone came to buy drugs there. It was almost on the edge of the road and at the start of Highway Eleven, which connected the *favela* to Barra da Tijuca. Tiny's den probably had the best location in the whole city, as it not only supplied the South Zone, but also the West Zone, the North Zone and the inner-city districts. He was certain he'd get rich in no time and this certainty was without doubt the biggest he'd ever felt. He'd buy a car, a shitload of houses, the coolest sneakers, some sharp gear, a launch, a color TV, a telephone, an air conditioner and gold, lots of gold to set himself up for life.

He felt like changing positions and needed to go to the toilet at the same time. He got up with his leg asleep, limped to the bathroom, urinated and took a long shower. Then he went into the messy bedroom, with no doors on the wardrobe and dirty clothes scattered all around. Before lying down he took a peek out of the window and saw five military policemen heading toward his block. He went back to the living room, cocked his gun, quickly made a rope out of his brother's sheets, tied it to the foot of the bed and went back to the window: three of the policemen were frisking a boy in the square of The Blocks, while the others were still heading his way. Tip-off. Some rat had squealed on him. He wasn't going to get arrested; he'd pull the trigger on that Officer Portuguese, and Runt too, those fucking bastards everyone was afraid of. He stood there watching the police and visualizing Street Keeper of the Land of the Souls to get his heartbeat back to normal. When he saw them cross the small bridge over the left branch of the river and disappear at Red Hill, he lit another cigarette and put his gun under his pillow, before lying down and falling asleep until the next day.

'Go to Sparrow's place. Go find out what the story is with that knife he got in the stomach. Go take this money to his brother. Be quick, OK?' said Tiny to Otávio at around eight o'clock the next morning. The boy went and came back with all the speed of his eight years of age.

'He's asleep. His mom wouldn't let us wake him up and she said she didn't want no money.'

'Is he OK? Fuck! Whew . . . Sparrow's OK! I knew it, I knew it. Hey, get me a car,' he said to the gangsters sitting next to him behind Building Seven. 'We gotta get a car to bring Sparrow over to my place. We can't leave him there—no way, the pigs'll go there, they'll go there if they find out he's restin' up at home. He's gotta watch his back!'

He went around the building, saw a car coming his way and threw himself in front of it. The driver slammed on the brakes. Cocking and uncocking his gun, he said:

'Lemme borrow your car real quick and I'll give you some money, lemme borrow it, c'mon, c'mon, get out, get out of the car, out of the car, quick, quick . . .'

Then he looked at Beep-Beep and said:

'What's up, Beep-Beep? Get outta here, go on . . . First call his brother and tell 'im Sparrow can't stay there. Tell 'im to wake 'im up and tell 'im to come quickly. Go on, go on . . .'

Beep-Beep put his foot down on the accelerator. Zigzagging down the main street of The Blocks, he crunched the first three gears, then the fourth, which he used unnecessarily, since he'd have to brake to turn onto the bridge. The car owner put his head down and buried his face in his hands, only looking when he heard the brakes squealing. He was relieved when he saw his car drive off the other side of the bridge. Tiny watched him with a benevolent chuckle, gave him the equivalent of two tanks of gas and promised that if Beep-Beep crashed it he'd give him another car in less than a week.

Sparrow arrived lying in the backseat with his gun cocked and a smile on his face. Fly, his girlfriend, was in the front seat. Tiny thanked God for delivering them alive to The Blocks, the car owner crossed himself, and Beep-Beep said naively:

'Wow! Your engine's hot shit, ain't it?'

Sparrow got out of the car and hobbled over to the entrance to the building where Tiny had spent the night. They had to carry him up to the fourth floor, where he then listened to Tiny's compulsive chatter about recent events. Tiny sat on the edge of the bed for a while making plans, then said he had to go meet a supplier. Before leaving, he gave Fly some money for groceries and medicine in case they needed it.

'A chick buying a chicken!' said Ana Flamengo, ending a short conversation with the stallholder who had just sold her a chicken at the Sunday street market. Then on she went, buying the ingredients for lunch with a wide, permanent smile, blowing kisses to the men, looking down her nose at the women and talking loudly at the stalls she stopped at. She was followed by a group of boys who talked a lot of shit, grabbed her ass and tried to pull her wig off. From time to time Ana Flamengo scowled, charged at them, swore and flashed a switchblade, but her smile was imperial when she came back to parade through the market in her teensy-weensy shorts, with silicone breasts, fancy flip-flops, gold necklaces, toned, shapely thighs that really looked like they belonged to a woman, the beauty mark on her white face, large earrings and scarlet-red nails.

Days after her brother had been killed by Detective Beelzebub, Ari, who now answered to the name Ana Flamengo, started living in the *favela* like any other resident. Before that, she'd only gone there to sleep from time to time. Not anymore. She no longer went to the Red Light District or Lapa Square; she plied her trade at the foot of the Grajaú Range with other transvestites and prostitutes. When things weren't going so well, she went shoplifting with a gang of women who met in the Alley to plan their operations and sell stolen goods.

Ana Flamengo was choosy about who she slept with; she liked pre-teens, who would line up in her living room to have her in the bedroom for a few minutes. But when she fell in love for real, Ana Flamengo belonged to just one man. She provided for Short Ass very well and gave him expensive presents in order to hold on to him. She was also affectionate, understanding and a good housewife. Her few friends who knew about her relationship with Short Ass said that if she were one of those young girls, she wouldn't be treating her husband with so much dedication and love. They were happy together for a year and nine months, but after being relentlessly razzed by his friends, who one by one found out about his secret love affair, Short Ass decided to leave Ana Flamengo, who couldn't accept that it was over. She tried everything she could think of to save her relationship: she started bringing him presents every day instead of once a week, lavished food on him, was more affectionate, and in the bedroom she gave him only the blow jobs he was so fond of so there was no need for penetration, which he'd begun to avoid. But there was no way she could maintain the relationship; it had been so secret in the beginning, but little by little word had got around. It was hard to hold on to him with so many people in the *favela* looking at him sideways, nudging one another whenever he was around, cracking little jokes. Even the friends he'd shared his secret with made mean wisecracks. He just couldn't keep it going.

On a rainy Monday he waited until Ana Flamengo had left the house, packed his things, took all the money stashed under the mattress and wrote on the paper the bread had come wrapped in: 'It's over, sorry about everything. Yours, Short Ass.' When Ana Flamengo read it, she felt cold: the cold of sleeping alone in the coming winter nights; the cold of no longer having a husband to kill the cockroaches that so frightened and disgusted her; the cold of having to cook for herself; the cold of not having anyone to bring presents to. The cold of loneliness. She paced through the rooms of the house with her head down, looked at the place in the ward-robe where Short Ass had kept his things: empty. Her tears washed away the powder on her sad-clown face, and she threw herself on the bed, sniffling in silence—the overwhelming silence that always accompanied that life of scorn and discrimination, in which she was always concealing herself, arriving when everything was over, receiving looks of disgust and getting beaten up by the police. It all flooded into her mind at once.

She got up, slowly took off her wig in front of the mirror and ran her hand over her face, mixing mucus, face powder, lipstick and tears. She undressed, running her hands over her private parts. An erotic scene: perhaps she'd feel pleasure acting out that scene, because all the actresses did it in films and on TV. She was an ac-tress: Glória Menezes missing Tarcísio Meira! Even better, she was Marilyn Monroe looking at the perfect body Short Ass had cast aside. Sometimes she stopped, flexed her muscles. She was a man, she was a woman, but sad, very sad for most of her life. Why did her desire have to be treated like something dirty, secret and em-barrassing? Her serious face, looking at herself, asked:

'Who are you? What else did you expect besides loneliness? Come on, throw yourself onto the bed and suffer in silence and tomorrow you'll get used to everything again. Nothing new's go-ing to happen, you fucking faggot!'

She decided to hurry up and get to sleep—she didn't want to toss and turn in bed thinking about Short Ass all night long. That being the case, she'd have to smoke a joint and drink about four beers and two glasses of brandy, then collapse into bed so out of it that she wouldn't even dream. She looked under the mattress and realized she'd been robbed. She couldn't decide whether to go after Short Ass to teach him a lesson or wait for him to come back; she was convinced the bastard would come back for money—he didn't work, nor was he cut out to be a robber. She remained in doubt the whole time she sat on the bed staring into space. She decided to do what she had planned minutes before. She went into the living room, fished two ten-cruzeiro notes out of her purse, splashed water on her face, pulled on the first thing she found in her wardrobe and slowly walked Up Top. She bought two bundles of weed and smoked the lot strolling through the alleys of the *favela*. Her depression returned, stronger this time, and she thought about going home and forgetting everything once and for all by shooting herself in the head. But instead she went into the first bar she saw, ordered a beer and sipped it slowly, without noticing the looks of disgust from the men playing pool. She lit a filterless Continental. The ash fell on her leg, burning her a little, but she didn't change the position of her cigarette. That little pain was nothing—real pain was the pain that ran through her soul and covered her body in goosebumps. She thought about the presents, the money she'd given Short Ass during the time they'd lived under the same roof, the special food, bowls of porridge and desserts she'd made with so much love. And the bastard had actually had the gall to rob her. Her blood boiled, hatred gripped her soul—she got up and sprinted off. The bar owner had to shout for her to pay for her beer. She zigzagged through the *favela* toward Short Ass's mother's house.

The person running with a thirst for revenge wasn't Ana Flamengo; it was Ari, six foot four, used to taking on policemen with his bare fists after midnight in Lapa and the Red Light District. That's right, he wasn't the Marilyn Monroe of Estácio, he was the tough guy from São Carlos who fought like no one else with a razor, delivered a mean sweep kick, and fought back viciously when attacked—and he wanted his money back, not because he needed it, but because of the betrayal, the nerve.

She clapped loudly at the gate of her ex-husband's house. The second time, on top of clapping even louder, she cupped her hands around her mouth and shouted the traitor's name. No one answered, but the light in the living room was on, and the third time she sensed someone moving. Her hatred grew when she noticed Short Ass peering out from behind the curtain. She warned him in a loud voice that she was coming in if he didn't come out with her money right away. Short Ass regretted having spent all of the money on drugs, put away the plate he was using to chop lines of coke, quickly tried to come up with a convincing lie, and went into a panic in the living room when he heard the gate creaking open, together with Ana Flamengo's voice saying she was on her way in. He went to the bedroom, opened the window and threw himself out. He fell on a pile of wood, making so much noise that he not only caught Ana Flamengo's attention, but also woke his parents. Ana Flamengo walked around the house and, no longer interested in explanations, attacked him violently. Short Ass tried to get away from Ana Flamengo, who called him a thief and a traitor at the top of her lungs, waking up the neighbors, who came outside to watch the fight. Ana Flamengo knew how ashamed of her Short Ass was, so she dragged him into the street. She beat him and shouted:

'You fucked me in the ass sayin' you loved me and now you've got the cheek to steal my money!! Motherfuckin' bastard! You left me 'cause I didn't give it to you up the ass when you asked me to, you slut . . . You're as loose as I am . . .'

Short Ass's mother tried to intervene several times. Ana Flamengo said it was a fight between husband and wife and it was nobody else's business. She only stopped beating up Short Ass when she realized he'd passed out.

After that day, Ana Flamengo avoided walking through the *favela* for a good while. She stayed at home, bitter with regret for having lost her head with Short Ass. She shouldn't have done it; she might have lost her chances of reconciliation. Going back to living alone was the thing she least wanted in life, and it wasn't because of sex, since she did it professionally and there would always be boys to deflower. All she wanted was a companion, but she'd have to get used to the idea of being alone; this was the second marriage that had ended in blows, in which she had been exploited and humiliated without being able to say a thing for fear of being abandoned.

Resignation, loneliness, hatred, fear. She gathered up the feelings locked in her room and tossed them out of the window, dressed provocatively, put on makeup and went to the market to buy a chicken.

After she'd shaken off the kids, she dropped in on some of the women in the shoplifting gang, to invite them to dinner.

'Look, it's like this—I'm sick of working in rich bitches' houses to give them hoods the lowdown. They always come out on top and give us jack shit, then the rich bitches give our descriptions to the pigs . . . The business is supermarkets now, know what I mean? We gotta do good joints and get expensive stuff that sells quick,' said Nostalgic to her friends while chopping onions at Ana Flamengo's house.

'This crap of doin' the street markets is also finished, you know. These days, the whities only carry grocery money and not a penny more. We stick our necks out for peanuts,' complained Joana.

'I'm tellin' you, the business is supermarkets! There's this woman that sews these panties with the bottom part stuck to your legs, know what I mean?'

'How?'

'They're sort of like bloomers, but you can tie 'em to your thighs and there's tons of space. All you gotta do is wear a loose skirt, doll yourself up, buy somethin' so they won't suspect nothin' . . . take a kid with you to look the part and you're all set. You can even get through with a bottle of whisky . . .'

'You girls've gotta do what I do: when I can't find a swinger to fuck in the ass, I grab a pocketknife and off I go . . .'

'But you're different, Ana Flamengo! You can turn into a man whenever you want,' argued Nostalgic, making everyone laugh.

'Guess who I saw actin' all ladylike in line at the clinic? Lúcia Maracanã!' said Joana, answering her own question.

'Who would have thought? She's really changed. All she says is hi when she goes past . . . She doesn't stop to chat anymore. It's all home and husband now . . .'

'One day I'm gettin' out of this life too, you know,' said Nostalgic, leaving a febrile silence in the air.

They returned to their discussion about new methods of stealing and came to the conclusion that Nostalgic was right, because supermarkets had the things everyone needed and it was much easier to steal there. It would put an end to the difficulty they had selling their loot.

They went to the seamstress's house that same day to get measured up and in less than a week they were operating in supermarkets in Barra da Tijuca, Jacarepaguá and the South Zone. They decided not to tell anyone else about their new business so it wouldn't catch on and start attracting attention. They were also careful to take turns in the supermarkets and work only on very busy days. A piece of cake, easy money. The women in the shoplifting gang were changed: they had enough money to live well above the breadline, without working in jobs that were bad for the body and soul.

They hated working as domestics—truth be told it was a life of contempt, drudgery and little money. Nostalgic always said she wasn't going to be the world's whipping boy just because she hadn't had everything a human being needed to make a decent life for herself. She wasn't the one who'd invented racism, marginalization or any other type of social injustice, and it wasn't her fault she'd given up her studies to polish the floors in rich bitches' houses. She wanted enough money to ensure a decent life for her kids, something she couldn't get by working, and so at the end of every month, like the other women, she hit supermarkets thirty to forty times, and was always successful. They had money to pay the doctor, the dentist, to buy food and their children's schoolbooks and stationery. All they wanted was a decent life, and so they added rooms onto their minuscule houses and replaced the furniture that had been carried away by the flood. They started dressing nicely, eating well, and using the cosmetics they'd dreamed of for so long . . . Their appearances changed, making their shoplifting, which went on for a long time, even easier.

'Nothing better than a bit of pandemonium to chase away the blues,' thought Ana Flamengo as she sat on the sofa after they'd left. The dinner with her friends had given her back her enthusiasm for life and she decided to go back to work, which she'd abandoned since Short Ass had left her. She hadn't felt like doing anything for a long time, nor had she wanted to talk to anyone about it, and she knew her work friends would ask after that bastard Short Ass, as always.

At that moment, everything indicated that her rough patch was coming to an end. She got up from the sofa and went to bed, with the intention of waking up refreshed to see—in gaudy lipstick, tight little shorts, discreet perfume, heavy makeup and a long wig—that old, permanent, imperial smile working as a facade of the night.

'Wow! Lookin' fantastic! Took some time out so you could come back better than ever, did ya?'

'Ah girl, even Sandra Bréa can't hold a candle to me! And that's not all: I've raised my price, I don't give head no more, I don't go to cheap motels and I only drink imported whisky. I'm back to knock 'em dead!' Ana Flamengo told her work friends.

'I've got some great gossip for you, gorgeous! You know Magalhães?'

'Yeah.'

'He's been married to just about everyone here, hasn't he? And, if memory serves me right, he's even had the odd screw with you . . . Well, while you've been away, he's been goin' for it with Gorete, and believe it or not, he hasn't even asked her for any handouts. Then one cold night, he asked her in a low voice if she'd give him one . . .'

'Speak of the Devil . . .'

'I bet you're talkin' about me . . .' said Magalhães, who'd just arrived.

'And I'm gonna keep talkin'. Um . . . now where was I?'

'He asked her to do him!' said Ana Flamengo, making obscene gestures.

'So then let me tell the story: she stuck that obscenity in slowly, and I felt my ring stretching, a bit of pain around the rim, then that smooth thing slipping in and out, my friend! I'm through with cunts—I just wanna get banged all day long!' finished off Magalhães, chortling along with those who heard him.

They stood around telling one another their news and laughing hard, until they decided to get to work and spread out after wishing one another good luck. As she'd been away, Ana Flamengo was allowed to take the best spot on the corner. She slid down her shorts and made erotic faces at the drivers, who went past slowly but didn't stop. Some swore, others cracked cruel jokes. Ana Flamengo felt the old desperation of having to steal something the next day if things didn't pick up, until a man pulled over close to her, opened the door and gestured for her to get in.

'I thought you were never coming back!' said the man, driving away quickly.

'You know me?' asked Ana Flamengo.

'I know you better than you could imagine, by sight, that is . . . I've had my eye on you for ages. I've been wanting to get to know you better, know about your life . . . Do you know a nice place where we can get comfortable?'

Ana Flamengo took him to a motel on Catonho Highway, the closest and most discreet place in Jacarepaguá, without taking her eyes off that man. He had a soft, slow, intense way of talking, and he spoke of discretion, understanding, his study of her and his desire. He didn't want anyone to know his name. He'd pay a monthly fee. He'd been watching her for a long time and was really turned on by her mouth. He wanted to have her body in every possible way.

At this, Ana Flamengo's jaw dropped.

They threw themselves at each other in the lift, went into the room groping one another and came in the bed, on the floor, in the shower, on the table, on the chair. It gave Ana Flamengo great pleasure to let that gorgeous man fuck her hard, and watching him howl each time he came was fascinating.

On the way back he reconfirmed everything he'd said on the way there, telling her emphatically that her disappearance had filled him with despair and that when he'd seen her again he hadn't wanted to miss his chance.

For two weeks the stranger returned to fill her with pleasure as no man had ever done and, above all, he was affectionate toward her. It was the first time she'd received a man's affection, the warmth of sleeping in each other's arms, breakfast in bed and long, passionate kisses: the happiness of receiving presents and making vows of eternal love.

But this happiness lasted only two weeks. Then it was just her eyes searching for her knight in shining armor in every car like his that drew close. She prayed for him to come back almost all day long. She'd never felt so distressed. She'd never thought she'd meet a man like that. A handsome, wealthy, polite man, who'd been wild with desire every time they made love. No, that happiness was nothing more than a dream. He would never have a relationship with someone like her—someone who'd committed and was yet to commit so many sins, someone who'd wanted to play with nature and in so doing had shamed her family. Her father had always said that it was better, much better, to have a son who was a gangster than a son who was a faggot. A faggot that everyone teased and beat up for no reason at all. That crazy man had only wanted to try something different, or perhaps it was revenge. Many men had told her that they were only having sex with her to get back at their wives. Yes, some men were like that; they liked to take their revenge in silence. Semi-revenge, since none of them would have the courage to tell their wives, fiancées, girlfriends or whoever. To be a woman —what she most wanted in life was to be a woman. And why hadn't she been born female, since she liked men so much? It was nature's fault—stupid, really stupid, and above all, unyielding. She wouldn't preserve her natural state because, while a single element felt a permanent and incurable pain, nothing in nature could be preserved. To love and be loved. That was all.

Guimarães was a changed man. He'd become quiet both at home and at work, staring off into space. Sometimes the routine of managing a bank forced him to stop thinking about Ana Flamengo, but most of the time he thought about the moments they'd spent together.

On Fridays, he imagined the people he passed on his way home from work were heading for romantic encounters. Maybe he could just have Ana Flamengo on Fridays? Perhaps he'd feel less guilty about cheating on his wife and his homosexuality: 'No, I don't want anything else to do with transvestites! Fucking her just once a week is the same thing—it's still a relationship. I'm never going to see that worthless dog again. If Fabiana finds out she'll divorce me on the spot. Oh God! Take away this desire! I don't want the kids to imagine me kissing a transvestite on the lips . . . I should've had the courage before I had kids . . . Why do I want it? Why does this shit have to happen to me? But what's wrong with being attracted to men? If only I could tell Fabiana . . . If only she understood me . . . I'm going to fuck her every day . . . I'd better fill the tank . . . Ana Flameeeengo . . . What a hot ass! Why are men's assholes better than women's? If mother knew how many times I took turns with Gilberto when we were young, she'd freak out. I've got to own up to liking faggots . . . No, no, no! This fucking traffic jam! I owe her an explanation . . . If I go there, I'll end up fucking her again. I haven't slept with Fabiana for almost a month . . . If she could just take a lover . . . I'm going to invite her out for dinner tonight . . . This business of taking work home sucks . . . '

Guimarães found his wife scowling and monosyllabic, as always. Even though she'd been invited out for dinner, she didn't change her demeanor and only accepted the invitation because of the children. She told him she needed to have a serious talk with him. Guimarães agreed, on the condition that they didn't fight. While they dined, Guimarães did his best to put his wife at ease, and tried to act natural. He was ashamed to think about Ana Flamengo when he was with her and his kids. He'd find a way to be more loving and initiate sex more often. This was undoubtedly what she wanted to talk about.

'Adriana, I love you, I've always loved you. There isn't a single second of my life that I don't think about you. You're the rose in my garden, the sun that lights my days, the light at the end of the tunnel. That's why I'm dedicating the next song to you with all the love a man can give a woman. A kiss from Marisol,' said the announcer at the traveling fair that had set up in a vacant lot near Main Square. His voice was romantic and a slow song was playing in the background.

Disconcerted, Adriana laughed in front of her friends, who clapped their hands and teased her on that rainy Sunday evening. Marisol watched Adriana's reaction from his hiding place. Her eyes searched for him in the far corners of the traveling fair.

Shortly after Adriana had broken up with Thiago, they'd started exchanging looks and affectionate gestures. In any conversation, they always pretended to agree with each other to show that they thought alike. Both on the beach and at the dance, Marisol always found a way to be near her and walk her home, and she, in turn, gave him every opportunity to do so. She knew Marisol was interested in her because his doting behavior spoke louder than words, but she had never imagined he would make his feelings public because he knew Thiago was still trying to get back together with her. Adriana told her friends that she thought the way he made his declaration was terrible.

As if that were not enough, Marisol sent a boy over to give her a caramel apple. He let her eat a little before walking slowly toward her with tearful eyes and arms ready for a hug and a kiss. Patrícia Katanazaka and Dóris found an excuse to leave the two alone. Marisol suggested that they head for The Plots. Adriana told him she thought using the loudspeaker to declare his love had been unnecessary. All he needed to do was say something and everything would have worked out fine; it would have been much better to keep it secret so Thiago wouldn't suffer.

'You saw with your own eyes how he tried to kiss me on Wednesday,' she said as they strolled through the streets of The Plots.

Marisol told her he hadn't said anything earlier not out of friendship, but because he was a man, and men had to respect other guys' girls. Now it was Thiago who should respect him and, when he found out they were together, he'd have to stop this nonsense of trying to kiss her. He said he was shy and that was the only reason he'd used the fair announcer. He hadn't even thought about Thiago—all he'd wanted to do was tell her how he felt about her. Still, if Thiago found out soon it would be easier for him to understand that she now belonged to another guy.

After a while they stopped in a dark place to kiss and caress one another. Marisol tried everything to get her to have sex with him but although she was turned on she said no.

Thiago strolled down Main Street with his hands in his pockets and his head down, dreaming up things to say to impress Adriana at the dance. He felt like the biggest dickhead for not being able to control his jealousy, which had made him attack two more of Adriana's friends at the rock 'n' roll festival. He couldn't even claim to have done it because he was high, because he'd stayed clean so he could keep an eye out. 'No way am I gettin' stoned and lettin' some guy make a move on my girl while I'm not watchin'!' he'd thought before they left.

He was the only one who'd stayed clean during the festival, acting like a guard dog, watching every guy who admired her out of the corner of his eye, putting his arms around her almost constantly to show she was his. Whenever she moved away from the tent, he grew surly, his rudeness knew no bounds and he threatened to beat people up. He lost it completely when Adriana ran into two friends from the beach almost at the end of the festival and started chatting with them. Without a word, Thiago attacked them viciously, which started a huge fight, since the two were with other friends who ran to their aid. The Boys from the *favela* ended up knocking three of them out and breaking the arms of another two in a fight that was, in Adriana's opinion, completely meaningless. She didn't even bother telling him that she didn't want to be with him anymore. She believed her silence would be enough to make Thiago leave her in peace. They each made their own way home from the festival. At first it seemed he'd accepted the separation without any problems, but after a while he started approaching her whenever he got the chance. Even when they were among friends. Adriana would ignore him.

Thiago found Patrícia Katanazaka and Dóris at the bus stop, asked after some friends, commented on the rain, made some small talk and then fell silent. Since he'd lost Adriana he'd said little, almost never saw his friends and could only think about making himself look better and dressing better. He thought he was already good-looking, and if he had a lowrider Beetle, with wide tires, metallic paintwork, tinted windows and a roof rack, there wouldn't be a single girl who could resist him; Adriana herself would run back into his arms when he drove past in sunglasses with his arm out the window.

He arrived at the dance somewhat guarded, shook hands with his thirty-two friends in the middle of the hall and put his hands in his pockets. His heart beat faster when he noticed that neither

Adriana nor Marisol were there. That fucking bastard had been acting all chummy so he could pounce on her as soon as he got the chance. He wanted to ask where Marisol was, but decided to stay quiet because he had the impression that everyone knew he was with Adriana and they'd rank on him for sure. He danced with everyone, then slowly sidled off and discreetly left the club. He wasn't sticking around to see Marisol strut in with his arm around his Adriana. He dashed to catch the 690, which went past full. He'd go straight home to bed, as this was the only thing he could do to get his mind off Adriana.

Adriana convinced her new boyfriend to come out of the rain after a great deal of effort, as he was dead set on having sex with her. They went back to the fair. When he saw the rain had eased up, Marisol invited her to take a ride on the Ferris wheel with the intention of keeping her by his side longer, and this was the exact moment that Thiago got off the bus a hundred yards away.

The square was deserted and there were only a few people at the fair. Thiago was still set on going home, but when he saw the fair he changed his mind: he could have something to drink and play roulette to loosen up. He headed toward the fair again with his hands in his pockets and his head down.

The raindrops became visible as they fell near the weak lights of the fair, a love song embraced the night, the wind-borne cold stung his face. He observed the people around him, who seemed to be wearing rags compared to his cool gear. He was good-looking, perhaps even more so than Marisol; Adriana wouldn't think of trading him in for Marisol. He crossed the square sneaking glances at the Del Rei Bakery and the pharmacy, where Marisol often hung out.

He entered the fair and went to the ticket counter, where he bought a shot of Fogo Paulista and two roulette chips. On the Ferris wheel Marisol's mouth was glued to Adriana's. Thiago saw them when he was halfway to the games stand. Everything spun so fast that the colors of the rainy night ran together, everything spun in his eyes, his whole body was tense, his hands shook, the sky came and went with the speed of the lightning that now lit it up, scribbling across the landscape. The long smooch, Marisol's hands stroking his princess's back, the Fogo Paulista burning his stomach, the music playing, his hatred growing, hot flushes pulsing through his body, the Ferris wheel stopping and Thiago running, unnoticed by the couple.

He went behind the gas station, along the right branch of the river, and slowed to a walk when he realized they couldn't see him. He couldn't think: all he had in his mind was the image of that passionate kiss on the big wheel and Marisol's hands stroking Adriana's back. He rambled through the entire *favela* heedless of the rain, feeling that life would always be a big mess.

Marisol woke after midday and, without eating, went up to the roof to smoke a joint. He had the habit of looking at the sky and thanking God for the good things that happened in his life. He couldn't wait to give it to Adriana and watch her come in his arms. He thought about her while he examined the double-barreled derringer he'd stolen from his father, who was a policeman. He had to give it a good cleaning so he could take it to the next dance at the Cascadura Tennis Club. In the last fight the guys from Cascadura had come in greater numbers and kicked out the Boys from the *favela*, who'd really taken a pounding. This had never happened before. He'd fire a few shots to give their enemies a fright. He oiled it, cleaned it with kerosene and washed his hands, then he got a bit of weed, wrapped it in a piece of paper together with a few bullets for the derringer, stuck the gun in his waistband, and came down from the roof. In the bathroom, he splashed his hands with rose-scented lotion and put in some eyedrops, then headed for Katanazaka's house to show the Boys the gun.

Mrs. Katanazaka opened the gate and said she was the only one home. They made some small talk, then Marisol drank a glass of water and said good-bye.

As he was leaving his friend's place, he ran into Thiago, who was holding a stick:

'What's up, man? If you're lookin' for me, here I am!' said Thiago with bulging eyes and a medieval seriousness, ready to fight to the death.

'What's up, Green Eyes? Don't go yet! Let's have another smoke!' said Acerola in Blonde Square one sunny morning.

'Hey man, today's Friday, I'm broke, and I can't hang around smokin' all day, 'cause I gotta work. I ain't a lazy ass like you, man!' answered Green Eyes jokingly, then headed over to The Other Side of the River, carrying tools to put an iron gate in at Whiskers' place.

He was on a happy high from good weed. From time to time he switched the hand carrying the tools. He lit a cigarette before crossing the bridge, then swapped it with his partner for the gate he had on his back and carried it to Whiskers' house.

Green Eyes and his partner had been in the business for a month, long enough to discover the tricks and secrets of the trade. The main trick they discovered was using as little cement as possible in the installation and the secret was ripping the gate out at night, painting it a different color and reselling it to someone else.

'Hey, Green Eyes. I'm not sure I wanna pull the scam on Whiskers, man.'

'C'mon! Whiskers might be a hood, but he won't come after us. That's not how he works . . . How's he gonna find out? All we gotta do is show up at night and rip it out on the sly . . . No one's suspected anything yet!'

'Well, it's up to you, OK?'

Whiskers was still asleep when Green Eyes clapped his hands in front of his house. He woke with a start. He thought Tiny had come looking for him again. He'd borrowed a gun from Tiny to do a holdup, because his was damaged, but before he could overpower, rob and kill the owner of a pharmacy in Madureira, he was chased and caught by two military policemen, who took the stolen money and Tiny's gun.

Tiny was hard on Whiskers when he told him what had happened.

'I want the same gun back, or five million cruzeiros, or a pound of gold in a week! If you don't get it to me, you're gonna bite the dust, got it? Got it?'

It was impossible for Whiskers to give Tiny what he wanted, even if he got lucky in all his jobs all week long. He looked out of the window and was relieved to see Green Eyes and his partner. Even so, he went outside with his damaged gun cocked.

When he'd made sure Tiny wasn't around, he put away his gun, took twenty cruzeiros from his pocket and gave them to Green Eyes to finish paying for the gate and its installation. He was happy to please his wife, who'd been asking for a new gate for a long time. The children wouldn't be able to run off anymore.

Green Eyes thought it odd that Whiskers was holding a gun, but he put in the gate as planned. All he had to do was wait until late at night, remove it and sell it to some other asshole.

Green Eyes went off to score some weed. He'd heard someone say there was some good stuff at The Blocks, so he headed over there feeling the friendly sun, his seventeen-year-old's happiness borne along on a gentle breeze. He'd buy three bundles so he could share them with his friends and laugh all the harder. The sky would be more velvety, the light would be brighter and everything he said or heard would be funnier and funnier. Among friends—it's always the best way. The gate scam would work out all right, but if Whiskers suspected anything at all, he'd give him his money back, roll him a joint, and everything would be fine.

Half an hour later he was smoking a huge joint with Orange, Acerola, Jackfruit and Mango. Green Eyes was enthusiastically telling them about the X Scorpion 1 scam, as he himself had named it. He waved his arms about as he showed them how he prepared the mixture to set the gate and how he stole it on Monday nights, which were always quiet. He'd sold the same gate to the same person on many occasions and, to throw people off the scent, he and his trusty sidekick, Valentin, painted the gate after every second sale so they could pull the X Scorpion 1 scam on another asshole. He was the only person he knew who sold the same product to a number of customers. He called himself a successful businessman. His friends laughed.

'If Whiskers finds out it's you, he's gonna be really pissed off!' said Orange.

'He won't give a shit if he finds out!' argued Mango, as they rolled their second joint.

They hung around until dinnertime. Orange and Acerola were the only ones who still attended school. Mango had dropped out of high school and started snorting coke, against the advice of Orange, Acerola and Jackfruit—friends his mother was always telling him to drop, because she preferred him to hang around with the rich kids from Freguesia, who were white and good-looking like he was. Mango's father, a Military Police lieutenant, had already disowned him for doing cocaine and stealing their money and valuables to buy drugs. But instead of kicking his son out of the house, he moved out himself.

Mango invited Jackfruit and Green Eyes for a bump at his place after Orange and Acerola had gone.

As soon as he got off the bus in Main Square after school, Acerola heard that Leaky Tap's den had received some good shit; Leaky Tap's assistant Victor had been handing out pot near Batman's Bar at around 5 P.M. to advertize the product. He decided to pick up some weed to smoke after dinner. He smoked a joint with Victor, then said good-bye. He wasn't sure whether to cross back over the State Water Department bridge or the big bridge, then decided to take the former, where he saw Tiny, Marcelo and Bicky dragging along Whiskers, who was crying and asking for more time to come up with the money. Acerola asked Tiny what was going on. Tiny told him half the story and said he was going to kill Whiskers over in the Cowshed. Whiskers cast looks at Acerola that were desperate pleas for mercy. At the outset Tiny was unbudging, but little by little he softened, until Acerola managed to convince him to give Whiskers another week to come up with ten million cruzeiros instead of five—for extending the deadline.

That same day, Whiskers went out and held up two businesses, five pedestrians and two buses. He stole a car and stripped it himself in order to sell the parts, but only managed to raise one hundred and fifty thousand cruzeiros. Although he was nervous, he thought he was onto something good and he'd make it if he went out every day with the same attitude as he had that first day, but come to think of it, if he managed to come up with more than one million cruzeiros, he'd leave the *favela* for good. That's what he had to do.

The second time he went out to strike it lucky, he only got a third of what he'd got the previous day. He spent the day in silence, desperately snorting cocaine, in a depression he'd never before felt in his life. He only left his bedroom to buy more cocaine, always with his gun cocked and flinching at the slightest noise.

The third time, he had to make a run for it because the security guards at the gas station he'd decided to hold up opened fire on him and he almost got killed. He arrived at the *favela* barefoot and limping, covered in scratches.

It was late at night and, although his thoughts were scattered, Whiskers happened to see Green Eyes just at the moment he ripped out his gate. He waited in ambush in an alley. What Green Eyes was doing angered him deeply—perhaps he was only doing it because he'd heard through Acerola that he was the next to go, his number was up. He was a real bastard, and depended on Tiny's protection in order to operate his scam. He waited for Green Eyes to get as close as possible so he could corner him.

'I'm takin' it so I can fix it, man! I even left a message with your wife,' said Green Eyes, putting the gate on the ground and getting ready to jump at Whiskers. Whiskers lowered his gun, trying hard to control himself.

Valentin, Green Eyes' trusty sidekick, trembled like a leaf in the wind and tried to hold his bowels so he wouldn't shit himself in front of Whiskers, who jumped when his wife and children came running up, saying that those two had stolen the gate. He fired at Green Eyes without batting an eyelid. He tried again, but the second bullet didn't leave the gun. It wasn't even necessary, because Green Eyes' heart had been blasted to shreds, and his trusty sidekick had already hotfooted it out of there, even before the first and only shot was fired.

News of Green Eyes' death spread fast. Acerola went with his friends to tell his mother and organize the funeral. At the wake, while smoking a joint, he told his friends how he'd saved Whiskers' life just days before. After the funeral, he went home thinking about the irony of what fate had dished up. He stopped to buy a cigarette and lit it. When he turned around he saw Tiny sitting on his bike with one foot on the ground, the other on the pedal and a look of disgust on his face. Acerola looked into his eyes, lowered his head and listened to Tiny's words:

'You see? You didn't let me kill the guy and the guy goes and kills your pal! But I killed 'im today!' said Tiny, and moved on, without waiting to hear Acerola.

Slick had been caught red-handed on his eighteenth birthday while he was mugging a couple in the city center. He had gone with Carrots, who'd taken off and left Slick behind when he noticed the police approaching; he sensed his partner wouldn't leave without trying to take the couple's belongings.

Slick was held at a police station in downtown Rio for a while. After he'd been tried and found guilty, he went to serve the sentence he'd been given: five years for the crimes he'd committed and for others he'd been forced to confess to under torture at the police station.

He'd arrived at Lemos de Brito Prison quiet and tight-lipped. He made himself a place to sleep in the cell, and didn't leave it for a week.

On the tenth day, at around midnight, he was woken by an inmate who told him that the chief wanted to talk to him immediately. He got up calmly, opened the cell and saw five men playing cards at the end of the corridor. Slick looked at the inmate who'd brought the message, then walked at a normal pace in the direction he'd indicated. The men kept on playing, pretending they hadn't seen him. Slick stood there for a while. When he was about to open his mouth, he was suddenly cut short:

'Where you from?'

'City of God.'

'What you in for?'

'Theft.'

'What gangsters d'you know in City of God?'

'C'mon, pal, let me sleep . . .'

'What's all this "pal" crap? We friends by any chance?' From the chief's tone of voice Slick realized the shit was about to hit the fan. He got ready for a fight.

'Got any money?' continued the man, who was wearing a Flamengo Soccer Club T-shirt, while the others continued playing as if nothing was happening.

'No.'

'How is it that you show up in the slammer and go for ages without findin' out who the chief is? You don't talk to no one, you don't share nothin' with no one. If you're broke, how come you've got smokes? You're gettin' off on the wrong foot! Look, there's these guys over in City of God that did this thing once, you know?' lied the chief. 'And it's you that's gonna pay their debt, know what I'm sayin'?'

He was quiet for a moment, then continued:

'From now on, you're gonna be Bernadete, and you're my bitch!' he finished in a voice loud enough to wake all the inmates in the corridor.

Slick flew at the chief, who dodged and stuck out his foot, tripping him up and making him hit his head on the bars of a cell. Dazed, he was kicked and punched for a considerable time, then, covered in blood and without the energy to pick himself up, he was carried back to his cell, where he stayed for a week. He received cigarettes, toothpaste and food brought in from outside the prison while he was recovering, and imagined that some friend had recognized him and was helping him out because he wasn't well. On the seventh day, however, he also received a bouquet of flowers that made him leap out of bed in a fury. He threw the roses on the ground and asked who the bastard was that was fucking with him.

'How come you accept everything, then freak out when the flowers come?' answered the chief from the end of the corridor.

Slick positioned his still-aching body in the middle of the corridor. With his hands he signaled that he was ready to fight the chief, who gave him another drubbing. After beating him, he ordered the other inmates to take him to his bed.

'Take his clothes off.'

While three held him down, another inmate pulled down his pants without much effort, despite Slick's attempts to stop him. The chief saw that he'd soiled his shorts and ordered them to let him go. With a knife at his neck, Slick washed and, without drying himself, was placed belly-down on the bed. He still tried to resist, but stopped struggling after he received a cut on his neck. The inmates held him down again so the chief himself could shave the hairs off his legs and buttocks before inserting his penis into Slick's anus.

From that day on, Slick had sex with the chief on a regular basis and behaved like a prison wife: he washed his jocks, folded his sheet every morning and set out the food from a cafeteria near the prison for them to eat together. Whenever he said or did something the chief didn't like, he was beaten. As time passed, he saw he wasn't the only one in his situation; other inmates belonged to the chief's friends, who were in fact a gang that dominated the whole row. Suffering is more bearable when you're not alone, and this eased his hatred somewhat, but he swore one day he'd get revenge. Life as the chief's woman guaranteed him good food, cocaine, sheets, a pillow, blankets, drinks, dope and chilled water. On visiting days, he was allowed to dress as a man to receive his family. In day-to-day prison life, however, he went around in red panties—red was the chief's favorite color—and had to wear lipstick and earrings. The first time he had diarrhea in prison he was forced to use menstrual pads.

'A faggot's diarrhea is his period!' they said.

When he was released, he was much more hardened, and pissed off at life. He remembered many occasions when he'd been woken by a slop bucket being tipped over his face, or the prison guards' truncheons thumping his ass for no reason. When the chief didn't have enough money for meals from the outside, Bernadete had to eat the prison's watery beans, rancid rice and unseasoned, dirty slabs of lard. When the chief lost interest in having sex with Slick, life went downhill, as he no longer had the perks of being a prison wife. All he had to eat and drink was prison food and dirty water. As for drugs—he only got them when a visitor smuggled them into the prison in their ass or snatch. The flu that settled into his body lasted the whole time he was there and his body was often oblivious to his head's commands.

But he was lucky to be alive and in full possession of his faculties, unlike Prawn, his cellmate. Prawn had never committed a crime until one day, tired of watching his family starve, he decided to steal a hunk of cheese at the supermarket, was caught red-handed by security guards and handed over to the Civil Police, who tortured him until he signed documents confessing to a number of crimes. Prawn was tried and found guilty, and did time in the same prison as Slick, where he lost the sight in his left eye as a result of a beating he received for resisting rape. His body was a parchment bearing many scars, stricken with tuberculosis. After a long period of beatings and illnesses, Prawn lost all notion of things and was first abandoned by legal aid, then by his family, as he had lost his sanity. When he was released, he took to begging in the city center. After six months he died in broad daylight without help or compassion.

Slick was afraid of going mad as he witnessed several cases of insanity, leprosy in the bodies of some of the inmates, and venereal diseases that spread throughout the prison. The many faces of death kept vigil even in his dreams. He hated the guards who brought drugs for some prisoners to sell, because in addition to charging extortionate prices, they also wanted to take commission. He was shocked when he heard the chiefs say that that place was their home. They were going to take holidays when they were released, but that was home. That was where they felt good. And those prisoners who didn't receive visitors, and consequently didn't even have the money to buy toothpaste or a fork to eat with, found themselves obliged to work for those who lent them these most basic items: they poured water over them so they could wash at leisure, cleaned their cells and, if they had smooth legs and tight buttocks like Slick, they had oral and anal sex with the chiefs. Slick had visitors who brought him money and his own toiletries, but the fact that he hadn't tried to find out who the chief was as soon as he got there had made him a prison wife.

As he passed through the last gate on his way out of the prison, he thanked his *pombagira* for not letting him get caught using drugs, or dealing at the chief's orders. He knew that paying a guard so you could deal in peace was not entirely safe, because sometimes he would turn you in anyway, or send another guard to confiscate the drugs and sell them to someone else. He knew inmates whose sentences had been extended because of it.

Slick arrived in the *favela* worried that someone might know what had happened to him in prison, so before going to see his friends, he sent Black Valter, his middle brother, to make sure there was no gossip about him. Luckily, his friends said they had missed him and didn't comment on his sex life in prison. Sparrow sent him a decent amount of money, thinking he was still locked up. Tiny ordered Black Valter to pass by Carrots' den to pick up three hundred cruzeiros to take to Slick; since Slick had been caught doing a job they were in together, he deserved a helping hand from Carrots. Tiny knew Carrots sent money to Luis Sting, so it was no skin off his back to send some to Slick as well. Carrots only gave him half. He said he'd send the rest later, and Slick stayed in hiding for another day.

He showed up at The Blocks after midnight and heard from Tiny's own mouth what he'd been up to in the *favela*, confirming and giving a blow-by-blow account of everything he already knew. He said a dry no when Tiny asked him if he'd been given a hard time in prison. Sparrow gave Otávio money to get several pizzas from a restaurant in Freguesia and lots of beer at the nearest bar to celebrate their friend's freedom.

'Slick's out! Slick's out!' shouted Sparrow, hugging him.

Tiny said he had to have his own den. He said he was going to talk to Carrots and promised that he'd agree to cut him in. Several times that night Slick talked about doing holdups, but Tiny was disapproving, saying that dealing was the way to go.

Out of Sparrow's earshot, Tiny made up a few lies about Carrots and suggested that he take over Carrots' den: if necessary he'd send three of his men with Slick to help him take Carrots out fast. Enemies had to be gotten rid of.

Slick accepted his suggestion, but decided to tell Sparrow, who begged him not to kill Carrots. Tiny agreed, against his will. Everything was decided before dawn on that sunny day: Carrots would only have peace when he came up with the rest of the money to send to Slick, who he believed was still in jail.

Instead of sending two of his men, Tiny showed up out of nowhere in front of Carrots, with Slick in tow. He told him it was bad form to have to be reminded to send help to a friend who'd been caught doing something they'd both been involved in. Carrots sensed something wild in Tiny's gaze, that gaze he knew so well.

He didn't question him and silently handed over the money to Slick who, after counting it, politely asked him to hand over his entire stash of dope as well, and to find a place far from the *favela* to sell drugs because he'd no longer be able to deal there.

Tiny prayed for Carrots to lash out so he could pull the trigger on him, but Carrots appeared as cunningly calm as Slick. He had an ironic smile on his face and, without looking at Tiny, said he'd been thinking of giving him the den all along because they were friends and that's what friends were for. Even though their conversation was discreet, people passing the dealers quickened their step, worried there might be a shoot-out.

Over in the prison on Grande Island everything was set. The bleeders, those who killed, and the bleater, the man who went to the Angra dos Reis Police Station to take responsibility for the murders, had already been chosen, warned, and were ready for action. Both the bleeders and the bleaters were chosen by the heads of the organization for different reasons. There were those who were chosen merely because they had very long sentences, and one more murder wouldn't change their sentence—everyone knew that in Brazil no one served more than thirty years. There were those who killed or took responsibility for murders so they wouldn't be killed for committing rape, going out with women whose husbands were behind bars, or mugging residents in their own neighborhoods. In short, they knew that if they arrived at that prison having breached the organization's code of ethics, they had three options: kill, be killed or assume responsibility for murders. Everything would happen when the samba started. The plan had been laid down during several brief meetings of the leaders of the newly formed faction, whose motto was: 'Peace, justice and freedom.'

The inmates in that prison who raped others, snitched when they were arrested, robbed, forced weaker inmates to pour water over them while they bathed, in other words, all those who subjected others to any kind of humiliation, were going to die.

Sting was first on the list, because he'd arrived terrorizing people as he'd done in the *favelas,* where he'd raped women, mugged workers, always kept the largest portion of the loot from robberies and every now and then had killed people he didn't like and thrown them into the river.

He'd been arrested, completely drunk, by police officers from the Warehouse the morning after doing two holdups and killing his victims with a .38. That same morning, Tiny broke into his house, took the rifle he kept behind the refrigerator and hid it in a place not even Sparrow knew about.

Sting was proud of having rammed Cruel—his nickname for his penis—up the asses of many inmates. He took their money, cigarettes, the food their families sent, and their blankets when it was cold; he said he was the boss of that shithole. Sting lay down on a blanket by the left wall of the courtyard. He ordered the first guy who went past to jerk him off, and the inmate obeyed without blinking. In a few minutes the entire courtyard became a single voice:

> *Portela parades its Carnival*
> *down this colorful avenue.*
> *The legends and mysteries of the Amazon*
> *we sing in this samba just for you.*
> *They say the heavenly bodies were in love*
> *but their marriage wasn't allowed to be.*
> *The love-stricken moon cried so hard*
> *that her tears gave birth to the river, the sea . . .*

As the samba ended, thirteen bodies lay bleeding in the courtyard. When he heard the first line of the samba, the man who'd been giving Sting a hand job pulled a knife from his waistband with his left hand, and slit Sting's scrotum in two in a single slash, cut off part of his penis, then stabbed him in the stomach, eyes and arms, his body writhing egocentrically, while the other prisoners drummed on anything they could, quickening the samba.

There was a momentary silence, soon cut short by the clinking of a knife on bars. One inmate, just one inmate, ran his knife across the bars and shouted that he'd killed thirteen bastards. The only reason this prisoner didn't die was because he took responsibility for the thirteen murders. He was the bleater.

Sparrow wasn't in the den in Building Seven when Tiny and Slick celebrated taking over Carrots' den. He'd borrowed Russian Mouse's bicycle and pedalled off in no particular direction. He was now following Daniel at a distance, admiring his style, his good looks enhanced by the sun. He was envious when he stopped to greet the most beautiful girls in the *favela* with kisses. He went out of his way not to be noticed following him. He wanted to be good-looking, dress like one of the Boys and go out with the girls who hung around with them, who seemed as happy as the rich: tanned skin, sleek hair, tattooed bodies. He continued to follow Daniel down Main Street, trying to work out what was written on his sneakers, T-shirt and shorts. Only Russian Mouse's Caloi 10 bicycle was the same as Daniel's.

They turned into Middle Street, and rode a few yards. Sparrow pulled even with Daniel and, out of the blue, challenged him to a race. The starting line would be the second bridge over the right branch of the river: they'd race to the New Short-Term Houses and return to the starting line. Sparrow knew he'd lose, as he was still weak from his injuries, but even so he pedaled hard and, to his surprise, kept the lead the whole time. He was as strong as Daniel, who was always at the beach and worked out all the time. He waited for him to arrive with a wide smile.

'Didja think I'd be easy?'

'You're fuckin' good!'

'Hey, where'd you get them sneakers?'

'I bought 'em over in Madureira, but any shoe shop'll have 'em.'

'What about your shirt?'

'In the South Zone.'

'And your shorts?'

'South Zone too. They're all top brands. The sneakers are Adidas, the shorts are Pier and the T-shirt's Hang Ten.'

'Hey, if I give you the money, can you buy me some?'

'Sure.'

'Let's go over to my place.'

Sparrow pulled a wad of cash from a plastic bag bulging with money and, without counting it, handed it to Daniel, who thought it was too much. Sparrow told him to go ahead and buy a shitload of size 7 sneakers, shorts and T-shirts, and also gave him the money to go and come back by taxi. He told him to take it all to Building Seven.

Daniel said good-bye, surprised at how nice Sparrow had been, and felt that he wouldn't even have had to let him win the race to be treated well by him. Sparrow watched him ride off. Daniel waved, then turned the corner and pedaled hard to Patrícia Katanazaka's place to pick up a Raul Seixas record she had promised to lend him. He didn't stay long, and headed off to do what Sparrow had asked.

It was already late when Sparrow finished trying on the dozens of shorts, T-shirts and pairs of sneakers that Daniel had brought to Building Seven earlier that evening. Now the only thing missing was a pair of hipsters. The three packages were so big that he'd had to take them to his mother's place in the same taxi. Even he admitted that the amount of stuff he'd bought was ludicrous, but that's how the rich live. The game was to spend money, have fun, enjoy life. He gave Daniel a bag of unpackaged weed and more money than he'd ever had in his wallet. There was enough to buy a surfboard, or even an imported skateboard.

'I'm a playboy!' said Sparrow to everyone who commented on his new attire. He had an enormous dragon breathing yellow and red flames tattooed on his arm, and Fly curled his slightly frizzy hair. Now he definitely felt like a rich kid because he was dressed like one. He got Fly to go and buy him a Caloi 10 bicycle so he could go to the beach every morning. Rich people rode bikes too. He'd start hanging around Pepino Beach as soon as he'd picked up their lingo. Everything in life was just a question of getting the jargon right. Some of the gangsters tried to rag on him about his new look, but he put his hand on his gun, saying he was no clown. Even Tiny suppressed a laugh when he saw him dressed like a playboy from the South Zone.

The generally homemade object made of fine paper glued together in a number of different shapes, launched into the air during the traditional June celebrations and propelled upwards by hot air produced inside it by fuses tied to one or more wire burners, is called a balloon.

There is the Japanese balloon, the smallest of them all, whose ascent and descent are instantaneous; the box-balloon, so named for its shape; the kiss-balloon, pure hot air designed as a short cut to romantic encounters; the tangerine-balloon; the hammer . . . The balloon only stays in the air while its fuse is burning.

The name 'balloon' is also given to the worker who slaves away every day of the week, then on payday, before going home, goes to settle his monthly account at the local watering hole, and while he's there gets more sloshed than usual, because the poor bastard thinks his pocket's bulging with money. The alcohol is the fuse causing him to puff up, up, up with hot air, rise, rise, rise, then come down, down, down, completely burned out. This is when the kids show up to pilfer his belongings and the rest of his money.

This activity, not only popular with juvenile delinquents but also among the kids from the Alley, was called spent-ballooning. It was banned by Tiny to stop people filing complaints down at the police station (thus reducing the number of police raids, making it look like City of God had become a peaceful place), and to gain the respect of the local barflies. The kids from Block Thirteen were flat broke, however, and woke up early on that Friday preceded by a full moon. They attacked all the newsstands armed with sticks and stones, then the shops on Freguesia Square armed with a penknife and a .22-caliber revolver, and spent-ballooned every drunk that didn't look familiar that night.

Zé Maria, who lived in Building Eight, liked to drink in Main Square. There, while chewing on chicken gizzards and sipping his firewater, he eyed up the women and gave his verdict on who was hot and who wasn't. He was drinking more voraciously because he'd received severance pay after six years of work. At the counter of Tom Zé's Bar, the kids were drinking soft drinks and watching Zé Maria sip his *cachaça*, nibble on gizzards and wash it all down with beer. Tom Zé had asked them not to rob anyone in the vicinity, offering them soft drinks in return.

Zé Maria staggered out into the already late night and the boys followed, waiting for him to get to a deserted place where they could jump him. The inevitable happened before he got to the Short-Term Houses at Red Hill. Zé Maria tried in vain to shake off the kids from Block Thirteen.

The next morning his stomach hurt and his head pounded, but nevertheless he decided to get up, wash his face and brush his teeth. He left home without answering his wife, who had asked him if he wanted breakfast, and went looking for Tiny. He didn't find him at the den and complained instead to Bicky and Russian Mouse, who promised to get his money back to him as quickly as possible.

'Yesterday I saw them kids from Thirteen all heading off together. They started actin' all weird when they saw me, know what I'm sayin'? It must've been them,' said Russian Mouse.

'C'mon then, off we go!' said Bicky.

'We'd better talk to Slick first, man. He's the boss over in Thirteen,' Russian Mouse warned him.

'No way, man! It's us that's gotta sort things out! They know they're not s'posed to go spent-balloonin' in the *favela*, don't they?' said Bicky.

'True.'

'So, c'mon then.'

They headed off on their bicycles through the alleys of Red Hill, crossed Edgar Werneck Avenue and turned into Miracle Street as calmly as if they were going for a morning ride. The kids were gathered in the first alley running off Miracle Street, trying to get their kites airborne with the glee of those with money in their pockets.

'Where'd you get the money to buy this string?' asked Bicky. 'None of your business, man!' answered Two-Wheeler, who glanced at him without raising his head, all the while tying the paper ribbons to his kite strings.

'Hey, kid! You think you're all grown up, don't ya? Everyone against the wall! Frisk 'em!' ordered Bicky, brandishing a 9 mm.

Russian Mouse frisked them looking for weapons and money, and gave Two-Wheeler and Toothpick a shove when they refused to lean against the wall. Their defiance made them hard to frisk properly, which is why he missed part of the money in Toothpick's pocket.

Bicky asked them several times if they were the ones who'd spent-ballooned Zé Maria. After each question they all remained silent. Two-Wheeler slowly sidled over to the drainpipe where his gun was hidden. Extremely thin, with bare feet, a runny nose and no shirt, he scowled at the dealers, who were threatening to take them to talk to Tiny. They stood there negotiating for a few more minutes until Russian Mouse convinced Bicky to let them go, and warned that they'd kill them if they caught wind of them spent-ballooning anyone else in the *favela*.

When they returned to The Blocks they found a still sleepy Tiny and, dispensing with greetings, launched straight into an account of what had happened. Their boss, who wasn't in the mood for talking, listened to everything without interrupting them, then said incisively:

'Only fools get spent-ballooned. Nobody forced him to drink . . . Forget about them kids! How much did they take?'

'Six hundred.'

'Give the old guy the money and tell 'im that if he gets drunk again he's gonna get another beating.'

Marisol stepped back and tried to persuade Thiago to talk things through. He wanted to explain that he'd only told Adriana what he felt for her after he'd heard they weren't together anymore. Thiago refused to listen. With clenched fists he darted back and forth, danced around, swore, and pretended to lunge at Marisol, who pulled out his derringer, cocked it and pointed it at Thiago saying he was going to kill him. Thiago ran no more than fifty yards, stopped behind a post and ordered his enemy to fire. Although he was holding a gun, Marisol tried to talk. He told him that if he wanted, he'd put away the gun so they could talk it over. Thiago replied that he was going to get his hands on a gun and kill him mercilessly, at which point Marisol fired. A thin smoke covered his face. The bullets began to lose momentum before they'd traveled twenty yards and fell to the ground.

The time it took Marisol to load the derringer was long enough for Thiago to try to attack him; Marisol would run while loading his gun, then fire two shots at Thiago, his tongue showing in the left corner of his mouth. Thiago would back off just twenty yards, wait for the two shots, then dash at his enemy. They spent the entire afternoon engrossed in this activity. A crowd gathered to laugh and egg them on. When Marisol fired the gun everyone ran, then onlookers would applaud Thiago's offensive. They ranged through the entire *favela* drawing a crowd until the ammunition ran out. Finally they locked horns in a fight. Everyone watching thought it was a draw.

Thiago and Marisol's fights went on for another two weeks, in the widest variety of places. The Boys persuaded Marisol not to use the gun against Thiago, since he was their friend. They also tried to convince Thiago to chill out, saying that the one who had to choose was Adriana, and she'd already chosen. Thiago wouldn't listen to his friends, saying the world was too small for the two of them and that Adriana was only with Marisol to make him jealous.

One Friday night, Sparrow fired two shots into the air in the Rec to separate them. Brandishing his gun, he threatened to kill them if they kept fighting and made them shake hands.

Everything had been arranged ahead of time with Sparrow, who'd become good friends with the Boys through Daniel and had started sending them dope morning, noon and night, every day of the week, as well as buying them ice creams, cakes and soft drinks at the Del Rei Bakery, where he always found the group hanging out together.

To celebrate the end of the dispute, he took everyone to a steak house, saying they could eat and drink whatever and as much as they wanted. He told them he'd pay for everything and that's what he did, always with a sincere smile on his face.

Now he was looking good too. The most beautiful girls in the *favela* greeted him with kisses on both cheeks. He went to the dances, messed around on the bus on the way there, and learned to bodysurf like no one else . . . He liked his new life.

The next day Peanut, the den assistant, said in front of the other gang members: 'The Boys give it like a girl.' Everyone laughed, including Tiny. At first Sparrow thought it was funny, but then he felt silly in front of his men, suddenly drew his gun and told everyone to run. At first they did nothing; it was only after the first shot that they all took off, running between the buildings. Sparrow went after them firing one shot after another. Tiny ran too, laughing like most of the gangsters, and Sparrow fired away with a serious look on his face, reloaded his gun, swore and dared the gangsters to shoot him. Although he was angry, he didn't actually want to hit anyone. His tone of voice was serious, however, and he chased his buddies for some time before heading for the shops, where he had a soft drink and some cakes.

Within a few minutes he was telling jokes to the barflies, clowning around and singing rock 'n' roll. Gingerly, his friends started to arrive. Sparrow treated them as if nothing had happened. He asked Peanut to roll him a joint and smoked it while leaning against Tiny, who showed him a scratch on his leg from where he'd fallen while running. Sparrow bought a Band-Aid and put it on his friend's little scratch. It had all been no more than an elaborate game of tag.

That evening, Sparrow told Tiny in private that he'd decided to get married. He'd been going out with Fly for a long time and was convinced that she should be the mother of his children. She was affectionate, understanding, she'd stopped stealing and smoking pot on street corners like a man, she was a good cook and knew how to keep house like no one else, his family liked her, and so on. He begged Tiny not to tell anyone, because he wanted to keep screwing the sluts and the pretty girls, who'd also started flirting with him.

'When're you gonna tie the knot?'

'Today!'

'Ain't you gonna buy a beer for the boys . . .'

'Since when do gangsters have weddin' parties, man?'

Sparrow had taken over the house of a dealer Tiny had killed. That very night, he sent Beep-Beep to buy his supper at the steak house and deliver it to his place at around midnight. The day before, he'd taken two men to paint and clean the house, and Night Owl had fixed up the masonry and plumbing, and assembled the wardrobe. The house was ready for the newlyweds.

As soon as he'd finished talking with Tiny, Sparrow said goodbye to his friends, got on his bicycle and went to the place where he'd arranged to meet Fly.

The night seemed empty after Sparrow had gone. Tiny felt like having a bump, but decided to smoke another joint to get to sleep. He rolled the joint himself and smoked it alone in the entrance of a building. The next day the whole gang was gathered near Building Seven when Bicky came down the street along the left branch of the river with two boys tied up with rope. Every now and then he clouted them over their already bloody heads with the butt of his gun. The boys had held up a number 690 bus full of residents from The Blocks.

'You can't rob the buses that come through the *favela*! We've already warned you! You're runnin' the gauntlet!'

The gangsters stood in two rows and made the thieves pass between them three times, hitting them brutally with the butts of their guns. Nine-year-old Bigolinha blacked out. Tiny thought it was just a trick to escape the beating and continued kicking and hitting him. Then, guffawing, he unloaded his 9 mm into the boy's body. He ordered Russian Mouse to shoot the other thief in the foot, then took another revolver, pointed it at the boy and ordered him to leave without looking back, otherwise he'd die.

The boy limped away using the side of the building for support. Tiny could fire at any moment, but if he walked a little farther away from the building, Tiny wouldn't be able to use the wall to take aim. He tried to move away, but couldn't walk without support and returned to the wall. If he got out of this one alive, he'd never steal in the *favela* again. His mother's voice shouting at him to hustle up some money recomposed itself in his ears. Miserable, his life was really miserable: he was going to be shot in the back. There were three yards left before the end of the building. He quickened his step and turned the corner with a relief that made him stop, breathe and look at his wound. He peered around the corner of the building to see if anyone was following him and got a bullet in the middle of his forehead, fired by Tiny, who'd had his gun pointed the whole time as he followed the building and kept it pointed after he'd rounded the corner, without changing position.

'Hey, Marcelo, get a car and dump the dickheads over in Saci Alley.'

Then, as if nothing had happened, he continued talking with his men, without looking at Sparrow, who called him a madman, his eyes brimming with water.

Two days later, a newspaper ran photos of the two dead boys saying it had been a heinous crime. Tiny listened as Sparrow read the article and asked him what heinous meant. Sparrow didn't know, but Daniel, who was there to collect five bundles of weed that were a present from Sparrow, explained the meaning of the word to everyone.

In the streets, the boys who studied in the mornings were spinning tops near their houses, while the girls played house in their backyards and on the stairs of their buildings. People's faces were calm. The river and its two branches ran slowly, since the dry season had settled in more than a month before. In the Rec, the Boys were talking about the latest fight at the dance; in the bars, the barflies were playing silly games, discussing soccer and telling old jokes.

It was a normal Monday, with the neighborhood women immersed in their afternoon gossip, people collecting bottles to sell for recycling, others looking for iron and copper wire to strip and sell at the junkyard. There were those who still hadn't had a meal that day. Some thieves had already gone about their work, muggers had already mugged and killed someone outside the *favela*, and the beggars who lived there were arriving back on buses.

Over in Block Thirteen, a woman checked the temperature of the water she had put on the stove to boil, having made two visits to the bar to call her husband, who was getting drunk with his friends. She'd thought about dropping the idea during the day, but when she saw him getting drunk she decided to go ahead with her plan to be happy forever. She'd made her husband take out life insurance the week before, and now she'd kill him in cold blood.

Over in The Blocks, a group of boys with the average age of seven had gathered on the stairs of Building Eight. They were known as the Angels, because they had all been born in City of God, and also as the Empty Pockets, as they didn't have money like the gangsters in Tiny's gang, who pulled off large-scale robberies and holdups.

Starving, they were devouring three chickens they'd got holding up a luncheonette on Taquara Square, where they'd arrived armed to the teeth with hunger.

With his mouth full, Highwayman said he'd never again do a job in order to eat. He swore he was going to pull off something big so he wouldn't have to risk getting caught every day. He'd follow the example of Bicky and Marcelo, who only robbed houses and brought home gold, American dollars and guns. This game of sticking their hands into their waistbands pretending to be armed could backfire one day. It was time to get guns to stick in the suckers' faces and order them to lay everything on the ground. It was humiliating doing favors for the gangsters in return for a little loose change, leftover food and weed.

Otávio was the one who enjoyed running errands for the dealers. He said he wanted to be a dealer when he grew up, but it took ages to get in with the dealer so you could become an assistant, then security, until you made it to manager. To head up a den you had to wait for the old guns to die or get locked up, or kill everyone as Tiny had done. No, they'd have to pull off big jobs so they could wallow in money.

That was what the boys decided as they fought to see who'd take the leftovers of the stolen chickens home.

Highwayman arrived home on tiptoes so as not to wake up his mother and stepfather. But his stepfather was awake, waiting to see if the boy had brought any money. Highwayman only offered him a chicken drumstick and got a beating, because his stepfather was no fool and wasn't going to support someone else's kid—he wasn't there so some lazybones could sponge off him. Highwayman's mother interfered, and got a beating as well.

The stepfather didn't say so, but he thought she was siding with that bastard because he reminded her of his father; she was so loving with him because this was a way of loving the other guy. One day he'd beat him to death so he wouldn't have to live with the traces of his wife's first husband. After the beating, Highwayman went to bed without spilling a single tear, because everyone knew and it could never be stressed enough that real men don't cry.

'When your wife starts bustin' your balls like that, the thing to do is fart, fart and fart at her all day long.'

'How?' asked the husband.

'Buy five pounds of oxtail, five pounds of potatoes and some watercress, get the bitch to cook it up and come to the bar to get sloshed. Then you go home, eat all that shit with red chilies and you'll fart sittin' down, standin' up, squattin', kneelin', awake or asleep. You'll do *phooo* farts, macaw farts, silent farts, whistling farts, bubbly farts, whining farts, exploding farts, runny farts and the works . . .'

'Today I felt like fartin' in the bitch's face . . . Why're women like that? Hell! I work my ass off all day long, I don't buy nothin' for myself so we're never short of anything at home, I'm not the aggressive sort, I don't hit her or the kids, I don't bother no one . . . What's it to her if I have a cold one or a shot of *cachaça* before dinner? She can shove it up her ass, you know. Hey, give us another shot of *catuaba* with that *cachaça* from Minas Gerais!'

'Why don't you fart today? If you eat some cracklin' it'll do the same thing.'

'Hey, Down There, give us some cracklin'.'

'Down There is where a snake's ass is, man!' answered the bar owner before serving him.

The crabby husband ate five pieces of crackling, drank another three shots of Cinzano-and-*cachaça*, washed it all down with a beer and staggered home. He opened the gate with some difficulty, feeling a real need to relieve his bladder, and hurried for the toilet, but the urine poured down his leg, wetting the living-room rug. He showered without taking his clothes off, thinking it odd that his wife was so quiet in the kitchen. He thought about saying something, but decided to keep quiet so as not to spark a fight. He pulled off his dirty, sopping clothes, stuffed them under the bathroom counter and went to lie down after putting on a pair of undershorts. In a few minutes he was snoring loudly. His wife dragged him into the kitchen and poured the boiling water over his head.

She was convicted of murder in the first degree and didn't get the insurance money.

'I wanna sell pizza, soft drinks, juices and that's it, got it?'

'You gotta have beer, man! Everyone drinks beer . . .'

'No, no, no . . . I don't want to put up with barflies. I've already got an industrial oven, two blenders, an orange juicer, glasses— the fuckin' works! Everything's all set—all I need is a nice little shop to get started, know what I mean? So, what d'ya say? I get fifty per-cent and the other fifty's for you and the head cook. But the money'll only start comin' in when I finish payin' off what I owe. OK by you?'

'Fine by me!' said Rocket with a gigantic smile on his face, hold-ing his arm out to shake hands with Álvaro Katanazaka, with whom he had already tried to set up a kitchen utensils shop.

They'd never had an actual shop, as they'd intended to start by selling from door to door. Later they'd open a little shop in the *favela* and, if they were hard-working and thought positively, they'd soon be opening other branches, hiring employees. However, not even with the little prospectus Katanazaka had put together, say-ing the profits would be directed to an orphanage, did they man-age to make more than one and a half times the minimum wages between them in their first month. Their progress at school was affected, they traipsed about the *favelas* and other districts all day long, sunk money into buying merchandise at the Madureira Mar-kets and only earned a pittance, half of which they had to set aside in order to restock their goods.

'We can't let anyone know, OK? Otherwise people'll be envious and that'll jinx the business,' warned Katanazaka.

'We've gotta buy a horseshoe and hang it in the joint the first day.'

They chatted a little longer. Ideas for the new undertaking arose at random, between drags on the joint they were smoking. When they'd finished, Rocket said good-bye and left Katanazaka's place, while his friend sprayed air freshener around the living room to get rid of the smell of marijuana: his parents would be arriving soon. Rocket took his Caloi 10, the bicycle every boy worth his salt wanted to own, pedaled five hundred yards, then suddenly did a U-turn and rode even faster back to his partner's house.

'You know that shop over in Araújo?'

'Yeah.'

'Well, the guy's renting the joint out! I was already in front of it when I remembered. My girlfriend's dad was thinkin' about rentin' it and all.'

'You think the guys're there today?'

'Might be . . .'

'Should we go?'

'Why not!'

Katanazaka got his bike and they rode down the street along the left branch of the river.

'You need to have a guarantor or pay a bond, and both the tenant and guarantor have to earn three times more than the value of the rent. Where do you live?'

'In City of God.'

'Are you the ones who want to rent it?' asked the landlord distrustfully, when Rocket told him where he lived. 'No. It's my dad.'

They left the shop enthusiastic about the possibility of renting it. The rent was a bit steep, but with their contacts and the good advertising they'd put out, they'd make that amount each month, no sweat. All they had to do was forge Katanazaka's dad's pay stub, and this was a job for Rocket who, as well as being a photographer, had turned out to be a very good artist. The bond money was already guaranteed: it would come from the severance pay Katanazaka was to receive that Monday, as he'd been fired from his job.

Braga, Álvaro Katanazaka's father, didn't hesitate: he did everything his son asked him to, not because he was indulgent with his children, but because he saw the prototype of a successful businessman in his son and knew he'd earn a lot of money—money that he himself had never known how to make. This didn't stop him from being a sensitive father or loving Álvaro with all his heart. His son would be what he hadn't been, and for this reason, he'd help him as much as he could.

Rocket accepted the invitation to have dinner at Katanazaka's house. It would be necessary and a pleasure. Necessary because he'd get started on the forgery, and a pleasure because Tereza Katanazaka's cooking was the best he'd tasted in his entire life.

'We've gotta fix up his last three pay stubs,' Katanazaka reminded him.

'Good point. Got a razor, glue and a typewriter? You'll have to make some doctored-up photocopies and everything, right?'

'We'll manage.'

Everything went as Rocket had planned. All they had to do was present Braga's ID and the three forged pay stubs in order to rent the shop.

Before three o'clock Braga shaved carefully, combed his hair, clipped his nails, put on the old suit he'd worn at his wedding, put on Tereza's glasses, and went with Rocket and Katanazaka to rent the shop. It went off without a hitch.

'You gotta dress like a waiter, man!'

'Look, man, I'm not wearin' no waiter's uniform, OK? What's the big deal? You know they're gonna rank on me!'

'Then you'll have to wear a white shirt so you look nice and clean, know what I'm sayin'? All bars are like that!'

'Not bar. Pizzeria,' said Rocket, correcting him.

'We gotta get there early tomorrow. OK? To give it the finishing touches. Tell everyone there'll be an opening-day special, but hey—only tomorrow.'

'What's the special?'

'Whoever pays the all-you-can-eat price gets two soft drinks,' said Katanazaka a month after renting the shop.

'Take some records down there—Milton Nascimento, Caetano Veloso, Gal . . .' Katanazaka continued.

'You reckon people're gonna like that kinda music?'

'Ah, who knows. But I'll take some rock 'n' roll records too.'

'We can change the music depending on the customers.'

'Good idea,' agreed Rocket.

They considered the opening a success. Sparrow arrived early and insisted on paying for all of the tables. Rocket managed just fine, the pizza was tasty, and the soft drinks were cold.

'You gotta put beer on the menu!' said Sparrow with his mouth full.

'I will, OK? It's just that I ain't got the bottles,' said Katanazaka with a pen tucked behind his left ear, giving him the air of a shop owner.

It was a rainy summer night. Rocket insisted on playing Caetano Veloso for the Boys, who laughed at silly jokes and always used the same jargon when they talked.

It was Friday, the day Tiny and Sparrow's dens sold much more than on any other. Good Life was now helping out with the management and Israel played samba in nightclubs, but had started going around carrying a gun and beating up hoods who stole within the *favela*. Israel was almost as powerful as Tiny and Sparrow. Every so often he'd swing by the den to pick up some money, but told the women he met that he didn't need to sell drugs to make a living. He was an artist.

Around midnight, Sparrow showed up at the shops with almost all of the Boys, and found Tiny and the rest of the gang there.

'Hey, these guys are my friends, they're all cool! I don't want no one givin' 'em a hard time, get it? No one. Anyone who gives 'em a hard time'll get a bullet in the ass, got it? Hey, grab yourself twenty bundles of weed. Go on, it's OK!'

Tiny carefully examined the face of each of the Boys so he'd never forget them; if they were Sparrow's friends, they'd be his too. Some he'd seen around the *favela*, others he'd known since he was a kid, as in the case of Leonardo, who lived in The Blocks, as well as Pedro and Rocket. He stared intently. Suddenly, he asked the bar owner to open a crate of Coca-Cola and left.

'Hey, man, there was only one bundle there.'

'We're out of weed! Who's gonna do the packaging?' Sparrow fell silent for a few minutes, then continued. 'Go to Carlos Roberto's house, get three pounds of dope and take it to my place. I'm gonna do the packaging with my pals. And I don't want no gangsters comin' lookin' for me, alright? You comin' to do the packaging? You comin' or what?' Sparrow asked the Boys.

At Sparrow's place the Boys folded the pot into sports lottery tickets, each puffing on a huge joint. Gabriel went to the bakery to buy cakes and soft drinks. Sir Paulo Carneiro went to the den Up Top to get cocaine, but soon came back saying that Teresa wouldn't give him the thirty papers of coke.

'Here, take this and go back. Show her this and she'll give it to you!' said Sparrow, handing over his thick gold chain with a picture of Saint George the warrior, also in gold, to Sir Paulo Carneiro, who was successful this time.

Rocket put a Raul Seixas album on the record player and said it would be better if they ate first, then had a toot. They hung around listening to music, snorting coke, smoking and bundling weed until Fly arrived home with her sister.

'What the fuck are these playboys doing here, Sparrow? Don't they have a house to go to? They come round to get fucked up, eat my food . . . Get out! Out! Fuck! Fuck! Goddamnit!'

Laughing, Sparrow signaled for the Boys to leave. The morning was dawning behind Gávea Rock. The cocaine they'd snorted had chased sleep away. They waited in silence for Sparrow to come out in swimming trunks, with a towel around his neck and dark sunglasses.

'Everyone to the beach. Meet me over at The Blocks, 'cause I'm gonna drop off the bundles and we can leave from there. Don't be long.'

As Sparrow closed the gate, Fly ranted and raved out of the window:

'You're not settin' foot in here today, you bastard! My mom's sick and all you wanna do is party. All you can think about is hangin' out with them fuckin' playboys! You shithead! Bastard!'

Sparrow laughed and headed off with the Boys under a cloudless blue sky. The sun blazed alone in a stupendous summer sky.

It was a busy Saturday at the beach, with big waves, surfers cutting the water, propeller planes trailing banners through the air, people selling iced tea, passion fruit juice, popsicles and suntan oil, people playing volleyball, others playing soccer and the Boys from the *favela* having bodysurfing races, accompanied by Stringy, who surfed every wave he caught with elegant competence.

For those who stay up all night snorting coke, the best thing to do the next day is smoke loads of dope to bring on hunger and sleep, which cocaine suppresses, and drink loads of coconut water to protect the stomach. Sparrow had already learned this lesson from the Boys, which is why he took some weed to the beach and loads of money to buy coconut water and sandwiches for the gang, as well as Adriana, Patrícia Katanazaka and the other girls, who were already on the beach when he arrived with his friends. He was rich.

On his way back from the beach, Sparrow got off on Gabinal Road with the others who lived in The Blocks, while most of the Boys continued on the bus. They arrived in The Blocks singing rock 'n' roll. Sparrow said he wasn't going to bed. He was going to get some more papers of coke so he could get fucked up, but first he was going to swing by old Aunt Vincentina's building. He knew that every Saturday she served a delicious meal, always accompanied by percussion and samba. He'd eat as much as he could, then snort some coke for a pick-me-up.

'Wanna come?' asked Sparrow.

'Yeah!' answered Leonardo and Rocket almost simultaneously. Tiny, Slick, Bicky and Russian Mouse were eating lunch with their .38s in their waistbands. They spoke with their mouths full, letting bits of food covered in saliva fall from their mouths in their haste, and discussed the beating they were going to have to give Hit-and-Miss, because it was the third time someone had accused him of rape since he'd been released from prison. OK, so he was a veteran among the gangsters, but he couldn't go around stirring up trouble in the area and terrorizing the residents, and if they didn't do something about it, the workers and potheads would think less of them.

'Leave him to me! Let's you and I go see him and if he gets smart on us we'll go ahead and take him out!' Sparrow told Tiny when he arrived.

Then he shook hands with each of his friends and hugged Tiny.

Sparrow ate two platefuls of cow-heel stew and snorted five papers of coke. Tiny snorted five papers too, and then they left. Rocket and Leonardo went with them as far as the bridge over the right branch of the river, then said good-bye. Sparrow said he'd be at Katanazaka's bar that night. They wound through the alleys at a fast pace, guns in their hands, with the solemnity of gangsters at work. They crossed the main streets quickly and slowed down in the alleys. In one alley, seeing the guns, a woman quickened her step and fell. Tiny laughed his quick, shrill little laugh, which alerted Sparrow, who knew that laugh well. He immediately said:

'I said I was gonna kill him if he got smart on us, but I was just kiddin', man.'

Tiny didn't answer and, seeing an acquaintance, arrogantly asked:

'Seen Hit-and-Miss?'

'He's over in Fifteen, havin' a beer.'

When Hit-and-Miss saw the two of them holding guns at the end of the square in Block Fifteen, he tried to slip away. He knew they were there because of the rapes he'd committed.

In the most recent one, even before he'd grabbed the fifteen-year-old girl near the old cinema, covered her mouth, dragged her behind the State Housing Company building, pulled her panties off from under her skirt and rammed his swollen penis into her anus, it had occurred to him that Tiny would get involved in this one, but he also figured that if he frightened the girl she wouldn't snitch. He threatened to kill her if she opened her mouth. As soon as he'd moved away, however, the girl began to scream:

'Pervert! Pervert!'

The news spread quickly, in spite of the fact that it was after midnight.

'Hold it! Hold it!' shouted Tiny when he caught sight of Hit-and-Miss, who'd never had sex with a consenting woman. While he was in prison he'd had sex with two homosexuals, and had once raped a cellmate.

'Is it true you raped a girl?' Sparrow asked firmly.

'Yeah, I banged her. OK? But she was hangin' around in a really short dress in the middle of the night and she came on to me, then changed her mind at the last minute, know what I mean, pal?'

'What's all this "pal" crap? We friends or something? And this story about her changin' her mind is bullshit. You're full of shit! No girl's gonna screw you with that ape face. Get your ass over here, 'cause I'm gonna give you an ass-kicking to remember the next time you wanna force a girl to have sex with you.'

'You guys don't let go of your guns, but I could crush you both with my hands.'

Sparrow handed his gun to Tiny and danced about in front of Hit-and-Miss, who followed suit. Sparrow gave him a thrashing and then, tired of hitting him with his fists, grabbed a pool cue and brought it down on the enemy's head. He then allowed him to flee the fight, his hand pressed to the deepest part of the wound.

'What's up, man? All spiffed up like a rich kid from the South Zone! Where you off to?' asked Daniel.

'The damn bar didn't work out. My mom's been sayin' she doesn't want to support a couch potato and I don't like bein' broke either, know what I mean, man? I'm headin' over to Macro to see if I can hustle up some work. I worked my ass off in that damn bar . . .'

'You gonna work in a supermarket, you nut? Fuck! That takes guts! But you gotta wear something square, man! You won't get anywhere in that playboy outfit.'

'Good point!' said Rocket.

'How come the bar went under?'

'Credit, man, too much credit, know what I'm sayin'? I told 'im: "Look man, you're sellin' too much on credit." And he said: "Don't worry, I've got things under control!" And look what happened. Katanazaka's really dumb, you know. Thinks he's always right . . . Hey, I'm goin' home to get changed, then I'm gonna see if I can snag this job, OK?'

'Good luck!'

One Wednesday night, Mango told his friends he was going to do a couple of houses with two buddies, Tião and Coca-Cola. He'd met them during the five days he spent in the lockup at the Drug Division after he was caught in the city center with two bundles of dope in his shorts. The policemen had thought it a good idea to leave him in the slammer for a few days, to see if he'd get his act together. The police usually treated white stoners like this. Even in the *favelas*, whites who weren't from the North enjoyed certain privileges when caught smoking marijuana. Most of the time the police didn't even arrest them. They just gave them a warning, then let them go. Because of this immunity, Mango always said that blacks were dopeheads, and he was just a user.

His life of crime began precisely when he met the two gangsters in jail. Before he was released, they asked him several favors which included going to a hiding place to recover four hundred thousand cruzeiros from a holdup they'd done, and taking it to them a little bit at a time in visits to Section B of Frei Caneca Prison, where they were going to do time. After a month, Mango made friends with other members of the dominant criminal organization in some of Rio's prisons. Not even Mango himself knew why he was so fascinated when he talked with the gangsters and listened to their stories of bravado, murders, robberies and holdups. His passion for crime grew even stronger when one of the inmates in Section B asked him to manage a den in the Quitungo housing project, a position that gave him power.

Within the *favela* itself, he started doing business with the guys from Tiny's gang; he bought and sold stolen goods and brought in loads of weed, coke, revolvers and ammunition.

On one occasion, before he started managing the den in Quitungo and dealing in guns and drugs, he'd had a serious run-in with Tiny, to whom he'd sold a stolen motor scooter with forged documents saying it was his. Tiny gave it to the son of one of the cool guys as a present, but two days later he swore aloud that he'd kill Mango the first chance he got because the police had arrested his friend's son for theft and fraud in Barra da Tijuca. If it hadn't been for Orange, Jackfruit and Acerola, Tiny would have already killed him.

When he became a fully-fledged gangster and supplier of drugs, revolvers and ammunition, he regained Tiny's respect. He'd heard of the organization and occasionally asked him how it all worked.

On one of his visits, Mango heard from Tião himself that he and Coca-Cola were about to get out of prison. Tião asked Mango to find them a nice hideaway, set aside some pistols and sell all the revolvers so that when they got out they could rob some houses and give the den a boost. Business wasn't going so well, due to a lack of stock.

By that Wednesday, there was only one revolver left to sell. Mango told everyone that he had a revolver going cheap, since revolvers were no longer of interest to Tiny, who now only bought pistols.

'Gimme a look at the piece then,' said a thief near Batman's Bar who made his living holding up buses and mugging people.

Something in the thief's gaze told Mango that he wanted to steal the revolver, and his mistrust was spot-on.

'Hey, playboy, this piece's mine!' he said without checking the weapon.

'Yours!?' said Mango, exaggerating an ironic calm.

'You're a playboy, man! Your dad's got money! You look smart, you can get a job anywhere you want, you don't need money . . . It's mine! The piece's mine!' he finished, not knowing that Mango was now a much more dangerous criminal than he was.

'OK then, keep it, but you know what?' said Mango. 'You're takin' it to hell, you fuckin' prick!' he said, pulling a 7.65 mm pistol from the back of his waistband.

It was only then that the thief realized the revolver wasn't loaded. He suddenly fell to his knees and begged Mango for God's sake not to shoot.

'Hit the ground!'

Acerola and Orange came over when they heard Mango's voice in Batman's Bar. Even after they'd heard their friend's story, they tried to get him to spare the thief, and eventually managed to convince him.

'But get out of the *favela* today, or you're dead!'

The three left together and spent the night at Mango's house snorting coke and drinking whisky. At first Acerola said he didn't want any coke, but after Mango said: 'Just once won't hurt,' he decided to keep his friends company.

They talked about crime, soccer and women. Only in the morning did Mango tell them that he and his partners were going to do a good joint that afternoon. They'd rustled up some doctors' clothes, 007 briefcases, sunglasses and prescription glasses, watches and new shoes to make them inconspicuous: Tião and Coca-Cola were white and tall like him.

'C'mon, man, don't get involved, you don't need it, your dad's a lieutenant . . . You should ask him for help, you know. Go back to school . . .' Acerola advised him.

Mango shook his head, said he couldn't hack studying anymore, and even if he did study, he'd never be as rich as he wanted to be. He said he'd only be a gangster for a while. He'd hustle some more dough, add it to what he'd already saved and buy a farm in the farthest-flung corner of the country. He might even go to Paraguay and take up beekeeping, a dream he'd had ever since he'd heard his science teacher talking about it.

Acerola and Orange said good-bye and went their separate ways, each thinking up excuses to tell their parents when they got home. Mango showered, had another shot of whisky, heard someone clapping outside and picked up his pistol. Peering through the hole he'd made so he could look out into his front yard without being seen himself, he saw his partners and shouted that the gate was open. They went over their plan, had a nap—his partners had also stayed up all night—then headed off after dinner.

Tiny's gang appeared on the street around midday, the waking hour for gangsters according to the teachings of Zeca Composer, a composer for the local samba school. One of his sambas went:

> As long as there are suckers in the world,
> gangsters will wake up at midday.

They all headed for Almeida's house. Almeida, one of the cool guys, had promised to prepare a nice lunch for Tiny and his gang.

'Cock-a-doodle-doo?' went Almeida's rooster, suspiciously eyeing Tiny, who'd asked Otávio to buy twenty pounds of potatoes and five chickens to put toward the lunch.

Otávio sped off. He couldn't wait for the lunch that everyone had talked about so much all week.

Before the sun had even risen, the rooster, having heard so much talk on the subject of his existence, cunningly pecked at the string that tied him to a bamboo stake in the ground until it was weak enough to break at the slightest tug. He was going to run away, but only after Almeida had thrown him the corn kernels he so liked, which he still hadn't done.

Almeida's rooster didn't actually understand things all that well—he thought like a rooster—but when he saw that bunch of niggers with their mouths full of teeth, drinking beer, glancing at him out of the corners of their eyes, smoking dope and saying they weren't touching coke so as not to lose their appetites, he didn't sing as he usually did. He kept to himself, waiting for his meal.

Otávio arrived by taxi with the five hens rolled up in newspaper, their feet tied together. Marcelo helped the boy take the hens into the kitchen. Tiny told them to throw them into the yard so the rooster could bang them and die happy. He believed this would make the meat tenderer and more tasty. Almeida's wife said the rooster should be the first to go into the pot, as it would take longer to cook. Forgetting everything, the rooster jumped on a hen, then quickly went after another one, and everyone clapped while Almeida waited, holding an enormous knife. The rooster didn't give the chickens a chance. Although he was certain that everything had to do with him being cooked, he thought he was going to die, and then again he didn't. Rooster logic. But when, out of the corner of his eye, he saw the knife in the hand of the one he'd always believed to be his friend, he realized that everyone around him was conspiring toward his death. On his first try he freed himself from the string, which had grown weaker as he was servicing the hens, dodged between the guests and took off running through the alleys.

'Grab 'im, grab 'im!' cried Tiny.

The gang took off after the rooster, but *favela* roosters are wild as hell. He wound in and out of alleys, as swift as a panther, dodged back and forth, forth and back, ran crouching so he wouldn't be seen from afar, only stuck half his head around corners to see if the coast was clear. From time to time he flew some fifteen to twenty feet, and ran desperately toward the New Blocks, making it difficult to catch him. The gang laughed their heads off as they chased their lunch. Turning into an alley, Tiny bumped into a man selling pots and pans and fell to the ground with him. He leaped up, told the guy to fuck off and shouted:

'Shoot the rooster!'

And the shooting began.

The rooster flew over the left branch of the river with bullets whistling past his ears and tearing up the ground, and went between Buildings Seven and Eight. By making short flights, he could climb The Hill or head for the square in The Blocks. He chose the latter. Never had so many shots been heard in The Blocks. Even those who always peered out of the window during shoot-outs to have a quick gawk didn't dare this time, for fear of stray bullets.

The gang did its best to catch the rooster. Whoever killed it would be more respected by Tiny, who was still in the alley beating the pots and pans seller with the butt of his gun so he'd never bump into him or swear back at him again.

At that moment Slick was strolling toward The Blocks, but when he heard the shots, he did an about-face and hid, thinking it was the police.

The rooster ran into the middle of a grove of guava trees, a place even the sunlight didn't really penetrate, looking for a perfect hiding place, but Tiny's gang plunged in after him, firing at random. Unable to fly, he panicked, ran even faster over that rough terrain and hurt himself, but had no time to feel pain. After a few minutes, the shots ceased. He hid under some dry leaves and waited for his hunters to give up trying to catch him.

After an hour the rooster came out of hiding, headed for the grounds of an abandoned mansion, ran to the other side, came out on Edgar Werneck Avenue and disappeared forever.

Back at Almeida's house, everyone was talking about the rooster's cunning. They laughed, smoked joints and drank beer.

'It was for the best, because rooster can be a bit tough,' said Almeida's wife.

Half an hour later there was a cry from Otávio:

'Bread for sale! Bread for sale!'

Five policemen were approaching, holding guns. 'Bread for sale' was their warning for when the police showed up. The gang was about to make a run for it when Tiny said:

'No one run! Guns cocked. If I shoot everyone shoots, but to kill, to kill . . .'

The gang stood up. There were more than thirty men holding .38s and 9 mm and 7.65 mm pistols. Faced with this offence Sergeant Linivaldo squinted. Both he and the other policemen immediately understood that to tell them they were under arrest would be to sign their own death warrants. They pretended nothing had happened and sidled off as if they hadn't seen a thing.

On their way back to the police station, Sergeant Linivaldo told his men they'd have to keep working as they had been: without going out on the beat. They didn't have the men or the weapons to arrest the gangsters and, since there hadn't been any complaints of muggings, theft or rape, they had no reason to worry.

Three o'clock, an extremely blue sky and stifling heat in the city of Rio de Janeiro. Mango, Coca-Cola and Tião went into the building dressed as doctors, wearing sunglasses, prescription glasses around their necks, fancy wristwatches and well-ironed clothes. They greeted the doorman and the elevator operator, and went to the top floor, the thirteenth, because both the gold dealer and the exchange bureau were there.

The gold dealer had a bulletproof glass door through which the whole inside corridor was visible. One of the security guards saw the three slowly approaching. Before any gesture from the trio, the door was opened.

'Good afternoon, sirs,' said the guard to the three.

Inside the room, there was only one other security guard, an employee and the owner of the establishment. Coca-Cola asked how much they were paying per gram. On hearing the answer, he

commented that the price was very low. He pretended to be thinking about it and coughed three times. Mango and Tião immediately drew their guns and said it was a stickup.

After making the owner open the safe, they tied everyone up with
telephone cord and hit them all over the head three times with the
butts of their guns.

Everything went off without a hitch at the exchange bureau too.

'Let's go!' said Mango in the corridor.

'No way—now that we're here, we might as well do the rest.'

They held up offices and businesses all the way down to the
sixth floor, where Mango looked out of the window and saw several police cars in front of the building and a crowd gathered on
the sidewalk.

The police had been called by the exchange bureau's office boy,
who'd arrived after the robbery.

Nervously, they checked whether it was possible to jump over
onto the neighboring buildings, but then decided to stick with their
plan. They ran down to the second floor and took the elevator,
where they straightened themselves up, mopped their sweat with
a hand towel they'd stolen from the bathroom of the last shop
they'd held up, and walked out. Coca-Cola asked a police officer
what was going on.

'The building's being robbed, sir! Where are you comin' from?'

'From the second floor . . . I didn't see anything strange.'

Three months later, Mango was back in the *favela*. Well dressed, a
new car in his name, documents to show he was self-employed, a
thick gold chain around his neck, two pistols. He'd become the
official driver for one of the leaders of the organization as well as a
cocaine distributor in the *favela* around Leopoldina.

'You know them bank robberies that happened all at once?'

'Yeah.'

'I did three, man! We called it Operation Pinpoint,' bragged
Mango to Jackfruit, Orange and Acerola. 'If you want a bump, if

you wanna smoke, go over to Fogueteiro and I'll fix you up with whatever you want,' he went on.

They hung around talking until around midday, when Mango went to Aristóteles' house. He'd known Aristóteles since he was a child, but they'd only become friends when they were older. They'd become such good friends that Mango was like one of the family; so much so that ever since he'd been disowned by his own family, he ate at his friend's house every day, slept there, borrowed his car and took various other liberties that only the best of friends can take. Aristóteles welcomed him with the same smile as always, went to buy beer and told his wife to serve dinner.

That night, the two of them snorted cocaine on the slopes of the *favela* with some friends, and when they were alone, completely drunk, Aristóteles looked Mango straight in the eye and said:

'Man, I gotta talk to you about somethin' serious, OK? Look, I'm unemployed and the wife needs to have an operation on a lump they've found in her stomach. She doesn't wanna have it done through the public system 'cause you know what it's like, don't ya?'

'You need some money?'

'No! I want you to hustle me up some stuff to sell on the quiet, know what I'm sayin'? I don't wanna sell my car and I wanna fix up the house a bit. I need to make some good money. I've got these pals over in Vila Sapê. If you get me the stuff, I'll sell it really fast.'

'Look, I can do business with you, but you gotta wise up—we can't afford to have any fuckups.'

'What day?'

'I'll give you an answer next week.'

Coca-Cola did everything he could to stop Mango from giving his friend the five pounds of weed to resell, but in the face of so much insistence, he gave him the green light to sell two and a half pounds, with a long list of conditions and warnings.

Aristóteles sold everything, earning enough credit to get another seven and a half pounds, which he also sold quickly.

After a few months, he was receiving fifteen pounds of dope a week. Even when he hadn't sold the last batch, he had enough money to pay up front with the cash earned selling pot to his friends and small dens in neighboring areas. His wife was operated on in a clinic for the rich; he built extensions to his house, bought a new car, a motor scooter for his son, and beers for the cool guys. After a time, he started pissing away money and then, one awful day, he received some old weed; because it was old, it was weak. He managed to resell it, but the guys who smoked it didn't feel a thing.

'This fuckin' grass only makes you hungry, thirsty and sleepy. You couldn't get stoned on it even if you smoked five big ones,' they said.

When Aristóteles had tracked down Mango near Batman's Bar, he complained about the quality of the weed. His friend told him that that's how things were between crops, and that he had to keep selling, especially now that Tião had been arrested.

'Bro, the pigs are chargin' a fortune to let the guy go. I'm gonna have to give his wife something today to take down to the station so he won't have to sign a confession. And next week we'll have to send more so they'll let him go, otherwise he'll be charged and slapped in the slammer. I wasn't even comin' down here today 'cause I've got tons of problems to sort out, but I wanted to ask you to lend us some dough, know what I'm sayin'? I'll pay you back on the tenth.'

'How much?'

'Fifty thousand.'

'Fuck! I've got a shitload of bills to pay. I don't reckon I'll be able to . . .'

'See! When you were up shit creek, we gave you a hand, but now that we're a bit tight, this is how you return the favor.'

'OK, OK! I'll help you.'

That same day, the owner of the den in Vila Sapê sent an errand boy for Aristóteles.

'Hey, man, the weed you sold us was really weak shit. I'm gonna have to get rid of a shitload of the stuff so I don't run the risk of gettin' caught for nothin'. Know what I'm sayin'? But hey—think you can get us some good shit so we can get things movin' again?'

'No problem!'

'Don't get me wrong, man. And don't tell your pals I'm bein' difficult. I'm askin' you to do me this favor, 'cause I'm really broke, OK?' said the Vila Sapê den owner, thinking Aristóteles was involved with big-time dealers.

Two weeks later Tião was back from the lockup. It was time to get finances back in order even though they only had stale weed to sell.

Aristóteles believed that the only thing he could do to be given good weed on Thursday afternoon was to think positively. It was the only way it would sell and the only thing he could do to get out of that situation. He should have taken his wife's advice: pay for everything up front and stop selling that damn weed. He'd been stupid, really stupid. The reason he'd bought things in installments was so he'd always have money in his pocket and could give everyone freebies. Now he was kicking himself.

Like Mango, both Coca-Cola and Tião believed Aristóteles had money stashed away; all his worrying was just greed, money-grubbing. In spite of their suspicion, they didn't hesitate to give their bad shit on consignment to Aristóteles, who claimed to be broke.

But when he smelled the dope, the owner of the den in Vila Sapê said he wouldn't be taking it. He rolled a joint, took a toke, and repeated that he wasn't going to buy it.

In spite of his problems, Aristóteles found a way to pay his friend back. Thinking he was in the clear, he got sloshed, then bought and snorted an excessive amount of coke even before paying his outstanding bills. He'd had enough money left over to clear his past debts and, God willing, he'd rustle up the money to pay off the following months' debts too. He also believed he could hold off paying for the consignment of weed. But Mango was tough on him.

'Look pal, the guys want the money by Saturday, OK? The guys've gotta help in a breakout. And we've gotta buy shit too, so think of somethin'.'

At around eleven o'clock on Saturday, Mango clapped his hands at Aristóteles' front gate. Aristóteles hid and told his wife to say he'd gone out early. Mango thought the wife was acting strange and left feeling suspicious. He stopped at Batman's Bar, where he asked everyone who passed if they'd seen his friend. He went to his girlfriend's house, had dinner and slept until six o'clock in the evening, when he decided to go to his friend's house again.

'You came earlier, didn't you?'

'Yeah . . .'

'I went over to Vila Sapê to try and scare up some money, but the guys there didn't have any.'

'But is our deal still on?'

'Fuck, man! I'm really broke . . .'

Mango stood there for a while in silence, ran his hand over his head and said:

'Look, I'll try and talk to the guys, OK, but keep tryin' to get it together.'

'You goin' over to Mangueira?'

'No, I'm goin' to Fogueteiro, 'cause I've gotta pick up some money there. But I bet the guys'll be there.'

'Hey, put in a good word for me, man!'

'I will, don't worry.'

When Mango got to Fogueteiro, an errand boy told him that both Tião and Coca-Cola were in Morro do Alemão in a meeting that had been hastily called by the leaders of the organization. Mango turned around and headed for Morro do Alemão. He wanted to know what was going on. He liked hanging around the big bosses; he hoped to throw in some ideas, get in good with them.

'Where's the money?' asked Coca-Cola as soon as Mango arrived, looking concerned.

'The guy's broke. He didn't manage to sell . . .' argued Mango.

'Kill 'im, kill 'im!' ordered one of the leaders.

Mango didn't have to go to his friend's house, because he found him in Main Square.

'Hey, the guys wanna have a talk with you, OK?'

'OK, I'll get over to Fogueteiro tomorrow . . .'

'It's gotta be now, man. Go get your car. I'll wait for you here.'

Mango drove the car in silence, his friend next to him making small talk, but after a while he also fell silent. Mango thought about Aristóteles' family—after killing him he wouldn't be able to look any of his relatives in the eye. He remembered the days when they spent the afternoons together listening to rock 'n' roll, drinking wine and smoking pot, the mornings on the beach, the dances, the drag races up in Alto da Boa Vista. He remembered the times Aristóteles had mooned someone out of the car window and told him to beep the horn, Aristóteles imitating Raul Seixas singing, certain that the Devil was the father of rock 'n' roll. He was going to kill his friend, but far from there and without anyone knowing about it.

The night was hot and Mango drove fast. When they passed through Mato Alto, a secluded place, he thought about stopping the car, ordering his friend out and shooting him in the back, but he decided to take him to Morro do Alemão, believing that with some persuasion the leaders might spare him. Cautiously, Mango started to talk again, secretly hoping the car could be sold to pay off the debt.

Mango told Aristóteles to wait for him on a corner, and climbed another five hundred yards to the shack where the leaders were still gathered.

'Man, the guy's saying he borrowed fifty thousand from him and paid it back on the date they'd agreed. When the shit was good he sold a shitload of it, so he was able to put something away, know what I'm sayin'? So look: get rid of him . . . No one told you to bring him here. Get out of here and get rid of him . . . We gotta send money for the guy's breakout, you know? This dickhead takes the dope then says he's broke—so get rid of him!'

Mango wanted to argue more on his friend's behalf, but he was afraid. After all, the man talking was one of the top leaders in the organization. He really needed to show them he could be cruel; he couldn't say no. He left with his gun in the back of his waistband.

'We've gotta go over to Fogueteiro, 'cause the guys headed over there.'

While he drove, Mango thought about where to kill his friend and regretted not having taken him out in Mato Alto. It suddenly occurred to him to kill him right then and there, to put an end to his suffering. He stopped the car before they got to Irajá.

'Get out!' he said, pointing his gun at him.

'What's goin' on, man? We're friends! You lost it?!'

From inside the car he fired twice into Aristóteles' incredulous chest, put the car into gear and took off. He drove for a few minutes, returned to the place where his friend's body lay bleeding and put him in the trunk. He was sweaty, cold, and thought that if he got help in time he'd be able to save him. He stopped the car, checked to see if his friend's heart was still beating but couldn't tell if he was still alive. He decided to leave the body right there and started pulling it out of the trunk again, then gave up and got in the car. He didn't have a clue where he was, numbness paralyzed his soul, his heart beat wildly. He pressed his hand to his chest, took a deep breath and drove through the heat of the night.

In the streets, people were sitting at the gates to their houses, children were playing dodgeball, teenagers were getting ready for potluck parties, bars were full. Mango only saw the road and didn't notice the traffic signals. Then it occurred to him to stop in front of a clinic, leave the body and take off. He shook, stepped on the accelerator of the Opala, remembered Aristóteles over in the abandoned mansion trying to save a girl from drowning in the pool. He had a good heart, and he didn't deserve to die like that. He heard a police siren behind him and went even faster. He crossed over onto the wrong side of the road, drove on the sidewalk, and regretted not having got rid of the body sooner. He went over the Madureira viaduct, spun the car around underneath and headed for Cascadura. Looking in the rearview mirror, he saw he was no longer being followed and slowed down, although he continued running traffic lights for another ten minutes. He drove up Grajaú Range, stopped the car halfway up, threw the body into the forest and went back to the *favela*, his thoughts scrambled.

'What's up, Old Pal? Seen Orange around?' asked Mango near Batman's Bar.

'I've been here for ages and I haven't seen him.'

Mango decided to go to his friend's house.

'Hey, Orange . . .'

When Orange shouted that he was coming, Mango opened the gate and the door and, without a word, hugged him, sobbing, his body still shaking.

'What's going on?'

Mango couldn't speak: he just sobbed. Orange sat him down on the sofa and fixed him a glass of sugar water. Mango drank it all slowly, then confessed:

'Aristóteles, Aristóteles—I got rid of Aristóteles!'

There was a mixture of disgust and pity in Orange's eyes.

'He told me he owed you money.'

'Not me . . . He owed the organization, know what I mean? I had to get rid of him, because it was me that got him in with the guys, but I didn't want to kill him . . .'

Orange turned his back on his friend. Silence invaded the room. He stared into the street trying to understand the absurdity of the situation. His mother came through the gate.

'My mom!'

Mango dried his eyes, pushed the butt of his pistol a little farther into his shorts and greeted his friend's mother. She looked at him suspiciously and sniffed the air to see if the two of them had been smoking marijuana.

Mango said good-bye to his friend and headed for Fogueteiro, where he smoked five joints, drank a bottle of whisky, vomited, washed his mouth out and slept only a little, because he dreamed horrible things and woke up shouting, frightening the neighbors. When he realized he'd been dreaming, he sat up in bed. And there he stayed until dawn.

'It's like this: set up a den there. OK? Put some weed and coke Up Top 'cause I'm sayin' so, right? Tiny and Slick had no right to take your den Down Below! Go ahead and get it up and runnin'! If anyone tries to give you a hard time, talk to me and I'll stick a bullet in their ass!' Sparrow told Carrots, when he ran into him in the Rec, downcast, asking a barfly for a cigarette. It was a year after he'd packaged drugs for the first time with the Boys.

'Want some money?' continued Sparrow. 'Hey, take this! And when you're back on your feet again you can pay me back, OK man? I'm sayin' it's OK!'

With a laconic smile, Sparrow watched Carrots leave. He told Breno what a nice guy Carrots was, and said Tiny and Slick had 'distreated' him. Sparrow went on his way after Carrots had turned the corner. He was going to the Katanazaka household to eat gnocchi, for which he'd bought the ingredients.

When he arrived, he asked Álvaro Katanazaka where the rest of their friends were; he and the Boys had become inseparable over the last few months. They'd spend three days in a row together snorting coke and camping out in towns along the Green Coast until they tired of camping. They went to the beach, disco and cinema together and visited the South Zone of Rio from time to time. Some of the Boys had started carrying weed and coke from The Blocks to the den Up Top and vice versa, and held Sparrow's gun when he was out of it. Sparrow got them to run errands for him as a favor, claiming that because they were white the police would never stop them. The more daring Boys became familiar with the daily chores of the gangsters and even shot rivals and troublemakers—as the playboy dealer called them—in the feet. They walked with a swagger, like gangsters. Sir Paulo Carneiro, who hung around with Sparrow the most, had become his partner in games of cards and prided himself on having learned all the tricks of the game in just one lesson from Russian Mouse, who, along with Bicky and Tim, had also started hanging around with the Boys, dressing like them and imitating their style. Even Tiny started going to the dances with them. Sparrow had managed to bring together the Boys and the gang from The Blocks.

Business in the dens grew steadily, and the use of cocaine increased by the day. Craving the drug, cokeheads from the *favela* and elsewhere showed up at the den with chains, rings, bracelets, TV sets, watches, revolvers, electric mixers, blenders and innumerable other household appliances to exchange for cocaine. The intersection of different worlds made it possible to trade anything. Tiny had bought a chest for the gold pieces that found their way into his hands at a low price, as the thieves from the Alley only sold their stolen goods to him now. Each day someone new joined his gang, not for money—because the only ones on salaries were himself, Sparrow, Carlos Roberto and his three assistants—but for fear of him and his men, and in order to gain respect and be able to pick on anyone they didn't like the look of. Even the Boys started picking on whoever they wanted. They were Sparrow's friends and, as such, considered themselves Tiny's friends too. They had influence. Up Top, the abuse became more frequent when Tiny decided he didn't like anyone who hadn't come from Macedo Sobrinho. He only liked people from the old days, the cool guys.

Slick had been locked up for six months. Even when he was being beaten up by five policemen at the Thirty-Second District Police Station, he didn't confess to the crimes the police wanted him to. While he was being beaten, he said he'd only sign a confession in the presence of a lawyer, because he knew that as soon as his brother found out he'd been arrested he'd immediately hire one to defend him. And that's what happened. The lawyer prevented the police from committing the crime of making him pay for offenses he hadn't committed. They charged him with possession of a firearm, his only offense. Tried and found guilty, he was to serve his sentence in Milton Dias Moreira Prison.

Sparrow quickly devoured the gnocchi so he could go and buy some fabric with the Boys; he'd decided that the whole group should dress alike. He was, in fact, trying to look more and more like the Boys. They were going to Botafogo to buy the fabric—only the poor shopped in the city center. After their shopping they were going to see a film in Copacabana and have dinner at a restaurant in Gávea, where they'd have a laugh and plan a camping excursion or a night at Dancin' Days, because the big thing now was discos. The rock 'n' roll dances were already on their last legs. The media was investing in this new trend and everyone had to follow it—otherwise they'd be left out, uncool, tacky, square, and any other adjective of the genre.

They ate dinner and had Kibon ice cream mixed with orange-flavored Fanta for dessert, which was all the rage. It couldn't be any other brand of ice cream—only Kibon. The only thing that remained in their minds of Raul Seixas was the concept of an alternative society, the utopia amidst so much nonsense that he represented. It was Sparrow's dream to buy a plot of land with running water, good soil for planting and little wooden houses for him and the Boys to live in. That's what he had to do in order to live among people whose faces glowed because they didn't live side by side with death. They never thought about killing anyone, although they liked pot as much as he did. That was his dream—to find himself a beautiful girl, live among beautiful people and disco-dance his days away without a worry in the world. No more toothless niggers with angry faces.

Sparrow looked at Russian Mouse with a certain disdain when he said he wanted to go to Botafogo with the Boys. But he gave it some thought because he was also white and fair-haired. He just didn't have the physique, but he'd get there if he started working out and bodysurfing. Russian Mouse's vocabulary wasn't promising (he used a lot of slang and too many swear words), but that didn't matter much, because neither was Sparrow's own. They left Katanazaka's place soberly, had a smoke in a quiet alley and took off for Botafogo on a high they wouldn't have been able to explain.

Tiny wanted to throw a much bigger party than any of those thrown by the numbers man, China White-Locks, around his numbers locations in São Carlos and Tijuca. He sent for dozens of presents, expensive desserts and hundreds of crates of soft drinks to make the kids happy. The numbers men had in fact been the first to invest heavily in the population of neighboring areas, but now that trafficking had fully taken root in the *favelas* of the Rio Metropolitan Area and the Baixada Fluminense region, the dealers also decided it was a good idea to invest in the areas they operated in. By pleasing the children, they not only ensured good relations with Saint Cosmas, Do Um and Saint Damian, but also with the locals, who did them favors and warned them when the police were around.

All of the desserts were first-class: the coconut sweets, for example, were made by Lúcia, an old black woman who cooked like no one on earth. Sparrow thought it would be a good idea to throw money into the crowd, on the condition that no grownups mingled with the kids. If they did, they'd get a bullet in the ass.

On September 27th, Tiny and Sparrow won the admiration of the locals for the party they threw in the square of The Blocks. They looked up to Tiny and Sparrow, flattered that they'd remembered the day of Saints Cosmas and Damian with festivities appropriate to the occasion. They had made the children happy.

Over the next few days, Tiny and Sparrow began to get the impression that the residents looked at them with gratitude, because the benefits the duo had brought to the *favela* were considerable; they'd put an end to theft, muggings and rapes, and were now handing out sweets. Spent-ballooning was allowed, as a way of punishing the drunks. Many barflies started drinking less, much to the delight of their wives.

The composer Big Voice wanted to meet Tiny and Sparrow. He'd heard of the gangsters through Zeca Composer. He knew that if he invited the two of them, many people from the *favela* would go to Portela Samba School to cheer for his samba, and this might be what he needed to become champion.

Zeca Composer wouldn't be competing for best samba that year, and was giving full support to Big Voice and Little Bird's samba for Portela. If Big Voice won, the record he was going to launch in the middle of the year was bound to be a success, and Zeca had already been promised two tracks. Zeca sent an errand boy to The Blocks to tell Sparrow and Tiny that a friend wanted to meet them.

It was no accident that he'd mentioned Sparrow and Tiny to Big Voice. The gangsters were always singing his songs and had all his records. He was careful to tell the errand boy not to mention the singer, as he wanted to give them a surprise.

It was a Saturday morning and Tiny picked up Sparrow to go to their friend's house. Zeca Composer's wife Penha would no doubt serve oxtail stew—it was her specialty. Tiny held a great deal of respect for Composer who, in addition to writing music, also painted, drew and conceptualized the school's parades. It was he who'd given him shelter in São Carlos when he was still a boy. He'd introduced him to his friends and now got him in to watch rehearsals without paying. He didn't like it when he started handing out advice, but apart from that, Composer was a good guy. He always had his wife prepare top-quality grub for his friends, and took him to the other samba schools' rehearsals and the bars where he played live.

'Big Voooice! Wow! Fuck me dead!' exclaimed Tiny when he saw the musician.

Big Voice laughed at his enthusiasm, hugged him as if he were an old friend and said:

'Composer tells me good things about you . . . I came here especially to meet you.'

'D'you like gettin' high?'

'Well, now that you mention it . . .'

'Pot, coke, a bit of everything? Hey, Composer, tell somebody to go fetch a pile of weed and coke for our friend here. Hey, this is Sparrow, he's a good guy! He's my business partner . . . Shake the man's hand, Sparrow! See our reputation? . . . This is Big Voice, man!' he said.

'Here's the story: Composer tells me everyone likes you guys, right? And Portela's picked up one of our sambas . . . The samba's good. Me and Little Bird are singin' it . . . I was wonderin' if you guys could invite a nice crowd to get behind us, know what I'm sayin'?'

'It's a deal! And don't worry, everything'll be fine.'

'I've already arranged with Composer to send three buses over, OK? There'll be tickets for everyone . . .'

'Sing us the samba, sing us the samba . . .'

They hung around talking while Penha cooked stewed tripe, her other specialty. Tiny got a boy to fetch some musicians so Big Voice could sing his hits. It was a happy day with Big Voice's gravelly voice singing sambas of love, accompanied by those present, who knew his songs by heart.

The buses arrived Up Top at around 10 P.M. on a suffocatingly hot Saturday, and stopped near Composer's house. Afraid of disappointing Big Voice, Tiny sent the gang out early to spread word in every corner of the *favela* that he was inviting everyone to go watch Portela, and those who weren't going would have him to deal with. Then he invited everyone he bumped into. His strategy got out of hand. Tiny himself had to get off the first bus, where the gangsters, the Boys and the cool guys were, to stop people destroying the other two buses. He punched them in the face, shot them in the foot and kicked them in the ass, especially the guys from Up Top.

The buses didn't leave until midnight, with red-hot samba, lit joints and lines of coke on the backs of wallets. At Portela, Tiny only paid for what he ordered. He'd already provided weed and coke and wasn't going to spend any more money. Russian Mouse and Bicky, who'd pulled off a good job in Seca Square, were the ones who ordered beer and whisky for their friends and the cool guys.

It wasn't for lack of supporters that Big Voice and Little Bird's samba didn't win, because in addition to the supporters from the *favela*, the composer had others who'd attended every day of the competition to get Portela's rehearsal hall buzzing when Big Voice's samba was played.

'OK, I know I was cheated, but thanks for the help,' Big Voice said to Tiny when the final results came out.

'You headin' Up Top?'

'Yeah.'

'Do us a favor and take this stuff over to Teresa—these deadbeats here are all sleepin'. And if you see Sparrow there, tell him to get over here,' said Tiny.

Against his will, Lourival took the supermarket bag full of bundles of pot, hung it on the handlebars of his bicycle and pedaled off. Tiny watched the boy leave and then, at the top of his lungs, told him to keep five bundles for himself. Lourival gave him the thumbs-up and headed through the main streets with the vague certainty that the police wouldn't stop him; this danger only existed in the vicinity of the den. He prayed for everything to work out. He'd get in good with Tiny and Sparrow.

Pretending to be calm, he rode slowly down Edgar Werneck Avenue. He turned into one of the main streets without any problems, but when he got to Middle Street, he almost flew into a panic when he saw the police officers Lincoln and Monster. He was now too close to them to turn around and the only thing he could do was to keep going as if everything was normal. It was probably even better to pass by as closely as possible, to show that he was cool. This occurred to him in a matter of seconds. He pedaled quickly when he felt that the policemen were far enough away, took the first alley after the Bonfim, crossed the square in Block Fifteen breathing a sigh of relief, turned into another alley pedaling more slowly and reached The Sludge.

'What's up, Teresa!?'

The old woman looked through a peephole and turned to Sparrow, who was counting money in one of the bedrooms: 'It's one of them playboys you hang around with.'

'Let him in, let him in.'

Lourival proudly told them how he'd passed by the police unnoticed. Sparrow patted him on the back and told him he'd always known he was bad.

'Wanna smoke a joint? Tiny told me to take five bundles . . .'

'Take ten and give five to Katanazaka. I'm not gonna smoke, 'cause I've gotta take this money over to Tiny.'

'The pigs are around . . .'

'Where was it you ran into them?'

'Over near Administration.'

'How many?'

'Just Lincoln and Monster.'

'Ah, if they give me a hard time I'll pull the trigger on 'em. I'm outta here. I'll head over to Katanazaka's later.'

Sparrow took the street along the river on his Caloi 10 bike, the money rolled up in a plastic bag in his underwear. Steering with his left hand and holding his .38 in the other, he pedaled fast. As he drew near the State Water Department Bridge he heard Lincoln's voice ordering him to stop. He went even faster. When he heard the police firing at him, he decided to put his gun in his waistband so he could steer better, but he fell and hit his head on the ground. He tried to get up, but his leg hurt. His only option was to throw the money onto the riverbank and, using gestures and threats, he told a boy standing nearby to take it to the den after the police had gone. He also got rid of his gun and limped through the first gate he saw, his head, legs and arms bleeding. Everything was spinning. He fainted and woke up in the cell at the police station.

'Are you Tiny or Sparrow?'

'Neither!'

'Go on and admit that you're Tiny, boy! Who is it that sends us money?'

'Dunno.'

'You work?'

'Yeah.'

'Where?'

'I do odd jobs.'

'Look, if you're Tiny, you might be able to get off . . . You know you've got two arrest warrants out on you . . . If we get some dough we'll put you back on the street,' negotiated Lincoln.

'Get the composite,' Monster told another officer.

'It's in the drawer and Linivaldo's got the key.'

'So you're not Tiny or Sparrow?'

'No.'

'Who are you, then?'

'Marcos Alves da Silva.'

'Nice name!' said Lincoln ironically.

'Why were you carryin' a gun?'

'I wasn't.'

'You think I'm stupid, man?' said Monster, kicking him in the back.

'Stick 'im in the cell. From what I saw in the picture, he's Sparrow.'

Sparrow went into the empty cell, sat on the ground and punched the wall.

'That's Sparrow, man. See the tattoo on his arm? He's got a tattoo in the picture.'

'Is there an arrest warrant out on 'im?'

'Yeah. Remember Beelzebub brought his brother in last week?'
'Did you know Beelzebub's been suspended?'
'No.'
'It was on the radio today.'
'What'd he do?'
'He hung a worker in the cell.'
'Beelzebub's totally crazy, isn't he?'
'I bet he's fucked now . . .'

Sergeant Linivaldo came on duty the next day. He recognized Sparrow immediately, although he looked a lot different from the first time he'd been arrested, accused of stealing money from the register at the bakery where he'd worked before becoming a shoeshiner. Still a minor at the time, Sparrow had sworn adamantly that he wasn't the thief, but he was still beaten up every day for the three days he spent there.

That was when he'd vowed to become a villain when he grew up, and give the police a real reason to beat him up.

In the afternoon, Sparrow was transferred to the Thirty-Second District Police Station. He was charged with several murders.

During his first day at the police station, Sparrow stayed in a cell by himself. His physical pain was slight now—only his conscience hurt intensely. If he were a painter like his brother Benite, he wouldn't be locked up. If he pleaded guilty to the crimes he'd committed with Tiny, he'd be put away for the rest of his life. He cried with his knees pressed to his chest and his arms around his legs.

It was dark. No sound reached his ears. He'd been afraid of silence and the dark ever since he was a kid, because when the two occur at the same time it's a sign that a ghost might appear. A tortured soul was surely coming to take him to hell. He curled up even tighter, hung his head, thought about God, and tried to recite the Lord's Prayer, but gave up after getting it wrong twice. He thought about the school friends he'd left behind in Vila Kennedy, where he was born, his first teacher, his father, who had died when he was still a boy. His memories came to him in a jumble, ignoring the precise chronology of his life.

Then his thoughts turned to the Boys, who were going camping during Carnival. He had to get out before then so he could spend a week near Patrícia Katanazaka. One day he'd pluck up the courage to tell her what he felt for her. If she wanted, he'd buy a house in Saquarema, Cabo Frio or even Barra da Tijuca so she could see her beloved ocean every day; he'd buy everything just to see that gorgeous little smile of hers.

He'd discovered he was in love with Patrícia when he heard she was going out with a playboy from Freguesia. The news, which came from the mouth of Álvaro Katanazaka, had destroyed his peace of mind, and he'd excused himself from his friends so they wouldn't see how upset he was. Until then, he'd thought it was only lust that he felt. When he got out of there, he'd tell her what he really felt for her and, if she agreed to be his girlfriend, he'd give Fly the boot. He thought about his mother back when he'd first turned to crime. The poor thing had been desperate. She'd gone out after midnight to bring him home, made vows to the Virgin, her blood pressure was always high, and she'd gone around the house crying all the time. She thought everything would have been different if her husband hadn't died. He bitterly regretted being a gangster. He was going to go straight.

'Man, in ten years' time no one'll be able to stop us. You could even stick the Army and all the police on the street, and we'd still be stronger, you know! First we're gonna take the prisons. When guys get caught they know they're gonna cross paths with us and if they don't do things our way, they're dead,' Mango told Jackfruit, Orange and Acerola on the corner outside Batman's Bar, at around 7 A.M. one Monday morning.

'Where are you now?' asked Jackfruit.

'I'm managing over in Santa Cruz ... The den there's selling fucking loads, but it's not like here, know what I mean? The whole gang gets money, everyone gets some dope and coke to sell and the manager gets fifty percent. The guards get something on the side too. You shoulda seen what happened last week: I was drivin' the Passat in the square . . . half asleep, 'cause I'd spent the night in a motel with the boss's wife,' he said in a low voice. 'Then suddenly, two police cars came into the square from the other side. I had a pistol, a .38, a bag of coke this big and for sure they was gonna frisk me. I floored it, the cops started shootin', a bullet hit the back window . . . All I felt was the car shakin' from the fuckin' gunshot. They shot holes in all four tires and I got the hell out of there, the chick in the car was bawlin' her eyes out. But I got lucky, I went down an alley, stepped on the gas, dumped the car, grabbed the chick by the arm, broke into a house, slipped through the back and scrammed. My .38 fell on the ground, but I went back and got it . . . Shit, man, it was a close call!'

'Did you really go back, man?'

'You think I'm gonna leave my .38?! I ain't seen another .38 like mine, man. Those knocked-off bullets that don't work in other .38s are like popcorn in mine. Mine's never let me down. You think I'm gonna give 'em my .38 on a silver platter? Hey, I'm gonna leave some stuff with you guys and I'm off, OK? I'd take you, but you ain't hoods, know what I mean? I'm not even gonna bother invitin' you. Only the heavy guys go there. I know you guys are cool, but if you're ever dyin' for a fix, just take a spin over there, 'cause it's fine, OK?'

Mango took a small bag of coke from his pocket, gave it to Orange, shook hands with his friends and got in his car. Before he got to Main Square, he beeped his horn at a friend and a couple of women. He drove calmly, as he knew the police rarely stopped anyone at that hour. Clean-shaven, wearing a suit, dark glasses and a wristwatch, with neat hair, a 007 briefcase and documents to show he was self-employed, no one would bother him. He headed straight for Santa Cruz.

In the main square of Santa Cruz, people hurried past on their Monday errands and children in school uniforms were everywhere.

He had to wait in the square to receive eight pounds of cocaine. He pulled the car over in front of a bar, handed his weapons to the owner to hide and walked to a street corner with his hands in his pockets. A little boy, also wearing a school uniform, walked up to him, asked him what time it was, then took three steps past him, pulled a .38 out of his schoolbag and shot him in the back three times.

In a house not far from there, when he heard the three gunshots, the owner of the Santa Cruz den said ironically to his wife:

'Your lover's dead!'

The boy walked calmly away from Mango's body, went into the den owner's house and received fifty thousand cruzeiros for his work.

Hit-and-Miss arrived in City of God one night after midnight, barefoot, shirtless, covered in scratches, dirty and ravenous. He went straight to his cousins' house, where he finally relaxed. He and five other prisoners had escaped from the police station where he was awaiting trial. His aunt didn't want to talk to him, and only let him have a shower, eat something and get dressed. Outside, one of his cousins told him that Carrots had got himself up and running again. The fugitive went looking for his friend. He was going to help him.

'If I go over to Realengo, I'll pick up some cheap stuff for you,' said Hit-and-Miss after Carrots had given him thirty cruzeiros. He went on:

'Thanks for sendin' me them funds over in the slammer . . .'

'I didn't send anything, man . . . The money was yours—right?'

'Some bastards don't send any, know what I mean? But you did the right thing by me.'

They stood there in a corner of the square in Block Fifteen talking about Tiny's gang. When Hit-and-Miss heard that Sparrow had been caught, he laughed heartily and swore that one day he'd kill him. Carrots frowned at him and said:

'If you kill him, you'll be killin' the nicest gangster in the *favela*.'

Hit-and-Miss went quiet for a while, took the paper lining from a pack of cigarettes and cut it. Carrots put a bit of weed on the paper, Hit-and-Miss rolled the joint and they smoked it, making small talk.

A new day dawned and a northwesterly breeze was blowing, bringing with it a mild chill. The den assistant, who'd remained quiet most of the time, counted the money, took his cut, handed the rest to Carrots together with the remaining drugs and left.

'Feel like a snort?' asked Carrots.

'A little pick-me-up before headin' over to Realengo'll do me good.'

'Your mom lives there, don't she?'

'Yeah, but I'm not goin' to her place. I'm gonna find a pal who did time with me . . . He's been out for a while, but he always sent me money while I was inside, dope, coke . . . He told me to go see 'im when I got out and he'd give me a hand.'

They snorted the coke in an instant.

'Thanks. Later on I'll bring you some good weed for the den,' said Hit-and-Miss.

Less than two hours later Hit-and-Miss was in Realengo. He knew it was more dangerous for a fugitive to walk around there than in City of God, but he was friends with the gangsters he'd met in jail and, since his friend knew a good supplier, he'd surely give him a few pounds of weed on consignment as he'd promised. He'd get the drugs and get out of there as quickly as possible.

The transaction with his friend went faster than Hit-and-Miss had imagined, but he'd only have a day to pay for the top-quality weed. He was also given the money to take a taxi to Cascadura, but thought he'd be better off taking a bus. Taxis were for whites. He believed that blacks who took taxis were either no-goods or at death's door.

He gave his friend the weed, got paid and decided to have a beer to celebrate. In addition to the beer, he had a few shots of whisky and some fried sausages. He talked loudly in front of his cousins, said he'd fucked more than one punk in prison, remembered the good old days, and improvised a samba. Completely drunk, Hit-and-Miss saw Sparrow's sister go past and, pretending he didn't know he'd been arrested, said:

'Tell Sparrow I'm gonna do your place tonight and I'm takin' down whoever's there: women, children, the fuckin' lot . . . '

Sparrow's sister arrived home in tears and had to drink a glass of sugar water before she could tell her brothers what had happened. Edgar, Sparrow's eldest brother, also an armed robber, decided to send the rest of the family to their aunt's house. Edgar prepared himself in every possible way for an encounter with Hit-and-Miss, who drank late into the night, had to be carried out of the bar by his cousins, and slept at his aunt's place. When he woke up, he had only a vague recollection of what had happened.

Enraged, Edgar went looking for him as soon as it was light. Although he wasn't friends with the men in Tiny's gang, he complained to a couple of them who asked him what was going on when they saw his gun cocked. Soon, Tiny's entire gang was looking for Hit-and-Miss, who luckily managed to get out of the *favela* unscathed.

On the bus, Hit-and-Miss panicked when he realized he'd either lost money or spent too much. He even wondered whether his own cousins had robbed him. The worst thing of all was not having a gun, and he had to sort one out urgently so he could hold up a joint and settle his debt.

Three days later, Hit-and-Miss got a gun from Carrots in an escapade that ended in the *favela*. He'd held up a gas station and was now at home alone with his aging mother, Margarida, who was shortsighted and suffered from asthma. He didn't listen to a word she said. He'd woken up in the middle of the night and was in the kitchen frying himself an egg. Afterwards, he was going to settle his debt. He heard a noise outside, immediately thought it was the police, ran to the bedroom, opened the window and jumped into the backyard.

A fine rain was falling that night, the streets were deserted, and the streetlamps were weak and far apart. He slipped over the fence into the neighbor's backyard and jumped the back fence with his lithe, long legs. The intruders called out his name.

'Antônio, someone's calling you,' said his mother, giving him away.

When he didn't reply, his mother walked over to the door saying her son had been there just a minute before but had disappeared. The man who'd sold him the pot, believing his mother was involved, opened fire against the flimsy wooden door. Hit-and-Miss's mother was hit several times.

Hit-and-Miss heard the shots and ran faster. He didn't notice a Military Police car in an adjacent street. Without shouting that he was under arrest, the police shot at him and he returned fire. When he realized he was almost out of ammunition, he decided to turn himself in.

'Let's kill the bastard now!' said the corporal.

'No, let's arrest 'im,' said the sergeant, thinking Hit-and-Miss might snitch on all the dealers in the area.

One Saturday at the end of the month, a tired Rocket went to work at Macro supermarket. He was already sick to death of his boring routine as a supermarket assistant. What he really wanted to do was take photos. He'd work a little longer, then do everything he could to get fired. He'd use his severance pay to buy the camera he so desperately wanted and enroll in a course. Problem solved.

The last Saturday of each month was good for those who stole from supermarkets, because they were always full. Two thieves from The Blocks were spotted by the floor manager waving at Rocket as they went by with a TV set, taking advantage of the confusion at the checkout. Rocket had no choice but to let the thieves pass: otherwise he'd have to move from the *favela* or be killed. He was scared, and when he realized his manager had seen everything, he pretended he hadn't seen the thieves in action.

The thieves were caught by the security guards and beaten up; they weren't handed over to the police so as to keep the supermarket's name out of the newspapers. Rocket worried for the rest of the day that the thieves might think he'd turned them in, which wasn't the case.

When he got to work at the beginning of the following week, Rocket was called into the office. He confirmed everything he'd told the floor manager. Looking his bosses straight in the eye, he told them honestly what could happen if he turned them in. The managers didn't understand and Rocket was fired.

His severance pay was enough to make a down payment on a Canon camera, but he'd have to pay the rest off in installments and help out at home . . . He looked in the papers for a used camera, which would be fine while he was learning. He saw he had less than half of what he'd need to buy the cheapest of them all. He tore up the newspaper in a fit, went to the den at The Blocks, bought some weed, and headed for the Eucalyptus Grove to smoke it alone. Along the way he ran into Stringy, from whom he'd grown apart ever since he'd started Bible-thumping. He made up an excuse so he wouldn't have to stop, crossed the bridge, and was walking along the river's edge when he heard someone call him.

'What's up, Ricardo?' he answered.

'Fuck! I'm really down . . .'

'You too, huh? I just got fired from my job and the money wasn't enough to do what I wanted to do. I'm fucked.'

'We need a joint.'

'I've got one here. Come have a smoke with me!'

'I knew you'd have one up your sleeve.'

They crossed the State Water Department Bridge, and Rocket's depression began to lift, not because of his friend's presence or the dope he was about to smoke, but because of the beauty of the place: that immense plain, the lake, the almond trees and the Eucalyptus Grove.

They raved on about other things while they smoked. The third joint from the generous bundle of weed was petering out and they were both staring into space, when Ricardo said:

'Wanna do a job?'

'OK!'

'We both need to get back on our feet, don't we?' said Ricardo emphatically.

'Damn right we do!' exclaimed Rocket.

Two days later, they got on a City of God–Carioca bus at around 10 P.M. at the last bus stop in the *favela*. They sat at the back. They were going to wait until the bus was full, then hold up the conductress and passengers. The operation had to be over before the bus went up the Grajaú Range, where Ricardo lived. Ricardo had stolen a double-barreled derringer from his grandmother. Rocket had also tried but failed to borrow a revolver from his cousin. They'd have to make do with the old derringer.

At the next stop, only one woman put out her hand. She had two children with her. She got on, saying the bus had taken a long time. The conductress said she couldn't help it, the owners of the company didn't put enough buses on the route, and she continued talking, now looking at Rocket and Ricardo. Rocket answered and within a few minutes the conversation had gone off in several different directions. At Anil Square, Ricardo told Rocket it was time to move, took the derringer from his waistband and said in a low voice:

'Now!'

When she saw them get up, the conductress, who hadn't noticed the derringer, said:

'Hop over the turnstile and just pay for one ticket.'

They looked at one another and decided in a second that it would be more strategic to do what she'd suggested. They hopped over. She said:

'Thank God this is the last trip . . .'

'How many d'ya do?' asked Rocket, as they sat down again.

'Four.'

'Takes ages, don't it?'

'Yeah. I'm so sick of this job.'

The bus stopped and a couple got on. Rocket waited for the driver to take off and said:

'Now!'

They both stood and looked at the conductress, who said: 'Getting off already? Take care!'

'No, we're not gettin' off yet—we're just gonna have a smoke.'

They sat down again and decided not to hold up the bus because the conductress was really nice.

They got off at Grajaú, wandered through the tree-lined streets of the suburb and agreed they'd be better off holding up the only bakery open in the area. They went into the bakery, ordered a Coke, and positioned themselves so they could see when another bus appeared at the end of the street. They'd do the holdup, catch the bus, get off two or three stops later and slip down the most obscure street they could find.

'You'll have to get a token at the register first,' said the shop assistant.

The girl at the till served Rocket with a smile. Rocket stared at her face with a Don Juan–like expression. She laughed again. As always, Rocket started chatting. The girl was sweet. She wasn't drop-dead gorgeous, but she was OK, thought Rocket. They drank their Coke in small sips so they wouldn't finish before the bus arrived. When another customer came in, they settled in and decided not to hold up the bakery because the girl at the register was really nice.

'Hey, let's get a bus that doesn't go through the *favela*, OK? But one that'll leave us somewhere nearby—then there won't be anyone we know and it'll be easier to get off and forget about it,' reasoned Ricardo.

'Good point!' agreed Rocket.

The 241 arrived empty. They got on, pretending not to know one another and bought tickets. Ricardo headed for the front of the bus, while Rocket went through the turnstile and stood close to it. The bus began to climb the hill. A compact view of Rio de Janeiro's North Zone slowly greeted their eyes. They could see the districts of Engenho Novo, Engenho de Dentro, Riachuelo, Méier and Penha, as well as

Fundão and Governador islands. To the far left was Bangu, Realengo, and Padre Miguel. It was a cloudless, moonless night.

Suddenly, Rocket glanced at the conductor. He was mulatto, and under his uniform he was wearing a Botafogo Soccer Club shirt. Botafogo had defeated Flamengo the previous Sunday and that was Botafogo's destiny: to beat the idiots. He was sure that every time Flamengo had beaten the Glorious Team it had been a setup, or the managers were lining their pockets. His gaze framed the conductor, then focused, clicked and that was it: he'd taken the photo he'd put beside the poster of his team. He thought about Ricardo. When he yelled: 'Now,' he was to stick his hand inside his shirt and announce the holdup.

The bus stopped at Cardoso Fontes Hospital, where two youths got on, helping a woman who looked sick. In five stops they'd be at Freguesia and that'd be it—they'd have hustled the money to buy his camera.

Rocket discreetly put his hand inside his shirt. All he had to do was wait for his friend to shout: 'Now,' and he'd hold up the Botafogo supporter. He waited, waited and nothing. He looked over the heads of a few passengers and saw his friend in an animated conversation with the driver. No way was he going to shout: 'Now!' He decided to go to the front of the bus, where his friend told him:

'The driver's a really nice guy!'

They got off at Freguesia Square. Staring at the only open bar, they decided to do the place. They were crossing the road when a car pulled over next to them:

'Hey, man, can you tell me how to get to Barra da Tijuca?' asked the guy in the passenger seat.

With the swift cunning of the thief he believed himself to be, Rocket said they were heading that way, and if they'd give them a ride, they'd be doing each other a favor.

'Get in,' said the driver.

As he got in, Rocket winked at his friend as if to say: 'This time we got lucky.' The driver started the car and turned up the radio.

'Luiz Melodia!' exclaimed Rocket.

'Like 'im?' asked the driver.

'Fuck, yeah!' he answered.

'Then you must like Caetano, Gil, Gonzaguinha, Vinicius . . .'

'I love Brazilian music!'

'Then I bet you like a bit of weed?'

'I won't say I don't . . .'

'I could tell by your faces . . . A head knows another head when he sees one!'

When they got to the *favela*, Rocket went to the den to get three bundles of weed for their new friends, who waited at the edge of Gabinal Road drinking beer. Rocket was given a bundle as a present and they exchanged addresses so they could get together sometime to listen to some good music and smoke a joint or two . . .

'Let's get together to do a job one of these days.' Rocket said to Ricardo.

'You're on!'

'Take some of this dope here 'cause I'm not in the mood for a smoke right now.'

'OK.'

'I'm out of here!'

'Take care!'

'Suck, bitch!' ordered Butucatu, and gave the pregnant woman another punch in the face, which was already covered in blood.

She had already performed oral sex on Potbelly. Now she was doing it to his friend and Potbelly took the opportunity to have anal sex with her. The woman screamed, bled and was punched in the stomach when she said she was pregnant. They did this for a while, taking turns.

'You gonna stick it in her cunt?' asked Butucatu.

'Nope, I just want her asshole.'

The woman had been kidnapped during the wake of her own father, who had died of a heart attack. For the previous two days, she'd trudged around the city center making arrangements for his funeral. Her mother had insisted on her not going to the wake, as she was worried about the baby. When she saw her daughter being kidnapped from the chapel, she fainted. Butucatu fired a shot into the air from inside the car while Potbelly stepped on the accelerator.

They tortured her in as many ways as they could, then cleaned themselves off with almond-tree leaves. The woman stood up, got dressed in silence, holding back tears, and said:

'Satisfied now?'

Without answering, Butucatu beat his former girlfriend dozens of times over the head with a stick. He'd thought it odd when she'd decided, without rhyme or reason, to end the relationship, but he hadn't been too concerned, believing that women were subject to such whims. Sooner or later she'd regret what she'd done and come back, saying she'd needed some time to figure out if she really loved him. He was wrong.

Potbelly had seen her with her arm around Stew and told his friend the first chance he got. At first Butucatu didn't believe it; he didn't think she'd have the nerve to go out with one of his enemies. They'd never fought or shot at each other, but only for want of an opportunity, because he'd sworn to kill him after a holdup in which he suspected Stew of having taken the lion's share of the loot. He hadn't said it to his face, but to a few close friends and his girlfriend, who had now traded him in for Stew himself. If she was capable of doing something like that, then naturally she'd tell Stew that he wanted to kill him one day.

He'd waited for the right moment to kill his ex-girlfriend. He could have pointed a gun at her from afar, but he'd preferred to wait for the chance to kill her slowly, because traitors have to die like that: carefully tortured, suffering like a cow, writhing like a chicken. It was pain he felt in his chest, it was passion in reverse, the suspicion that his cock hadn't been big enough to make her come twice, three times in a row and tell him, as she climaxed, that he was everything, the best of them all.

He stopped beating her and checked to see if she was still breathing. He saw that she was alive and was overjoyed. He marveled at his infinite fortune, not because he wanted to spare her, but because his revenge was not complete and it was in the vagina that the pain of betrayal would hurt her the most; she'd have to feel it twofold. He grabbed the largest branch he could possibly break off a tree and hung from it, pulling it down, his eyes narrow with revenge. His strength alone wasn't enough to break the branch, but combined with his fury it was easy. Then he rammed it into the pregnant woman's vagina. News of the murder spread from mouth to ear, ear to mouth until Tiny heard about it. He thought the incident might affect business in the dens because the police were going to be all over the place.

Tiny had been sad of late; he didn't say much, and was giving the gangsters Up Top a harder time than usual. He almost always confiscated the gold chains the thieves tried to sell him. His humor only improved when he took a resident's dog, thinking it reminded him of Sparrow. Then, one Monday morning, Tiny's friend appeared in front of him with his arms open and a smile plastered across his face.

After he'd gotten out of the dark cell, Sparrow had been put in a cell with dozens of other prisoners who, if they didn't know him personally, knew him by name.

On his first visit, Benite took him a lot of money. Some of it went to the chief inspector, and the rest was spent on drinks, weed and coke supplied by one of the detectives at the station. All his visits were like that. While he was there, he drummed and sang sambas and hard rock, and when he got out he promised to send the chief inspector money every month.

The sun was bigger than anything and everything in the Rio de Janeiro sky that Sunday. The Crown carnival group was having a party in Ipanema, a dress-up party at the beach. Tight drumming, well-rehearsed dancers, sizzling samba. Somewhat hesitant, Butucatu decided to cross the *favela* and get on one of the buses taking the carnival group to Ipanema. At times along the way he thought Tiny would kill him; at others, he thought the dealer would mind his own business, since his murder in the *favela* had been a crime of passion, a man's crime.

Tiny and Sparrow were with the percussionists waiting to leave, and drummed along to the sambas everyone was singing. Tiny was surprised to see Butucatu there, but pretended he hadn't seen him so as not to scare his quarry. He continued drumming with his hands and whispered in Sparrow's ear:

'I'm gonna get rid of Butucatu!'

'Yeah, I heard about what he did, but don't get rid of 'im. Just rough him up a bit, OK? He did somethin' that was his own business, know what I mean?'

'Yeah, but he should've done it somewhere else . . . He grabbed the girl over in Tanque and brought her back to the *favela*!'

'He was desperate. Just rough 'im up a bit!'

'Shit, man! Ever since you started hangin' out with them fuckin' playboys, you've turned into a wimp!'

He walked away from Sparrow, took the gun from his waistband and shouted:

'Butucatu, come have a chat!'

When he saw the gun in Tiny's hand, a shiver ran down Butucatu's spine. He walked toward him with his hands visible so Tiny wouldn't think he was going to draw his gun. He knew he might get killed, even if he could justify the murder, but on the other hand he believed he'd be spared, because he'd never stolen anything in the *favela*, he'd never trafficked and was on friendly terms with Sparrow.

The conversation started calmly. Butucatu insisted that it was a man's crime:

'I was defending my honor, man! And I'm already fucked. Her

family's already snitched on me, so this story ain't gonna affect you,' he lied.

Tiny didn't listen and repeated over and over:

'You should've got rid of her outside the *favela*, you bastard!'

He spoke in a particularly loud voice to catch his men's attention. They'd help him beat up Butucatu. When Bicky, Russian Mouse and Marcelo came over, Tiny gave Butucatu the first punch in the face. Butucatu danced around, saying he was going to fight back, and that if he had to die, he'd die fighting—he'd die like a man. The gangsters helped beat him up. Bicky drew his gun, and didn't shoot only because Sparrow intervened:

'Don't shoot, don't shoot!'

During the bus ride to Ipanema, Tiny repeated several times that he should have killed Butucatu, because he could see in his eyes that he was a backstabber.

'Get over it, man. He's just a jackass!' said Sparrow, as always.

Butucatu remained on the ground, unconscious. By the time he came to, the buses had already left. It was a dark night. He got up slowly, his entire body hurting and bleeding. He tried to walk, his legs buckled and he ended up back on the ground. He only managed to get up and walk home the next morning.

'I'm pregnant!'

'You're kiddin'!?'

'I am. I haven't had my period in two months . . .'

'Fuck, I'm gonna be a dad! Let's have a beer!'

'We're not havin' any beer, Sparrow. I'm too young to be a mom, and I don't wanna throw my youth away for a kid! Kids tie you down. I'm gettin' rid of it,' said Fly when Sparrow came to bed after the beach party.

'What you talkin' about, girl? Fuck, we've been livin' together for a long time, ain't we? Is there anything you ain't got?'

'I ain't got you, Sparrow! All you wanna know about is that bunch of playboys, going to dances, sometimes you disappear for a week at a time at them crazy campouts . . . You think I don't know you fuck them white girls? I'm gettin' rid of it and that's that. I've already talked to my friend, I'm drinkin' coffee-leaf tea and I'm havin' the abortion tomorrow.'

'I won't let you!'

'It's too late now—I've already drunk a shitload of tea and if I don't get rid of it, it might even be born deformed.'

Sparrow didn't say anything. He got up, pulled on his clothes and walked through the night until he got to Tiny's apartment. He told his friend what had happened and Tiny consoled him:

'Don't worry man, when women have kids they go to the dogs . . . Go get one of them white girls knocked up . . . nice and young . . .'

Yes, it was better that Fly got rid of the brat. It would actually be good, because he'd kick her out and she wouldn't be able to say a thing. He decided to roll a joint, then smoked it with his pal as a kind of celebration for making the right decision.

'How 'bout a shot of whisky?'

'Why not?'

Tiny drank from the bottle, then passed it to Sparrow. They sat on the sofa and smoked a joint, talking and laughing while they drank the whisky. Sparrow was the first to fall asleep right there on the sofa. Tiny staggered to the bedroom and threw himself on the bed.

At around midday, someone pounded at the door. Gun in hand, Tiny opened it. Benite, looking sad, said he had some bad news.

'Spit it out, man, spit it out!'

'Sparrow's wife . . .'

'Is she dead?!'

Sparrow's brother lowered his head and walked over to the kitchen. Tiny hugged his friend, who, bug-eyed, fell silent for a few minutes, an expression of deep sadness on his face.

'Where is she?'

'At Xinu's place. People're saying it was an abortion.'

'Who's there?'

'No one, everyone got the hell out of there.'

'I'm not goin' there, OK? I'm not goin' home either . . . Can I crash here, man?'

''Course!' answered Tiny.

'Give my brother some money for her funeral.'

Tiny gave Benite the money to give to Fly's family. Sparrow's brother went downstairs together with Tiny, who went out to search high and low in The Blocks for a girl who was always smiling at him. She was pretty, she wasn't a slut, she studied, and she didn't hang around in the street all the time. He'd never had a woman like that. He started going out with her that very day. Sparrow locked himself away in his friend's apartment for three days, without eating, showering or brushing his teeth. When friends dropped by, he'd exchange a few words then head back to the bedroom.

'Get yourself protected, man! You're really jinxed. You've been stabbed, arrested, and your wife's just kicked it . . . You gotta get yourself protected so you can relax, man!' Tiny told Sparrow a month and a half after beating up Butucatu.

'OK! OK!'

Tiny called in Aunt Vincentina. She'd known him since he was a kid and had told him about some strong magic over in Vigário Geral. They went by taxi after dinner on the last day of the year. The priest gave him a quick session because he had to leave with the devotees for Copacabana, where they were going to see in the New Year.

They went back to the *favela* by taxi, believing that everything would go swimmingly for them in the year that was about to begin. There would be no shortage of money or women. Vincentina thought the session had been badly done, and insisted that the two of them go to the beach for another session.

'Ahh, Auntie, I'm not goin'. I've already made plans with the Boys to have a party over at Katanazaka's place. I need to have some fun so I can stop thinkin' about Fly . . . Comin' Tiny?'

'I'm gonna drop by your parents' place, then I'm gonna keep quiet in The Blocks.'

And that's what happened. That night Tiny was the only non-member of Sparrow's family at the gathering, but he was treated like one of them. After midnight, everyone went their separate ways. Before saying good-bye, they arranged to have dinner the next day at Composer's house. They missed Penha's cooking.

It was already morning when Sparrow left the Katanazakas' house and walked to The Blocks. He was going to shower, change clothes, have a nap, then go with Tiny to the other side of the *favela* to enjoy Penha's cooking. He found Tiny at Tim's place, drank another glass of wine and did what he'd decided to do.

At around three o'clock in the afternoon the bosses of the streets of City of God crossed the *favela*, discreetly armed. Tiny walked along looking serious, greeting the cool guys with just a nod of his head. Sparrow laughed and wished even those he didn't know a Happy New Year. The sun was hot and the streets were busy, as they were only on holidays.

Butucatu's sister saw Sparrow and Tiny crossing Edgar Werneck Avenue near the yellow church and rode home to tell her brother that that bastard Tiny was heading Up Top, accompanied only by Sparrow. Butucatu got his gun from the wardrobe, his ammunition from behind the fridge and lay in wait in the yard of a house.

Tiny got irritated each time Sparrow stopped to make a fuss over someone. He told him he was acting like Father Christmas and hurried him along, saying he didn't like taking so long to get somewhere.

'I'm so glad you guys showed up!'

'What's up, Penha?' asked Sparrow.

'This week I had a bad dream . . . I dreamed they filled you full of lead, son!'

'Then it's more years of life for me, especially since I got myself protected. Don't worry, Penha, it means more years of life for me!'

They ate dinner and listened to the samba schools' record at a high volume. They chewed the fat for another hour after dinner, then said good-bye. Penha warned Sparrow to take care.

'Hey, you know them chickens at my place?'

'Yeah.'

'You can have 'em. I haven't been over there to give 'em any corn since Fly died, and my brother keeps complainin' and doesn't go either . . . You can have 'em. Two of 'em lay blue eggs! I'm outta here then, OK?'

'OK!' replied Composer.

'Let's take a stroll past the Two-Story Houses,' said Tiny.

Butucatu took position when he saw them appear at the end of the street and cocked his gun: he only had to wait for Tiny to walk twenty yards to pump a shitload of bullets into his ass.

Sparrow walked along singing one of the sambas they'd heard at Composer's house. He didn't know his friend wanted to pass through there to find Potbelly so he could rough him up a bit too: if Butucatu had copped it, Potbelly would also have to cop it.

Butucatu was extremely nervous, and could still feel the pain of the kicks, punches and blows with sticks and gun butts he'd got from that bastard's entire gang. He'd only kill Tiny and would spare Sparrow, who hadn't attacked him at any point, and he'd stopped them from killing him. Not only that, but a few days later, Sparrow had sent him a message telling him to spend some time away from the *favela*, because if a gang member saw him when he wasn't around, they might kill him just to win points with Tiny.

Butucatu's whole body shook. When Tiny came within firing range, he held his breath and squinted. But Sparrow, still singing, passed in front of Tiny, making it hard to see him. He lowered his gun, breathed, took aim at Tiny again, steadied his arm, fired twice in a row and slipped away through the backyard of the house.

Sparrow fell, writhing.

Tiny ran, bleeding. Although he'd been hit, he still had the strength to return fire, but he feared Butucatu had several supporters in the area because of the murders Tiny had committed there. He made his way back to Zeca Composer's house, but before he sprinted off, he caught sight of Butucatu through the holes in the bricks at the top of the wall where the murderer had placed the barrel of his gun and fired.

'Go see Sparrow, he's down, he's down, go, go . . .'

'Who was it?' asked Composer.

'Butucatu, it was Butucatu, I shoulda killed 'im, I shoulda killed 'im . . . I told Sparrow, I told 'im, I told 'im!!! They got Sparrow too! Sparrow's down! Go see Sparrow . . . I'm gonna die, I'm gonna die!'

'Calm down, stay cool, man! You're not gonna die!'

'Go help Sparrow, he's like a brother to me! Go help 'im, help 'im . . .'

Composer was unsure who to attend to, and on an impulse decided on Tiny, who was bleeding a lot. Tiny's mother lived a few yards away.

'Take my gun . . .' said Tiny to Composer when they started walking.

He was finally going to see his mother—she'd surely help him.

'You were asking for this to happen to you. I don't let murderers into my house,' said his mother so bitterly that Tiny lowered his head and stayed in that position even after his mother had violently slammed the gate shut.

'Let's go to my real mother's place!'

'Let's go to the clinic!' said Composer.

'Not the doctor, no, not the doctor! Take me to my other mom's place—she's a nurse now.'

In front of the chapel there were only the Boys sitting on the sidewalk with several lit joints, singing 'Alternative Society' by Raul Seixas.

Before leaving the *favelas*, the gangsters had decided not to stay long at the wake, but the night turned out to be a good one: women were showing up left, right and center, someone brought a bottle of whisky, wine, lemon cocktails . . . Russian Mouse perked up and sent someone to buy five crates of beer, while family members were given handshakes, pats on the back and the shoulders of others to lean their heads on, prayers, blessings and words in verse and prose, recited and sung. Tambourines, rattles and *cavaquinhos* appeared. People were snorting coke and joints were passed from mouth to mouth.

Only Sparrow's body, in the center of the chapel, got in the way of the proceedings. They decided to push the coffin into a corner and paid homage to the deceased from time to time by singing his favorite samba: 'I live where no one else lives.'

As at any good party, there was no lack of flirting; the men were under a spell at the sight of so many beautiful women. And the guys who managed to hook up with one had sex in the bathroom, in the empty chapel next door or in the nearby streets, and some said Sparrow was enjoying it all—he'd always been one for a bit of a romp.

A bright, round moon made the eternal mystery of the night even more enchanting, and the funeral was the biggest ever seen. It was a hundred and nine degrees out.

TINY'S STORY

THE LATE 1970S AND EARLY 1980S

'I hardly ever see Rocket anymore.'

'Yeah . . . he's really fallen off the map.'

'He's off doin' his own thing, ain't he?'

'You can say that again!'

'I only see him around . . .'

'He hangs around with those guys from the Residents' Association . . .'

'He's a real photographer now!'

'You can say that again!'

'All the guys he hangs around with are from the university. He loves all that political stuff . . .'

'I know them, man . . . They're the ones who block off the street every May Day with them workers' demonstrations and they're always holdin' a shitload of meeting's . . .'

'Residents' Association, huh?'

'Yup . . .'

They fell silent for a time.

'Rocket used to be the biggest head!'

'You can say that again!' They laughed. 'That was all he could think about, wasn't it?'

'You can say that again!' They laughed again.

'Think he still smokes?'

'Ha! I ran into him one day on the stairs of his building—shitfaced.'

'But he has a puff on the quiet, don't he?'

'You can say that again!'

'But everyone's disappeared!'

'What? They're all still here, man!'

'No, they ain't! Look: Sir Paulo Carneiro left the *favela*, I think he's livin' over in Taquara, Vicente's gone, so has Katanazaka, Thiago . . . Tonho ran off to the United States . . .'

'What? Who told you that?'

'Marisol. Bruno and Breno are still around, but they're off doin' their own thing, Paype got married . . .'

'What about Adriana?'

'She got married to some rich guy she went to school with . . .'

'The last guy from the *favela* to get it on with her was Aluísio . . .'

'She was really hot, wasn't she?'

'You can say that again! There's more, let's see . . . Hey, everyone's disappeared! We're the only ones still around . . . you know, that hang around together . . .'

'Everyone's off doin' their own thing . . .'

'What about Tiny?'

'Fuck, man, that guy's a piece of work . . . It was him who killed them guys Up Top yesterday, him and Bicky . . . They're killing people left, right and center . . . I talked to 'im yesterday . . .'

'We should get rid of 'im, man!'

'No, he doesn't mess with us! Let's get rid of Ox, OK? He hit Marisol twice in the face over at Cascadura Tennis Club . . .'

'You gonna get a move on and cut the rest, man? How many papers you got?'

'There's ten left! Enough for us to play all night.'

'So cut the rest of that one then.'

'There's this house near the canal and the owners are rich as fuck—seriously! Me and Xinu was walking along, right, and we saw the whole family going off to the beach. I felt like doing the place alone . . . If I'd've had a partner . . .'

'Once Chocky did three houses over in Barra and Recreio and

he hit the jackpot, man! He got gold, two hot-shit cameras, a watch, a film camera and a shitload of other stuff!'

'And he did that Flamengo player's house over in Araújo . . .'

'It was him and Old Pal . . .'

'What was the guy's name again?'

'Dunno, all I know is that he played for Flamengo . . . They got two revolvers, a shotgun and a shitload of trophies. They gave the trophies to the kids down at the Rec to have soccer tournaments with.'

'They nearly got into deep shit with Tiny for thievin' near the *favela*.'

'Did they?'

'He sent for 'em and broke their balls . . . Russian Mouse was ready to lay into 'em.'

'He's really got some pull, don't he?'

'Yeah, he's in good with Tiny.'

'We should get rid of him too!'

'Fuck, man, cut that shit properly!'

'I am . . . This bit here's almost soft.'

'Chocky had a fuckin' awful death! The day he died, he went to the beach with Leonardo, came back with 'im and had dinner at his place. He said he was goin' to the dance later on, then he disappeared . . .'

'You really think it was Rogério who took him out?'

'Folks are sayin' he went through Rogério's place lookin' for gold, but only took a TV set. Rogério found out it was him and took him out!'

'Who would've thought that Chocky would turn into a gangster? Good lookin', never lived in the *favela* . . .'

'Who got 'im in with the group?'

'Patrícia Katanazaka . . . him and Ricardo.'

'They live in Freguesia, don't they?'

'Yeah.'

'Was he rich?'

'So-so. But he always looked sharp.'

'He turned into the biggest thief!'

'You can say that again.'

'The plate's cold, man!'

'Heat it up.'

'Gimme the matches.'

'Get the lighter, over there on the table.'

'That job's still on, isn't it?'

'Depends on Shrimp, man! He said he was gonna case the joint.'

'Was he goin' today?'

'He said he was, and then he was comin' straight here. I just hope he doesn't screw things up.'

'Are all five of us goin'?'

'Sure! Three go in and two stay outside to keep watch.'

'That pistol's got a nice shine on it, man!'

'Yeah, you wipe it down with kerosene?'

'Kerosene my ass! I used lubricating oil!'

Daniel snorted his line of coke then passed the plate to Rodrigo, who snorted his eagerly. They poured two small glasses of whisky, lit two cigarettes and continued:

'After Sparrow died, Tiny got even worse. D'you see what he did over on Highway Eleven last month?'

'Marisol told me a bit, but I wasn't in the *favela* at the time. So what happened?'

'Someone saw Butucatu over in Gávea gettin' into a Kombi . . . one of them minibuses that come to the *favela* . . .'

'Yeah?'

'So Tiny staked out Motorway Eleven with the biggest gang and everything, and he stopped and searched every Kombi that came along . . .'

'Fucking shit!'

'But wasn't Butucatu in the slammer 'cos of that inquiry about the girl they raped?'

'He escaped, man! Him and Potbelly got out in some jail-break . . .'

'But you know what I heard?'

'What?'

'That they got 'im again. The pigs busted him over in Serrinha.'

'What about Potbelly?'

'Potbelly . . . I was talkin' to his sister the other day. She said he's given up smoking and snorting. He's over in Minas Gerais, workin' with an aunt and uncle that live out in the country. He's really cleaned up his act, you know.'

'You can say that again!'

'What about Slick?'

'Slick's out. He's running things over in Thirteen . . . him and Night Owl . . .'

'Them kids from Thirteen are bad. They steal left, right and cen-ter! That Earthquake guy's the biggest Judas—we should get rid of him too . . .'

'We're only gonna get the ones who want to give us a hard time, OK?'

'True.'

'This whisky really hits the spot, doesn't it?'

'Marisol gave it to me.'

'You still gettin' it on with that girl, what's her name?'

'I gave her a good one yesterday! I made her suck me off, then I fucked her in the ass . . .'

'Yeah? When you fuck a girl in the ass, if she ain't already done it, she'll only forget you when someone else does it, and if it never happens again, she'll never forget you.'

'Hear that whistle?'

'Yeah. Must be Shrimp, wait for him to whistle again.' Shrimp used the code.

'What's up, man? How's things?'

'Not good. Ox gave Marisol another roughing up on the beach . . . He punched him in the face just 'cos Marisol didn't want to lend him his bike . . . He's such an asshole!'

'I hadn't heard . . . The other day he was walking through the square and you know what he said?'

'What?'

'"The Boys give it like a girl after shakin' their asses at the dance." Then he said: "I roughed up Marisol on the beach. I punched him in the face . . . I asked him to lemme borrow his bike, but he wouldn't."'

'He's the next one to go!'

'That Israel's a bastard too! He killed a rich kid over at the shops yesterday for nothin'!'

'Yeah, I heard . . . Cut me a big line, 'cos I only just got here, man.'

'Do it yourself.'

'Gimme the razor. I need a joint to calm down. Where's this coke from?'

'Leaky Tap.'

'His den's doin' a shitload of business! Roll me a joint, man.'

'Hold on, man, we'll have one in a minute.'

'So what's the story with Israel again?'

'It was this guy . . . some rich kid . . . I think he was from Pau Ferro. He showed up in The Blocks asking where the den was. Bicky said they were still doing the packaging . . . So the guy goes to the shops and orders a Coke and a pack of smokes . . . and Israel's watching him . . . Wasted man, completely wasted!'

'He loves pickin' fights when he's drunk.'

'The kid was a bit of a looker, right? Blond, huge tattoo on his arm . . . So he lit his smoke, put the lighter on the counter like this and stood there, minding his own business, drinking his Coke. Man! When he went to pick up the lighter, Israel whacked him in the face. He'd been watching the guy out of the corner of his eye . . .'

'He's got it in for anyone good-looking, don't he?'

'When the guy picked up the lighter, he jumped up and planted the guy in the face and went: "Tryin' to take my lighter? This lighter's mine." So the guy says the lighter's his, man! He smashed his face in with his 9 mm and really messed him up!'

'Good Life's the only nice one of the lot: he doesn't give anyone a hard time. He treats everyone nice . . .'

'True!'

'You're right!'

'Another one we've gotta take out is that Bicky guy . . .'

'Let's make a blacklist! See if there's a pen down there.'

'First, The Blocks: Ox, Bicky, Russian Mouse, Beep-Beep and Marcelo . . .'

'But no one can find out, and if anyone sees, they die too.'

Ana Flamengo went down Middle Street looking more gorgeous than ever, but she was discreet, since Guimarães had forbidden her to wear clothes that were outrageous or psychedelic, as he called them. As happy as could be, she bowed to her husband's wishes. Husband? Yes, husband, who had bought a house in a peaceful place and furnished it with impeccable taste. He didn't let Ana Flamengo ply her trade anymore; she was now a one-man woman and, to add even more sparkle to her life, he'd let her adopt the baby of a friend who was behind bars.

She went to the street market—the only reason she went to City of God—pushing a really fancy stroller. Very chic. Scowling at the few who insisted on cracking jokes, she complained about the price and quality of the goods and stopped to talk only to those she held in high esteem, for now she despised the poor; they were noisy, toothless and didn't have the slightest understanding of homosexuality. Ana Flamengo was no longer a faggot—now she was a homosexual, and proud of it.

Ana Flamengo had been through a lot as a working girl: things on the streets had taken a turn for the worse—the police were always breathing down their necks, making it difficult to work, she'd taken several beatings, and had been brutally raped by two Military Police officers, who shot her three times after they tortured her.

'It's a miracle I didn't die!' she said.

Unable to work in peace, Ana Flamengo turned to mugging, theft and smuggling drugs into prisons in her anus on visiting days. She was caught red-handed stealing from a supermarket in Barra da Tijuca, and did a year in prison, where she never lacked sex—someone was even killed in Sector B in a dispute over her attentions. But she was beaten when she didn't want to sell drugs and run the risk of getting caught for a crime she wouldn't have committed of her own accord. Many inmates had seen their sentences extended for doing this kind of work . . .

After their dinner at the restaurant, when Fabiana said everything Guimarães had expected her to, he made an effort to lead a normal life with his wife. He wanted to come clean, speak of his desire, tell her about his love for Ana Flamengo, but he limited himself to saying he was having some personal problems that he couldn't even tell her about. Fabiana tried to drag it out of him, but he said he wouldn't tolerate an invasion of his privacy and promised that he would do everything in his power to save their marriage.

It was difficult for him to resist seeking out Ana Flamengo, and on several occasions he pulled his car over near her street corner to watch the one he truly loved, before going home to debase himself in the sex that he forced himself to have with his wife. His home life was harmonious for a time, and it seemed as though his problem had been solved but, as the days went by, the familiar monotony set in: having to fuck that shriveled snatch, covered in hair, made him feel sick. The architecture of the vagina was ugly and badly finished: it was hard to get it up for that red hole with those dead-looking bits of flesh. But worst of all was when Fabiana asked him for oral sex; touching that slimy thing with his mouth made him queasy, and the damn woman always refused anal sex, which depressed him and made him miss Ana Flamengo even more. That enormous shaved butt, winking asshole and naughty feeling gave him pleasure, lots of pleasure.

One fine day, sometime later, a drunk Guimarães went looking for Ana Flamengo. He showed up out of nowhere, grabbed her, planted a steaming kiss on her lips, after which he didn't even need to say that he'd live with her forever. That same night he went home, woke up Fabiana and, without the slightest shame, told her the whole truth.

After many fights, expletives and threats, Tiny lost his girlfriend. The girl's parents won her back and managed to rent a house in a faraway neighborhood to safeguard the future of the girl who had been the greatest love of Tiny's life. She had been the only decent girl to get close to him of her own accord; the others were all sluts he'd met in the night, who only went out with gangsters. He went around observing women and for a long time he didn't have sex with a slut.

Respectable girls, who didn't hang around at night, didn't steal, didn't spend the weekend holed up in a bar, who worked and studied, attracted him. Unfortunately, in addition to being a gangster, he was ugly, short and chubby, with a thick neck and a large head. The new car he'd bought, the gold chains he wore, the fashionable clothes—none of this caught their attention. He didn't tell anyone of his torment, but instead took it out on small-time criminals and started raping the women he had the hots for.

Sparrow had died more than a year earlier. Whenever he got the chance, Tiny roughed up someone from Up Top to avenge his friend's death. He hadn't liked that crowd from Up Top from the start, but he began to hate them after Sparrow died. He thought they were all Butucatu's friends. Whenever he heard that someone from Up Top had stolen in the *favela,* he went and caught the thief and made him wash dishes and clothes and clean his or a friend's house; some he killed, others he beat with a chain. He let them know he was a mean bastard.

He tried to find out who in the neighborhood had a telephone, so he could rough up the bastard who'd called the police when his gang had surrounded Ferrite's house. Ferrite was a military police-man, and Butucatu had taken cover there after killing Sparrow. They'd been about to break into the house to kill Butucatu when three police cars arrived, forcing the gang to take off.

At the request of Sparrow's family, Tiny decided to allow Fer-rite to continue living Up Top. He promised himself, however, that he'd send him off to rot in hell if he ever crossed paths with him.

One Sunday, he went out with Russian Mouse, Bicky and Beep-Beep for a saunter Up Top. He lied, telling them a customer had seen Potbelly in the *favela* two days in a row. His real objective was to see a woman he was enchanted with. The green-eyed blonde—with her firm ass, small breasts, long hair and beautiful face—had never looked at him, not even that day he'd surreptitiously followed her for several blocks, watching her body, imagining himself hold-ing her and giving it to her.

He and his friends walked around Up Top, but the blonde was nowhere to be seen. He decided to have a beer at Noel's Bar, where he stayed until 10 P.M. He smoked a joint, drank beer and whisky, and chewed on some crackling. Russian Mouse and Beep-Beep took off for the dance well before he and Bicky left the bar.

Bicky suggested they head back along Front Street, saying it would be all clear at that hour. They wouldn't have as far to walk. Tiny refused, still hoping to find the blonde, because what if she looked at him and fell in love? There was no harm in dreaming it might happen. Nothing ventured, nothing gained, he thought.

Middle Street was deserted, except for a tall man standing out-side the Bonfim. They could tell he wasn't a hood from his de-meanor. Tiny put his gun in his waistband and ordered Bicky to do the same, so that if he ran into the blonde he'd look like a nor-mal guy.

He passed close to the man; he was tall and black with an ath-letic build, wavy hair and blue eyes. The man's good looks made him angry, the anger of the ugly, but he didn't let on to his friend. He lowered his head, took a few more steps, and when he lifted his head he saw the blonde coming in his direction, dressed in black.

'Hey gorgeous!' he murmured.

'Go look at yourself in the mirror!'

Without looking back, the blonde walked over to the man on the corner and gave him a hug and a kiss. Bicky was startled by the expression on his friend's face as he watched the scene, frozen and unblinking, as the blonde walked away with the guy. Tiny took off running toward the couple, and Bicky, without understanding exactly what was going on, followed his friend, who pointed his gun at them and took them to a quiet place. Bicky got the man in a stranglehold, while Tiny tore the woman's clothes off. The man tried to free himself. Tiny fired a bullet that grazed his foot and said if he had to fire again he'd blow his head off.

Then Bicky pressed the barrel of his automatic to the guy's head, while his friend undressed. Tiny ordered the woman to lie down, then spread her legs and tried to penetrate her. She slapped him across the face, and was punched several times in the arm. Tiny got up and spat on the head of his dick, because the blonde's cunt just wouldn't get wet. He grabbed her arm and forced her up against the wall with her back to him. He lifted up her left leg and managed to enter her slowly, with some difficulty, from behind. Again the man put up a struggle and got thumped with the butt of Bicky's pistol. The woman begged her boyfriend to keep quiet.

'C'mon, move, move your hips . . .'

Although she was crying, she moved her hips. Her boyfriend closed his eyes. Bored of that position, Tiny made the blonde lie on the ground, lay on top of her and gave it to her hard. Stopping from time to time so he wouldn't come, he sucked her breasts roughly, sucked her lips and tongue, then ordered her onto all fours. He went around to her face and said:

'Suck it, suck it!'

Then he went behind her again and rammed his thick penis into her anus.

Tiny sighed with happiness; he was happy to be performing that act, not only because he was giving it to the blonde, but because he was making the man suffer. It was his revenge for being short, squat and ugly. When he'd come, he looked at the blonde's boyfriend. He considered killing him, but if he killed him he wouldn't suffer much, and what was the point in only a little suffering? On the spur of the moment, he went back to the blonde, gave her a kiss, got dressed and left.

They clapped their hands at the gate of the nearest house. Luckily, the house belonged to an acquaintance of the man, although they hadn't known it until then. Ashamed, he told the acquaintance everything that had happened while he found some clothes for his girlfriend, treated their injuries, and made them each a cup of hot coffee.

He took his girlfriend home and wandered through the streets with his eyes on the ground, waiting for his family to go to bed.

José worked as a bus conductor, taught karate at the Eighteenth Military Police Battalion headquarters, was finishing high school at night in a state college on Seca Square and played soccer every Saturday afternoon—the only time he was ever around people his own age, because he wasn't really the chummy type. He kept to himself to avoid hassles. As he was considered very handsome in the *favela*, he was always surrounded by women, and had even been nicknamed Knockout.

He slowly turned the key in the door and tiptoed across the living room so as not to wake his younger brothers, who slept there. Thirst. He went to the bathroom, positioned his mouth under the tap and turned it on.

'Honey?' called his mother, making sure her son was home so she could sleep in peace.

'It's me.'

* * *

He was unable to lie on his back and stare at the ceiling like he usually did, so great was the pain he felt in his neck. He barely blinked. Wandering through the streets, he'd felt hatred and shame. Lying there in bed, these two feelings gathered new momentum. Tiny's penis moving in and out of his darling's vagina, the very woman he'd chosen to be his bride, with whom he was dying to have sex, but was holding out until they were married. That bastard had deflowered his beloved like a bulldozer. He remembered his girlfriend thrashing around, trying to break free from her rapist, him punching her in the face, thumping her across the back to make her shut up, the blood trickling out of her vagina.

He changed sides, his body shaking. How could a man do something like that? And to him—he who was incapable of the slightest cruelty, who'd always avoided fights and had never wronged a soul? His head throbbed in time with his heartbeat. He hoped the acquaintance wouldn't tell anyone, and regretted having told him about the rape. He'd keep it a secret until he'd taken out that lowlife. If he had the money he'd leave town the next day. Each time he remembered the scene, he felt like crying. But he didn't cry, just tensed his muscles. His face tingled. The taste of blood in his mouth. The need to get up, get himself a pistol and cover Tiny in blood.

He was careful not to leave his flip-flops upside down, because if they stayed like that his mother would die. He drank stonecrop and milk for colds, rubbed Vicks VapoRub into his chest when he had a cough. His dad liked the singer Marlene, while his mother preferred Emilinha Borba, he watched *Bonanza* on his neighbor's TV, listened to *Geronimo—Hero of the Backlands* on the radio, played tag, was allowed to join in the older kids' games, was a member of the church youth group, flew kites, played marbles, pushed trolleys at the street market, listened to ghost stories, and whenever he lost a tooth, he'd throw it onto a rooftop so the tooth fairy would bring him a new one. He drank Calcigenol and Fontoura Biotonic, collected Beetle windshield-washer nozzles and soccer cards. His mother bought cheap encyclopedias from door-to-door salesmen, he enjoyed the adventures of *National Kid* and Roberto Carlos films and watched *The Life of Christ* on Good Fridays. He played soccer on Alfredo's under-thirteens team, went to the pharmacy and the bakery for the neighbors and refused tips, as his father had taught him. He sold river sand to construction sites, and sold bread and popsicles in the streets to help his mom out at home. He was the best student at primary and secondary school, was always the best-looking wherever he went, and every woman he met was smitten with his blue eyes, curls and black skin. He didn't drink milk after eating mangos because it was bad for you, at his house they were careful not to sleep with their blankets the wrong way around so they wouldn't have nightmares, he put a shoe on the window ledge for Father Christmas, did square dancing during the June festivities, chased balloons, ate Saint Cosmas and Saint Damian candies, and played the car-spotting game . . .

He woke early, still aching in places, and went to work without breakfast. When he realized he'd have to pass near the scene of the rape, he turned down an alley.

He worked in silence, which no one found odd because he was like that, nor did they think anything of the bandage on his neck, because he was always turning up with karate injuries.

He wanted to sit there in his conductor's seat forever, wishing that life was just people getting on and off, the bus coming and going, children messing around, women staring at his face, traffic jams. Every blonde that got on the bus reminded him of his girlfriend. He never wanted to see her again, because how could he bring himself to face her? What kind of man was he who hadn't saved her from that predator? If he ever saw her again, what would he say to her? He was ashamed, deeply ashamed.

He went to school straight from work. He sat through five classes without taking any notes, didn't go downstairs at break time and was the last to leave. If he could have slept there, he would have.

He took the bus home. If he'd had the money he'd have left town . . . He felt disgusted at everything in that place when he got off in Main Square. Feeling withdrawn, he took a convoluted route home so he wouldn't have to see anyone. With each step he tried to dream up a way to leave the *favelas* with his family. If he, his sister and his brother all got fired from their jobs, they could pool their severance pay and put a down payment on a house, perhaps even in the Baixada Fluminense region. He'd put it to his family, find a way to leave there forever. His footsteps were firmer now. Why hadn't he thought of it before? He'd been at his job for three years, and his brother and sister about the same. He crossed Middle Street almost at the end, took a back street and, turning into the lane where his house was, noticed a handful of people standing around a body. He ran. It was his grandfather, full of bullet holes.

'It was Tiny, it was Tiny!' shouted Antunes, his middle brother.

'But . . . ?'

'He came looking for you saying he was going to kill you! When he tried to force his way in, Dad stabbed him and he did this!' his mother explained.

He clutched his grandfather's body, kissed his face and whispered something in his ear. He shook him slowly thinking he might come back, or that he wasn't dead, then checked his pulse, got up, looked at his mother leaning against his sister, grunted an incomprehensible monosyllable and went inside.

A group of people from the Assembly of God Church was praying. Wide-eyed, he couldn't decide whether to stay inside or outside. His grandfather's body bleeding at the gate, his younger siblings leaning against the wall. Outside, more and more people arrived, an old woman lit candles around the body and covered it with a white sheet, which quickly became soaked in blood. Grandpa Nel's blood. His grandmother was telling family members that God knew what he was doing. The dog lying near the body, a few plates of half-eaten food on the table, his grandfather's half-drunk mug of water. He paced through the house, the backyard, went back inside, went to the gate. He retraced his steps with his hands on his head. At first his steps were slow, then he quickened his pace, going faster, faster, now running in the tiny space. Someone tried to put their arms around him and was shoved away. He ran back to the body again, his hands and chest clenched, and let out a long cry—rather, a mixture between a cry and a roar. He blacked out.

Bad news travels much faster in *favelas*, and not only does it travel, but it grows: by midday the locals were already talking about the rape, for there is always someone—no one ever knows who—who sees it and spreads the word. Word got around that Tiny had also raped Knockout. In an attempt to get in with Tiny, one guy—who didn't even know Knockout—told Tiny in no uncertain terms that Knockout was going around saying he was going to kill him. Everyone looked up to Tiny's friends, and even more importantly Tiny didn't give them a hard time, which is why the guy did him this false favor.

When he heard the story, Tiny laughed his quick, shrill little laugh. He'd kill Knockout so that what had happened to Sparrow wouldn't happen to him. At eight o'clock on the dot, he clapped his hands at Knockout's gate. His mother went to the gate saying her son wasn't at home.

'Send him out here, otherwise I'm comin' in to kill him inside!' he shouted, pointing his gun.

When Knockout's grandfather heard the threat, he grabbed the knife on the table and concealed it, then, with his mouth full, hurried to the gate and tried to talk to Tiny, who kept repeating:

'If he won't come out, I'll kill him inside.'

The grandfather considered himself the head of the family and wasn't prepared to let someone wreak havoc in his house for anything in the world. He stepped back and told the gangster to enter. As Tiny walked through the gate, he launched a single jab at his stomach. Tiny's reflex was to protect himself with his arm, and the

knife sunk halfway into it. At almost the same instant, Tiny unloaded his 9 mm into the old man's chest.

The nursing assistant assigned to treat Tiny told him that only a
doctor could confirm whether he'd get the movement in his left
hand back; she said it was a shame he hadn't gone to the doctor
immediately, because there was a chance that if he underwent sur-
gery he'd soon get back the movement in his fingers.

Tiny said it was better to live with a disability than run the risk
of being arrested in a hospital.

'Go to a private clinic,' his friends argued.

'It's all the same shit! I'm not going!'

At the wake, the few friends standing around Knockout said he'd
be better off leaving the *favela*, as Tiny was dangerous. Knockout
said he wouldn't be able to leave that fast. Someone suggested he
build a shack as quickly as possible in Salgueiro, where he'd been
born, because his plan of trying to get himself fired might take ages,
and Tiny would have time to do more harm. He could go straight
to Salgueiro from the funeral, get some planks of wood, buy some
zinc roof sheeting and build a shack where he could put his family,
then find a way to buy a house. It was decided; he'd take his family
to Salgueiro, where they had a few relatives who could put them
up until he was able to build a decent shack.

His family accepted the idea of going to Salgueiro. They'd stop
off home just to pick up their personal belongings. They were given
a lift to Main Square, and tried to keep to the main streets. They
avoided the alleys, where hoods hung around. Knockout was the
first to turn into their lane and again he saw a handful of people at
his gate. This time there was no body on the ground, but even if
there had been, it couldn't be a member of his family, as they were
all together. He quickened his step and saw his house pockmarked
with bullets of every imaginable caliber, the windows splintered,
his dog riddled with holes.

* * *

'Hey, can you lend me your pistol?'

'Whatcha talkin' 'bout, kid? Forget it! You're a good guy, nice and friendly . . . One day that Tiny'll get himself killed or wind up in the slammer. Go spend some time away from the *favela* . . .'

'You gonna lend it to me or not?'

'C'mon pal, you're in with the cops down at headquarters. Go have a word with one of them and they'll round the guy up in no time . . .'

'Look, man, he could show up at my place any minute! The guy's a maniac! He's got it in for me . . . if I leave, he might even come after me! I haven't done a thing and the guy wants to kill me. I've gotta defend myself . . . If you're not gonna lend it to me, hurry up and say so, 'cos I haven't got time! My family's there and no one knows what to do!'

'Listen to me, man . . .'

'So you're not gonna lend it to me, are ya? Thanks for nothin'. I'm outta here . . .' he said.

'Hold on, hold on . . . You're fuckin' nuts! I'll lend you this shit so you can defend yourself, but be careful what you get yourself into, OK?'

Knockout handled the .45 with the skill he'd acquired during his time in the Parachute Regiment. He loaded it, put two extra clips in his jacket pocket and thanked his friend. Images of the rape, his grandfather covered in blood and his house riddled with bullets flashed through his mind as he headed down Middle Street.

His friends realized what was going on when they saw the bulge of the gun.

'Where're you off to?'

'I'm gonna kill that bastard!'

'You can't go alone, man! The guy's a killer! Forget it! This isn't your thing. You're a good-looking guy, you got everything goin' for you, don't get mixed up with gangsters, man . . .'

Knockout didn't listen. When his mother heard he was going looking for trouble, she ran after him and tried to stop him. Knockout was unbudging; he left her and carried on. He walked Middle Street from end to end, went through Block Thirteen, took Miracle Street, crossed Edgar Werneck Avenue, strode down two alleys and slowed down when he neared the third. He took the gun from his waistband, cocked it and turned into the alley that ran past Building Seven, where Tiny usually hung out. He saw his enemy and three other gangsters, took aim and fired again and again.

Tiny laughed his quick, shrill little laugh, returned fire and took shelter. Two of his men also fired, then followed Tiny, but the third tried to exchange fire out in the open and received a fatal bullet to the forehead.

Knockout walked over to the body and shot it three more times in the chest. He then stood with his left foot on the head, his right on the belly and shouted:

'This one's the first! Whoever follows that bastard'll come to the same end as this guy!'

Knockout's deed made Tiny freeze for a few seconds. He stopped laughing and wove his way between the buildings. Knockout reloaded his gun, then ran. He caught sight of a gang member behind a post, went after him and ruthlessly blasted his head open. Bicky, Beep-Beep, Tiny, Slick and Israel appeared at the end of a building. Knockout let the bullets fly, walking toward them without dodging the return fire. Fearing their enemy's determination, the gangsters retreated and took cover. Knockout combed The Blocks until he gave up the attack.

It was the first time someone had fired at Tiny in the *favela*, killed two of his men and forced him to hide. Things were quiet at The Blocks for the rest of the day.

'Tiny just went past with more than twenty men . . . all packing guns . . . He asked your assistant how much your den was sellin' a day.

He said he was gonna take your den again . . .' lied Ana, Carrots' wife, to her husband and two of his friends.

Ana lied in keeping with her sixth sense, because she believed that sooner or later Tiny really was going to take her husband's den. She made up the story so he'd get prepared.

'If he tries to get smart with me, he's gonna get a faceful of lead this time!' said Carrots.

'Knockout's got them freaked out, hasn't he?' said Ana.

Tiny's gang patrolled the alleys Up Top and fired shots into the air. Furious and in a cold sweat, Tiny shouted that he was the one in charge there. Knockout surprised the gang from a rooftop. One of his bullets grazed Beep-Beep, he killed another of Tiny's men and then disappeared from the view of the other gangsters who surrounded the building, dumbfounded.

'You're fucked, playboy! You're gonna die!' shouted Tiny.

Knockout reappeared out of nowhere in front of some of Tiny's men and fired without trying to dodge their bullets, causing his enemies to beat a quick retreat. When they arrived at The Blocks they were surprised by Knockout over near Building Seven. Without a word, he fired, hit another of Tiny's men in the head and again made the others run for it.

Two days passed without any shooting. Tiny couldn't believe what was happening. That playboy had more balls than he'd thought. He bitterly regretted not having taken him out on the day of the rape, and stayed locked away in his apartment with Slick and Night Owl, snorting cocaine. All they talked about was the new enemy.

Knockout spent those two days awake, combing the alleys Up Top. Many people cheered him on and women who didn't even know him, having heard of his good looks and bravery, hung around on street corners hoping to see him. At around eleven o'clock in the morning, Carrots approached him. He was standing on a street corner, explaining the reasons for his revolt to a small group of acquaintances.

'I wanna have a word with you.'

Knockout nodded and Carrots went on:

'My name's Carrots. I heard about your run-in with that bastard, you know. I don't like him. We've had loads of misunderstandings, me and him, and it's like this: if you want ammo, you got it, if you want guns, you got 'em, and if you want me to go with you to kill that bastard, I'll be there, OK man? You know there's no negotiating with him now! You've gotta get rid of him and everyone that hangs around 'im, right? You can't mess around with him.'

Carrots' lingo sounded strange to Knockout, but he answered:

'I want the guns and ammo, but I prefer to go alone.'

'I know you've got the balls, man, but he's never alone. There's always a shitload of pawns hangin' around . . . If you like, we can get organized over at the den . . . Then we can take Teresa's den, which is actually his, know what I'm sayin'?'

'I'm not interested in dens. I'm not a criminal. I've got a score to settle with Tiny himself . . .'

'Fine, fine, but if you try to take 'im on by yourself, you're gonna bite the dust!'

The small group stood there listening to the conversation. Among them were gangsters Tiny had beaten up and the relatives of gangsters he'd killed. Everyone there knew that Carrots was trying to team up with Knockout. Maybe they could help take Tiny out; they had more than enough reasons. Little by little, they chimed in.

'Hey man, I once did this huge house and got a shitload of stuff, right? But I had the bad luck of running into Tiny and he took it all . . . him and Slick,' said Seagull.

'He killed my brother,' lamented Mousetrap. 'One day he grabbed me like this, took me down to The Blocks and made me wash the whole gang's shorts . . . he ordered guys to take their shorts off just for me to wash,' said Rascal.

Knockout was silent.

'C'mon, man! Let's team up!!' urged Carrots.

'Once we were hangin' around on the corner playin' cards, right? He held up the game, took the money, punched everyone in the face and walked off laughing,' said Mousetrap.

'I mean, come on, that gang's completely worthless. When he tells one of 'em to do somethin', they do it just to get on his good side. A bunch of ass-lickers . . . I've got ten guns!' stated Carrots.

'Got any pistols?' asked Knockout.

'No, but I can get some.'

'We can hold up a gun shop . . .'

'I'm not a criminal! I'm not stealin' a thing!' replied Knockout.

'You didn't used to be, man, but now you are and your enemy ain't gonna rest 'til he's killed ya. He raped your girl, killed your grandpa, filled your house with bullets and you've already taken down four, right? If you're not a criminal, take your family and get out of here, or he'll kill every last one of you,' said Carrots testily, then went quiet and pretended to leave.

'Hang on, hang on. Look, I just wanna kill Tiny. I'm not gonna steal or do holdups and I'm not interested in anyone's den!'

'If that's how you want it, that's how it's gonna be, but the den's mine and that's how it's gonna stay. Alright?' said Carrots, looking at the others.

'It's all yours!' said Knockout.

'If you gimme a gun, I'll come help you take him out!' said eight-year-old Steak-and-Fries, who'd been beaten up by Tiny.

'Take him out, my ass! You need to stop stealin' and go to school . . . You're just a kid!' said Knockout.

'Look man, I smoke, I snort coke, I bin beggin' since I was a baby, I've washed car windows, shined shoes, killed, stolen . . . I'm not a kid. I'm a man!'

Tiny was still thinking about Knockout. For the first time, he knew fear. The bastard fired without dodging return fire. He was a good shot and worse: he wasn't afraid of him. He had to be got rid of fast, he decided with Bicky and Slick over a beer at the shops at exactly the same time that Knockout, Carrots and the other gang members were talking Up Top.

Tiny suddenly thought of Carrots. Carrots could kill Knockout on the sly, because Knockout probably knew who everyone in Tiny's gang was by now, but he wouldn't suspect Carrots because he lived Up Top.

'Hey, Sidney, come here!' he said as soon as he'd decided how to kill his enemy. Of course Carrots would do him this favor to get on his good side. He was sure his childhood friend was afraid of him.

Sidney walked over.

'Go tell Carrots he's gotta kill Knockout, otherwise I'll get the guys and go take his den. Go on, get outta here. If he don't like the idea, tell 'im to come see me.'

'Now you're talkin'!' exclaimed Bicky.

Sidney sped off on his bike, took the road along the river's edge to the first street after the big bridge, wove through another three alleys and reached the square in Block Fifteen, where Carrots was telling his assistant to get the rest of the guns to give his new partners. He heard Sidney's whistle. Carrots looked up and Sidney waved. He walked over, listened to Tiny's message, and said:

'OK, but it's gotta be now! I've been wanting to take him out. There, there he is. Come with me so he won't think it's a setup.'

Sidney began to pedal. Carrots walked beside him.

'You strapped up?' he asked.

'Yeah.'

'Don't touch it. Let me kill him. You only get involved if someone decides to side with him. Don't let on.'

They went slowly.

'You shot at me too!' said Knockout when he set eyes on Sidney.

Suddenly, Carrots pressed the barrel of his revolver to Sidney's head.

'Tell him, what was the message your boyfriend sent you to give me!?'

'W-w-what . . . !?'

'W-w-what my ass, kid! Spit it out or you're dead!' said Carrots, frisking the errand boy's waistband until he found his revolver.

'He told you to kill 'im, otherwise he was gonna take your den.'

Knockout shook his head and said:

'Get out of this life, kid. You're young, don't get caught up in that maniac's game. I don't know what you've got in that head of yours!'

'Ass kissing—that's what!' said Carrots and fired a bullet that grazed Sidney's backside. Then he added: 'Go tell your boyfriend that Carrots and Knockout are the bosses Up Top now! Fuckin' asshole!'

Gray, gray all the way from the Recreio Range to Gávea Rock, from Barra da Tijuca to the Grajaú Range. Heavy, still, dark gray clouds hung in the sky over the *favela*. It was going to rain hard. The river would surely burst its banks, flooding the houses along its margins. The people who had moved there because of the 1966 floods foresaw a catastrophe, with the waters destroying everything, bringing snakes and alligators with mouths full of teeth. Lying on the sofa near his living-room window, Tiny ran his tongue along the barrel of his revolver and watched the raindrops splatter against the glass. Now the rain was sheeting down; it looked as if someone had thrown an enormous bucket of water at his window.

Sitting there alone, he saw Knockout's blue eyes staring straight into his with every bullet that left his pistol, with every step he took, unafraid of getting shot. Dangerous. He'd got himself a dangerous enemy, and to top it all the bastard was a looker. He'd never seen a good-looking gangster in the streets or films. And now, since the guys were getting together Up Top, he'd best work on consolidating his friendships. He decided he wasn't going to take any more money from Slick's den, and he'd give Bicky and Russian Mouse each a den, to strengthen their loyalty.

Slick came back into his thoughts. He found his friend more sinister since he'd got out of prison. He hardly ever spoke, was always alone and, in conversations, he never looked you square in the eye. And what about that asshole Carrots? He should have been killed a long time ago! But that was all Sparrow's fault, with his fucking habit of letting things go, not letting him kill people . . . That's why he was dead. Dickhead! He thought about the blonde, became aroused and unzipped his fly. The movement hurt his left arm, but he fixed his thoughts on the blonde's cunt and jerked himself off. He came, then cleaned himself up with the blanket and took a nap.

He got up half an hour later, went into the bedroom, climbed onto the bed, cleared piles of objects off a black box on top of the wardrobe, got the box down, opened it, took out Sting's rifle and pretended to fire in all directions. Knockout's goose was cooked. He looked out of the window, saw Bicky rolling a joint and went downstairs.

'Hey, man, wanna take a stroll in the rain? We might catch that asshole off guard. And look what we've got for 'im,' said Tiny, holding up the gun. 'Think he's gonna just stand there with this pointed at him?'

'Fuck!' exclaimed Bicky.

They thought it best to go on foot. Goalie, who didn't care that he was less than ten years old, went ahead, checking to see if the coast was clear. They decided to head through Block Thirteen. Although he couldn't use his left arm very well, Tiny kept a tight grip on the rifle. The gangsters from Block Thirteen, used to seeing a hostile and abusive Tiny, were taken aback by his handshakes, pats on the back and unprompted laughter. They hung around for a while smoking a joint rolled by Butterfly, Slick's manager, and then moved on. Tiny said he was off to kill Knockout and then he'd buy everyone a round of beer to celebrate.

Up Top, Knockout was examining a pistol. Carrots grumbled that it was the only one he'd managed to get his hands on. Knockout silently filled a clip, expertly loaded the .45 and tried to think of somewhere to try it out. He asked his partner to suggest a place.

'Over by the big lake,' he said at once.

Knockout walked along still staring at the pistol, with Carrots trailing behind.

Tiny, Bicky and Goalie crossed the Rec and turned into the street that ran past the church, where they caught sight of their enemies in an adjacent street. They hid. They could keep going straight and surprise them from behind, or take the parallel street and jump out in front of them. Tiny couldn't decide. He regretted not having tested the rifle. In fact, he didn't even know how to shoot it. He was kicking himself for lugging that heavy thing around and not being able to use it. Bicky looked at him as if waiting for orders. Tiny gave up on the rifle, cocked his pistol and took off running down the street perpendicular to the one they were on.

When he'd checked the gun thoroughly and put it in his waistband, Knockout quickened his pace. Only now did he look to make sure there were no adversaries around. He wasn't yet in the habit of fearing the police and therefore wasn't as alert as Carrots, who noticed a police van driving slowly down the street along the river's edge.

'Let's double back and take the inside route—the pigs just went by!' said Carrots.

They turned back onto the street where they'd been seen by Tiny, who'd already taken the street parallel to them and reached the end, where he was lying in wait at the corner. They were taking a long time to pass, so he risked a look. To his surprise they weren't there—maybe they'd seen him? He looked the other way and saw Knockout and Carrots going by.

Tiny ran, thinking he was surrounded. The only way to escape death would be to run to the river and cross it, he thought. From the river's edge, he saw Knockout and Carrots cross the bridge and turn left.

'They're in with Leaky Tap!' he concluded.

'Hey, Leaky Tap, how's things?'
'Things're good, man. Out for a stroll?'

'Yeah, I'm takin' a walk,' said Tiny, accompanied by more than twenty armed men.

Leaky Tap's calm made Tiny uncertain. If he was in cahoots with Knockout he wouldn't be so calm at the sight of Tiny's gang, but still he asked:

'Been talking to Knockout?'

'Don't know him.'

'I saw him over here in your area yesterday . . .'

'Ah, so it was him that was firing them shots, then. I just heard the noise . . . I even thought it might be the police . . . But then people said there was a guy tellin' the kids to get out of there 'cos he was going to test a gun . . . but I didn't see nothin' . . . Hey, there's this supplier around that's got some hot-shit coke! I told him to have a word with you, OK? I don't handle coke . . . He said he was gonna pay you a visit.'

They made small talk until Leaky Tap wrapped things up: 'Look, I've gotta split, OK? I've got this job to do—there might be some big money in this one.'

'Good luck!' said Tiny, certain that Leaky Tap hadn't teamed up with Knockout.

With the intention of storming The Blocks, Carrots and Knockout met with their allies in Block Fifteen, where Tiny's gang had gone after saying good-bye to Leaky Tap. They separated when they got close to their enemy's area, inching along, checking every alley they turned down.

Tiny went ahead of his silent gang. The eldest were Slick, Night Owl, Tiny, Little Bicky, Russian Mouse and Tim, all in their early twenties. The rest of the gang were no more than fifteen years of age. Some were twelve, like Blubber, Black Stump and Marcelo, while others were only nine or ten. They were heroes in a war film. They were the Yankees and the enemies were the Jerries. They were all children of parents who were unknown or dead; some supported their households, and none had finished elementary school. They were going to try to kill Knockout.

Peering over a wall with his left eye, Tiny identified his enemies. There were nine of them. He thought they could surround them and kill them all at once. Knockout would be his—he'd put a bullet through the middle of his forehead with the rifle. He now knew the secrets of the weapon. Imagining he was a general, under the effects of the dope he'd smoked beforehand, he organized the ambush in a near whisper.

'Look, we've gotta take out Tiny, Slick, Bicky and Russian Mouse as soon as we can. They're the most dangerous, but we can't forget about the pawns 'cos they all wanna get on Tiny's good side, know what I'm saying? We've gotta go in through Gabinal Road, 'cos they probably think we're gonna hit through Red Hill, OK man?' said Carrots, oblivious to the ambush.

Nervous and ready for action, the soldiers were waiting for Tiny's first shot before they attacked their enemies. Examining a pistol that the father of one of Tiny's murder victims had given him as a present, Knockout fired several shots into the air. And the shoot-out began. Knockout saw two of his allies fall to the ground writhing. Carrots skillfully shot an enemy and jumped over the nearest wall, which he then used as a shelter from which to fire. Knockout ran into the middle of the square firing with both hands. Tiny leveled the rifle, took aim at Knockout's head, held his breath, fired and missed. Luckily for his opponent, the rifle jammed. Tiny's shot rang out and frightened the members of Knockout's gang, who beat a quick retreat to the Two-Story Houses, where they ran into Blubber, Slick and Night Owl. Two were grazed by bullets and another keeled over dead with one of Slick's bullets in his head.

Knockout pointed both the revolver and the pistol at Tiny and walked toward him with his tongue in the corner of his mouth, staring, which perplexed Tiny. The bastard wasn't even afraid of rifles. When one of Knockout's bullets whistled past his left ear, he turned and ran. Knockout turned to face the members of his enemy's gang still cowering there, and shot at them, forcing them to disband.

Bicky, Russian Mouse and Beep-Beep managed to corner Steak-and-Chips. They grabbed the boy's gun and took him to a place far from the combat zone, beating him as they went.

'Kill 'im and get it over with!' ordered Russian Mouse.

'No, if he tells us where Knockout holes up, we'll let 'im go . . .' lied Bicky.

'Go fuck yourself, you son of a bitch . . . I ain't tellin' you shit.'

Tiny appeared with Black Stump. Bicky, infuriated by Steak-and-Chips' response, ordered him to the ground. The boy said he'd die standing, because real men died standing. A single tear slid down his smooth face. That's how tough guys cry—the only thing that changes at the hour of death is a tear. Black Stump hit him over the head with the butt of his gun and said:

'One way or another you're goin' down.'

Steak-and-Chips fell to the ground unconscious. Bicky asked Tiny for the rifle, placed the barrel in the boy's mouth and fired eight times, moving the barrel of the rifle in a circle so he'd never again insult his mother. Then Black Stump stabbed him repeatedly so he'd never again disobey his orders. The boy's body was reduced to a mass of bloody pulp.

Knockout sent for candles and lit them himself around the bodies of his men. Steak-and-Chips' mother's nervous breakdown, as she tried to gather up the parts of his head splattered across the ground, looked like an epileptic fit. Knockout felt responsible for that horror. A piece of Steak-and-Chips' head on one side of the alley, one of his eyes sitting there intact, as if looking at him, small pieces of bloody flesh scattered around, and only the bottom of his head attached to his neck. The previously deserted streets filled with people in an instant. Mothers crying over their children's bodies.

Over in The Blocks, the atmosphere was festive: just one casualty. Bicky bragged about how he'd blown Steak-and-Chips' head to smithereens. Tiny praised him, bought him beers, put his arm around him, said he was the coolest guy in the gang, hoping to encourage the other pawns.

For the next few days, Knockout was not seen on the streets. In hiding at Carrots' place, he saw his name in all the newspapers; he, Tiny, Night Owl, Slick and Carrots were even mentioned on TV. The reports said the war was over dens. When Tiny found out his name was in all the newspapers, he was so excited that he got Russian Mouse—the only member of the gang who could read and write—to read him the newspapers every morning. Russian Mouse said they only had to read the police pages, but Tiny insisted that he read every section of every newspaper in the city, including the classifieds, hoping to find his name. The police patrolled Up Top and The Blocks day and night for the rest of the week.

To Knockout's surprise, he received overwhelming support from the residents Up Top. After the deaths of some of their men, new allies appeared—people he didn't even know offered to do him favors and reported where they'd seen Tiny's men. Men from the Two-Story Houses and the Short-Term Houses also joined his gang. But they were unarmed—there weren't enough revolvers or ammunition to go around. Mousetrap suggested a gun shop in Madureira, saying it would be a piece of cake to do. If they had three more partners they could trust, they'd land themselves a lot of guns. Carrots promised to help, as did Hairy Beast and Turtle.

The robbery didn't yield enough guns for the entire gang, but half of the twenty-six men were armed. Carrots took it upon himself to get the ammunition. They decided to take Tiny's den Up Top to raise the money to buy weapons. Carrots also thought it a good idea to take over Slick's den in Block Thirteen. They needed to dominate the parts of the *favela* where there were houses because, they if managed to pull it off, it would then be easier to take The

Blocks, since Block Thirteen was strategically located in relation to Tiny's area.

One Friday at two in the morning, Knockout and Carrots led eighteen men through fine rain and deserted streets to attack Block Thirteen. They were hoping to find Slick working the den.

They headed down the street that ran along the right branch of the river, crossed the small bridge, passed Augusto Magne School and reached the Nut Cracker, where they planned the raid. They split up: one group took the street where the kindergarten was and the other crossed Middle Street. They entered a square parallel to the Block Thirteen Short-Term Houses and, at 2:15, broke into them as planned. Everything was deserted. They searched high and low, but found nothing. All of a sudden, a shoot-out began. From a rooftop, Slick, Butterfly and My Man hit two of Knockout's allies, fatally wounding them. Then, from other rooftops, the rest of the gang began shooting at the invaders, who took off in fright when they heard the machine-gun fire.

Predicting that Carrots might be plotting to take Block Thirteen, Slick had armed his assistant and put two lookouts around the Rec day and night. One of them had seen Knockout arriving with his men and ran to tell Slick.

Carrots and Knockout were now the enemies of two gangs.

Butterfly, My Man, Butterfly's brother Moth, Two-Wheeler, Foxy and Earthquake were Slick's main allies. Gangsters since childhood, they were streetwise and held up buses, homes and pedestrians. They and Slick commanded twenty kids with a similar background to their own. Truth be told, they weren't all that fond of the members of Tiny's gang. But they'd join forces with them to safeguard the den, which was, after all, on their turf, even if they didn't have a share in its profits. The gang was made up of brothers, brothers-in-law, friends, cousins and childhood friends. Two of the members were Niftyfeet's kids and one was Hellraiser's only son. Knockout would have to fight a clan.

*   *   *

Furious at having lost the den Up Top, Tiny and the gang from Block Thirteen showed themselves to be superior in weaponry and men in another two raids. They killed two of their enemies and sent the rest of the gang running for their lives. At the shops, Tiny spoke in a loud voice and cursed Knockout, as he desperately snorted coke, then suddenly turned to Slick and said:

'Call the gun guy, call 'im . . . Tell 'im to get his ass over here now.'

In less than an hour, the gun supplier was at the shops. Without greeting him, Tiny demanded:

'I want ten of the most up-to-date guns you got! The sort they're usin' in the Falklands War. Send me ten 'cos I'm gonna blast the shit out of everything. I want the ones that you fire like this and the bullet goes after the bastard until it gets 'im. Bring me that kind!'

'What's this about guns from the Falklands?'

'It was in the paper, Russian Mouse read it to me . . . Ain't that right, Russian Mouse?'

'Yeah. It's this type of rifle that's really fucking powerful!'

'It's gonna be hard to get my hands on them.'

'I don't give a shit! I want that rifle! I'll pay whatever you want.'

'I ain't got that kind.'

A week later, the supplier had only managed to get one machine gun and five sawed-off shotguns from a civil policeman.

Knockout's gang also grew, but its new members were practically children and had never handled guns. Even without them, they went to the front line as scouts or got together just to scare their enemies in Block Thirteen with pieces of wood tucked into their waistbands and toy revolvers. They'd creep up to the enemy zone to swear and throw stones, then run back when fired at.

Knockout's decision to move from the *favela* was completely forgotten after his first attack on Tiny. He'd learned to kill and even found it easy. Besides, killing a gangster wasn't a sin—on the contrary, he was doing the locals a favor in sending those hoods off to the Devil. He wasn't leaving with his tail between his legs, because he wasn't the one who'd gone looking for trouble. He was going to avenge his grandfather, his ex-girlfriend's rape and the deaths of his friends killed in combat. His mother entreated him to place everything in God's hands and tried to make him abandon his foolish ideas of revenge, because only the Lord can judge us. She begged him to resign himself to the truth in the face of the test placed in his path by the Lord. When she didn't manage to convince him, she threw herself into prayer at the Assembly of God Church, together with her husband and others of the congregation. Faced with the possibility that Tiny might storm his house, Knockout gave his brother Antunes a pistol and always left two of his allies on guard in the area, day and night.

Antunes had also given up his job. He slept little, didn't leave the house, and was alert, always alert, like a scout. He'd taken it upon himself to help Knockout in everything he needed, because he believed in the justice his brother was seeking and would support him to the end. Since he was out of work, Knockout found himself obliged to carry out his first holdup. He went through with it, but told his partners not to shoot anyone under any circumstances. But on his third job he was surrounded by several security guards, and ended up having to kill one of them during the getaway.

Carrots was against doing holdups because it was dangerous. Again he offered half of his den's profits. Knockout accepted because he knew that the risk of killing innocent people in holdups was very high. Faced with the options, he decided that selling drugs was the safest. Besides, people only bought drugs if they wanted to.

One Saturday, Tiny's entire gang went to attack Up Top. Otávio stayed at the shops in The Blocks to take care of the den. Scrawny and short, he could barely handle the weight of the pistol. He'd recently been promoted from errand boy and was happy with his new position as assistant. He laughed at anything and everything and made a point of showing off the pistol and a plastic bag containing a stash of weed and coke. He sat on a chair in a bar in the shops and ordered a beer, having hidden the drugs under a rock.

He lit a cigarette, gulped his beer down, ordered another one, colder this time, and drank it in the same manner. Elated, he greeted everyone that went past, whistled at women, and bought candies for the children under a relentless sun.

The traffic flowed down Gabinal Road toward Barra da Tijuca beach. Hundreds of cars went past on sunny mornings. Highwayman and his friends had piled up dozens of paving stones by the edge of the road. They did this because they only had two revolvers. They knew Tiny could give them a hard time for staging a holdup there, but feeling they had no alternative, the nine Empty Pockets threw the paving stones at nine cars all at once, then waited for the drivers to lose control so they could hold them up. They smashed in the heads of a man and two women, killing them in their first and only attack, and took everything they could in a matter of minutes. Everything had been planned by Highwayman, who'd got up early and left home forever the morning after he was beaten up by his stepfather for arriving home with no money. He'd started sleeping at friends' houses or on the street. He didn't join Tiny's gang because he didn't like taking orders. Of the five revolvers he'd got in a house robbery, Tiny had confiscated three. The plan was to hold up the cars, head through The Blocks to the bush, and come out at Quintanilha, where Tube, another gang member, had rented a shack. Otávio spied them during the getaway. At gunpoint, he made them stop, took them behind Building Seven, took the loot and money from the holdup in addition to their two guns, and hit the kids his own age. Satisfied with his work, he let out a little laugh. He ordered them to put their noses against the wall and their hands up until Tiny got there.

Two hours of shooting in the alleys Up Top. Tiny killed another of Knockout's allies. There were now fifty of his men against thirty-five hiding in the bush. The superiority of Tiny's gang in terms of weapons grew with the Block Thirteen gang on their side. His men fought with two revolvers each. Slick had a machine gun, Tiny had the rifle and his five main soldiers had the sawed-off shotguns. In the bush, some of Knockout's men were taking turns with a single revolver. Even Knockout beat a retreat. The only man killed was riddled with almost one hundred bullets in the Soviet-style attack that Tiny so enjoyed: the whole gang stood around the body and fired two bullets all at the same time.

News of the tragedy on Gabinal Road tore through the *favela*. Tiny decided to stay in Block Thirteen because The Blocks had been surrounded by the police. Otávio let the Empty Pockets go and went home to lie low.

Vitor, Leaky Tap's assistant, announced Out Front that the dealer had a sawed-off shotgun for sale and would sell to the first buyer. One of Knockout's neighbors, who was having a beer, overheard Vitor talking to one of the gangsters from Block Thirteen. The guy told him he'd have to wait for Slick or Tiny to wake up before he could talk to them, because they didn't like to be woken up. The neighbor, a working man with a family to support, had never been involved with villains or drugs, but when he learned of the tragedy Tiny had caused Knockout, he sympathized with him and wanted him to win, although from a distance. But this was very valuable information and he thought it best to let Knockout know as soon as possible. He knocked back his last glass of beer in a single gulp, paid and repeated what he'd just heard to the first of Knockout's men he saw. Knockout lost no time. He and Carrots went to The Other Side of the River and bought the gun.

That same day, Knockout headed downhill with Carrots and Mousetrap. The idea of taking Block Thirteen had grown on him, and he knew how important the area was to his objectives. He had two pistols in his waistband and carried the sawed-off shotgun.

Over in Block Thirteen, Buzunga had just sold two papers of coke to Old Pal, who'd arrived from a holdup and was now strolling down Middle Street.

'Who's over in the den?' Carrots asked him.

'C'mon, man, don't ask me that kinda thing! It's between you guys, right? I'm no go-between!'

'Don't worry!' said Knockout.

They entered a square parallel to Block Thirteen and observed the enemy area for a while. Knockout was anxious to go in but Carrots insisted on waiting, so they waited a little longer and invaded Block Thirteen when it was deserted, at two in the morning. Some of the Block Thirteen gangsters were sleeping, while others were down at The Blocks. Only Buzunga was there, hoping to sell the five papers and ten bundles that were left quickly so he could go straight to a motel with his girl. There he'd spend every last penny, because that's where he most liked spending money. It was good, really good. All you had to do was pick up the phone and the stupid waiter brought you fries and a cold beer. He'd never be a waiter—they reminded him of rich bitches' maids.

He looked around, chewing his lips because of the coke he'd snorted, and thought about his girl. He'd set aside some weed to smoke at the motel to counteract the effects of the coke, which was ill-suited to nights of lovemaking. But everything was different after a joint: fantasies took form and anyway, he'd never seen a tastier piece of black ass. If he weren't such a man he'd come quickly. As he'd learned from talking to other men, he'd think about something else when he was about to come. He could hardly wait. Although he was snorting coke, his penis moved in his shorts. He'd have her little asshole again. He opened another paper of coke. When the time came he'd give it to her good—he was a man through and through.

Carrots signaled to his partner that the guy was his, then took aim and held his breath, as one should, and fired. Buzunga jumped up and ran. He turned down Miracle Street, took the third alley and regretted it. In front of him an enormous wall blocked the alley. He couldn't go back. If he'd known there were only three of them he'd have exchanged fire without a worry. He dropped everything he was holding and tried to jump the wall, but failed. He was going to make it; all he had to do was steady one of his feet for support and he'd be OK, since he'd already managed to get a grip with both hands. Knockout took aim, waited for him to swing up and blew his spine to pieces. Buzunga fell with his head facing one way and his feet facing the other.

'That's how you shoot a gun!' he said in a serious voice.

'Let's get outta here, c'mon . . .'

'Hang on!' said Knockout, taking the cocaine, pot and pistol.

Buzunga's body appeared in every newspaper in the Rio metropolitan area. According to the press, City of God had become the most violent place in town. The conflict between Tiny and Knockout had been labeled a war. A gang war between drug dealers. The daily atrocities were always in the papers and terrified those on the outside, who could only follow the conflict through the media. Newspapers sold out early and the audience for news programs and specials on the subject increased dramatically in the *favela*. Besides massaging the gangsters' egos, puffing them up with all the fame and the fear they caused, these programs were a rich source of information. It was through them that the gangsters found out about police suspects and their ways of dealing with the situation. There was no better barometer for assessing how much the press and the police knew.

Tiny gave the green light for muggings, rapes, the charging of tolls and theft in the enemy area. In response, although Knockout didn't approve of it, his men did the same. The two zones were delineated; even those who had never been involved in crime could be killed at any minute, just because they lived in this or that zone. Anyone could be related to the enemy, or a friend, which is why they couldn't allow the free passage of residents between one area and another. The armed lookout standing there in broad daylight was now more necessary than ever—just as much as the night watch. For the locals, heavy weapons became a part of the landscape. Friends no longer got together, and relatives couldn't pay each other visits. Keep your nose clean and your head down. That's what they said.

'Hey, you guys've been with me for ages, right? You're my buddies and you've never done wrong by me. I been thinkin' . . . Slick's got his own den and I've got two here in The Blocks, ya know? So look—go ahead and set up your own dens 'cos that's fine by me, OK? Dope is sellin' well, and soon we're gonna kill that Knockout and I'll be able to put a den Up Top again.'

'But where can we put a den?' asked Russian Mouse.

'Wherever, OK? Wherever you think is best.'

The next day Russian Mouse's den was up and running in the Old Blocks and Bicky had one in Red Hill.

'Why'd you go and do that, man? You know a den in Red Hill's gonna set me back, you know I . . .'

'He said I could put one wherever I wanted, right? I thought it was the best place and that's where it's gonna stay!' said Bicky to Slick that night.

'I'm just tellin' you what I think, man. I'm not lookin' for trouble, OK?'

'Fine, but if it's trouble you want you've got the right man! The den's stayin' there, no matter what.'

Slick fell silent, as was his habit, gave his partner a shifty look, left without shaking his hand and turned into an alley. He cocked his gun and crept back, imagining Bicky pulling the trigger on him from behind. Halfway down the alley he turned back; the bastard might go around the block and surprise him from the front.

Bicky watched everything from the roof of a house.

'Go ahead and get rid of 'im, man! If he's gonna make life difficult for us, get rid of 'im. I can do it if you want!' said Butterfly, believing what he was saying, although he'd never killed anyone.

'He's a fighter. If we lose 'im now, it's one less that might kill Knockout.'

'Forget it, man! Knockout's gonna bite the dust any day now! That Bicky's not such hot shit.'

'Leave 'im . . . When he thinks he's winnin', we'll take 'im out . . . I'm gonna head home. Get the money, put Two-Wheeler in charge and go get a stash of coke from Tiny. I'll pay 'im later.'

'Two-Wheeler went to check the lookouts over in the Rec.'

'Call 'im back and put 'im in charge,' finished Slick with his usual seriousness.

Butterfly watched Slick walk down Middle Street until he reached his house. He wondered if Two-Wheeler was going to replace him as manager. He could see him trying to get closer to Slick, his readiness to steal, his shrewdness in combat. It wasn't the first time Slick had sent him on an errand on which he might get caught, leaving Two-Wheeler in charge of the den. Slick could even be setting him up to get caught. He knew that if Slick and Tiny were finished off, he'd be the owner of the den in Block Thirteen. He wasn't about to let Two-Wheeler take his place. He did as he'd been told, and took his time about it. Two-Wheeler's excitement at being in charge of the den, if only for a short period of time, irritated Butterfly. The biggest bicycle thief in the *favela* slung the machine gun over his shoulder, sent Earthquake and Wildcat to the corner outside Dummy's Bar, sent a seller to work near a square behind Block Thirteen, called in three more lookouts, told them to tell customers where the seller was and ordered the whole gang to stay together precisely where the drugs were being sold.

'Why do we have to stay here?'

'Haven't you noticed the Jerries only come through there and there?' he said. 'So next time they're gonna change their route.'

Butterfly returned from The Blocks, hid the cocaine at his place, had lunch, then went to Two-Wheeler and told him his setup was wrong. Two-Wheeler tried to justify it. Ignoring him, Butterfly went about redoing everything. He fired two shots into the air to get the attention of the lookouts on the corner outside Dummy's Bar. They turned to look and he waved them back to the den. Two-Wheeler rolled a joint. He was peeved and didn't really understand Butterfly's attitude. When it was time to hand over the money he kept almost half of it for himself, just to provoke Butterfly, and gave his friend a caustic smile.

The night was slow. A fine rain came and went, whipped by a strong wind. Knockout had already spotted the lookout at the Rec. He was alone. He stood on the street corner, waiting for a way to pass without being noticed. He was lucky. A truck came slowly down Middle Street. He stepped back, jumped onto the truck, told the driver to speed up and thought about jumping off when he reached a place where he couldn't be seen, but decided to keep going. He got off near the square where Two-Wheeler had placed the lookouts and hurried over until he was very close to Block Thirteen. He fired the sawed-off shotgun twice, hitting one of Slick's men right in the head. He took out his pistol and waited for someone else to appear. Butterfly came out shooting his pistol. Knockout crouched down and returned fire, one of his bullets grazing his enemy's leg. He retreated without being followed.

When Two-Wheeler saw his friend's head blown almost completely off, he sent Earthquake to get the machine gun and took off running along the river's edge. He didn't slow down at corners and ran like the Devil. He went into Block Fifteen, didn't see anyone, and headed for The Sludge. Deserted. He decided to go to the Two-Story Houses but ran into Knockout's gang when he turned the first corner, and sprayed the air with machine-gun fire. He returned to Block Thirteen, leaving his enemies dumbfounded as they counted one dead, two wounded and a lifeless passerby.

He arrived at Block Thirteen dripping with sweat, and reorganized the gang so that all routes in were under surveillance. Butterfly secretly hated him, but was unable to say a thing.

* * *

'Why didn't you give Night Owl a den?' Slick asked the first time he was alone with Tiny.

'Night Owl's a drinker, know what I mean? He'd make a mess of things, but from time to time I'm gonna give 'im a bit of hush money . . . You had a misunderstandin' with Bicky, didn't you?'

'Sure did, man! So many places to put his den and he went and stuck it right next to mine . . . It's not right!'

'Don't get so steamed up—soon we're gonna take out those guys Up Top and set up some dens there . . . Hey, let's see if there's any news from the slammer. The guys are back from their visit,' said Tiny, changing the subject.

They headed for the shops, where a few people were drinking beer. There was only one message for Slick: Skinny, a friend he'd made the first time he'd gone to prison, was about to be released and had asked him to find him a place to stay. He couldn't go home due to constant threats from old enemies he'd made in the neighborhood after he'd killed two members of the same family. Before his friend spoke, Tiny said:

'Send 'im over. We'll find 'im a place to crash . . .'

'Thanks. He's a good guy!' said Slick.

After five years in prison, Skinny arrived in the *favela* to swell the ranks of Tiny's gang. Tiny shook his hand, looking him straight in the eye. From the guy's face, he judged him to have balls and, to attenuate the clash between Slick and Bicky, he told him that he and Slick could set up a new den in The Blocks. Skinny eagerly snorted the line of coke Tiny cut to celebrate his freedom. They hung around talking until Skinny, drunk on beer and brandy, was taken to Tiny's house, where he fell asleep despite an excruciating headache.

The dead passerby was an uncle of Sparrow's friend Gabriel. In the heat of the moment, seeing his mother's brother lying on the ground, Gabriel swore revenge. He forgot his vow soon after the funeral, but his brother Fabiano, a private in the Army, went looking for Carrots to ask him for a revolver.

'Look, I can't give you a revolver, man, but you're one of us, right? The guys've been abusin' everyone, man! But we're gonna get 'em, OK? Ya know Knockout?'

'I've seen 'im around . . .'

'I'll introduce you!'

'Great.'

The news that Fabiano had joined Knockout's men spread among those who were not connected with either gang. A couple of friends tried to convince him to drop the idea of revenge, but he was determined. When he heard that Fabiano had become a gangster, Dé became scared—he'd had a fight with him in the past over a girl, and now he might want to kill him. At the time, he'd beaten up Fabiano, broken one of his teeth, given him a swollen left eye and twisted his right arm. And it was all Bete's fault for having gone out with both of them. He'd never got caught up in anything more serious than street fights. Now what was he going to do?

'Get out of the *favela*, man! The guy said he was gonna take you out!' lied one of his friends, just to add fuel to the fire.

He was up shit creek. From that point on he changed his ways. He dropped out of school, broke up with his girlfriend and didn't dare leave the house for anything in the world. He asked his father to go to the Navy to find out about joining up. If he got in he'd go and live for two years at the barracks in Espírito Santo, enough time for Fabiano to be killed or put in jail. He made plans.

'Enrollments have closed, son.'

One Friday sometime around noon, the shoot-out in Block Thirteen began: Knockout and thirty men invaded the Short-Term Houses. Dé climbed onto the roof of his house and saw Fabiano firing away with a .38. He was sure that if his former friend saw him he wouldn't forgive him. He'd have to get his hands on a revolver as soon as possible, to defend himself.

After hearing him out, Slick decided to lend him a revolver and told him he didn't have to go into combat Up Top. His sole function would be to defend him and his partners when the enemies attacked. That way everything would be fine.

Weeny, the son of the snitch murdered by Hellraiser, was invited to join Knockout's gang, but refused. Tiny had never harmed him and he wasn't interested in getting involved in other people's fights. But when Carrots told him his father's killer's son was in the Block Thirteen gang, he decided to accept the invitation. He became a cruel thug, developed a taste for killing his victims when they had no money, raped women in the enemy area and mugged people in the *favela* at any hour of the day or night. In his first attack on The Blocks, he took out a Jerry with a .32–caliber revolver, and in the second, he wounded Night Owl in the leg. He was daring enough to attack alone and considered himself master in the art of surprising the enemy. Meanwhile, in Block Thirteen, Hellraiser's son felt obliged to be as dangerous as his father had been. His mother Berenice, now an alcoholic, encouraged him when there was nothing to eat in the house, saying his father had never taken shit from anyone and had never let her go hungry. Outside of the home, both Tiny and Slick exaggerated Hellraiser's feats in the world of crime in the hope of making his son a perfect soldier.

'Mom, everyone's sayin' that Maria Rita's going out with a guy from Thirteen.'

'What's the problem, boy? Your sister's fourteen. She's old enough to have a boyfriend . . .'

'Mom, you don't get it, do ya? The guy's from Thirteen. He's a gangster. People're sayin' she's even smokin' dope.'

'Well why didn't you tell me before?'

'I've only just found out, but apparently the whole street knows.'

When Maria Rita got home, Dona Maria watched her ravenous daughter clumsily taking the lids off the pots and pans on the stove, and noted her red eyes. After heaping too much food onto a plate, Maria Rita wolfed it down, drank almost a liter of water and sat down to watch TV. She was soon fast asleep. Dona Maria waited for her to wake up and asked:

'You're smokin' dope, ain't ya, girl? You're hangin' round with gangsters, ain't ya?'

'Who, me?'

'Yes, you, young lady.'

'Who said so?'

'Your brother. He heard on the street and he told me and I saw the color of your eyes when you got home. Are you goin' out with a gangster?'

'Earthquake ain't no gangster. He just lives near them . . . And my life's none of Paulo Groover's business.'

Dona Maria went on and on, giving her daughter a tongue-lashing. Maria Rita got angry, hit the lamp and confessed:

'OK then, you really wanna know? I have been smokin', and the guy is a gangster, but I like 'im and that's all there is to it.'

Blind with rage, Dona Maria flew at her daughter, kicking and punching her. Maria Rita dodged her, managed to jump out of the window and, straightening her clothes, hastened up Middle Street to her stomping ground.

'Where's Earthquake, where is he?' she asked a group of people on a street corner.

'I'm here,' he answered, walking toward her.

'My dickhead brother told my mom a load of bullshit and she beat me up . . . The fuckin' bastard!'

'Is he in with Knockout?'

'No, he's the biggest asshole . . .'

'I'm gonna get 'im for the beatin' your mom gave you! Where can I find him?'

'He goes to Alberto Rangel.'

'What's his name again?'

'Paulo, but people call 'im Paulo Groover, 'cos he likes discos.'

'So he shakes his tail and wags his tongue? I'm gonna give 'im a goin' over so he'll learn to keep his mouth shut.'

That was the end of Paulo Groover's peace. Some days he got beaten up as he arrived and left school, so he soon dropped out for fear that the abuse would go on indefinitely. Desperate, his mother decided the best thing to do was to go to Block Thirteen to talk to her daughter's boyfriend.

'If you're going, I'm going too,' said her son.

They set out determinedly for Block Thirteen and had no trouble finding Earthquake, who was with Moth and Butterfly. The conversation got off to a bad start. Dona Maria didn't listen to what Earthquake was saying, nor did he listen to Dona Maria. Groover tried to keep everyone calm, but couldn't stop Earthquake hitting his mother in the shoulder with the butt of his pistol and landing her a swing kick. Groover picked her up with great care and carried her far away from her aggressor. But Earthquake and his pals didn't anticipate that Groover wouldn't let things go.

That very same night, Groover went looking for Knockout.

A rumor went around that the businessman Luis Prateado had sent dozens of weapons to Knockout's gang, including sawed-off shotguns and machine guns. People were saying that the businessman's objective was to encourage the war, so that, in cahoots with the government, he could have the population of the *favela* moved elsewhere. He was planning to build middle-class residences in the region where the *favela* was situated, between Barra da Tijuca and Jacarepaguá, because it had gone up in value considerably over the last few years. No one knew if the story was true or false.

Luis Cândido, the dyed-in-the-wool socialist carpenter who had once made a shoe shiner's stool for Tiny at his mother's request, in keeping with his Marxist-Leninist principles, thought it was all a conspiracy by the dominant class and savage capitalism against the poor and oppressed. In his daily struggle to defeat these forces at the helm of the City of God Residents' Association, he preached: 'The people, as one, shall never be undone.'

The rumor reached Tiny, who dismissed it. At around eight o'clock on a cloudy Saturday, he called the gang together to launch an attack Up Top. He'd have to see it to believe it. He rounded up all the men from the Block Thirteen gang too, and divided them into three groups. They headed Up Top along different paths.

'Listen out for where the shots are comin' from and run to where-ever things are happenin'!' he ordered.

Lincoln and Monster headed up Front Street with six other police-men. Knockout and his men were testing weapons in the square on Block Fifteen. Fatso insisted they should attack right there and then, arguing that it was crazy to only go out after midnight—the Jerries had wised up and were expecting them.

'There's too many kids on the street right now,' replied Knock-out.

'Fuck 'em!' replied Fatso, and continued, 'We'll only do what you want, right? But gangsters can't afford to be nice! Get it into your head that we've gotta take that bastard out quickly! You know we've lost tons more than they have . . . You can't afford to worry about kids! Ever heard of strategy?'

Fatso was pedantic in his speech. He'd finished high school, was white, had never lived in a *favela,* and felt like big noise among those illiterates. He'd arrived there on the recommendation of Messiah, with whom he'd done time. He didn't return home because his father, a general in the Army, didn't want anything more to do with him after his involvement in drugs: he'd been arrested at the Novo Rio Bus Station with eight pounds of weed. Messiah told him to talk to Carrots, sure the dealer would help him. Carrots took him under his wing. As a way of paying him back, Fatso decided to go on a trip to get guns. During his travels hitchhiking around the country, he'd discovered a gun shop in a small town in the state of Minas Gerais. No one knew why, but he wouldn't reveal the name of the place to anyone. He held up the shop and brought back rifles, revolvers and even a BB gun, which won him his peers' respect. He started talking louder and often questioned Knockout and Carrots' decisions.

He dried his face with the towel he always had around his neck because he sweated a lot, then left to have a soft drink at a bar on Middle Street. He walked along with his head down for a while, carrying a machine gun and a 7.65 mm pistol. Members of the Block Thirteen gang moved in single file down the side of the street in a crouching position. Fatso saw them without being noticed and went back to warn his friends. They lay in wait on the corner.

After checking the alley, Butterfly headed in. When he was pulled back by Two-Wheeler, he exclaimed:

'The coast's clear, man!'

'How d'ya know?'

Two-Wheeler aimed his gun at the wall and fired twice. Fatso pointed the barrel of the machine gun in the same direction and fired.

'See?!' said Two-Wheeler.

Tiny appeared at the other side of the square flanked by eight men, while the police approached the Block Thirteen gang from behind. Tiny fired when he saw the enemy.

'Motherfucker! Bastard!' shouted Tiny.

The shoot-out was massive. Knockout's gang had no choice but to jump the walls of nearby houses. Knockout and Weeny took on Tiny's men alone. Not seeing Hellraiser's son anywhere, Weeny decided to run to where the Block Thirteen gang was also trying to jump walls, to look for him there. As soon as he saw his most hated enemy, he aimed his gun at his head and fired. Hellraiser's son fell to the ground, dead. In the square, Knockout forced his adversaries to run for it, killing one and wounding another two. Other gangsters appeared behind the policemen. Bicky only fired so the police would give his friends some respite. Lincoln returned fire and hit one in the leg, while Monster cornered one of Knockout's men, who hadn't managed to jump the wall.

Eight hours later Tiny did two more raids Up Top, but had to beat a retreat both times.

'Those guys really did get themselves some guns!' complained Tiny to Slick and Skinny.

'But we've got more men . . .' said Slick.

'We need even more, man!'

'We should have another talk with those parachutists and get them to join us,' suggested Slick.

'You reckon I haven't already talked to 'em?! But they said they'd only shoot if those guys show up here.'

'What about the Empty Pockets?'

'I haven't seen the Empty Pockets since that day. And if they show up in the area I'm gonna kill 'em one by one.'

'We should let 'em come back, have a talk with 'em and if they join us, let 'em off the hook . . .'

'Good idea! You're an old fox now, ain't ya? Someone said they're all lyin' low over in Quintanilha. We'll have to send a message for 'em to come back,' said Tiny.

'Hey, go get me some food, man,' said Fatso.

'What're you thinkin', man? Do I look like an errand boy?' asked Mousetrap.

'C'mon on, just do it and don't get so worked up!'

'No fuckin' way, man!' said Mousetrap, getting up.

'If I was Knockout or Carrots you'd do it in a flash . . . If you don't go, you'll get a bullet in the ass!'

'They wouldn't ask me in the first place!'

Fatso pointed his pistol at the leg of the guy he considered the stupidest member of the gang. Something told him that at some stage he'd fuck up, because he didn't know how to deliver a message or count, much less read. A worm. He pulled the trigger and hit his target.

The other villains present said nothing. They just watched Mousetrap limp over to The Sludge. Gun in hand, Fatso asked if anyone was going to side with Mousetrap. Silence.

The next day, staring at the ground, Knockout listened to Mousetrap's account of what had happened. He remembered the hard edge to Fatso's voice when he'd wanted to storm Block Thirteen during the day and remembered Carrots telling him that this Fatso guy was really hotheaded, and that he should watch his back when he was around, not only because of his attitude, but also because he wasn't from the *favela* and no one really knew who he was. Mousetrap showed him the hole in his leg with tears in his eyes. Enraged, Knockout sent for Fatso.

'Hey, man, where do you get off orderin' the guy to buy you food? The guy's one of us! You can't go round roughin' up one of our men!'

'Go fuck yourself! You think I'm like those kids you boss around? I'm an ex-con, man! I'm not takin' orders from no one!'

'You know I don't like swearin' and if you wanna stay with us you'll have to do what Carrots and I say!'

'You tellin' me you're a gangster and you don't like swearin'? That's a first . . . You deserve to lose your grandfather, dad, mom and your whole fuckin' family, you know! That'll teach ya!'

Knockout shot him first in the stomach. Knowing Knockout was too good a shot, Fatso didn't draw his pistols. He ran across Block Fifteen, but when he got to the other side he fell to the ground squirming, his towel wrapped around his neck. Knockout strode over and shot him three more times in the head.

Head down, he left without looking at his gang and went to his new girlfriend's place. He hadn't wanted to do it, but the bastard should've had a bit of respect for him and shouldn't have mentioned his grandfather or brought his mother into it.

* * *

'To be honest, I think he had a point, you know. This thing about only attackin' at night's all wrong. If we show up at a time we've never showed up before, we might get lucky. We might even catch 'em sleepin' . . .'

'You think?'

'Might be worth a try . . .'

'Let's go now then! Hey, Wart! Round up the guys 'cos we're goin' down.'

The eleven o'clock sun was strong. Knockout's gang slid through the alleys. None of Tiny's lookouts were on duty. In Block Thirteen, Slick and Night Owl were smoking dope with the other gangsters. Most of them were as high as kites and more than thirty joints were lit. Two-Wheeler didn't notice Butterfly's hatred whenever he gave Slick a friendly pat on the back.

Knockout and his men were faster now. Instead of going through the Nut Cracker, they decided to take the road along the right branch of the river all the way to the end, then took the last alley parallel to the river and came out in front of Block Thirteen. They stopped, checked their guns and ran to the enemy area.

The attack was quick; their enemies beat a retreat before they were hit and then Lincoln, Monster and eight other policemen arrived, shooting.

A few minutes before the shoot-out, Renata de Jesus had been sitting in her stroller looking at everyone who went past. She puckered her lips, laughed and cried, as seven-month-old babies do. Her mother tried to get her away from the front of the house, but the spray from a sawed-off shotgun arrived first and blew her head off.

'Stop!' shouted one of the policemen chasing Knockout's gang. Bira had fallen in the rush and was picking himself up, giving his pursuer time to take aim.

They handcuffed him and took him to the police post. Bira, a fugitive from the Esmeraldino Bandeira Penal Institute, was then accused of having raped a nine-year-old girl who lived near Block

Thirteen three days before. The victim herself had gone to the Thirty-Second District Police Station, accompanied by her mother, to file a report. At the post, Bira confessed to the rape after a severe beating and then, to boot, signed a confession saying he'd murdered the baby.

After the death of the baby girl, there was a spontaneous lull in the fighting. Knockout didn't speak to Carrots for two days for having supported the idea of attacking by day. A child had been killed by one of his gang's bullets as a result. No one actually knew who had hit her, but only he, his brother, a pawn, Fabiano and Weeny had been armed with sawed-off shotguns. He wasn't going to go along with any more suggestions he didn't really agree with, and his remorse at having killed Fatso disappeared forever. He couldn't accept the other death. To stop it happening again, every time they planned an attack, he sent a boy ahead of time to warn the gangs from Block Thirteen and The Blocks of the day and time it would take place. Tiny laughed and told his friends that Knockout was an idiot, because only an idiot would tell the enemy when he was going to attack. Once, Huey warned them that Knockout was planning an attack on The Blocks the following Friday at midnight. Tiny set everything up to ambush him and Knockout didn't show, because the police had closed everything off Up Top. The next time Huey went there to pass on a message, he got three shells in the head from a sawed-off shotgun.

'Wanna make some easy money?'
   'Only bankers make easy money, man!'
   'Hey, I'm serious . . .'
   'When did you start handin' out tip-offs?'
   'Get rid of a guy for me.'
   'Who?'
   'Two-Wheeler.'
   'What're you talkin' about? Ain't the guy your friend?'

'I thought so too, you know, man. We grew up together . . . But here's the story: remember that day they killed the baby?'

'Yeah.'

'He made the death sign behind my back when we were makin' our getaway! He doesn't know I saw.'

'But if I get 'im, I'll have the whole gang after me!'

'No you won't, man. I'll give you a nice little bundle so you can disappear from the *favela*.'

'Fuck, Butterfly. You're not up to somethin', are ya? I ain't got nothin' against the guy, OK? You know I don't take sides—I don't want no enemies. I bet he told you to tell me this story to test me! Didn't he?'

'I'm not fuckin' around, man! I'll give you ten thousand cruzeiros to take him out.'

Double Chin thought for a while and took a drag on his cigarette. He realized it had gone out and lit it again with his lighter, took a long drag and squeezed his nose. His movements were slow.

'OK, but I want five thousand up front.'

'It's yours.'

Butterfly fished a plastic bag full of money out of his underwear, took out five thousand cruzeiros and handed it to Double Chin, urging him to act fast.

Double Chin had never held so much money in his hands and his look of happiness was genuine. If he killed Two-Wheeler, he'd have double the amount. He thought he'd struck it lucky, because only a week earlier he'd been released from a five-year prison sentence, the second he'd served. It really was his chance to start a new life. Double Chin knew all the tricks of the trade, not because he'd been involved in crime since he was a kid, but because he'd learned them in jail. He'd been caught red-handed in the only two robberies he'd tried to pull off.

'What's up, Two-Wheeler? Feel like a puff?' asked Double Chin two hours later.

'Sure!'

'Let's go this way 'cos the pigs've just headed down to Block Thirteen . . .'

'On foot or by car?'

'On foot.'

'I've got some stuff here too . . .'

'Is it from here?'

'Yeah, from the den.'

'I've got a brick . . . it's from Padre Miguel.'

They left the Nut Cracker. Double Chin went ahead. Two-Wheeler broke up some weed, tore the paper lining out of his pack of cigarettes, cut it into a rectangle, placed the weed in the middle and rolled the joint. Double Chin scanned the entire square behind Leão supermarket, didn't see anyone familiar, let Two-Wheeler go ahead of him, took his .38 from his waistband and shot him three times.

Nothing in a *favela* goes unnoticed. There is always someone who sees and tells. The law of silence works only for the police. Slick went out to comb the *favela* just minutes after Two-Wheeler's death. Together with the brothers of the dead man and another four men, he was going to make a mess of Double Chin, who by that time had already met Butterfly in a prearranged place. He had already received the rest of the payment, shaken the traitor's hand and was just leaving when Lincoln and Monster announced that he was under arrest.

'That one there robs buses. He had more than five thousand in his pocket! And this guy's one of Tiny's mob,' said Monster, pointing out Double Chin and Butterfly for the journalists milling around the police station.

Butterfly and Double Chin were placed next to two other prisoners to have their picture taken. Butterfly covered his face with his hands, while Double Chin lowered his head.

'Go ahead and take 'em to the cell,' said Lincoln.

'No, let's leave 'em here—the car'll be here soon to take 'em to the station.'

'Can I go to the toilet?' interrupted Double Chin.

'Yeah.'

'No, not prison again! You fuckin' asshole, Monster! I'm outta here, I'm outta here . . .' thought Double Chin.

Certain the police wouldn't fire in the presence of the journalists, Double Chin dodged sideways, pushed Butterfly at them, took the first left when he reached the street and got a bullet in the neck.

'I want cars, man, but new cars, the newer the better, this year's models, OK? For every car you bring me I'll give you five pounds of weed and three of coke. It's better for me and you, know what I'm sayin'? It ain't gonna cost you nothin' and I'll make more money,' Tiny's supplier told him one Friday night.

'Deal.'

The supplier got into his car, accompanied by two civil policemen, and headed up to Carrots' den, where they struck the same deal. They then visited Rio de Janeiro's twenty other dens and made the same proposal.

That same day, Tiny issued an order for all stolen cars to be left in the vicinity of the abandoned mansion with the pool. There was a huge area of dense forest where the police didn't go, and should one of the gangsters see the police heading that way, they were to fire a shot into the air to distract them and stop them finding the hiding place, as Tiny had instructed.

The very first day he went out to steal cars, Skinny got three, and the following day he got another four, which encouraged the rest of the gang. But three of Tiny's men were caught red-handed and, the next day, two more were killed by the Civil Police after a long chase.

Skinny's run of luck stealing cars continued. After a time, the supplier came to deliver the drugs near Building Seven, and Tiny divided them into equal parts, even though he hadn't been pressured to do so. Skinny looked Russian Mouse straight in the eye and tossed him two pounds of dope and one of coke, saying he was a good guy. When Bicky realized he wasn't going to get anything, he turned his back on them, stroking the handle of his pistol.

The following week, the supplier came back to call off the car deal. Things hadn't gone the way he'd wanted, as he'd had to fork over an arm and a leg to the Federal Police to get across the Paraguayan border with the cars.

Marisol, Daniel and Rodrigo were the only ones of the Boys who still hung around together and kept getting tattoos, wearing hip-huggers and perming their hair at home, even though the Boys thing was coming to an end—disco fever was all the rage now. They hadn't become involved in the war, and only did robberies. They had several types of screwdrivers, pliers, crowbars, saws, knives and pistols to help them break into houses and cars. They kept their tools and weapons in a guitar case and went out to do their jobs as if they were going to a party.

It worked because they were white, didn't attract the attention of the police and didn't arouse suspicion in places frequented by whites. Marisol didn't blow the money he got. He used it to fix up his house, then bought a car. They continued until they were able to open a bar and give up crime.

Of the many houses in which he could hide, Knockout had chosen Brickie's place that day. Brickie left him alone, which is what he wanted. He sat on a bench, his tears splashing down onto the rough cement floor. The forty-watt lightbulb barely lit the small room. The air smelled of cooking oil and the cobwebs were still. Since there wasn't a breath of wind, no little hand dared move to show the passing seconds. All was still. He was a criminal, a killer, the creator of a gang, a person who led youths astray. This wasn't why he'd learned to pray when he was a child, this wasn't why he'd always been the best student at school, this wasn't why he'd kept to himself in the *favela*. His diploma in physical education had gone down the shithole, as had his honeymoon with his loved one after he'd witnessed Tiny's penis pounding into her like a bulldozer, his grandfather's bloody body, his house riddled with bullet holes, Steak-and-Fries' mother picking up the scattered pieces of her son's head from the warm asphalt. More tears welled up. He had the awful feeling he hadn't prayed enough for God not to abandon him, and felt fury taking root in every pore of his body. He didn't sleep that night.

The next morning Knockout heard that Slick was in the habit of going to parties at Skinny's friend's house in Cruzada de São Sebastião. Both Skinny and Slick went almost every Saturday night, stayed until sunrise, then on Sundays went to the beach in Leblon. A friend of the family had seen Slick at the housing project on weekends. He'd kept an eye on the gangster without him noticing and, as soon as he knew his movements, had given Knockout the lowdown. Carrots had always said that Slick was as dangerous as Tiny and that, if they managed to kill him, they'd knock the wind out of the Block Thirteen gang's sails. Knockout gave his friend a phone number to call if he saw the enemy in Cruzada de São Sebastião, and the phone rang the very next Saturday.

'I'm comin' with you!' said Fabiano. Fabiano drove the car slowly while Knockout kept his head down to avoid the police, because he thought that two men in a car would attract attention.

It was ten o'clock at night, the sky was full of stars and the moon was in its last quarter. The Leblon nightlife enchanted Fabiano.

'Get up, get up . . . Check out all the gorgeous girls!' he said, driving slowly.

They watched the colors of the Leblon night. Perhaps that really was normal life—young people just like them intoxicated with a happiness they themselves hadn't felt in a long time. The cars, the clothes, the lights . . . They thought nothing in the world was worse than poverty, not even disease. They stopped at some traffic lights and a black boy offered them a Sunday paper. Fabiano shook his head, the lights turned green and they only drove off when the cars behind them honked their horns. They saw a police car parked at a corner and suddenly reality returned. Their reason for being there became clear again when they saw the .38 in the holster of the policeman leaning against the car. They sped off toward Cruzada.

Slick, Skinny and Kicks were snorting coke on the stairs of a building in Cruzada. They were talking about Bicky, who thought he was hot shit and was always sucking up to Tiny. He'd really put his foot in it with this nonsense of setting up a den near Block Thirteen. Perhaps they could take him out during a raid and blame the enemy.

'Let's wet our whistles, then go to the party,' said Kicks after he'd snorted the last line.

'Where?' asked Slick.

'In the bar on the corner over there. The guy pours a mean shot of Jack Daniel's.'

'That's really good whisky.'

'Let's leave the guns at your place.'

They hid their guns, went downstairs, turned left and headed into the bar. Fabiano parked the car on the next street. They retrieved their two .45s from inside the torn upholstery of the backseat, put them in the back of their waistbands and headed into Cruzada.

Over in the square on Block Fifteen, Paulo Groover was counting the takings from the sale an assistant had just made. He ran to the bin, grabbed a new stash for another assistant, then headed back to the square where the enemy usually appeared; he was on lookout duty that Saturday. If he saw one of the enemy, he'd fire his gun to warn the rest of the gang who were scattered throughout the area. He reached a corner and saw the police in a poorly lit alley. He steadied his gaze, cocked his gun, waited for them to pass beneath the only lit streetlamp, decided they were customers, and relaxed.

* * *

Inside the projects, Fabiano and Knockout stayed away from each other. The samba was sizzling in the best-lit corner of the third building, and a little farther on there were two dealers selling only cocaine. One of them asked Fabiano how many papers he wanted.

'Three,' he said emphatically.

The other asked Knockout the same question.

'Just one.'

Then Skinny appeared on their right, sauntering along with his arm around Kicks, with Slick to his left. Knockout subtly signaled to his friend and positioned himself behind a customer. Fabiano followed. The trio's steps were drunken and they were speaking louder than normal. They were off to have some fun at the party and pick up some hot chicks. They were less than a hundred meters away when the man in front of Knockout moved. The avenger drew his .45.

Bicky, Tiny and Russian Mouse were chatting at Tim's place. Tiny was sorting out gold chains from rings, bracelets and earrings. He wrapped them in paper, then filled a chest with the package, saying he was going to hand it all over to a friend who could be trusted. Bicky remained quiet for a time, staring at a point in space.

'Whatcha thinkin'?' asked Tiny.

'I'm thinkin' 'bout Skinny . . . I'm pissed off with him! He bought a brand-new car, you know. He's always loaded, and he don't come Up Top with us no more, know what I'm sayin'?'

'The guy's thing is holdups, man!' said Russian Mouse.

'Holdups my ass. He's got his den in the best spot here in The Blocks! You know his den sells more than all the rest together? You really handed it to him on a platter!' said Bicky.

'You'll have to sort that out with him, OK? In fact it ain't even with him, it's with Slick, know what I'm sayin'? You're my buddy, but you know Slick is too,' said Tiny, opening the door with the chest of gold on his back.

Groover didn't recognize the policemen and waited for them to pass so he could take another look from the next corner. He started creeping along the wall, but stopped suddenly when he heard the police cocking their guns.

'If you lift a finger you'll bite the dust right where you are! Don't turn around.'

To Groover's relief, Oswaldo handcuffed him. It wasn't the enemy —better to be arrested than to die. 'Where's Knockout?'

'Dunno.'

'You can tell us, 'cos we're not after him, OK? Don't you know he used to teach us karate down at the barracks?'

Groover shook his head.

'Well then! We wanna have a word with 'im. Tell us where he is!'

'Look, I don't think anyone knows where he is, know what I mean? Some days he disappears, then he shows up again, then disappears again . . . He's gotta watch his back.'

'If you were to tell us, we'd let you go, but since you don't wanna help . . . Let's go, get moving.'

Groover was placed in the police station's only cell, where he found himself face-to-face with Blubber. Both of the same age and build, they glared at one another. Groover tried to keep as far as he could from his enemy. Blubber laughed, said he was going to beat the shit out of him, and flew at him in a flurry of punches and kicks. Groover didn't know how to fight, as he'd never hung out on the streets. Blubber, on the other hand, was adept at swing kicks, dodging and hitting his opponent's vitals. It only took five minutes for Groover to black out.

Thinking they were armed, Knockout didn't take perfect aim. He moved too fast, not wanting to give his enemies time to draw their guns. The first bullet got Kicks in the forehead, then he fired the others at Slick, who rolled back and forth on the ground. He emptied his gun at them. Skinny ran into a building, kicked down the door of an apartment on the third floor, went into the bedroom, opened the window and got ready to jump if they came after him. While Knockout reloaded his pistol, Fabiano pointed his gun at the dealers and took their drugs and weapons. Slick had time to follow Skinny, but went into a second-floor apartment. Knockout and Fabiano backed away firing, jumped in the car and returned to City of God.

Kicks' brother awoke suddenly to his youngest sister's screams and ran downstairs. When he saw his brother's head blown open, he threw his arms around his bloody body and stayed that way until the morgue van arrived.

Slick's brother swelled the ranks of the Block Thirteen gang, just as Knockout's younger brothers swelled the ranks of his. Brothers, cousins, uncles, all manner of relatives and friends of gangsters joined one gang or another because they felt obliged to avenge a rape, a hold-up, a robbery or any other offense, and so became soldiers.

In some cases future gangsters had no crime to avenge, but they joined the war because the gangsters' courage and readiness to kill gave them a certain charm in the eyes of some girls. They thought it would impress them. They admired so-and-so or such-and-such for being involved in defending the area, and they in turn felt powerful, and therefore understood. The cool guys, however, said they were born pawns, the very antithesis of born gangsters. Unsuspecting youths joined gangs and went to war, sometimes armed only with a stick, while they waited to be given a revolver.

Shocked residents commented among themselves that in times past only the truly miserable became gangsters, driven by their own misfortune. Now everything was different. Even the best-off people in the *favela*—young students from stable families whose fathers had good jobs, didn't drink, didn't beat their wives and had never been involved in crime—were seduced by the war. They fought for silly reasons: kites, marbles, girlfriends. The areas dominated by the gangs became veritable fortresses, soldiers' barracks, accessible to few, and those who were unaware of this found themselves publicly humiliated and pushed around because they lived in the area of this or that adversary or because they were friends with an enemy gangster. So the war took on greater proportions, and the original reason behind it no longer mattered.

The demarcation of territory made it necessary for the gangs to use special codes to identify allies and rivals, so as not to be pushed around, or worse, accidentally killed. Existent in the *favela* since the golden days of the Boys, designer clothes had begun to inhabit the imagination of the dirt-poor. The gangsters turned to this resource, which afforded them distinction, status and ease of identification, and designed a kind of gang uniform out of the nylon fabrics used by gymnasts which were so in vogue at the time. Thieves took it upon themselves to meet the gangs' needs, each with their brand of choice and favorite color. And so, at the beginning of a harsh winter, more than two hundred gangsters were meticulously following fashion trends.

One hazy day, one of Knockout's pawns, Félix, was waiting on a street corner near the house of the girl he had a crush on. When she appeared at the gate, he adjusted a short piece of wood in his waistband and took off running toward Block Thirteen, pretending he was going to make a raid on his own, like the best gangsters. He ran along, stopping at corners, pretending he hadn't seen her. He'd turn the corner, cross the Nut Cracker, get close to where the Block Thirteen lookouts were stationed, pretend to attack and take off running. The enemy would no doubt fire a few shots, and his beloved would hear them and think him the most courageous of men.

He crossed the Nut Cracker, reached Middle Street, caught sight of Earthquake and My Man, and swore at them with his hand on his hip:

'You bastard. You're gonna get an assful of lead, you fuckin' asshole!' he yelled, then turned down the first alley he saw to double back and return along a parallel street. But he ran right into Moth and Black Valter, Slick's brother, who fired at him. Félix had no alternative but to run closer to Block Thirteen; he couldn't go back the way he'd come because of Earthquake and My Man. He took another street in an attempt to get to Edgar Werneck, but My Man and Earthquake followed him, firing. The first shot hit his left arm, making him spin, the second, from a sawed-off shotgun, blasted off his right arm and made him spin in the other direction. The third brought him down and the fourth just put him out of his misery.

Knockout heard straight away that Félix was dead. He couldn't remember who he was, but it meant yet another casualty for his gang. He angrily called together his men and headed straight down Middle Street followed by some seventy gang members.

The shooting had been going for three hours when Knockout penetrated the labyrinths of Block Thirteen alone and kicked down the fragile wooden doors. Nine-year-old Othon fired a .32 from under the table when his front door was kicked in, and the bullet grazed Knockout's left arm. He jumped to one side and, with just one hand, riddled Othon's body with lead from his sawed-off shotgun, then returned to his friends and beat a retreat.

The five policemen on duty that day didn't dare pass the Prospectors' rehearsal square. They showed up half an hour after the shooting had stopped to deal with the bodies of Othon and yet another newborn baby killed in the war.

As soon as he heard about Knockout's attack, Tiny called together his gang and headed for Block Thirteen. The policemen flew into a panic when they saw the gang. Tiny himself shouted that he wasn't going to fire at them. They passed by the policemen as if they were ordinary residents, rounded up the Block Thirteen gang and headed off to attack the enemy on its own territory.

The first few shots were few and far between, since it was no longer possible for Tiny to barge straight in as he had in the past. Knockout's gang had almost as many men as his. The Block Thirteen gang split up when they got to the Rec and headed up the river's edge. Tiny's gang split up and took Middle Street and the alleys. The youngest enjoyed that feeling of war, thinking they were TV heroes. All Tiny could think about was the money he'd lost ever since the war had begun. He shouted, swore, pretended he was going to attack then didn't. Whenever an enemy bullet whistled past, he'd laugh his quick, shrill little laugh. With his gang all together, Knockout ordered them not to go into the firing line and to do only what he told them to. He called Carrots over, reached into a bag and pulled out two hand grenades that a gang member had stolen from the barracks he worked at. He had already explained how to use them. He said he'd taunt Tiny so he'd come closer.

'No way, man! You should run off so they go after you and I'll throw it.'

'OK, do it.'

Knockout fired two shots with his sawed-off shotgun and Tiny responded with a spray of machine-gun fire, destroying a section of the wall they were using as a trench.

'Let's go, let's go, let's go!' shouted Knockout.

Tiny, Black Stump and Slick advanced and Carrots threw the grenade.

They crossed the square, reached The Sludge and found themselves face-to-face with the Block Thirteen gang. The dozens of shots fired had no specific target; they just had to shoot straight ahead. Only Knockout, Carrots, Mousetrap and Antunes actually aimed at the enemy. It wasn't very different for their adversaries: their bullets lodged in the most diverse places. Approximately one hundred men exchanging fire and only two casualties for Knockout's gang, and another two for the Block Thirteen gang, whom he'd killed himself.

The grenade exploded, but only gave Tiny and his men a fright; it had fallen into a drainpipe without a cover and only split and shook the ground. Startled, Tiny looked at Slick and said:

'This shit's dynamite!'

'Fuck!'

Knockout took three Molotov cocktails out of his bag and told the rest of the gang to stay put. He asked Mousetrap to cover him and headed back to where Tiny was. This time he appeared right in front of his enemies, firing at them with a machine gun and, with his left hand only, lit one of the bombs and threw it at the head of one of Tiny's men before running away. Tiny and company were horrified to see Couscous running around, blue flames covering him from head to foot, his deep cry contrasting with Tiny's quick, shrill little laugh, his gymnast's clothes melting and sticking to his body which, with slowing movements, fell to the ground and burned in silence.

Tiny realized his machine gun was out of ammunition, tossed it to Slick, took his pistol from his waistband and went out alone into the alleys. He found his enemies in one and ran at them, firing. Knockout's men retreated a little, and he stood there alone returning Tiny's angry shots, but his machine-gun fire failed and didn't hit its target. A clash of titans. A shoot-out with no hide-and-seek, some of Knockout's men peering out from behind a wall, Tiny's from another. Knockout ran out of ammunition. The second he placed his hand on the butt of his other pistol, he was hit in the stomach. He fell and rolled backwards hoping to find safety in the trench, while five of his men went after Tiny.

'I got 'im, I got 'im, I got the bastard, I got Knockout!'

Just as Knockout was being rescued, My Man emerged alone from an alley and killed another two of Knockout's men.

Over in The Blocks, happy that Knockout had been hit, Tiny bought beers for whoever wanted them and gave away free drugs in his dens. Euphoria reigned.

At that stage in the war, Carlos Roberto's friends advised him to quit managing Tiny's dens; anyone who was tight with Tiny was, naturally, his enemies' enemy. Carlos Roberto, who was already managing rather half-heartedly, started handing over his duties to

Good Life, who liked handling money. After a short time, Good Life took over everything and, to get on his brother's good side, started going around armed, giving orders and participating in the decision-making. He bought two houses, one in Realengo and the other in Bangu, for Tiny to hide in when he needed to. He bought himself a brand-new car, a boat and diving equipment, as he thought his own was out-of-date. He rented a house in Petrópolis, where he often went horse-riding, began to dress more smartly, always frequented posh restaurants, and went water-skiing in the Barra da Tijuca canal. The bastard knew how to spend money.

'What's up, Leonardo? I always see you with the guys, but you keep to yourself, dress sharp, like to swim, and you've always got a nice girl on your arm. Wanna make some easy money so you can have even more fun?'

'That depends. I'm not lookin' to get into trouble!'

'This is a piece of cake, man! You've got your license, haven't you?'

'Yeah.'

'All you gotta do is drive for me, OK? Didn't you like it those times I took you horse-ridin' in Petrópolis? Didn't you like it when we went divin'? Well now we can do this stuff every week, know what I'm sayin'? You won't have to use a gun, right? We'll only be spending about two days a week here, and the rest of the time we'll just be having fun. You just drive, OK? I'm gonna get my brother out of here every week and when he goes we go too. But don't tell anyone, right? I've rented a huge house in Petrópolis.'

'With him?!' scoffed Leonardo.

'No man. We're goin' somewhere else.'

'What's it worth?'

'Money's no problem, man. I'm the one runnin' my brother's business, know what I'm sayin'?' said Good Life.

Tiny walked along with his head down, believing the rumor that Knockout was dead. Now the only one left was that motherfucker, Carrots. He went up to Leonardo and his brother and said:

'Here's the story: in that last attack, loads of ammo was used and almost no one got killed, right? Hey, you—you're not doin' nothin',' he said, looking at Leonardo. 'Round everyone up and take 'em over behind The Hill—we're gonna practice target shootin'. Tell a kid to get us some bottles to practice on, OK?'

'OK!'

'And you listen up,' he went on, talking to Good Life. 'Go buy me some clothes, OK? But don't give 'em to me in front of anyone.'

Over on The Hill, where more blocks of apartments were being built, an irate wind tugged at the low green vegetation. The muddy, rocky slope extended all the way down to the abandoned mansion with the pool, and halfway down there was a flat area overlooking most of the estate, the back end of the neighborhood of Araújo and part of the North Zone of Rio. There was also a view of the Recreio dos Bandeirantes hills and Knockout's neighborhood, which Tiny squinted at suspiciously, then laughed his quick, shrill little laugh.

Dozens of bottles were lined up on the muddy slope, and each man had the right to ten shots. The one who missed the most had to buy beers for the gang. Leonardo didn't waste a single bullet, prompting Tiny to say:

'I don't like this kid, I don't like 'im!'

On the way back, Tiny went up to Leonardo.

'Did you tell Skinny to come?'

'Yeah.'

'What did he say?'

'He didn't say nothin'.'

He quickened his pace until he caught up with Bicky.

'That Skinny thinks he's hot shit, you know. He had nothin' when he got here and now he don't even listen to me, know what I'm sayin'? He's makin' more than the rest of us put together. You see the car he bought?'

'It's all legit. It's not hot . . . The car's brand new!'

'Remember that time he didn't give you coke for your den and he gave some to Russian Mouse?'

'Yeah!'

'Well, I reckon he's got it in for you, and another thing: the day I got Knockout I saw 'im makin' the death sign behind your back.'

'You're kiddin'!?'

'It's true, man. But I've already been to the *terreiro* and the guy said everythin's fine, you're not goin' down . . . but the guy's got it in for you.'

They walked down The Hill and stood around in the square for a few minutes. They could see Skinny washing his Beetle. The radio was on, there was a half-empty bottle of whisky sitting there, and Skinny trotted out a few dance steps from time to time, his revolver near the bucket of water and kerosene.

'Get rid of 'im!' Tiny told Bicky as he watched him.

'Do we have to get rid of Slick too?'

'Let's wait a bit, 'cos he's on good terms with the kids on Block Thirteen, know what I'm sayin'? We don't know if Carrots is gonna continue the war, but don't worry—I'll take care of 'im.'

Bicky reloaded his pistol and went around the building, leaving Tiny with a grim smile on his face. Skinny was lying on the ground rinsing off the mud flaps and didn't notice Bicky walking over. Bicky fired twelve bullets, at point-blank range, into his friend's head.

After a month, the newspapers were saying that the death toll in City of God was higher than that of the Falklands War in the same period of time. It had become one of the most violent places in the world. A TV camera showed pictures of Knockout at Miguel Couto Hospital. He answered all of the reporter's questions without blinking. At the end of the interview, he stated that the war would only end when he or Tiny died.

'Then the war ends today. It's gonna end today 'cos I'm goin' down to Miguel Couto to get 'im. I'm goin'!' shouted Tiny when he heard about the report. 'Leonardo, you're drivin' me down there . . .'

'Why don't you cover your arm in Mercurochrome and say you're hurt?'

That night, Tiny doused his arm with Mercurochrome and tied his pistol to his ankle. He laughed his quick, shrill little laugh. He got in the car and slid down in the backseat. Leonardo started the engine and a shoot-out began.

Ten civil policemen had gone in disguised as dustmen, hanging off a dump truck and firing at any black face they came across. Leonardo accelerated and took the road behind the square, where he and his brother abandoned the car and disappeared between the buildings.

In his apartment, before the shooting started, Sharky had punched his mother in the head, kicked her in the stomach twice, head-butted her in the mouth and hit her across the back of the neck with the butt of his gun, bringing her to the ground. The old cow was always telling him to put his clothes away and to not leave his belongings scattered around the house. Every time he went to the toilet, she checked to see if he'd wet the toilet seat. It was as if she was possessed. He'd already told her that if she insisted on bossing him to do this or that, he'd bash her head in. The bitch hadn't believed him.

When he heard the shots, he thought it was Knockout's gang and went out to fight: if he killed Carrots, he'd be looked up to and Tiny might even give him a den. At that moment the Military Police showed up. Without shooting, they wove their way quietly through the buildings and came face-to-face with a confused Sharky, whose pistol wasn't even cocked. He tried to cock it. A spray of bullets cut him through the stomach. His sister came after him and shouted:

'Kill the bastard—he bashed up Mom and almost killed her!'

When he heard Sharky's sister, Sergeant Linivaldo went into the middle of the street, motioned to the policeman driving the van, took the steering wheel and ran the back left wheel over Sharky's head several times.

The policemen grouped together and the sergeant counted them; one was missing. He appeared with a pawn in handcuffs. They put him in the back of the van and headed for Knockout's area. They hid the van in an alley, took the pawn into the middle of the square on Block Fifteen and removed his handcuffs.

'Now run that way, run, run!'

They fired a shot into the air and left. Knockout's men found the pawn and killed him.

Carrots told everyone to lie low. He'd only resume fighting when Knockout returned. He was afraid; he didn't have what it took to run the gang. The police were breathing down their necks, the newspapers ran stories on City of God every day and his name was always splashed across the front page.

He took cover at the house of a friend whose wife had disappeared more than a week before. Now he was able to take Carrots in without having to listen to the bitch going on and on because he'd brought a gangster into the house. Carrots' hands were shaking, his heart beat fast. His friend was asleep in the bedroom, completely drunk, grinding his teeth, farting and tossing around in bed. What a fucked-up life he had. He didn't even want to be in this stupid war. He'd always liked money, money was what he wanted, and there was that dickhead wanting to take over his den. The greedy bastard; he'd never liked Tiny. He remembered the days when he'd worked as a cleaner at the Catholic University, the only time he'd donned a sucker's uniform. He knew he wouldn't get rich cleaning up white kids' mess, and only suckers worked knowing they'd never enjoy the good things in life. That was why he'd given it up, and he'd never gone back to that bitch of a life. Weed, coke, that was where the money was. If it weren't for Tiny he'd be rich.

He thought about his kids. He wanted them to study at the Catholic University; he'd always heard that the best schools were the Catholic ones. Two kids. What did he have to leave them? The most obvious inheritance was the war. Knockout had better come back soon, to help him fly at Tiny with all the hatred he felt at that moment. Kill him, take the den on Block Thirteen and work hard for a year. He'd buy property in the countryside, where he'd raise chickens, put in a pool and build a bathroom with a sauna. He tried to remember how to make Molotov cocktails, but nothing came to him. His soul was filled with anguish. His gastritis came back to punish him. Milk. In the fridge there were only some rotting potatoes and a blackened piece of steak on a layer of dirty white grease. There was a bottle of brandy on the shelf. He didn't hesitate, and drank it all to get a good night's sleep. If one of his enemies arrived there'd be no problem; he'd die in his sleep. There are moments when one's own death seems imperative.

No one knew how, but Butterfly appeared on a street corner in the middle of one night. When people asked how he'd got free he replied that he had a few tricks up his sleeve. He knew about everything that had happened. The only thing he couldn't understand was why they were all standing on the street corner if Sergeant Linivaldo was on the prowl.

'If he comes, we'll give it to 'im in the chest!' said Tiger seriously.

Butterfly looked at him. He only knew the gangster by sight, and there were others with him he didn't even know were in the gang, but Tiger was the only newcomer to come forward and had been so incisive that Butterfly fell silent. Tiger continued:

'We should be Up Top right now, you know. There's a shitload of guys up there that only dare come out when Knockout's around.'

'Go get the guys from The Blocks,' said Butterfly to a pawn.

'What's this about gettin' the guys from The Blocks, man? We can take care of this ourselves. That Tiny's messed up in the head. He wasted a friend that Slick brought in and only shows up to give orders.'

'He let Bicky take out Skinny because the guy'd made the death sign behind his back. I was in the slammer, but I heard about it.

Look, you're with us, but the only ones who give orders round here are me, Slick and Tiny!' said Butterfly.

Tiger grew serious, looked at the entire gang, scratched his nose and said:

'OK, if you're the boss.'

Tiny's gang appeared at the other end of the street. The Block Thirteen gang waited for them to approach in silence.

'Hey Slick, I'm broke, you know. I need a little somethin' to buy some guns with, know what I mean? So here's the story: you give me what you used to give Skinny, OK?'

'OK,' he said through clenched teeth.

Tiger looked at Butterfly and My Man, then screwed up his nose and moved off.

The two gangs headed up Middle Street together, with orders to pull the trigger on anyone, even the police. Butterfly looked at My Man with knowing eyes, doing his best to make his friend understand that he didn't agree with Tiny's instructions. My Man understood, but tried to hide his reaction amidst the two uniformed gangs.

Over at the police station, Lincoln and Monster were arming themselves. They were going with six other police officers in two vans to The Blocks to try to take the enemy by surprise.

Up Top, members of Knockout's gang were in a meeting at Groover's house, where the pawn was telling them what had happened in the cell down at the police post. He said the policeman wanted to have a serious talk with Knockout, believing he really was a friend of the chief. They were eating bread and mortadella. They were filling their bellies so they could snort the half-ounce of coke already chopped out on the plate. First they'd smoked some dope and now they were thirsty.

'Eating this shit dry sucks!' said Mousetrap.

'Hey, kid. Nip over to Palhares' Bar and buy us a family-size bottle of Coke.'

The pawn stood up, took the money and asked:

'Anyone got an empty bottle?'

'What's this shit about an empty bottle, kid? You're a gangster, ain't ya? You should be stealin' it.'

'Take my gun!' said Mousetrap.

The white, curly-haired boy walked with small steps, his eyes bulging. The fear of losing his life only came to him in that instant. He'd never felt it before, but now, in the deserted streets, after Carrots had ordered the entire gang to lie low, his regret at having dropped out of his second year of secondary school, at having left his part-time job to fall into the clutches of the war out of sheer fascination, was patent.

In the next street, Tiny ordered his gang to be quiet. Something told him he was about to catch his enemies unawares. The boy walked faster. It was best to act quickly; the next day he'd give up his life of crime. Tiny, who only had his sawed-off shotgun cocked, silently cocked his machine gun. Gangsters, cats and the police are all alike—they pop up in the most improbable places and bring the silence to life.

Shivers ran down the boy's spine, he slowed his pace and his mother's voice asking him how he was getting on at school resounded in his ears. Tiny motioned for the gang to stop, and aimed his machine gun at the corner with his finger on the trigger. The boy also stopped without a sound, cocked his pistol and started to walk quickly again. He was less than ten steps away from entering Tiny's firing range.

He took seven steps, then one of Tiny's pawns cleared his throat. The boy breathed a sigh of relief, believing that someone honest and good was coming around the corner—a gangster wouldn't make any noise. He quickened his step and walked into Tiny's firing range.

'Hands on your head, asshole!' said Tiny, and asked his gang, 'Is this kid a no-good?'

'Yeah!' said Tube.

'Let's fuck 'im up, let's fuck 'im up!' said Russian Mouse.

'Put the gun on the ground and lie down! Wanna pray?' asked Tiny with every evil bone in his body.

The boy said nothing.

'Where's your friends?' Tiny asked.

The boy knew he was going to die whether he talked or not, so he kept quiet. He pissed his pants, tensed his body, and at that moment his parents' advice came flooding into his mind. Tiny stared at him for a time, uncocked his gun and ordered the gang to go take a walk. Alone with the boy, he ordered him to get up and asked:

'Know how to sing?'

'Yeah!'

'Then sing "Maluco Beleza"!'

The boy started at the chorus, stuttering at first, then sang in tune. Tiny looked at the moon, and felt the wind lightly brushing his face. The boy's voice was like Sparrow's singing the same song, except that Sparrow had always sung with a smile on his face and his arm draped around Tiny's neck, jumping around like a child. In a flash the memory touched several points, it wasn't just one Sparrow that he remembered, but many, in many different places and situations, always laughing or singing. If Sparrow were alive, maybe Tiny wouldn't have raped Knockout's girl and none of this would be happening; he'd certainly have a lot more money and no enemies.

The boy stopped. Tiny told him to sing again. Again, looking at the sky, he sought Sparrow's image leaning against a star, because his voice had sounded in his ears the very moment he was going to fire the gun pointed at the boy's head. He saw nothing. Sparrow wasn't on a star; only his soul was there, beside him, showing him that the boy wasn't a real enemy. He stared into space and winked, believing Sparrow would see it.

'Get out of this life, boy . . . Get outta here! Did someone do somethin' to you to make you join the war? Go find yourself a school!'

Almost unnoticed, Lincoln's gang took cover on The Hill after they'd hidden the police vans in the bush. A security guard at the construction site on The Hill jumped in alarm, but Lincoln himself motioned to him, telling him to relax. With the help of a pair of binoculars, he was able to see everything going on in The Blocks. Sergeant Linivaldo came to the conclusion that they were in Knockout's area. They'd have to wait.

Tiny told the gang the kid wasn't a gangster.
    'The bastard wasn't a Jerry! He was after some guy 'cos of a girl.'
    They went back to The Blocks.

Lincoln told his men to stay calm when Tiny's gang gathered in the square. They needed to watch where they were going next.
    'The one next to the lamppost is Tiny,' said Sergeant Linivaldo. 'Which one's Slick?'
    'He's the one that's leavin', goin' down that alley there . . . He's the boss of Block Thirteen.'
    'Gusmão, go to the van and send out a radio message that a guy in a blue tracksuit is going to cross Edgar Werneck at the bridge at the start of the avenue. He's dangerous and armed. Tell 'em to bring 'im in, but I want 'im alive, 'cos he can give us a lot of info.'
    Slick did not resist when he was told he was under arrest. He answered everything the policemen asked him at the police post itself.
    'You takin' 'im down to the Thirty-Second, Sergeant?'
    'Only on Monday. First let's see if everything he's told us is true.'

Cocaine sales in The Blocks increased, and in spite of the war it was common for cars to arrive with people from elsewhere wanting to buy coke, as it was the easiest area in the *favela* to get to. Tiny laughed whenever Good Life told him how much he'd sold on a particular day. The addicts kept bringing in household appliances, weapons and jewelry to exchange for drugs. There was no way the police could arrest so many addicts, so they only arrested those who were armed. There had still been no word from Slick. It was only when Sergeant Linivaldo shouted out in Block Thirteen that he wanted two hundred thousand to release him that his friends discovered what had become of him.

Butterfly went to Tiny, who at first didn't want to fork over the money. He said that Slick hadn't kept his wits about him and he wasn't about to give money to the police to free a fool. But after much grumbling, he sent Good Life to give Butterfly the money.

Slick heard it all from Butterfly half an hour after his release. Butterfly beefed up the story, saying that Bicky had repeated twice that Tiny shouldn't hand over the money. Slick ground his teeth.

'Look, that Tiny owes me money, and if I ever run into 'im when I've got my gun on me, I'll pull the trigger,' said an addict after making some small talk, and snorting the first line of coke through a ten-cruzeiro note from the third wrap that he'd bought from Carrots' assistant. 'One day, I went over to his area to get some stuff and he gave me a hard time. He even punched me in the face.'

'You're kiddin'!?'

'Kiddin'? No way! He thinks we're stupid, man. He hasn't got a clue that we can get nasty too.'

'Where're you from?'

'São José. So,' he said, pausing to snort another line of coke, 'if anyone wants to get together to take 'im out, count me in, OK? I can't bring anyone from my area 'cos we don't have anywhere to crash here.'

Carrots' assistant let the addict run Tiny down for a good while, always agreeing with him, then said:

'You can say that again. But hey, go have a chat with those guys over there. Everyone there wants to get rid of 'im too.'

Mousetrap heard the same story that the assistant had heard. Then he pressed the barrel of his revolver to the addict's head, ordered a gang member to frisk him and took him to meet Carrots. After a great deal of talking, Carrots sent for another three papers from his den and continued to ask the names of the inmates the newcomer had done time with.

A short time later, Mousetrap arrived to say the car was ready. The mechanic had promised it would no longer stall for no reason.

That night they went to fetch Knockout from the hospital. The operation was a success. The policeman on duty at the time was screwing one of the nurses and only reported the prisoner missing two hours later.

Antunes told Knockout that he'd been thinking a lot about their mother over the last few days. He was tired of that life of bullets, death and drugs. He was going to get a job and rent a room for himself, their sister, mother, father and younger brother.

'The guy said there's cheap rooms to rent over in Catete . . . I'm not interested in this life anymore, see. I'm gettin' out before I get a record . . . We don't have any peace. C'mon, man, forget this shit about revenge. You almost got yourself killed and you've killed tons of people.'

'I'm getting out too, but only when Tiny's dead!'

'Well, it's up to you, but it's a hell of a way to live! I never thought I'd ever hold a gun . . . It's a dog's life . . . All you have to do is go out into the street and you end up in trouble over nothing. Just yesterday I had a run-in with Altar Boy and Screw.'

'What about?'

'They were dealing and ended up snorting the den dry—more than twenty papers. I went to talk to them, but they said they were gonna take me out . . .'

'I was gonna get rid of those two but Carrots told me not to, so I let it go . . .'

'All I know is that I'm out of here, right? Here's my pistol. I'm going home for a shower and a change of clothes, then Tribobó and me are going down to that gas station on Miguel Salazar to look for a job, OK? There was an ad in yesterday's paper saying they were looking for help. I'm going to see if the guy'll give me a job and then, if he's got other stations, 'cos they always do, I'll ask for a transfer.'

'Good for you, man. Good luck!'

For Antunes, that morning had the purest air. It was the morning he was going to let go of the madness of revenge. God Almighty would see to it that Tiny got punished. Who was he to deliver justice if divine justice was stronger? He was leaving to look for a job, leaving City of God, leaving the war. Knockout would leave too. That was what his mother had said—that if he left, his brother would end up leaving too. The gas station owner would give him a job, because he was well-spoken, knew his math, and even though he was black, he had straight hair and his brother's blue eyes. He looked good; that was important, very important. He showered, chose his best clothes, put on some cologne and slicked back his hair. He was meeting Tribobó at 8:30 on the corner of the former Doorway to Heaven bar. He asked his mother to pray for him to get the job and hurried into the street.

'You're so handsome, my boy, so sharp-looking. Forget this revenge thing. That Tiny won't last long. The police'll end up killing him!' said a woman gossiping with three others at her front gate.

People greeted him as he walked along; he was the brother of the avenger, and almost as handsome. He walked through the streets Up Top without that tense face he'd been wearing of late, without a gun in his hand or waistband, greeting housewives as he'd done in times past, without peering around corners to check for the enemy.

There on the corner, duly spruced up for the occasion, Tribobó was waiting for him with the same smile. So many times they'd gone out together to launch an attack and now they were going to look for work! It was doing wonders for his soul. And what about his grandfather's soul? He prayed for God to take it to a good place, together with the souls of those who'd died in combat. He'd pray for them always.

'You'll have to fill out a form. Have you got all your documents on you?' said the employee who received them. 'Where do you live?'

'City of God.'

'That's gonna make things difficult. The boss isn't accepting people from City of God.'

'Why not?'

'I'm not sure, but fill out the form. You never know, right?'

Altar Boy and Screw watched them from behind a truck on the other side of the street. The sun was hot and the traffic heavy. Firing from there would be stupid. If they went a little farther down the street, crossed over and doubled back, keeping close to the walls until they got to the gas station, they could surprise their enemies easily. This was what they did, unnoticed.

The first bullet came from Altar Boy's revolver. It only served to warn their enemies and the gas station employees. The attendants headed into a condominium next door, the employee who'd been talking to Antunes and his friend jumped into an oil drum, and Tribobó jumped a small wall and fled. Antunes got two bullets in the head, spun and fell to the ground.

Without putting him out of his misery, Altar Boy and Screw ran into the middle of the road, stopped a car, got in and headed for Taquara, where they abandoned the vehicle and stole another one, then drove up Grajaú Range and were never seen again.

The news spread quickly and Antunes' body was surrounded by people. Several police officers arrived to ask questions.

Knockout was drinking the tea his girlfriend had prepared, missing his mother's affection and homemade remedies. The sparkle in his brother's eyes had renewed his zest for life. He hated black tea without sugar, and held his nose as he drank. He felt pain and peered out beneath the curtain. It was already midday, but it still seemed like morning. The fresh air met his face. Perhaps if he smoked a joint time would go faster. No, no drugs. Passion fruit juice made you sleepy, yes, he'd knock back a whole jug. He called Mousetrap, who was keeping guard in front of the house. Silence. He called again. He wanted to ask his friend to buy the newspaper. There'd no doubt be a story about his escape.

'Wait a minute,' answered Mousetrap.

Mousetrap, Carrots, Turtle and Hairy Beast were talking in low voices about what had happened. No one stepped forward to report Antunes' death to Knockout, who was lying down. His few movements had caused his two wounds to bleed. His friends decided to go in and tell him about the tragedy together. They opened the gate in silence. Knockout cocked his gun and slid from the bed to the ground.

'It's OK!' said Mousetrap.

With their help, Knockout got back into bed, and asked Carrots to turn on the fan. He found their silence odd. Ever since he'd got back from the hospital his friends had been overly cheerful. And now this seriousness for no reason, with everyone hanging their heads and dragging their feet. He screwed up his forehead, looked them each steadily in the eye and asked:

'Who's down?'

Nervous silence. A cry. The desperation of his friends as Knockout stood abruptly, weak at the knees. He knew it was Antunes. He held Carrots by the shoulders and said:

'It was Antunes! It was Antunes! Where's his body? Where is it?'

'Over at the gas station past the Wella building.'

'It was Tiny, wasn't it?'

'No, it was Altar Boy and Screw.'

Without a word, he pulled on clothes and headed for the door, his hatred giving him the strength to walk. His friends tried to hold him back, but he jerked away, shook them off, reached the yard, went through the gate and crossed the threshold of his fate, the fate of being punished for not having prayed enough. His wounds bled and left a trail through the alleys, through the streets now full of people. His eyes stung, but that's all—the tears did not come, and what good were tears anyway? Crying didn't change a thing. All he could do was allow his desire for revenge to well up. He had flashbacks of the sheet covering Grandpa Nel stained red, Steak-and-Fries with his head blown off, his darling being abused, the wall of his house riddled with bullet holes, his dog full of lead, and now the image of a blood-stained Antunes was about to be embedded in his memory. He reached Miguel Salazar Street, where the morning breeze was stronger, but fuck the breeze and the sun burning his face! What he really wanted was for it all to be an illusion, for his brother to be alive. He caught sight of the crowd. Blood ran down his pants legs and made the inside of his sneakers slippery.

He approached the body. Even the police were silenced by his arrival. Just like his brother, no one seemed to move in his presence. He embraced the dead man's body, brothers' blood mingling, kissed his cheeks, and whispered something in his ear. Then he carefully let go of his body, backed away, looked around, grabbed a stump of wood he found nearby, took it to the gas pump, doused half of it with fuel and held it to the flame of one of the candles around his brother's corpse, raised the torch and ran, his heart pounding like the Devil, toward Altar Boy's house, without even noticing the two bullet holes in his body. Physical pain was nothing—hatred could supplant any debility. He turned down an alley, where he found some gang members, who followed him. He arrived at Altar Boy's house, took the machine gun from Carrots, handed him the flaming piece of wood to hold, and fired a spray of bullets at the door and windows. He went back to Carrots, handed him the gun, took the torch, went into the house and set fire to the curtains, asking someone to get some cleaning alcohol to splash on the doors and the roof beams. In no time at all, the small house was in flames. He stood there for a few minutes, then went to do the same to Screw's house.

At Antunes' funeral, Carrots ordered his entire gang to stand outside the graveyard holding their guns. Knockout had insisted on going, even though most of his friends thought it was a bad idea.

'If the police or any hoods show up, let 'em have it til Knockout can get out. He can't run.'

But not one policeman or villain appeared.

Two days after Antunes' funeral the combat between the gangs gained new momentum; when Tiny heard Knockout was back in the *favela* he decided not to give him any peace. Sometimes the fighting went on for three or four days at a time. Tiny always swore at the top of his lungs. When the battles were taking place, the police thought it best not to interfere. It was better to let them kill one another.

School classes were cancelled and no one went to work. There were deaths, especially among the pawns in Knockout's gang who became easy prey in the ambushes—they hadn't been brought up among villains and weren't skilled in fleeing from the police. When the parents—always the last to know their kids were involved in the war—eventually found out, they started taking preventive measures: they moved house, sent their kids to stay with relatives far from the *favela* and even took them to work when they had no other choice.

After a while, a desperate Knockout banned the pawns from going to the front line. He took away their weapons and went to their homes to tell their families. He only wanted real villains with him. Tiny, on the other hand, even forced workers to fight. When they didn't go into combat, they got a bullet in the ass.

Tiny's dog reminded him of Sparrow, and he carried it everywhere he went. It ate top-quality food, no leftovers, and he only allowed

Black Stump, whom he treated as if he were his own son, to take care of the dog. It was Black Stump who fed the animal, bathed it with special shampoo to protect it from fleas and ticks and took it for obedience lessons. When the dog was bigger it also went into battle: Tiny set it loose and followed its steps.

The families of the dead pawns called the newspapers in an attempt to get the media to pressurize the government into putting an end to the war, which had been going on for two years. Complaints to the police had no effect, because most of the gangsters had been arrested at some stage, but almost all had been released in exchange for bribes from Tiny. Only the pawns were taken down to the Thirty-Second Police Station, where charges were pressed against them, because Tiny refused to spend money on weak soldiers.

When he heard classes were about to start again, Groover began to miss the days when he used to study. He remembered teaching his school friends to dance, the potluck parties and girlfriends. Granted, he hadn't been the best of students, but he'd been sure he'd finish elementary school, go on to high school and try to get into Physical Education at university. But that bastard Tiny had spoiled his dream when he killed his younger brother in one of his attacks, just for the sport of it.

When he thought about Tiny his face twisted once again into a scowl. He got up, opened the fridge, grabbed a bottle of water, drank half of it in three gulps and ran his eyes over the two-bedroom Short-Term house: his mother sleeping, the empty place where his brother used to sleep. The hatred he felt at that moment gave way to compassion. He looked on top of the wardrobe and decided to have a read through his old schoolbooks.

He flicked through them slowly, went over lessons, notes from test days, messages from girlfriends forgotten between the pages, a heart with an arrow through it dripping blood into a chalice. He picked up another textbook that contained only questions:

What song has marked your life?
Who would you take to a desert island?
Who was the first person you ever kissed?
Do you have a weakness?
What kind of girl are you attracted to?

He found a pen and set about answering the questions. He wrote something down, scratched it out . . . He tried in every way possible to pass that test; yes, it was a test, perhaps the most difficult he'd ever taken. If he managed to answer the questions he could imagine he was still a person who had something healthy about him, but absolutely nothing came to mind; his eyes just welled with tears. He threw himself onto the bed, on top of the book, and cried himself softly to sleep.

He woke up early, thinking himself the biggest idiot on the face of the earth for having joined the war, because if he'd asked to change schools and disappeared from the street, Earthquake and his friends would surely have forgotten him. He'd been stupid. If there hadn't already been a war he would never have got involved in one of his own accord. He walked through his tiny house to the stove, where he found a piece of buttered bread, a cup of white coffee and a note, saying: 'Son, take the money from the top drawer in the wardrobe and go somewhere far from here.'

All of a sudden it occurred to him to go to his school. He'd ask his teacher to get him a place somewhere else. He'd get out of there, study every day and, who knows, he might even get a job. He washed, dressed and headed for his school just as Slick and Night Owl were leaving Block Thirteen, intending to kill enemies.

Groover crossed the Rec without noticing anything unusual. Not even his friends were in the street. Poking half his face around a corner, Night Owl watched his footsteps, cocked his gun, and hid as Groover crossed the bridge. He assumed he was going to take the street along the left branch of the river to attack Block Thirteen alone, which he'd been doing lately. He waited long enough for Groover to come close and stepped out into full view, ready to fire. He didn't see him and, thinking he'd gone around the block, ran to wait on the next corner.

'I heard what's been going on with you, son . . . How awful! I was even thinking about coming to talk to you, but your own friends said it'd be dangerous.'

'Just as well you didn't come, what with the stray bullets and all . . .'

'Why haven't you got out of here? This business of taking justice into your own hands is nonsense.'

'It's only just sunk in and I've come to see if you could help get me into another school!'

'That's no problem, but how're you going to live here now with all these enemies?'

'I'll leave . . . I'm even thinking about getting a job . . .'

'Why don't you try getting into technical school? They've got technical courses and the students study all day long. I'll talk to a friend of mine. Come back and see me and I'll let you know what she said.'

They talked a little longer, then Paulo Groover left, taking care not to let his teacher see the .38 in the back of his waistband.

Groover decided to head back past Leão supermarket, cross Middle Street, cut through Blonde Square to Penguin's bar and head up through the alleys.

His enemies followed his steps with their eyes and this time didn't wait for Groover to come closer before firing at him again and again. One bullet grazed his leg, and another went through his abdomen. Even so, Groover had the strength to draw his gun, shoot Night Owl in the arm and Slick in the leg, and run back into the school.

Slick and Night Owl followed him: they continued the chase despite the fact that they'd been shot and tried to break into the school, but Groover's teacher confronted her fear and nervousness, and the gangsters themselves. She argued that the school was official government grounds and as such the police wouldn't give them peace until they'd caught them. Slick called her every swear word under the sun and fired his gun into the air. The principal called the police while the argument grew heated outside. In the toilets, Groover's bladder emptied itself when he heard the sound of the sirens.

The teacher, calmer now, talked to the police, but only told them that the gangsters had tried to invade the school. Then, with the help of other teachers, she hid Groover in her car and drove him to a hospital.

A rumor went around that Knockout had gone off the deep end since Antunes' death. He didn't eat, didn't sleep and had taken to snorting too much cocaine. His determination to kill Tiny grew with every passing second. When he heard that another pawn had been shot by Night Owl, he had a nervous breakdown and was taken to a clinic, where he spent three days before escaping from his room. When he got back to City of God, he was immediately involved in a shootout with several gangsters from Block Thirteen, who had gone Up Top to launch an attack. He killed one and was hit by a bullet in almost the same place where Tiny had hit him before.

The day Knockout got out of the hospital, his enemies were still hopeful that he might die, so Tiny's gang had relaxed a little. They were gathered behind The Hill, now inhabited by hundreds of new residents, indulging in beer, whisky and cocaine. Joking around in a loud voice, Tiny said that Night Owl's game was to kill loads of pawns so he could call himself a killer. This riled Slick, who was actually the one who did the killing; Night Owl only covered him and put his victims out of their misery. Tiny wanted to put Slick down in front of his men because he'd noticed that most of the gangsters had been hanging around him lately, which made him afraid that he might lose his leadership.

Bicky stayed quiet, watching Slick's every move, thinking that Tiny might have ordered Slick to kill him. Slick, equally quiet, expected Tiny to betray him at any moment. Russian Mouse was sitting in a corner, laughing at everything Tiny said. Marcelo was giving Beep-Beep the full rundown of the sex he'd had with some slut the day before. He gesticulated and made faces. Good Life motioned to Leonardo, then told Tiny he was going to meet a supplier to receive a load of cocaine. Leonardo went with him and Good Life suggested they go for a swim at the beach. Alone in another corner, Otávio was flicking through a pocket Bible his mother had given him the last time he'd gone home. Tiny got tired of joking around with Night Owl, looked at a pawn known as Marine—he'd earned this nickname for deserting the Marine Corps to join the war and snort coke to his heart's content—and, with a serious expression on his face, asked:

'You're goin' out with that hot piece of ass from Block Eight, ain't ya?'

'Yeah.'

'She's really hot, ain't she? When you're about to fuck her, d'you kiss her snatch?'

'Yeah,' he answered, embarrassed.

'Do you really? You must be suckin' cock and everything!' he finished and laughed wildly. His men joined him.

Knockout arrived Up Top at around midday, to the joy of his men. There was much celebrating, with several rounds of shots fired into the air by the addict who said he'd been given a hard time by Tiny. He was now living in the *favela* in the house of a gangster who'd been arrested, and his job was to look after the guns and ammunition. On the corner of Block Fifteen, Knockout shook the hand of each soldier with a sad smile on his tired face. Thin and anemic, he moved with difficulty. He went to Carrots' house, where fifty of his men were milling about.

The news that Knockout was back in the *favela* spread quickly Up Top. Several residents sent him food and juices to help his recovery. His parents were taken to Carrots' house for a short visit, but they kneeled on the living-room floor and prayed for almost two hours without even touching their son. In silence, Knockout looked at his mother all in black and thin as a rake; he'd never seen a greater expression of bitterness. Tears spilled from his eyes, his body shook. The gangsters were also silent outside, with that sad, mute prayer inside.

'You need to get those wounds blessed, then have someone work some magic to protect you,' advised Carrots after Knockout's parents had gone. Knockout said nothing.

When the news reached Tiny, he was still behind The Hill. He started pacing back and forth, and laughed his quick, shrill little laugh, cutting the silence, which was so intense it seemed old. He looked at Night Owl and bellowed:

'Didn't you kill a shitload of pawns? So go kill 'im then!'

An apprehensive silence was resumed for a short time.

'Leave it to me—I'll kill 'im!' growled Slick, who now wore a red and black top hat. Where and when he'd started wearing it, no one could say for sure.

This time the silence was not cut by Tiny's laughter. With bulging eyes, he left without saying where he was going.

A beverages truck was making a delivery at the shops at around eight o'clock at night. Part of the gang was drinking beer there. Slick held his revolver to the driver's head, said something to him, then climbed into the back and called Night Owl, who also clambered up. As soon as his helper returned to the vehicle, the driver maneuvered the truck in the square and turned left. The gangsters watched in silence as the truck drove away. It headed down the street along the right branch of the river, turned left again, crossed the bridge and followed the river's edge to Block Thirteen. Slick climbed down, talked to Butterfly and went back to the truck, which then turned slowly into Middle Street. Under the tarpaulin, Slick and Night Owl watched everything through two holes they'd made on the way there with a piece of metal they'd found in the truck, which now turned into a street adjacent to Block Fifteen. It drove all the way down the street, turned, drove back and stopped at the entrance to the square.

'Let's take a walk. It's too hot here!'
  'Yeah, I'm boilin'!'
  'Stay put, man! You're sick!' said Carrots.
  'You guys smoke too much. Fresh air's good for you.'
  After his parents had left, and confused at the path his life had taken, Knockout went overboard snorting coke and smoked one joint after another. Then, always calm and polite with his friends, he said he was just going to stretch his legs and that he'd come right back to lie down. He strapped up and headed out with his buddies to the square on Block Fifteen, where his friends usually hung out.

Knockout stayed at one end of the square talking with the cool guys from Up Top. He said he'd never expected the war would assume such proportions, and repeated that he had nothing against most of the guys in Tiny's gang; his wrath was reserved specifically for Tiny himself. The driver and his helper got out of the truck unnoticed.

Butterfly divided seventy men into seven groups of ten, decided where each group was to attack from and headed Up Top. Earthquake, My Man, Butterfly, Tiger, Moth and Cererê were carrying machine guns and five of the pawns carried sawed-off shotguns. They had orders to keep firing, even if only into the air, to split up the enemy gang.

The first shots were fired at the river's edge, then gunfire was heard in a number of places. Knockout's men were disorientated, and ran in all directions, firing at random. Although debilitated, Knockout cocked his gun and headed for the middle of the square. On the back of the truck, Slick and Night Owl waited for the right moment. More than one hundred shots were fired at the same time.

Knockout shouted at the top of his lungs that he didn't need protection, and that each man should fend for himself. He ordered his men to split up, then decided to leave the square and head for enemy territory, imagining he'd catch some bastard returning to Block Thirteen. He ran with difficulty toward the truck, the addict following behind. He was the only one who decided to cover him.

Over in The Blocks, Tiny was talking with Bicky in his apartment. He said Slick had to be killed as soon as possible because even though he didn't believe in *macumba* anymore (after Sparrow's death, he'd stopped going to the *terreiro* to talk to Street Keeper, and he no longer recited the prayer he'd taught him or lit candles), he had a bad feeling about this business of him wearing an *exu's* top hat. He'd set him up in the next attack Up Top.

'How?'

'I'll get 'im when he least expects it, man! When the bullets are flyin', know what I mean? I'll just wait 'til his back's turned and pull the trigger. I've already taken out about five like that . . . Bernardo, Giovani, Alligator . . .'

'Fuck! Was that you? What for?'

'I had a feelin' they were up to no good, know what I mean? They were givin' me the evil eye. When I feel someone's got it in for me, I get 'em quickly . . . But hey: no one knows, OK? Keep it to yourself.'

Slick nudged Night Owl and said in a low voice that he didn't even need to shoot Knockout. Since he'd knocked back a few that afternoon, however, Night Owl understood that it was time to shoot Knockout and suddenly lifted up the canvas to fire, shouting:

'Nooooow!'

Dumbfounded, it took Slick a few minutes to work out what was going on. Knockout was also taken by surprise, but still he was quicker and fired three shots, although he didn't take aim. The pair jumped from the truck and ran. Without much agility or speed, Knockout went after them firing his gun, not giving them time to shoot back. Slick and Night Owl zigzagged back and forth as they ran. The addict looked behind him, then to both sides and, not seeing anyone, shot Knockout three times in the back. Knockout still managed to turn and point his revolver in an attempt to kill him. The addict shot him again.

Knockout fell.

And along came the wind to make little dust whirls on the dry ground, to carry the sound of the gunfire to more distant places, to destroy poorly made birds' nests, to tug at kites caught on wires, to weave its way through the alleys, to creep under roof tiles, to make a kind of inspection of the tiniest cracks in that hour, to nudge along the blood running from Knockout's mouth, and along came the rain with heavy raindrops ricocheting on the rooftops, flooding the streets, increasing the volume of water in the river and its two branches. It was so heavy that some thought it was trying to drench the course of time forever, from that moment on.

'Get someone to bring an ox, I want an ox . . . find a good cook and have her make some oxtail stew, get another to make cow-heel soup, and another to chop up the meat for the barbecue . . . Run over to the butcher and tell him to bring us everythin', quick . . . Hey, you there, start rolling joints . . . The stuff's on the house at the den . . . just dope, not coke, the coke's only on the house for the gang,' said Tiny, his left arm draped around Slick's shoulder and his right hand holding his dog's collar. 'I knew you were gonna kill 'im, I knew it! When you said it, I knew you meant it!'

'I was facin' 'im like this, right? Firin' away . . . So was Night Owl. I sunk the first one in his balls. Night Owl was shootin', too. We had more than twenty of his men shootin' at us, so we got out of there . . .'

The party to celebrate Knockout's death went on for three days, while Up Top everything was silent, the streets were deserted, and bars and shops were closed. A wake was held for Knockout in his own home, without any gang members present. In numbers his funeral surpassed Sparrow's and Niftyfeet's.

The day after Knockout's death, the addict asked Tiny's men, who were gathered in the square on Block Fifteen, for the gang's two best weapons. He said he was going to inspect them to keep them in good shape, walked off as if heading toward the house where he was staying, then turned down an alley, crossed Middle Street, pointed a pistol at the first car he saw, ordered the driver out, got in, put the two guns in the backseat and took off. He took Edgar Werneck Avenue at high speed heading toward Barra da Tijuca, happier than ever because he'd finally taken out the man who, while trying to kill Slick and Skinny, had killed his brother in Cruzada de São Sebastião.

'Kicks, my brother, I got 'em back for you!' he thought aloud.

Near Jacarepaguá Lake the motor began to splutter, and a little farther along it cut out completely, even though it was traveling at high speed. The addict turned the key back and forth in the ignition, but the car kept starting, then cutting out. He began to get nervous and pulled the car over onto the shoulder, without noticing a police patrol car drawing near. He was about to get out when he saw the police car and tried again to get the car to start. The police officers, who had only intended to give him a helping hand, noticed his desperation and told him he was under arrest. First they frisked him, then they searched the car, where they found the guns. They started beating him up right then and there. Down at the station, he told them everything he knew about Knockout's gang.

After talking a lot to Butterfly in private, Tiger ended up convincing him to break ties with Tiny and Slick. He said that this nonsense of only the two of them earning shitloads of money without fully exposing themselves and everyone else having to risk getting caught in robberies and holdups was wrong—it was unfair. They decided that some of the gang members would take turns selling the drugs and give seventy percent to the den, while the others would just stay on guard to protect the den from their enemies and the police. My Man would be the manager and the two of them would run the show. They'd use the seventy percent to give the main soldiers and lookouts a weekly wage and health insurance plan, help the local workers when they were in need, buy more weapons, hire a lawyer to work for the gang, and restock their merchandise. Butterfly thought there were too many people and that the money wouldn't stretch that far, but agreed with his friend nonetheless.

'We ain't got nothin' to do with Tiny no more, didn't you know? Or with you guys either. The money that comes in here stays here. How come we gotta give it to you guys? Tell your partner that Block Thirteen ain't got nothin' to do with The Blocks no more—alright?' said Butterfly with My Man, Earthquake, Moth and Cererê beside him, guns cocked.

Slick looked them quickly in the face one by one. He saw that the boys were no longer so boyish. They'd grown not only in height, but in shrewdness and cunning. The rest of the gang, more than ninety men, were posted on the corners of Miracle Street. It was best to be friendly and agreeable, because he was pretty sure he'd be killed if he weren't.

Tiny got angry when he heard of their decision and said he was going to send off all the hoods on Block Thirteen to meet their maker. But he relaxed a few minutes later when Good Life told him it was better to leave things as they were than to make more enemies, and that the Block Thirteen den wasn't doing much business.

With so much newspaper coverage of the violence in City of God, the Department of Public Safety and the Military Police told the press through the Department's chief press secretary that a large-scale police operation would be put in place in the region. Two days after the official press release, in the middle of a stifling hot May, Lieutenant Cabra assumed command of the police station, which had been completely renovated and extended. The station, where there had previously been only ten officers, received thirty well-armed men, and six new patrol cars joined the lone car that had been there.

Colonel Marins, commander of the Eighteenth Military Police Battalion, told Lieutenant Cabra to tell his subordinates that gangsters should be arrested, but if they reached for their waistbands to draw guns, they could shoot to kill.

This battalion was responsible for public safety in Jacarepaguá, Barra da Tijuca and Recreio dos Bandeirantes, and the commander also ordered all men to report to headquarters an hour and a half earlier, and all patrol cars to pass through the *favela* before heading for their beat.

The police action plan was primarily based on intelligence work. Dozens of police officers disguised as customers had gone to the dens to buy drugs. Others, taking advantage of the fact that mentally handicapped patients from Juliano Moreira Hospital in Taquara were always running away from the asylum and wandering through the *favela*, had pretended to be runaway patients, wearing the asylum's uniform, making funny faces and acting weird. They kept an eye on the gangs and followed their behavior. In this way, Lieutenant Cabra arrived with a substantial list of gangsters and their respective addresses. Their first raids failed, however, because most of the newspapers had divulged the information beforehand. The gangsters kept an eye on the city's main newspapers and when they discovered the authorities' intentions, they moved house and went to ground during the first week of the new police presence in the *favela*.

Even with all the police infrastructure, drug dealing was still rampant. The dealers sold at different points each day of the week, and posted pawns on street corners to cry, 'Bread for sale! Bread for sale!' whenever the police approached on foot or by car. On the other hand, the gangsters began to live in fear when they heard there were plainclothes police officers around, ready to pounce on them. Their lives were threatened by anyone willing to snitch, so if in doubt, they'd take out the potential traitor with no time for explanations, pleading or pardon. No room for screwups. Already wily, they became even more violent. Workers, cool guys, addicts—anyone at all could find themselves at the mercy of the gangsters' whims and discrimination.

Paranoia reigned in the *favela*. Even the addicts, previously valued customers because they kept the dens running, found themselves in danger. For ordinary residents this was yet another fear they had to live with. The police on one side, the gangs on the other, both spreading fear and putting lives at risk.

Earthquake was dealing one Saturday, and to get up Bicky's nose, crossed Edgar Werneck Avenue to sell his drugs near Bicky's den. A few pawns were left at his original spot to tell the stoners where the drugs were now being sold.

Bicky only learned of the affront that afternoon. He'd spent the morning at Violeta's office. Violeta was a lawyer who sold primary and secondary school diplomas. He could score police clearance certificates, ID cards, driver's licenses and other documents, and the bastard could even get you clearance certificates for cars and real estate. It was God in heaven and Violeta on earth.

Without consulting Tiny, Bicky got a machine gun and went alone to Block Thirteen to fire a few rounds. He didn't kill anyone, but his gesture could have sparked off a war between the two gangs. So very early the next day, Good Life asked Tiny to go tell the leaders of Block Thirteen that Bicky's attack had been an isolated incident, and that no one agreed with what he had done.

Tiny passed the task on to Slick and, as he talked with him, noticed that he kept laughing and putting his arm around his shoulders. He asked himself why he was afraid of Slick if they'd been friends since they were kids. If Slick had never shown signs of be-traying him, why kill him? He had flashbacks of his childhood, the days back in São Carlos, the shoeshiner's stool . . . He'd be a real bastard to betray his friend just because he was afraid of him; he was ashamed of being afraid. But he'd already planned Slick's death with Bicky, and if he backed out Bicky might think he was the trai-tor. He'd really screwed up and didn't know how to put things right. Now one of them would have to die, but whichever one stayed alive would be his friend if he warned both of them. He took this deci-sion on an impulse and, without actually listening to what Slick was saying at that moment, said:

'You know, out of everyone around, our friendship's the best. That's why I'm givin' you this tip-off—Bicky wants to get rid of you. Once I heard 'im sayin' somethin' strange to Sharky before he died, know what I mean? And when he saw me he started actin' all shady. If I was you, I'd take him out! I didn't tell you nothin' 'cos I wasn't sure, OK? But after what he just did, I dunno . . . I know the guys ain't workin' with us no more, but they're still buddies, you know? And you're still friends with Butterfly and his bunch there . . . Get rid of him, man! Get rid of him!'

'I'm getting rid of him today!' said Slick, then got on his bike and headed for Block Thirteen.

Tiny watched his friend ride off, then asked a pawn to go get Bicky.

'I've got somethin' important to tell ya. But don't say a word, OK? It's time for you to take out Slick, know what I'm sayin'? He wasn't happy when you pulled the trigger on that mob, you know. It might even have been him that told 'em to sell weed on your turf. Get rid of 'im! Get rid of 'im!'

As he crossed the square a few minutes later, Tiny saw nine police officers near the shops and dashed off without being seen. When he got to his new apartment he spotted another six policemen over on Red Hill.

'Good thing Good Life's arranged a hideout for me outside the *favela*,' he thought out loud.

'Go get Leonardo. Tell 'im we're going to Petrópolis. Tell 'im to fetch the car—we're gettin' out of the *favela*. There's too many cops around. I don't like cops! I don't like 'em. Then go to Good Life's place and tell 'im to send me all the money, send it all, 'cos I'm going to Petrópolis . . . Off you go, get a fuckin' move on!' said Tiny to Casserole, the oldest pawn to join the gang at the age of twenty-five.

Leonardo parked the car at the entrance to the building. Tiny took a little while to come down, as he was stuffing money into his shorts, his shoes, his shirt, his pants and jacket pockets, and under his cap. He rolled up the rest in a plastic bag, stuffed two 7.65 mm pistols into his waistband and went downstairs.

Leonardo took off at a moderate speed along the right branch of the river, crossed Gabinal Road at the end, took Highway Eleven, put the car in third and heard a police siren behind him. He was changing into fourth gear when the Military Police car pulled alongside him:

'Pull over!' shouted Sergeant Roberval, pointing a machine gun at him.

Leonardo stopped the car.

'Both of you out with your hands on your heads!' ordered Roberval.

'Tiny, that one there's Tiny! I'll get the picture! I'll get it!' exclaimed Pedro, one of the privates.

He returned holding a piece of paper, which he showed to Roberval after he'd ordered the two captives to the ground. Osmar frisked Tiny first.

'He's got a revolver and money everywhere! So you're rich are you? Get up, get up and take your clothes off! You stay on the ground,' ordered Pedro.

'You know there's more than ten warrants out on you? Yeeeaaah, man, things're lookin' bad for you!' said Osmar.

'Now, you answer everything I ask you. And if I think you're lyin'
I'm gonna beat the shit out of you. You read me?' said Roberval.

Tiny gave him the thumbs-up.

'Is this car yours?'

'Yeah.'

'Is it in your name?'

'No.'

'Whose name's it in?'

'A woman over in The Blocks . . .'

'Who bought the car?'

'Skinny, a guy Carrots killed!'

'Ahh, right, but it was Bicky who killed 'im! We know everything!
Here's the story . . . You frisked the other one?'

'He's unarmed and got no money.'

'Tell him to get outta here.'

Leonardo got up and walked slowly down Highway Eleven toward Gabinal Road.

'Now we can talk better. You're gonna get the car papers from
this woman and get someone to bring them to me tomorrow
morning, got it? And no funny business! I'm gonna let you go,
but I wanna see the documents and don't go around with your
pockets empty or you're dead. If you get caught and blab, I'll have
you killed in the slammer. When I'm on duty, I want half the den's
earnings, OK?'

'No problem.'

'Leave the money in a bag in that grassy area over in the square
when I arrive and I'll cut you some slack, know what I mean? OK?
You'll be fine!'

Tiny nodded.

'Leave 'im with a gun!' he told one of the privates. 'Now go
home and say the Lord's Prayer 'cos you've met God, but if you
go round with nothin' in your pocket, you're gonna meet the
Devil. Understood?'

* * *

It was late at night. The square in The Blocks was deserted, and there were only a few people drinking beer at the shops. Creeping along the walls of the building, Slick surreptitiously watched the barflies at the shops: there were no gangsters.

'Anyone seen Bicky around?'

No, no one had seen the person he wanted to kill. But turning the corner he saw Bicky, who tried to cock his gun. Slick pumped him full of bullets. The day dawned gray. Tiny called the gang together in an alley and ordered everyone to lie low for as long as possible. He only wanted his assistant and lookouts in the street— no strutting around with revolvers on street corners, but if they happened to run into the police they'd have to shoot first and if for some reason someone was arrested there was to be no talking. Tiny then headed for the shops, said something to a woman, went down an alley, emerged on Gabinal Road and waited apprehensively by the roadside until Good Life pulled over in a car. Tiny got in and they left the *favela*.

Got It Made and Seagull were caught with forty bundles of weed by two plainclothes policemen Up Top.

'Fuck! You've only got weed! Ain't you got any dough? What useless pieces of shit! C'mon, down to the station . . .'

Down at the police station, Sergeant Linivaldo greeted the dealers with punches and kicks, then ordered an officer to truss them up with nylon rope. They put them in the patrol van and Sergeant Linivaldo ordered the officer to head for Bandeirantes highway. They turned onto Highway Five and stopped.

'Get out,' said the officer as he opened the back. 'Run! Run and don't look back, 'cos now you're gonna be sellin' dope to the Devil.'

The dealers ran no more than five meters before they were shot in the back.

To tell the truth, Whitey only fired his gun when Knockout's gang was in The Blocks, and even then only when Tiny ordered him to.

This life of crime wasn't for him, and he was happy about the police presence because he could go out without worrying that Tiny might order him to stand around on a street corner with a revolver waiting for Knockout's men.

One Sunday, he left home early to go to his ex-girlfriend's place to try to get back together with her. He arrived at her building, cupped his hands to his mouth and called her name several times. When no one answered, he decided to go into the building. He knocked on her door three times, and she opened it on the fourth, still sleepy. She left him in the living room, went to the bathroom, and came back after a few minutes:

'Look, if you're here to try and get back together, don't hold your breath, OK? I'm tired of being strung along . . . You don't make any plans, you don't save any money, you don't talk about getting married, and you've already had your way with me. I don't want to be strung along anymore.'

'I promise I'll start puttin' somethin' aside each month.'

'You always say that, then you say you couldn't manage it . . . You're always buying clothes, spending money on coke . . .'

'Keep your voice down, girl . . .'

'My mom's not home. And I'll tell you somethin' . . . I've already got myself a boyfriend, OK? So don't bother me, 'cos he's the jealous type and he's a policeman . . . You'd best keep your distance,' she said, opening the door.

Whitey left hanging his head. He'd never thought that one day she'd tell him she had someone else. He'd been stupid, because if he'd been more considerate with her this never would have happened. When he got to the bottom of the stairs his eyes were full of tears. He didn't want anyone to see him like that and turned back.

His ex-girlfriend also opened the door crying, and they hugged, kissed and had sex right then and there in the living room, on the condition that he wouldn't come inside her. But as soon as they'd finished she repeated that she really was seeing Officer Morais and that she wasn't going to dump him, because in less than a month

Morais had taken her to meet his parents and had promised to rent a house so they could live together.

'Don't you think you're goin' too fast, Cida?'

'Well, he's better than you—you haven't made a move in three years.'

They showered, had sex again in the bathroom and when Whitey said good-bye she said: 'Maybe we can do this again sometime.'

A few minutes later, she got a message that Officer Morais was waiting for her in Freguesia Square, quickly fixed herself up and went to meet him. He took her to a motel.

'Don't come inside me, OK!'

'It ain't right that Carrots gives all the orders and has both dens to himself, you know! We lost brothers and cousins in the war, we helped him take Tiny's den and we didn't let him lose his own den, ain't that right, man? We need to have a word with him . . .' said Fernandes to two friends in the New Short-Term Houses.

'And he don't want no one else to set up a den in the area,' said Farias.

'Why did Fatso fall?' asked Messiah, who'd escaped from jail that day.

'He was givin' Mousetrap a hard time so Knockout took 'im out,' answered Fernandes.

'Hang on, hang on, it wasn't just 'cos of that, you know. Carrots was dyin' for Knockout to get rid of him. He really egged him on . . .' said Farias.

'Is that right?'

'And he'd given the gang a shitload of weapons.'

'Fuck! He really helped me out in jail, you know. The whole time he was there, I always ate food from the outside. He was cool . . . I was the one that sent 'im here . . .'

In the days prior to this conversation, Fernandes, Farias and Messiah had started plotting against Carrots with the gangsters from the New Short-Term Houses and the Two-Story Houses. Everyone agreed with them.

One day, they woke Carrots at around ten in the morning. He woke with a start, thinking it was the police, but when he looked through the window and saw Fernandes, he relaxed. His calm did not last long, however. When he saw the guys from the Two-Story Houses and the New Short-Term Houses on the corner outside his house, he guessed that they'd come about splitting the den.

'Let's go over there, 'cos the guys wanna have a talk with you, OK?'

Carrots walked over to his friends and asked what was going on. Silence. Then a gang member spoke up:

'You're the ones who've gotta answer him. It was your idea. You were the ones who talked to everyone. Spit it out, man!'

Fernandes blurted out what he thought, then Farias piped up and reaffirmed what his friend had just said.

Carrots laughed, said everything was OK, shook everyone's hand and went back inside.

After two months Cida still hadn't had her period. She was pregnant. The baby could be Morais' just as easily as Whitey's, but she wanted it to be Whitey's. In fact, she had a feeling the baby was his, which was why she went looking for him.

'Ahh, now you want me? Go find your policeman.'

Her belly grew and Morais, head over heels in love, took her to the house he had rented.

His defeat caused Whitey great suffering, because her moving in with the policeman made him feel he'd lost her forever. The only reason he wouldn't accept a reconciliation immediately was revenge. He wanted her to grovel and suffer as much as he had. The news that Cida had moved in with Officer Morais got around overnight and Whitey's friends teased him:

'Ha ha ha, lost your girl to a pig!' they laughed.

To get his own back, Whitey said loudly:

'But the kid in her belly's mine!'

Word got back to Morais.

Carrots got strapped up before sunrise on a Monday morning and went to Mousetrap's house. They chatted in his yard for a while, then shook hands.

'I knew I could count on you . . . Get your gun, maybe we can find those bastards now.'

Minutes later, Fernandes and Farias were dead.

The next day, in an alley near the square on Block Fifteen, the entire gang listened to an argument between Carrots and Messiah, who were both holding guns. Allegiances were spatially defined: those siding with Carrot stood on one side, next to him, and those siding with Messiah stood on the other. Those who didn't want to take sides tried to calm them down.

'I was the one with the den up here! Tiny killed everyone here and I fought him off—me and Knockout! The den's always been mine and it's gonna stay that way, got it?'

'But the guys put their lives on the line. We've lost a shitload of friends, cousins and brothers!'

'You haven't lost anyone, and you didn't kill anyone, so why're you stickin' your nose in?'

'I'm stickin' my nose in 'cos I sent a friend here, the guy donated some guns to the cause, and you took him out.'

'It wasn't me!'

Lieutenant Cabra headed up Middle Street with ten men.

My Man, Earthquake, Butterfly, Tiger, Moth and a pawn wound their way through the alleys.

Over in The Blocks, the Empty Pockets got off a bus and walked through the Old Blocks.

'Did you *fuck* him?'

'No! I haven't spoken to him since we've been together. His pride's hurt 'cos I left him for you.'

'If I find out you screwed him, you'll get a bullet in the face! You got a photo of the bastard?'

'I did, but I tore it up!'

'Have any of your neighbors got a phone?'

'Yeah, but I don't like asking to use it!'

'Well, here's what we'll do: the next time I'm on duty you take a stroll as if you're just passing through, and as soon as you see 'im, you come to the station and tell me.'

'You're not gonna kill 'im, are you?'

'No, I'm just gonna give 'im a fright!'

Lieutenant Cabra waited a while behind a wall on the corner opposite the square on Block Fifteen, waved to his men, got his machine gun ready and gave a little jump as if about to surprise someone; he did this at every corner he came to. No villains. He motioned to his men and they walked down one side of the square.

The argument became heated, with everyone talking at once. Carrots shouted for silence at the top of his lungs and fired a shot into the air, which sparked off a shoot-out punctuated with shouts and pleas:

'Calm down!'

'Hey, pal, we just wanna talk!'

'Take it easy!'

'What's up, man?!'

'Cool it, man, cool it!'

Cabra's men positioned themselves behind posts, cars, walls, and some even broke into houses. The Block Thirteen gang thought Tiny was attacking and hurried to fend off the assault. Paulo Groover, still not fully recovered, ran through the Short-Term Houses. He wanted to get away from that mess that no longer made any sense to him. No one in the Short-Term Houses had hit his mother, no one had beaten him up. He was going home, already with the intention of turning himself into the authorities. He thought that behind bars he'd be safe, he could learn a trade, but then he found himself face-to-face with the Block Thirteen gang.

Over in The Blocks, the Empty Pockets found it odd that there were no gangsters on street corners. They kept close to the walls. Only Highwayman and Tube were carrying revolvers tucked into the back of their waistbands. They wanted to tell Tiny that they'd go with him to shoot Carrots, hoping to be given revolvers too. Israel came along carrying a machine gun and a bag of cocaine. He was taking it to Good Life's house to mix with boric acid, before packaging it in tiny plastic bags and selling it. He saw the Empty Pockets and raised the machine gun.

Groover ducked sideways, fired his gun to try and escape, doubled back and shouted that the Block Thirteen gang was in the area. He was greeted with a hail of bullets from Carrots' men, ducked again, ran into someone's backyard and managed to get away. When he reached his own yard, he saw his mother's finger lying in a puddle of blood: his sister had hacked it off with a carving knife. He found his mother and walked with her to the bus stop. As they got on, he threw away his gun, and after his mother had been seen to at Cardoso Fontes Hospital, he headed for the youth detention center.

The Block Thirteen gang moved in on the enemy and froze when they saw Carrots' men shooting at one another. Then they joined the shoot-out and soon Cererê from Block Thirteen fell twisting to the ground, along with Mallet, a friend of Messiah's. Lieutenant Cabra's men, armed with machine guns, had also reached the combat zone and joined in too.

'Where you goin'?' Israel asked the Empty Pockets, pointing his machine gun at them.

'We wanna have a word with Tiny.'

'Tiny's not around, and I'm running the show. Anyone got guns on 'em? If you do, put 'em on the ground, 'cos if I find one when I search you, you're dead.'

Those who were armed followed Israel's orders. He searched the entire gang, which had several new members, and then, for no reason at all, smacked Highwayman, Tube and Bruno several times in the face.

'We came to join you guys!' protested Tube.

Only then did Israel stop harassing them.

The shoot-out had been going on for half an hour and there were five dead. The shots were fewer now, because only the gangsters who hadn't managed to make a run for it were still fighting; most had split when they saw Cabra and his men. After another twenty minutes of gunfire the police had taken down eight men. The shoot-out came to an end.

Cabra ordered an officer to go to the station and get five officers to bring five police vans. Then they put the bodies in the vans and disposed of them in different places.

Tiny returned to the *favela* on Sundays to collect money; Sunday was the best day for gangsters to be out and about, the day workers packed bars, played soccer in vacant lots, went to the street market . . . He believed that the hustle and bustle confused the police, because they thought all blacks and northerners looked alike. Whenever he went to the *favela*, he held barbecues and killed a member of Messiah's or Carrots' gang. Sometimes he killed one from his own gang for no apparent reason, just saying he'd felt the guy was up to something. If his German shepherd barked at anyone, he shot them in the foot.

One Tuesday, Good Life, Beep-Beep, Marcelo, Twit, Whitey and a pawn were packaging coke and weed in a building. Whitey didn't want to be there, but Israel had insisted.

'Get your ass over there. There's loads of customers waitin'! Good Life's in charge!' Israel told him after sending Otávio to fetch him from home.

Whitey's ex-girlfriend was strolling through the buildings. When she saw Whitey at the window throwing more money to the pawn who'd gone down to buy food, she headed off, more quickly now, for the police post. She gave her boyfriend the address of where Whitey was, like he'd asked her to. She also told him they were probably packaging. Morais immediately called fifteen officers and told them he'd just discovered Tiny's gang's new hideout. Sergeant Roberval ordered them all to take machine guns. They got in the van and headed for The Blocks.

'The building's surrounded! Throw your weapons out the window!'

When the dealers saw the number of policemen around the building, they quickly ducked back into the apartment. Tiny's German shepherd woke with a start and barked loudly. They heard Morais' voice again: 'Throw your weapons!'

Good Life took the cocaine and flushed it down the toilet. In a panic, the gangsters called to the neighbors for help, and shouted for their families and friends. They were trying to bring together a crowd of onlookers to intimidate the police, who wouldn't dare kill them in front of a large audience. Many begged the police to spare the gangsters' lives, while many others were praying for them to get on with it and finish them off. Good Life ordered his men to throw their weapons out the window.

'Now we're coming up. If everyone stays nice and quiet no one'll get hurt. Leave the door open and everyone wait by the window!' said Morais.

The villains followed his orders, as Morais and his men came up the building's three flights of stairs. They entered the apartment. The German shepherd leaped at them and was shot.

Only three officers remained downstairs at the entrance to the building, and they stopped Marcelo's and Whitey's mothers from going in.

After searching the entire apartment, they ordered the five to face the wall, took aim, and fired.

There was a great commotion downstairs, with the gangsters' family members and dozens of residents in panic. The officers called for reinforcements. One resident called Cardoso Fontes Hospital for an ambulance.

Sergeant Linivaldo, who wasn't on duty, was talking with other police officers in Taquara Square after leaving the bank. After hearing the call for reinforcements on the radio, he got in his van and headed for The Blocks.

Marcelo and Beep-Beep were still alive and Marcelo was shouting, 'Mom, mom!' thinking she'd hear him because she lived in the next building.

Sergeant Linivaldo arrived at the same time as the ambulance. He ordered the officers not to let any of the ambulance workers into the building, galloped up the stairs, drew his revolver, put four more bullets in Beep-Beep and six more in Marcelo. Morais saw an umbrella with a pointy tip lying on a table, grabbed it and perforated the eyes of the bodies lying around the room, including the dog's.

'Shoot each one two more times from the front, so we can say they tried to resist,' Roberval told Morais, who carried out the order straight away.

'That guy you hang around with is a joke! You can't stay with him, 'cos he's a joke! Stick with me! I'm the one you should be kissing, not him!' Israel told a woman passing through the square in The Blocks.

Israel had taken over the running of the den since his brother Good Life had been murdered. He was always drinking at the shops and when he was drunk he was all over the women, even the married ones. He was always asking whoever happened to be nearby to lend him their car, and if they refused, he shot them in the foot. Even his mates were afraid of him when he was drunk.

Tiny had the misfortune to be approached by the Civil and Military Police six more times. Both used extortion on him. On one occasion, he was taken into custody and the police made him phone to ask someone to bring them the documents for the houses, car and boat that Good Life had bought, which the Military Police's Secret Service had tracked down. All of Tiny's assets were signed over in the policemen's names. Even the chest of gold ended up in the hands of the police.

One Friday the Civil Police approached him again. This time he was in a stolen car with three pounds of weed and two hundred thousand cruzeiros, a couple of pistols and Sting's rifle. He immediately offered the drugs and money to the police, but this time they didn't accept the bribe.

Down at the station, Tiny revealed the places where Carrots, Butterfly and Messiah might be found, with the intention of weakening his competition's drug trade. After being found guilty of several crimes, he went to serve his sentence at Milton Dias Moreira Prison, where enemies from both São Carlos and City of God were also doing time. There were even two men who had once tried to sell weapons to Slick on Block Thirteen, but ended up being robbed and beaten up. They were all there now, united by the Red Command, the dominant faction in Rio's prisons.

Tiny knew he'd die in jail. His only way of staying alive was to pay the prison chiefs a weekly bribe. He called his brother on a daily basis and always said the same thing:

'Send another fifty thousand during visiting hours.'

On one occasion Black Stump answered the phone and said that Israel was drinking a lot, spending money in motels and restaurants and pushing the sellers around. All Tiny was concerned about

was the fact that his brother was spending money and he yelled
down the phone:

'Take the den, take the den and don't give 'im any more money!
I was the one who did the killin'—he didn't kill anyone. Take the
den and if he don't want to hand it over, get rid of 'im, get rid
of 'im . . .'

'And that's not all. He's kicked the Empty Pockets out again, and
he's killin' addicts, givin' workers a hard time and takin' girls by
force. The pawns're all gettin' out. One day Russian Mouse gave
him loads of beer, waited for him to get trashed, took that week's
takings and disappeared . . . Ah, and I almost forgot—Night Owl
got taken out yesterday. The pigs got 'im in his sleep.'

'I don't give a shit! I already said, if Israel keeps screwin' up,
kill 'im . . .'

Black Stump, Blubber and Slick listened to and followed Leonardo's
advice: to let Israel live. All they had to do was tell him he couldn't
drink or spend money anymore, because Tiny was paying to stay
alive in prison. He agreed and started saving money.

Slick had started to dress with great distinction. Linen trousers, a
watch with a leather strap, sometimes suits, sunglasses, and he
didn't catch the normal buses to avoid police raids. The special bus
was much safer, because the police never searched anyone.

It was on the special bus that Slick saw her for the first time and
gave her a romantic look. Luckily for Slick, the school teacher got
off at the same stop as he did and continued the conversation he'd
started as they waited for the lights to change so they could cross
the street, before continuing toward Middle Street.

From that day on, Slick went out of his way to bump into her
every day as she left school and, although she found him a bit rough
around the edges, the primary-school teacher started seeing the
gangster. His passion softened his seriousness. He started laughing again, and went back to playing around and cracking jokes with

his friends. He spent less time in the streets, stopped launching attacks Up Top, didn't hang around chatting with other gangsters on street corners and went to his girlfriend's house whenever he could, just to get away from the *favela*.

But it was also on the special bus that the teacher heard from a resident that the guy was called Slick, a dangerous criminal, and if she wanted she could show her his photo in the newspapers.

'He might be your brother, but he's a Jerry, know what I'm sayin'? Forget this stuff about family, man! You've gotta get rid of 'im!' said Carrots to Fizzy-C, who was only thirteen years old.

'I know, man! But I've gotta get 'im during the day, know what I'm sayin'? My mom's home at night.'

'So let's do it now. If he's around, we'll get rid of 'im.'

'You comin' too?'

'Sure!'

They ran through the alleys as Carrots had planned, searched high and low and didn't bump into any enemies in the streets. To show he was faithful to Carrots, Fizzy-C himself suggested:

'Let's go to my place. Maybe the bastard's sleepin'.'

And he was. He was woken with the barrel of a revolver at his neck and was taken outside. His only defense was to threaten his brother:

'If mom finds out you killed me, she'll be really fuckin' angry with you!'

'So fuckin' what! Who told you to join the Jerries?'

Alexander was taken to the river's edge and his own brother shot his ten-year-old body three times.

'You gotta score ten grand, OK? Ten thousand in two weeks to get me out of here. If you bring it Sunday, I'll be out the same day,' said Tiny six months after going to jail.

Black Stump did two holdups, Blubber and Israel did the same, they added what they'd stolen to the den's takings, and the following Sunday Tiny shook the guards' hands and left the prison with the other visitors.

Black Stump warned Tiny not to return to the *favela*, because although the police had reduced their patrols, the place was still risky. Tiny went to the house of the only friend he'd made in prison.

Israel went to the *favela* of São José to buy cocaine, because it had been two weeks since the supplier had paid him a visit. He was going to buy ten papers to mix with boric acid, package it up in smaller amounts and sell it to the addicts. He parked his Brasilia at the foot of the hill and climbed the steep stairs singing a popular samba. At the den, he found Tube chatting with one of the den's owners.

'Hey, man, this kid's a dumbass. Don't talk to dumbasses or you'll turn into one.'

'Why am I a dumbass?'

''Cos you're a dumbass, OK? And if you talk too much, you'll bite the dust here and now!' said Israel reaching for his waistband.

Tube was quicker and fired just one shot into the middle of his forehead. Then he felt Israel's waistband and realized he was unarmed.

'The guy wasn't armed!'

'What a dumbass!' said Tube's friend.

With a great deal of effort, the teacher convinced Slick to turn himself in. It was better than living a life of crime. She promised not to leave him and that her own father, who was a lawyer, would work to get him out of prison as soon as possible.

Slick had been feeling reborn ever since he'd fallen in love with the school teacher. In the routine of visits to his girlfriend's house, he'd begun to believe in the possibility of a future different to the life he'd led until then. The Saturday afternoon sessions at the movies, followed by a cold beer and healthy conversation, had made him realize how simple life could be, although no less attractive. He had begun to see beauty in married life, dreamed of a future with her and imagined how nice it would be to grow old together, bringing up children and counting Christmases. In spite of the suffering a prison life would bring, he turned himself in to the Thirty-Second District Police Station.

Tried and sentenced, he went to do time in Sector B of Lemos de Brito Prison, where he had several enemies. They didn't say a word to him and left him alone the first time they were let into the courtyard to take some sun. The second time they stabbed him in the stomach forty times.

Right after Israel's death, the Empty Pockets attacked The Blocks four times in a row. The fourth time, they arrived shooting at everything in sight and established themselves as top dogs in the area. They'd killed Black Stump, Tiny's last henchman, and the only reason they didn't kill Blubber and Otávio was because they'd both fled the *favela*. However, the pawns who'd given up crime during the police crackdown and thought they wouldn't be harassed by the Empty Pockets because they hadn't given them a hard time in Tiny's day were mistaken. The Empty Pockets told everyone that they weren't going to kill anyone, but the pawns were killed one by one, and whenever one of them was found dead, they invented lies to justify the murder so the others wouldn't leave the area. Even those who had never been on the wrong side of the law were killed because they'd argued or fought with one of them.

Rapes and muggings gathered new momentum. The cool guys were also being harassed, even though they hadn't been involved in the war, but there were no casualties among them. The dens in The Blocks began to lose custom because the Empty Pockets didn't know any other suppliers and those who had dealt with Tiny disappeared when they didn't get paid.

Carrots was under constant attack from Messiah's gang, the Block Thirteen gang and the police, and he lost five men in less than a week. With no alternative, he took his den's takings, rented a shack in the Baixada Fluminense region and left Mousetrap in control of drug sales. He claimed that the police wouldn't rest until they'd caught him.

'Tell everyone I've gone clean . . . Tell 'em I'm a sucker now and I'm drivin' taxis, OK? We'll split the den's takings fifty-fifty, alright?'

Mousetrap was happy. Now he was in charge of the den on Block Fifteen. Even though he had to fight off two gangs with only a few men, the power was seriously exciting.

With the poor management of the den in The Blocks, the ongoing war Up Top and the difficult access to Leaky Tap's den, the Block Thirteen gang was now selling more drugs than anyone else. My Man and Earthquake took to drinking only soft drinks, because water was for the poor.

The gang grew, while the attacks Up Top became fewer and farther between. They'd wait until they'd all killed one another, then try to take over the dens in that area.

'*K* plus *i* is ki, plus *t* is k-i-t, kite. Fuck! It's kite!' said Tiny, spelling it out next to his new friend's wife in Realengo.

The same week he got out of prison, Tiny spent time with the buddies of his new friend from prison. He went on holdups with them fifteen days in a row. His cunning in the holdups and the shrewdness he demonstrated when they took the dens in Realengo earned him the position of second-in-command: he earned forty percent on the sale of the drugs. Now he was realizing the dream he'd nourished in jail, because he always had to ask someone to read out the letters he received and that could be dangerous; someone might find something out about him. He already knew how to sign his name, and if he managed to track down that lawyer, Violeta, who could solve any problem, he could have an ID card and a check book, something he'd always dreamed of.

One Friday, a pawn brought the news that the Empty Pockets had splintered and were at war. Highwayman didn't want to share the command with Tube and they started fighting right there. This first battle went on for three days. The police, who had been more concerned with the war between Messiah and Mousetrap, once again stepped up their activities in The Blocks and killed four Empty Pockets in ten days.

One Saturday morning, five Empty Pockets showed up in Block Thirteen looking for Butterfly and Tiger. They wanted Block Thirteen to help them take The Blocks.

'Is it just you guys?'

'Yeah, man. The others've split . . . But we're here to join you all!'

'Then what?' asked Tiger.

'You guys keep the dens in Block Seven and Red Hill and we keep the ones in the shops and the Old Blocks.'

'It don't work like that, man! The dens are all gonna be ours, but you can join us!'

'OK!'

'So you're with us then! I'll score a house for you guys to crash in!'

'Hey, we know where they're stayin'. Where they meet . . . It'll be easy!'

'How many of them are there?'

'Eight.'

Up Top, the war was practically over, Messiah's men had killed most of their opponents, Mousetrap had been arrested and the rest had managed to flee the *favela*. The residents of the New Short-Term Houses were thankful the saga had come to an end, because Messiah and his men had made holes in the dividing walls of their tiny houses to escape from their enemies and the police. They entered the houses at any hour of the day or night, went through the holes and left again, far from their pursuers.

*   *   *

To take the dens in The Blocks, the Block Thirteen gang divided up into groups of ten, who took different routes in. The fighting lasted two days. In this battle eight Empty Pockets, two gangsters from Block Thirteen and a police officer were killed, and several more were shot.

Although they were greatly outnumbered, the Empty Pockets didn't run, and fought to the death.

Messiah sent a message to Butterfly and Tiger saying that if they didn't attack Up Top, his gang wouldn't raid Block Thirteen, and if Carrots showed up, they'd kill him themselves.

'Agreed!' said Butterfly to Messiah's errand boy.

Peace reigned once again, and the only man who, for a time, continued to kill those who stole, mugged or raped in the *favela* was Otávio, who put thirty bodies in a single hole, and when he didn't kill them, chopped off their hands with an axe. Then, out of the blue, he became a Protestant and started preaching near the dens, saying he'd committed those murders because he'd been possessed by the Devil. The gangsters left him in peace because they always left the evangelists alone. He was arrested one night on his way home from church and spent two years in jail. After he was released, he got married and had children. Every Sunday, he visited prisons to try to convert the inmates. The police didn't believe he'd converted, however, and when they saw him they beat him up, even in front of his wife and children.

One day Otávio tore up his Bible, burned the suit he wore to church and went to the den to ask Butterfly for a pistol just to kill policemen with.

Jackfruit, Orange and Acerola, now married, still got together to smoke a joint and remember the old days. Their meetings had been rare during the war.

* * *

Old Teresa went back to working as a domestic for rich housewives, but only to keep herself occupied, since she no longer needed the work. Her eldest daughter had married a Canadian, who had taken her to Canada, and every month she sent her mother a decent sum of money.

After several years of fighting for rights on the Residents' Association, Rocket got married and moved away. He managed to establish himself as a photographer, and returned to the *favela* from time to time to visit his mother and friends.

Leaky Tap was caught during a bank robbery in Copacabana and his assistants gave up dealing. Some time later, Leaky Tap's den became the headquarters for a new gang, whose bosses were Carrots' cousins. Carrots started frequenting the *favela* again and fighting the villains Up Top, but was arrested early on in the conflict.

One rainy Christmas Eve in Blonde Square, thirty men got out of several taxis, all armed with machine guns. Only Tiny was carrying a pistol. Fat, wearing linen pants and a silk shirt, he told his men which path to take. They arrived at Block Thirteen, where there were no lookouts on duty because it was Christmas and the gangsters always started drinking early on holidays. He searched high and low until he found Butterfly, who tried to run, thinking Tiny's men were policemen.

'We've come to talk . . . It's me, man, Tiny!'

Butterfly stopped behind a wall, recognizing his voice. 'Here's the story, OK? I want The Blocks back because that area's mine!'

'Sure, OK!'

'When you guys wanted to keep this den, I didn't say nothin', right? We fought side by side and there was never any backstabbin'. Bicky was the only one who tried somethin' smart, but that was it, right?'

'We only took The Blocks 'cos the Empty Pockets were givin' everyone a hard time, alright? Go ahead and take it—just let us sell the merchandise we've got there and we'll be out.'

After they had talked, they drank from the same glass, Tiger fired shots into the air, they snorted coke, drank wine, whisky and beer, and Tiny left, certain that he'd return for good on December 31st.

Tiny's sense of self-importance was renewed and he had plans to be the boss of City of God once more. To this end, he and his friends from Realengo had already planned a surprise attack on Block Thirteen in the very first week of his new reign in The Blocks. Then they'd attack Up Top. He believed everyone there was afraid of him, because he'd always been mean—that was the best way a gangster could be respected. For Tiny, there was no peace or remorse, he never did anything he couldn't get something out of later, and he rubbed every good deed in the face of the person he'd done it for, because he suffered when it wasn't returned, thus destroying everything that didn't feature in his cruel understanding of the world, of life, of relationships. He had the ability to bring out violence in anyone and multiply it at will. He talked to himself in the corners of the living room, the bedroom, in prison and at liberty, and anything he perceived as aggression toward him was returned in the guise of death. He was lord of his own disillusion, and it was his evil fate to be unable to forgive, to annihilate everything his villainous mind was unable to grasp, to invent what others hadn't done to justify his own cruelty. He was vermin born under the sign of Gemini.

The almost-dead moon above the clouds showed signs of life from time to time, the stars were faint and only the New Year's Eve fireworks lit the night, Tiny's night, the night he'd be the boss of City of God again. He stopped by Block Thirteen, but didn't find any of the bosses, so he left a message for Tiger and Butterfly saying that he was already back in The Blocks and that if anyone was still dealing in the area, he was ordering them to stop. He headed for The Blocks, driving a blue Corcel. He went straight to the shops, where he slapped the cool guys on the back and bought sweets for the children, saying he'd learned to read and drive, that he was boss in Realengo, but this was the place where he most liked to be in charge.

At 11:30, a boy told him that Tiger and Butterfly were over on The Hill waiting to have a talk, but for him to go unarmed because a talk was just a talk. No fighting.

'What do they wanna talk about? Hey? Hey?'

'They said it's for your own good.'

He was quiet for a minute and considered not going, but if he didn't they might think he was scared of something. He was Tiny—he was afraid of nothing.

'OK, OK, tell 'em I'll come as soon as I finish my beer . . . Off you go, off you go, go tell 'em, go!'

He waited for the boy to move off, looked around and saw there was no one from Block Thirteen watching him, took a pistol from his waistband, and put it in a holster strapped to his ankle. His friends adjusted their own weapons and they headed for The Hill.

The square in The Hill was empty, except for Tiger and Butterfly crouching between a post and a wall. They'd ordered some of their men to hide in the buildings and join the fight at the sound of the first shot.

Tiny and his friends walked up to Tiger and Butterfly.

'We've decided we're keepin' the den, know what I'm saying? This story that the den used to be yours ain't right, you know. We didn't take the den from you, we took it from the guys that took it from you, OK!' said Tiger.

'What's all this, man? Didn't we agree that . . .'

Butterfly cut him off, reiterating what his pal had just said. Ignoring him, Tiny subtly raised his hand to his forehead, glanced at one of his friends and made the sign of the cross. Tiger, who was watching him intently, whipped his pistol from his waistband, shot Tiny in the abdomen and took off running with Butterfly. The sound of this first shot sparked off a commotion and the pawns, who had been hiding, disbanded in disarray. Tiny and his buddies took advantage of the confusion and headed downhill, firing in all directions. During their escape Tiny shot a pawn right through the head.

The quartet crossed the square in The Blocks, ran into the first building, and entered an apartment where a family was celebrating New Year's Eve. The gangsters ordered them to shut the door, then Tiny sat on the sofa, his eyes rolling back in his head, went into convulsions and died as the New Year's Eve fireworks began.

His friends went up another three flights of stairs, entered another apartment and aimed their guns at the owners. At daybreak they calmly left the building, caught the bus and headed back to Realengo.

Over on Block Thirteen, early in the morning, Tiger had a boy grind up glass and pour it into a can together with wood glue. When it was ready, he stretched a kite string from one post to another and coated it with the mixture. He waited for it to dry, made the bridle, the tail, and hoisted the kite into the air to tussle with others in the sky.

It was kite-flying time in City of God.